I0736114

Mattie

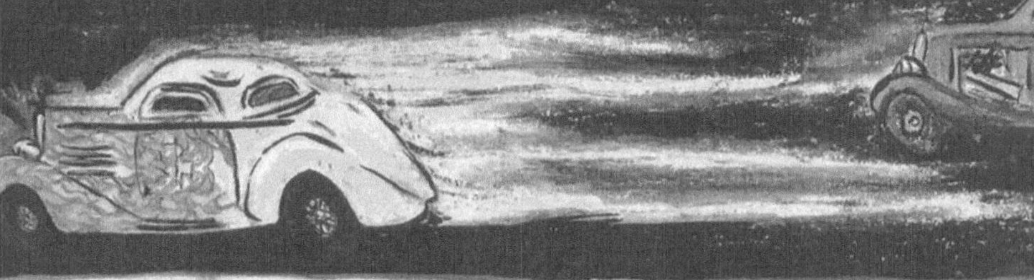

JOHN ROBERTS

Copyright @2022 by John Roberts

All rights reserved. No part of this book may be reproduced in any form or by any electronic or mechanical means, including information storage and retrieval systems, without permission in writing from the publisher, except by reviewers, who may quote brief passages in a review.

This publication contains the opinions and ideas of its author. It is intended to provide helpful and informative material on the subjects addressed in the publication. The author and publisher specifically disclaim all responsibility for any liability, loss or risk, personal or otherwise, which is incurred as a consequence, directly or indirectly, of the use and application of any of the contents of this book.

WORKBOOK PRESS LLC
187 E Warm Springs Rd,
Suite B285, Las Vegas, NV 89119, USA

Website: https://workbookpress.com/
Hotline: 1-888-818-4856
Email: admin@workbookpress.com

Ordering Information:
Quantity sales. Special discounts are available on quantity purchases by corporations, associations, and others.
For details, contact the publisher at the address above.

Library of Congress Control Number:
ISBN-13:   978-1-961845-67-1 (Paperback Version)
              978-1-961845-66-4 (Digital Version)

REV. DATE: 08/31/2022

MATTIE

JOHN ROBERTS

INTRODUCTION

Flames, the first thing I noticed about the coupe was the flames. They were not the more common, symmetrical flames with perfectly defined lines and directions, one fender the same as the other, one side of the hood a mirror image of the other side. These flames looked like real fire, raging out of control, consuming the entire front of the severely modified antique Buick which had been converted into a powerful quarter mile drag racer. The long hood and the huge sweeping front fenders were engulfed and the flames were licking at the huge number thirteen painted in red, white and blue on each door, just catching the front and top edges of the numbers on fire. The entire coupe was rare and special, but the flames were a major contribution to its individuality, it was one of a kind, special beyond words, an incredible work of art on a canvas of steel, beauty that stopped you in mid thought and held your eyes captive and blocked out everything else so that you had to make a conscious effort to look away. And even then, you looked back.

I stood and stared, in love, lusting, wanting, unable to bring another thought to my mind or to speak, as if I were twice my tender age of twelve and in the presence of a beautiful bikini clad young woman giving me a come on look. Whether I was aware of it or not, I wanted this car, this car named Mattie. The very first moment I looked at it, it grabbed me and held me and threatened to pull my soul from my body.

The year was 1990 and I was twice my age. In car years. The result of being raised by my grandfather, an avid classic car and race car enthusiast, retired with the time and money and good health to enjoy his hobby to its fullest, with me tagging along, fully participating in restoration projects, overhauls and car shows as if I were a grown man. I had sat on the floor of his shop, in my diapers, and cut my baby teeth on nuts and bolts, and later, home schooled by this brilliant, personable, self-made man, doing my history lessons and my spelling exercises and math problems aloud, as we overhauled engines, set gaps and clearances, and sanded sheet metal preparing it for paint.

He had searched for this car for over five decades, this very car that stood in front of us now, and he would have it. For all my years with my Paw Paw, and I could remember life no other way, having been orphaned as an infant and taken in by him shortly after he was widowed by the same accident that killed my parents, he entertained me with his memories of this coupe, memories of it new, bought by his Paw Paw in 1934, and three years later, sold, traded in, his protests and tears dismissed as the misguided ramblings of a child. And then there was his, almost, lifelong vow to find it and own it, resulting in an obsession that controlled a part of him for fifty four years. Now, here it was, but different, changed, no longer the antique machine he remembered but a full blown, modified, jacked up, custom painted, chopped and shaved modern hot rod. Would he still love it? Would he still right the wrong of so long ago, despite such radical changes? I loved this car, I had known it for but one minute but I dearly loved it, and for the first time, I understood my grandfather's love for it too. And so began my quest for the same machine. I was certain that I, Joseph Raymond McClane III, would someday possess the long time object of affection and memories of the architect of my entire world, Joseph Raymond McClane Sr., or Paw Paw as I knew him.

It required no convincing from me though, that very hour we had that car on our trailer and were on our way home, filling the three hour journey with adrenaline enhanced plans for the newest addition to our stable of fine classics and hot rods. And this one would be the star of the show.

But the coupe came with passengers of its own, ghosts, residing in the car, unable to escape it, some perhaps not even wanting to, others desperate for release. And they wasted no time in extending their haunt to me, mistaking me for my grandfather as a young boy, or so I thought. In the coming days and years they would appear, semi-transparent and illusive, but definitely there. They would whisper to me, tell me their stories, take over my dreams, brush against my face and hands while I worked on the coupe. At first they frightened me, especially the widow Ferguson, but I quickly realized they were no threat to me, they were but a mysterious part of something I loved; inseparable, dug in and determined, creating a private world for me to explore and indulge and to utterly enjoy. As they shared the past with me, made me aware of their history with the coupe, I realized that I had to record it all, it was too special, and much too important to let fade away. After all, the coupe would live on forever, and some day pass to another owner who would be visited by these same ghosts, ghosts of former owners, which by then would certainly include Paw Paw and me.

Mattie pulled me in, quick and deep, embedded herself in my soul and took over my life. But even when I finally realized the control she had over me, I offered no resistance. And if I learned anything from the entire experience, it was that Mattie had chosen me and she would never let me leave her, never.

CHAPTER 1

A deep rough voice answered the phone, an obvious east Texas accent drawing out the words, adding extra syllables here and there. "Yeah, this is Frank."

"Hello Frank, my name is Joseph McClane, I'm calling about the '34 Buick coupe you have advertised for sale. Is it still available?"

"Yeah, but I don't know for how long, got a guy comin' tomorrow, might buy it, sounds like. Said he's bringin' a trailer with him, and cash."

"Well, I could come today, if that's okay with you. I'm near San Antonio, about four hours away. But could I ask you some questions about it first?"

"Yeah, sure, what do ya' wanna know?"

"Uh, well, does it have the side mounts or the continental kit?"

"It ain't got neither one, man. This car's set up for drag racin'. There's some extra parts out back that came with it though, I think I remember seein' a continental kit in with 'em, might be the one for that car."

"Oh, yeah, no bumpers either, right? Okay look, I know the drive train is all new, but the body, it's a real steel 1934 Buick body, right?"

"Yeah, yeah, right, it's a real 34 Buick body, minus bumpers and running boards and hood panels, and the interior is changed too, of course. But most of the original stuff is still layin' around here somewhere if you want it, ain't nothin' but junk to me."

"Okay, one more question Frank, does it still have the original frame? That's where they stamped the serial numbers, you know."

"Oh yeah, I remember lookin' for those, to see if they matched the title. They're there, and uh, somebody stamped somethin' else there too, right by the serial numbers, not no factory stamp though, a girl's name, Mindy or Mandy or somethin' like that. Probably some love sick, high school, hot rodder a generation or two ago. Anyway, ya' wanna come see it or not?"

Paw Paw and I hitched our twenty two foot car hauler trailer to our big, black, one ton, dually, Ford pickup and headed for Houston. It was about a two hundred mile trip from where we lived in the hill country west of San Antonio. Las Casas was the name of our sleepy little town of about five thousand people. Rumor was that it was originally named Las Casas de Los Pobres, Houses of the Poor, but at some point in time it was shortened to just The Houses, or The Homes. Like most south Texas towns, Las Casas was predominately Mexican in population and culture which to me was normal since I had lived there all my young life. Actually I enjoyed the Mexican culture, the food, the music, the celebrations, and the skinny young Mexican girls sure were pretty. At twelve, I was just starting to notice girls and I really liked the jet black hair and dark skin, and especially the bone structure of their faces, the cheekbones, small noses, some with a little bump, and the low hairline on their foreheads. A Mexican girl from church had caught my eye, Anita Cantu, she was beautiful, but so pretty I decided she probably wouldn't like me back. She attended public school and was probably one of the popular kids, probably had boys calling her all the time.

As we traveled, I watched for cops and Paw Paw negotiated the traffic a full twenty miles an hour over the speed limit while he related to me his memories of the car we were pursuing. I had heard the stories before, many times, but listened intently anyway, and mused at the glow radiating from him as the realization set in, his quest of five decades was about to produce the ultimate reward. Paw Paw was the kid who had stamped Mattie on the coupe's chassis, right by her serial numbers, and that was the car's name, Mattie, short for Matilda.

"Joey, I fell in love with this car when I was about your age, maybe a couple of years younger. My Paw Paw would let me ride in the rumble seat, it was a king's throne to me. I was certain the whole world was envious of me as we toured the neighborhood and down town with me smugly encased in my throne, half in, half out of the body of the car. I told him from day one that I wanted that car someday. He never took me seriously, just a silly child, the next one would capture my heart too. But it didn't. Three or four years later he traded Mattie in on a new car, a sedan, big and cumbersome, no rumble seat, sluggish, and not at all fun. Maw Maw never liked the coupe, no back seat, no trunk, and too fast. A "hot rod" she called it, not a fitting car for an older businessman. After he traded it in on the new car, it was quickly bought by old widow Ferguson. She didn't even know how to drive, she had been totally dependent on her husband and now he was gone. It wasn't a good car for her to learn on either, heavy and hard for a woman to steer and stop, and hard for a short person like the widow to see over the long elegant hood and sprawling fenders. First she ran into her own garage with the coupe, and soon after that hit a tree right by her driveway, then she ran over a dog. After that she just gave up, parking the coupe in the small dirt floor garage that was originally built to be a carriage house. She never drove it again."

"When I saw the damage she had done to my beautiful coupe, I cried, then I went to her to beg for the car but was not received well. I had a fist full of dollars to show her, and a very well-rehearsed plan for coming up with the rest of the money I'd need to buy it."

"Why, you're just a child." She told me. "You can't have a car."

"Please, I love that car. Her name is Mattie, she was supposed to be mine someday."

"Oh, don't be silly. Go on now, and leave me alone."

"But, please, I've got fifty dollars saved up, I'll pay you something every month, I'll work and earn money and pay you. I'll work for you, clean, paint, dig, I'm strong, I know how to work, please!"

"There's a depression going on child, people are broke, starving, losing their homes, you can't buy a car. Go on now."

"But you're ruining it! You're running into everything and ruining it! Please!"

"And she shut the door in my face, my face with tears streaming down, eyes begging, lips trembling, desperate, but to no avail. Old widow Ferguson died in that car that very night, she was having seizures of some kind, no phone, neighbors not home, looked like she tried to drive, probably to get to a doctor, but she never made it out of her own garage. She sat there all night in Mattie, dead, vomit caked on her clothes, a nasty mix of fecal matter and urine in her dress under her, horror etched on her face. Ashamed of my own emotions, I secretly felt that she got what she deserved for depriving me of the car I so loved. I didn't know if Mattie would ever forgive her, but I sure wouldn't."

I tried to keep track of the car after Mrs. Ferguson died, finding out that her nephew got it next; a crazy, spoiled, undisciplined kid, given whatever he wanted, caring for and appreciating nothing. He wrecked it, pretty bad, damaged the front end, bumper and hood and fender, worse than his aunt had already done. His father got it fixed but not right, just left the bumper off, and the used fender that replaced the damaged one was for a slightly different model and never did fit right, and it wasn't repainted either. My beautiful coupe was slowly being destroyed and I was powerless to stop it. Finally the boy blew the engine up and his dad refused to buy him another car because he had not taken care of this one. Eventually the kid realized his options were to get the coupe running or walk, so he had it up on jacks trying to remove the ruined engine and it fell on him, crushed his chest. They said he lay there for hours, pinned in place, and slowly suffocated. His dad found him later that day. After that the coupe was abandoned in a field."

"I remember seeing it one August day when I was on my way out of town, leaving for college, it had been that long. I drove my car into the field, right up to the coupe, got out and inspected it. The driver's side window had been left open, allowing rain to get in and damage the interior. I rolled the window up. I walked around to the rear and opened the rumble seat, climbed up and sat in it, reliving younger and happier days, crouching down to make myself small again, ten years old again. I talked to the car, promising to return from college one day and rescue it. Someone shouted in the distance, telling me to get off the property. I looked around and saw the source of the voice, a shirtless old man standing in an open doorway of a house some one hundred or so yards away. I waved. He responded by siccing a large black dog on me. The dog had a lot of ground to cover but was coming fast. A quick goodbye, a hasty repeat of my promise to the car, and I resumed my journey. I talked to the car, promising to return from college one day and rescue it. Three years later I finished school with a degree in petroleum engineering. World War two had ended the depression, everyone claimed, but times were still hard. I went right from school to the army, with only a few days visit home, and the coupe was gone. I asked family and friends to try to find it for me and one day at mail call, sitting in a makeshift barrack in Northern Africa, a letter from my dad informed me that the car had been donated to the war effort and had been melted down for the steel in it.

Paw Paw fell silent and stared out through the windshield, lost in another time and thoughts of youth and war and Mattie.

"But it hadn't, right? A man named Amos had it, right Paw

Paw?" I was familiar with the story, but loved it anyway, never tired of hearing it, and wanted him to continue. But now we were nearing Houston and needed to concentrate on finding the right landmarks and turns.

"Heard that one before, eh?" He asked, with that knowing smirk that expressed gratitude for my willingness to let him recant this personal piece of history once more. "Okay Joey, watch for Sunset Acres Avenue, it'll be on our left pretty soon now."

On the eastern outskirts of Houston, Texas, imposing city skyline in the distance, we entered the Sunset Acres Subdivision. The neighborhood was a mixture of small, needy looking houses and old single wide mobile homes with broken down cars in the yards and Pit Bull dogs chained to trees, the Pit Bulls running half circles, barking and straining against their chains to warn us. A few blocks down, the pot hole pocked pavement turned to gravel, and dust boiled up behind us, even though we were only going about twenty five miles per hour. Finding the right address without much difficulty, I noticed that it blended in well with its neighbors, trashy and unsafe looking, strewn with broken cars and pickups and parts of cars. But to my relief, no Pit Bull chained to a tree. Why would anyone want one of those? Sparky crossed my mind. I smiled at the thought of him snuggled up to me in bed at night. I loved my little terrier.

The large, wide, concrete driveway, which looked new and out of place, led directly to the shop's front overhead door and it was open. The shop was a tall, green colored metal building with white trim. We both paused a moment to still our racing hearts, before getting out of our truck. The moment was a collage of emotions.

"Yes, I see it!" Paw Paw exclaimed and threw the pickup door open. Then he hesitated, looked me in the eye and reminded me about our strategy, "We don't know this car, okay? If he knows we're looking for this particular car he'll not be willing to negotiate the price, right?"

"Right." I replied and put on my poker face. "We're looking for a 34 coupe, but not any certain one." Secretly though, I wondered how either of us would be able to contain our excitement. Fifty four years of wanting this car, forty five invested in what most of the time must have seemed like a futile search, and here we were at the finish line. And we were supposed to 'put on our poker faces' and 'contain our excitement'. Yeah, right.

We bailed out simultaneously and, as I rounded the front of the pickup, I glanced at Paw Paw. His gaze was fixed on the bright yellow coupe at the back of the shop. The shop was cluttered with tools and jacks and car parts, two car lifts, and eight whole cars. The cars were performance models from the sixties and seventies including a couple of the larger bodied seventies MoPars and a green 1968 Hemi Cuda, sort of like the one we had but not in as good of condition. Paw Paw saw nothing but the coupe. I walked in an angle to him until we brushed against each other. As we touched, he allowed his eyes to be diverted to mine for only half a second and then returned his full attention to the coupe. I swear I could hear his heart beating.

Paw Paw was a negotiator and horse trader of the highest caliber, second to none in bluffing while reading his opponent's mind, he could have been a professional gambler. I had watched him several times and tried to learn this art, this standing toe to toe, eye to eye, with someone seemingly just as determined, and yet coming out victorious over them every time. But this time I worried about him, this one was personal, fifty something years worth of personal. Could he get past that and dig down deep and get a deal on this coupe that he'd vowed as a boy to someday own? Or would he dispense with the game this time and just pay the man's price and have his prize?

"Be right with ya'" Came the shout from under the pickup. Feet in oil stained, laced up leather work boots stuck out from under what must have been the shop truck, it was up on jack stands, rear wheels off and lying nearby. The creeper rolled out and

Frank emerged, struggled to his feet and I began to observe and read him as Paw Paw had taught me to do. Caucasian , fiftyish, tall and slim but bent over, balding, bad teeth, very dirty even for a mechanic, like he maybe didn't start the day out with clean clothes. He was also unwilling to look either of us in the eye for more than a second, as he hobbled toward us, wiping his greasy hands on a red shop rag. That was in our favor in the price negotiations, he couldn't read Paw Paw if he couldn't look him in the eye. Maybe that would balance out Paw Paw's nervousness.

"Frank." He introduced himself with outstretched, oil stained hand. I could smell alcohol on his breath as he spoke, even from several feet away.

"Joseph McClane. Nice to meet you, Frank." They shook hands and I knew Paw Paw was reading something from the handshake, firmness or flightiness, something. "And this is my grandson, Joey."

"Hi."

That and a nod was all I got. I raised my hand to shake but he'd already looked away. I was disappointed. I wanted to test his handshake too, the way Paw Paw had taught me. But it looked like Paw Paw needed something to wipe his hand on now so maybe I didn't miss much.

"You're here for that Buick coupe, right?" He motioned with his hand. "It's in the back there." Frank turned and led the way through the shop, still wiping his oily hands on the red shop rag, around cars and tools and parts, placed here and there with no sense of order whatsoever. As we drew near the coupe, a phone rang from somewhere back in the front of the shop. Frank quickly reversed his direction and broke into a limping sort of trot to catch the phone and yelled over his shoulder for us to go ahead and look the car over, adding, "Out the back, around the corner of the building to the right's most o' the old parts to it, take a look at them too, if ya' want. Gotta take this call, be right back."

Paw Paw and I looked at each other and he let out a sigh, and we proceeded toward the coupe without Frank. Being left alone with the car at that point was probably the best thing that could have happened. It gave Paw Paw a chance to see it for the first time and be honest with his reaction without tipping his hand.

I stopped a few feet away and watched, allowing him his long awaited moment of reunion. He walked to the car as if in a trance and touched it on the left front fender, just behind the huge chrome headlight bucket. As if oblivious to the thick coat of dust, he ran his hand along the massive fender, across the passenger side door, and stopped where the door handle should have been, and breathed, "Shaved."

"Shaved?" Slowly, I approached.

"Shaved, no door handles, electronic door controls. Everything is different, everything's been changed."

He seemed in a stupor and I worried that it was too much for him. His car had been put through so many changes over the decades. I worried he wouldn't be able to love it again. I wanted to defend it, to help him in his disappointment in what was supposed to be his finest hour. I was sad for him, it wasn't supposed to be like this.

"We can fix it, Paw Paw, you and me, we've fixed worse, come on, it's okay." I reached out and touched his forearm. His gaze remained fixed on the coupe.

"Yellow." He breathed in and out heavily as though trying to rid himself of his burden. "Flames." A wooden, three legged stool was nearby and he sat, wearily, put his hands on his knees and leaned forward. Shook his head slowly. "Not much left of the old coupe I knew, not anything the same."

While searching my mind for some comforting words, staring at the car, I noticed the sealed beams had been removed from the headlamp buckets. It was wired for modern headlights but the wires were just hanging and the massive chrome buckets that had been modified to house modern sealed beams were empty. Looking into the engine compartment, I saw that the horns were there but the wires to them had been cut, and not just severed, but several inches of wire had been cut out of the wiring harness. That seemed strange to me, why would someone do that?

"I like it, Paw Paw, it's beautiful." I needed to counter his negative thoughts, but the truth was, I didn't just like it, I loved it. It was the most beautiful thing I'd ever seen. And in my life with my grandfather, I'd seen thousands of hot rods, show cars, and race cars but this one had just stolen my heart. In fact, I almost hoped he didn't want it anymore, because I did. If he tried to go home without it I'd beg him for it, through tears, just like he did Mrs. Ferguson all those years ago. I'd even remind him of that, just so he'd feel guilty and let me have it. I'd offer to pay for it, work it out, I had some money.

"Paw Paw, if you don't..."

He raised one hand to stop me. "No, I'm okay, Joey. I'm just shocked, don't know what I really expected, after all these years. He told me it was customized and set up for racing, it's just so..." His head slowly shook from side to side, breathed deeply, in and out.

"Paw Paw, it's beautiful, I could love this car. Please, if you don't want it, I do!"

Our eyes met and he saw in mine what I needed him to see. He smiled, that knowing smile of his, and nothing else needed to be said aloud. He placed his hand on my shoulders and patted me in the small of my back. Paw Paw had raised me with love and gentleness, never hitting me or even raising his voice. And I had always responded with admiration and obedience. He was my hero, my best friend, my family, my trainer for life. And we were good for each other, filling in the gaps left in each other's lives by the loss of the rest of our family.

"How do you open the door?" I asked, now happy in my confidence that we would be taking the coupe home. "I want to see the interior."

I could see through the windows that it had a roll cage, which I knew meant it turned quarter mile times of under eleven seconds. Unable to find the remote control for the doors, we turned our attention to the hood and the engine. Originally, the car had been equipped with a hood that opened in gull wing style, and now, though the top section of the hood was still in place, the side panels had been removed, leaving the engine compartment in almost full view. In it was the famous 426 cubic inch Chrysler Hemi Head engine, but it was broken, frozen up, ruined, and the fuel injection system had already been robbed off of it. Closer inspection revealed a gaping hole in the block, down low near the back on the driver's side where the rear piston and rod had blown completely out of the block. Wow, I'd never heard of one blowing apart that bad.

The transmission was some kind of serious drag racing automatic with trans-brake and switch pitch gear changing mechanics, but its condition was unknown, and it probably wasn't suitable for street driving anyway. A peek under the coupe told us the driveshaft had been removed and we saw it on the floor several feet away. Maybe Frank had started to remove the whole drive train and just hadn't gotten very far with the project. Changing all that out wouldn't be a problem for us though, we were master mechanics, my Paw Paw and me, smart and skilled and with a very well equipped shop.

Two quick beeps startled me and I jumped back a step as the driver side door sprung open a few inches. "Here's the control for the doors." Frank offered it to Paw Paw as he approached. He held it out at arm's length, and stepped back. "I just put the battery back in the car earlier so you could see inside, and that the controls work."

"Why did you have the battery out?" I asked, intending to also ask about the disabled headlights and horns.

"To shut the damned thing up!" He snapped. His eyes looked so serious.

"What?"

"Nothin', never mind, it ain't important!"

I shrugged off the awkward conversation and climbed inside the coupe and sat in the only seat, a high back, padded aluminum, professional racing seat, safety harness and all. I draped the harness around me and smiled. Man, this car must be fast, this is exciting. I griped the wheel with my left hand, covered the shifter with my right, and fanaticized. I was racing Mattie, I could see it, the track, the lights, another car next to me. My foot went down on the gas and we shot off the line, taking the lead instantly and I watched the tachometer rush toward the red line, and it was time to shift and the shift got me back to peak horsepower and I was adding to my lead. The end of the quarter mile was coming up fast, I was winning, I was flying across the line!

Paw Paw tapped on the windshield from the other side. I jumped. My heart was pounding. For a moment there I thought I really was racing Mattie. I struggled to focus. He was saying something. He mouthed silently, "Mattie" and pointed downward. He had found her name on her frame, where he had stamped it so many years ago. He smiled and looked down at it again, ran his finger tip over it, reliving that very moment, I guessed. I smiled as I wondered at the thoughts, the memories going through his mind.

I looked down at the hole in the floor, about as big as a man's fist, a little bigger, near the gas pedal, a steel floor where there had originally been a wood one, jagged edges pointing inward. It was right in line with the hole in the engine block so it must have blown metal through the floor when the engine came apart. Frank was watching me, suspiciously I thought, from twenty feet away, I looked at him. "Looks bad, did it hurt the driver?"

He bristled and frowned at me. "You ask too many questions, boy." He quickly walked around the car and toward Paw Paw. "Did ja' see the parts outside yet?"

"No, not yet." Paw Paw answered and moved around the open car door to inspect the interior. I was still perched in the racing seat. Once again his happy smirk turned to a concerned scowl. The original dash panel and gauges were still in place though no longer connected, a new set of racing gauges were mounted in their own spaces inside an unpainted homemade sheet metal console which extended from the bottom of the old dash to the floor. The console appeared well built, nice craftsmanship, just awkward and out of place with the original dash attached to it. The old Mohair covered bench seat had been replaced by the padded aluminum racing seat with all the harnesses and seat belt mechanisms, and the entire steering column and steering wheel had been replaced too, with something more modern and suitable for racing. Upholstered door panels and headliner were gone as were the seat cushions and upholstery for the rumble seat.

Paw Paw stood and stared, too long, I knew, but he was lost in time, seeing the coupe as it had been before and not as it now was, remembering days of old, and perhaps even going through the coming restoration in his mind, removing the racing interior and replacing it with one that would look as it did when he was a young boy in love with the car.

In an effort to shake him back to reality, before Frank noticed how the car was pulling at him, I slid from the seat and stood in front of Paw Paw. "Let's go see the other parts, Paw Paw." I gave him a gentle shove on the shoulder.

"Yes," He agreed slowly, as he reluctantly tore his attention from the coupe. "Let's go see what all goes with this car."

"Did you race the coupe, sir?" I asked Frank as he led us toward the open rear overhead door.

"What, me? Oh no, not me, a customer of mine."

"What kind of times did it turn?"

Frank shot me a sideways glance with suspicious eyes. "You a drag race fan, son?" He spat on the floor as he gimped along and wiped his mouth on his sleeve and squinted his eyes. "Well, he turned in the low nines with it all the time, high eights on a good night, that car could fly. See them boxes of old trophies against the wall over there? They go with the car too, if ya' want 'em, otherwise they'll just go in the dumpster. Seems like a lot of old worthless crap's been followin' this car around for a long time."

I glanced toward the wall, there were maybe a dozen cardboard boxes, big boxes, you'd have to carry one with both hands and lean back to balance it. Trophy parts were randomly protruding thru the tops, as if they'd just been carelessly tossed into the boxes. I wondered how many had been damaged. Of course I wanted them.

"So why did he quit racing it, just because he blew the engine?" I felt a sudden breeze or something, for a second I thought it was a moth or maybe a spider web brushing up against the right side of my face and I tossed a slow one handed swat at it, back and forth, but nothing was there. For some reason I was compelled to look back at the coupe. Something inside the car moved. Was someone in it? Who? Why? Where did they come from? A chill swept over me and I shivered and stopped in my tracks, wide eyed, wondering. I looked at Frank and he avoided my eyes, but I could tell he saw it too and it made him really nervous. I looked back at the car. Nothing. But it certainly was an eerie nothing.

"Come on around here, come on boy, lots of parts, and I'd just as soon they leave here with the car so I don't have to haul 'em off."

I followed them out and around the corner of the building and there, outside in the elements, was a wealth of parts; seats bare of fabric but the seats, even the rumble seat, the running boards, the original steering wheel, bumpers, even the old continental kit, not all in the best of condition, but a lot of hard parts to find for the restoration that would be sure to quickly follow the purchase. This had to convince Paw Paw to buy the coupe, now I was really hopeful.

"Look, Paw Paw, look at all the original parts that are still with it!"

He gave me a look that said, "Don't show excitement and destroy our edge in the deal."

We examined the parts, separated what we wanted from the rest of the pile, and made sure Frank agreed to exactly which parts would be included with the coupe. Then we needed to inspect the car some more. My eyes were on it from the moment I stepped through the shop door, remembering the movement in it just a few minutes earlier, wondering, watching a very nervous Frank for some clue to the mystery I was now sure came attached to the coupe.

Frank didn't like this car, it was almost like he was afraid of it. I watched him out of the corner of my eye, and while we examined the car, he stayed back, never came close, walked around it in a looping circle while eying it with suspicion, maybe even fear.

What did he mean, he took the battery out "to shut the damned thing up"? And why were the headlights and horn disabled? Was that "to shut the damned thing up" too? Why was the driveshaft out on the floor? It couldn't go anywhere, the engine was blown, and froze up too. I wanted to question him some more about it but he was already complaining about too many questions from me, and Paw Paw wasn't making an issue of any of it, so I decided to not pursue it.

Back at the coupe, Paw Paw climbed inside, slung the harness over his shoulders, and gripped the steering wheel with one hand and the shifter with the other. I watched and remembered how that same position had, just a few minutes prior, sent me into a dream world. It didn't seem to do anything for Paw Paw though. "I guess I'm a little old for this." He said, looking around inside the car, trying to make peace with what he saw, perhaps trying to convince himself he could put it all back right. And I could tell his hesitation worried Frank, just as it was meant to do.

"Thought you wanted to restore it, it'd be good for that, all steel body in good shape. This is a hard model to find, probably ain't more'n a couple a' dozen of 'em left. Might be worth fifty thousand, restored. No rust, that's a real good thing for a car this old."

"It's come a long way from 1934. Be hard to put back, needs a total rewire, and a whole new drive train, interior. I don't know. The right model, but..." He shook his head. "It's been chopped, and shaved."

"Well, ya' know, ya' gotta look at both sides o' the coin, right?" Frank nervously wiped his mouth with his hand, looked at his own dirty fingernails and gnawed on one of them.

I looked at Paw Paw and his sly but barely visible grin said, Yes, Joey, watch the body language, we've got him on the run.

"Some pretty expensive upgrades already done; disc brakes, four wheel disc brakes, and power steering, and twelve volt conversion... I mean, if you're a purist, and everything's gotta be one hundred percent original, then it ain't gonna work 'cause ya' gotta go all the way back to cable brakes and primitive mechanics like that for this one. But if you were gonna do a resto-mod, then the hard work is already done, just redo the interior and bolt another engine in and you're set." Frank was exaggerating the car's value, even when restored, and minimizing the work needed and we all knew it, but he was arguing for the sale.

"Yeah, it's got some things going for it, but... Sixty five hundred dollars, I don't know." Paw Paw squeezed his eyes up in an obviously forced smile, wise crow's feet showing, more body language, I thought. "Maybe I should just keep looking for a while, find something else. I'd have to put another twelve grand in it easy, and hundreds of hours, and that paint job, good for the race track maybe, but, no, I don't think so."

I couldn't have disagreed with him more about the paint job, I liked it, even the huge number thirteen on each door. I liked the coupe as a race car and didn't want it changed from that. And later on our way home, or back at our shop I'd argue for it to be left alone; flames, painted on numbers, shaved door handles and everything. Well, yeah, it needed an interior but the seat frames and stuff were included in the deal, so that part would be easy enough.

Frank shrugged his shoulders and tried to appear unshaken. "Make me an offer. But don't insult me, I ain't desperate, just need it out of the way."

Something told me, as I watched the negotiations, and I always loved this part, Paw Paw was so good at it, but something told me Frank was "desperate" to get rid of it, he wanted it gone, but not just because it was taking up space in his already overcrowded shop. It wasn't about money either, something about the coupe bothered him and a lot. And he kept it in the corner of his eye, always looking back at it, checking, nervously, like he thought it was going to come after him or something. He was afraid of this car, it didn't make any sense, but I was sure of it.

"Forty five hundred dollars, cash, hundred dollar bills, right now."

Frank flinched. "No! No, I couldn't take that." He blurted indignantly. "Got way more'n that in it. It was supposed to win big, then the owner could pay me, he'd racked up a pretty big bill with me. But when it blew apart that night and... Well, he was no longer able to pay me, so…" Frank coughed into his rolled up hand and looked away and inhaled and exhaled heavily. Paw Paw had him.

"Counter offer, then." Paw Paw said in a challenge, looking directly at Frank.

"Six thousand. Man coming tomorrow will pay that at least, I know he will." Frank looked back at the coupe again, shuffled his feet, wrung his hands together, and turned back around to where he couldn't see the coupe anymore.

"I could go forty nine hundred, but that's it."

"No, I need six thou." Frank was shaking his head, looking down at the dirty concrete floor, hands in his pockets now.

"Okay, well, sorry, I guess it's not going to work out this time." Paw Paw put his hand on my back, gave me a gentle shove, and we started toward the driveway. I knew this was a bluff, he wasn't going to leave here without that car, and I wasn't going to let him.

"Come on, man, work with me a little." Frank pleaded to our backs. "You want it, I can tell. Gimme, gimme, fifty five hundred. That's cheap, dirt cheap."

I stopped on cue with Paw Paw, we turned to face Frank. We could probably get it for the forty nine hundred if we played this game out, I figured, pull the money out, count it off in front of him, start to walk off again. But something I'd never seen before happened, Paw Paw gave in. He knew he'd won, he was too good at this to not know, but the moment was special and I think he decided to honor the moment and not cheapen it by making this just another win negotiated over just another car. This was his coupe, his long sought coupe that he'd begged his grandfather and Mrs. Ferguson for, sat in it in an abandoned field and promised it he would come back for it, and now he could have it.

After the money and title exchange we helped Frank move cars and car parts and tool cabinets out of the way so we could push the coupe through the shop to the trailer we had waiting in the driveway. I wiggled under the front of the coupe on my back and connected the cable to the frame and then hurried around inside the car to steer as Paw Paw operated the winch to pull her up onto the trailer. We had done this before.

Sitting in Mattie, I looked around, trying to be careful to not lose my focus on steering her onto the trailer, and I looked out over her long hood and sprawling fenders, at the flames. They looked like Hell Fire to me, and they made her look as if she was hauling ass and fanning the flames to a frenzy and I imagined myself racing her down a drag strip. One hand on the wheel the other on the shifter, I guess I just got pulled into a vivid imaginary situation, a very deep day dream, and I was older, maybe seventeen, maybe eighteen, and I was racing Mattie down the track at the San Antonio Drag Raceway, and things in my peripheral vision were a blur but I could tell I had a comfortable lead on my opponent and I shifted gears and I watched the time board as I passed by it as I always did even though I knew my time wouldn't flash on that sign until I was well beyond it. I could look around at it after I did the turn around and was on my way back to the pits. And I did. 8.982 seconds, 147.66 mph! I finally broke into the eights! I was ecstatic, I had worked so hard for this!

The trailer winch stopped, Mattie jerked to a halt and I looked around, trying to figure out which world I was in. It took a few seconds, quite a few. I felt as if I was being pulled between two worlds, or maybe the same world but two very different points in time, I gripped Mattie's steering wheel tight with both hands and glared into space, frozen, thinking but not thinking, unable to react, or maybe unwilling. I was shaking, all over, trembling. Mattie had a tight fisted grip on my soul and wouldn't let go, and I didn't want her to let go. I heard music coming from Mattie's dash, an old song, from the fifties, or sixties maybe, acoustic guitar, drums, violins, beautiful young female voice. "Tonight you're mine completely, you give your love so sweetly, tonight the light of love is in your eyes, but will you love me tomorrow?" Where was it coming from? Mattie had no radio. The music faded.

Paw Paw stepped up onto the trailer and jostled my shoulder through the open window. "Come on, Joey, let's get the rest of the stuff loaded up."

I looked in the mirror, I needed a shave. I did a double take, I don't shave, I'm twelve years old. I looked in the mirror again, I didn't need a shave. Paw Paw opened the door and motioned for me to get out. I reluctantly swung my feet around, still fuzzy headed, avoided Paw Paw's eyes but caught a glimpse of Frank's. He knew, maybe not in any detail, but Frank knew Mattie had just done something to me. I stopped just before sliding off the seat and stepping down to the trailer, looked back inside the car, I wanted to stay there, in that world, in that time.

"You all right, son?"

"Huh? Uh, sir?" I was unable to make that last movement to separate myself from Mattie.

Paw Paw was craning his neck to look me in the eye. "Are you okay, Joey? What's wrong?"

I was in a daze, struggling to clear my head but not really wanting to. "Oh, um, yeah, I'm okay. Let's, uh, let's get the stuff loaded." Moving away from Mattie felt like pulling against a powerful magnet.

We stacked the extra parts and the driveshaft on the trailer, around and under Mattie and in the pickup bed and tied them down, put a few small parts inside her, being careful to not scratch anything. I carefully placed the boxes of trophies in the rear seat and floor of the truck's double cab, it held all but two of the boxes and I found slots for them among the parts in the bed. Now we were ready to head home with Mattie.

Paw Paw and Frank shook hands and wished each other well. I

saw a different look on Frank's face now, relief, and desperately needed peace. He could even look me in the eye now, briefly. He looked like a man who had just had a heavy burden lifted from him, like now everything was going to be okay. When our eyes met I knew he had something to say, something about Mattie, maybe the answers to my earlier questions, even the ones I didn't ask.

Frank looked down and back up to me, to Paw Paw and back to me again, hesitated, took a deep breath, in and out, ran a dirty hand over his mouth, over the two or three days' salt and pepper beard stubble, and told us.

"Listen, uh, you're gonna think I'm crazy, but, be careful with that car. I mean, I was watchin' the boy in it, and, it's already takin' over... Well, what I mean is, the damned thing's haunted or somethin'. I mean, it's pretty scary goin' down the track a hundred and forty miles an hour and suddenly seein' a face in the mirror, or on the other side of the windshield. And other stuff too, like voices, whispers, playin' music without no radio, old music, an' doin' things you can't explain, doin' stuff on its own, things not possible..." He had worked himself up over whatever he was trying to tell us about and he was breathing fast and kind of shuttering. His eyes were huge and he shook his head. "Well, just be careful." He started to turn away, turned back and added. "It was fine for a long time, but somethin' happened one night at the drags, it was like the car got real upset, angry, and then vengeful and dangerous, wanted to hurt people, willin' to destroy itself in the process. Never seen nothin' like it, and never want to again. We had to disable it to get it under control, as if a blown engine shouldn't already have it disabled. I'm just glad to get the spooky son of a bitch out of here." Once again, Frank's eyes met mine, then he glanced at Mattie on the trailer behind us, and back at me and I saw genuine fear in those eyes. He turned and hurried away and we did too.

Paw Paw and I didn't speak much for a few miles, except about the turns and roads we needed to take. Frank's weird story had dampened our spirits a little, but we soon remembered that we had Mattie, Paw Paw's Mattie and we were taking her home. And once we began talking about the coming restoration we got all excited and the travel time then filled with ideas and plans and schemes about how we would build this car. We talked about our options for everything from engine to upholstery to wheels, her modifications, what to leave, what to correct.

Paw Paw mentioned the time when he tried to buy Mattie from Mrs. Ferguson, laughed a little, and added, "You know something, Joey? I'd like to see Mrs. Ferguson's face now."

Something about that statement made me shiver and I looked at the car on the trailer behind us. The movement again, and this time it had some color, blue, light blue, baby blue. Startled, I jumped and turned completely around in my seat and stared, wide eyed, heart racing.

What is it, son? Everything all right with the car back there?"

"Um, yeah, I guess so, Paw Paw. Just a shadow maybe, or a reflection from a passing billboard." Still staring at the coupe's windshield, I again caught a hint of blue inside, something being blown about by the wind. "Stop!" I yelled, and immediately wished I hadn't.

"What? What is it?" He let off the gas and eased on the brake and began moving over onto the shoulder of the highway.

"Um, I think we left a window open, something's blowing around in there."

We stopped and walked back to check on the coupe, windows all closed, doors securely shut. Paw Paw opened the driver side door and I hopped up on the trailer and stuck my head in. I looked around, nothing blue, nothing even cloth, or paper, nothing that would blow around, even if there was wind inside the car, which there was not. I decided to not look back at it anymore for the rest of the trip, and I didn't, no matter how hard it pulled at me, but I never quit thinking about it.

I started to remember some things about my fantasy of racing Mattie. It had been like one of those dreams that are so vivid, but when you wake up the dream escapes, you know you dreamed something and you want to remember it but you just can't, but then maybe later something triggers the memory and it comes back to you. That song, it was playing in my head, continuously, not all the words but the tune and the chorus for sure. Did I really hear it? Was it really coming from Mattie? No, it was coming from Frank's shop, had to be, no radio, no tunes. Right?

"Paw Paw, do you remember an old song that said something about, "But will you love me tomorrow." Like from back in the fifties maybe? A girl band I think, there was a violin and the lead singer had a real pretty voice, remember a song like that?"

"Hmmm. Oh yeah, Joey, let's see, that was by the Shirelles I think, yeah that's right, late fifties probably, Elvis era, pre-Beatles. Why? Where did you hear something like that?"

Now why didn't I expect that question? "Um, uh, I don't know, I think maybe it was playing in Frank's shop."

"I didn't hear any music in Frank's shop, no radio or anything at all."

"Oh, I don't know, I don't remember then, where I heard it. It was just going thru my head is all, and I wondered if you remembered it." I started to look back at Mattie on the trailer, but remembered the blue movement and stopped myself. I turned half way around, hesitated awkwardly for a couple of seconds, and turned back facing forward.

Paw Paw noticed, he knew I was spooked. Paw Paw was a very perceptive man, I could never hide anything from him. "Don't let the delusions of an old alcoholic trouble you, son. There're no such things as ghosts, the car is not haunted."

I nodded in agreement, wanting to believe him but avoiding his eyes, because in my mind I wondered. The coupe obviously had a lot of history, had been through the hands of several people, each one with a life of stories and problems and agendas and experiences. Could they have left little pieces of themselves behind in the car, unsolved and unresolved troubles? Could the car be holding them captive and punishing them for wrongs they had committed against it? After all, two people that we knew of, had died in it, well one in it and the other under it. And I know I heard that song in Mattie.

Now I was being silly, it's just an old car, one that survived owners and wrecks and modifications and even abandonment at times. It was my Paw Paw's car now, or again, and it would be whatever we wanted it to be. And what would that be? Fast intrigued me, speed, drag races, very much my favorite, I loved the drag races and hoped to compete in them someday, and Mattie was already set up for that. But with Paw Paw pushing seventy and me still just twelve years old, professional racing of any kind was not an option for us, not for now anyway. Mattie needed to go back to being a street machine.

As our conversation strayed back to what we would do with Mattie, our excitement and anticipation returned. We agreed the interior should go back to as close to original as possible. The electrical should remain the modern twelve volt system it had already been converted to, but it needed circuits and harnesses added to accommodate updates like a sound system and turn signals, a heater and interior lights, maybe even an air conditioning system.

Before we were half way home, day turned to night as we continued to plan the rebuild of the coupe, and I refused to look back at it anymore, half fearing what I might see. Within half an hour or so of home, I fell asleep, vaguely aware of Paw Paw turning on the radio and finding a station to listen to. We'd be home soon, on our own turf, and things would be back to normal and tomorrow we would make a detailed assessment of our new toy and find a starting point.

We'd probably just start taking it apart first, or preparing the loose parts that came with it for paint and installation.

"Joseph, Joseph McClane." The old woman's voice whispered to me. "I'm sorry, Joseph, I should have let you have the car. I didn't know, I just didn't understand..."

I awakened with a violent jump that hurt when the seat belt and shoulder strap stopped me. "Paw Paw!" I was fighting, slapping out with my hands. "Get her away, get her away from me!" I slammed my right hand into the dash and the resulting pain to my fingers brought me out of my fitful daze. My breathing was hurried, gasping, and my eyes open wide though not yet seeing clearly. A strong hand rested on my shoulder and I jerked away, afraid, confused.

It was my grandfather's hand and he touched me again, trying to reassure me. "Joey, come on Joey, wake up, you've had a bad dream. It is okay, son, we're home now. It's okay, relax."

And we were home, easing thru the brick columns that held the black wrought iron gates and the automatic gate openers, the gates still swinging open for us. It was good to be home where everything would be familiar; my room, my bed, Sparky, my little Rat Terrier dog. It had been a long trip to make in one day, Houston and back, especially after getting started after noon. A fog had moved in, adding eeriness to the coupe. I glanced back at it. No ghost this time. I breathed a quiet sigh.

"Paw Paw, what did Mrs. Ferguson look like?"

"Mrs. Ferguson? Why would you ask that?"

"I don't know." I lied. "Just curious, I guess. What did she look like?"

"Oh, Joey. That was so long ago, and I was just a kid. Just an old woman, squatty, gray stringy hair, I can't remember much about her, just that she had the car I loved and wouldn't take me seriously. If not for that I'd probably not even remember her at all. Hey, buddy, it's late and we're both tired, let's leave the coupe on the trailer for the night and unload it in the morning."

It was unlike him to leave a car outside for even just one night, but he got no argument from me.

CHAPTER 2

Once in my bed, tucked in and kissed goodnight by Paw Paw, Sparky snuggled up to me under the covers, I lay there thinking about the events of the day; the coupe and Paw Paw's smile when he saw MATTIE stamped on the frame even though he already knew it was there, Frank and his spooky warnings about ghosts in the car, the movement in the car, the unexplained blue movement, the blue cloth that wasn't there, the music playing with no radio, and my fantasy run down the race track that seemed so real. In spite of its ghosts, I loved that car, and it was love at first sight. I began to think about the restoration, and I fell asleep rebuilding the coupe in my mind. Mrs. Ferguson did not revisit me during the night as I feared she might. Or if she did, I was so deep in my exhaustion induced slumber that I was not aware of it.

I awoke early in the morning to the sound and smell of Paw Paw cooking breakfast and I joined him as quickly as I could get dressed. Bacon, the sound and smell of bacon frying was definitely the way to wake up. Paw Paw was a good cook and we usually ate our meals at home and we always ate well. Breakfast was his favorite meal, he claimed, and he prepared it and consumed it with an amusing enjoyment. This morning we had fried eggs sunny side up, we liked the yolks runny, whole wheat biscuits with real butter and honey, turkey bacon, and sliced tomatoes. I could have done without the sliced tomatoes, I thought, but once I took a bite of one I enjoyed it, cold and crisp, a good opposite from the other food. I drank orange juice and snuck bacon scraps to Sparky under the table while Paw Paw sipped coffee and pretended to not notice.

"All right." He announced, standing up and stretching his arms and back, reaching for the ceiling. "Let's go find a place for Mattie in the shop and figure out how to get started on her."

I was ready and ran ahead of him, out the door, down the sidewalk, across the drive to the truck. I climbed up into the big four wheel drive dually, pushed the remote button to open the shop's overhead door, and started the truck's diesel engine to let it warm up. Paw Paw always insisted on a full minute long warm up before moving any vehicle. Let the fluids warm up and reach proper operating pressure, he would say. I scooted over and Paw Paw slid behind the wheel, turned the rig around in the wide concrete drive, and backed the trailer with Mattie on it to the shop door.

"I could have done that." I declared.

He reached over with one long arm and gave my knee a gentle squeeze. "Yeah, Joey, I bet you could've. You're getting to be a real man. Next time, okay? Remind me."

Paw Paw was a tall man, about six feet four inches, with long features; arms, legs, fingers, even long facial features. He was ruggedly handsome for his age, like Clint Eastwood, I always thought. I hoped to be tall like him and all indications were that I would be, at twelve years old I was already five feet nine inches tall.

Within minutes, we had the coupe on the lift and were walking around under it looking up. We each held a shop light, examining, exploring, commenting. Looking at the bottom of the engine, I thought about Mrs. Ferguson's nephew and how he died under the car. Was his ghost in it too? I was sure hers was. And that gaping hole in the floor, it looked like a shotgun blast from underneath Mattie. I'd never heard of a blown engine sending shrapnel through the floor. It looked more like an attack to me than just parts flying. Was it aimed at someone? Was it pay back for some sin committed against Mattie? Was Mattie so angry at someone that she wanted to hurt them? Stop the silly thoughts, I told myself. Mattie is a car, not a person, she can't willfully do anything on her own. You love this car, stop spooking yourself about it. Enjoy this restoration, it's special, it's Mattie, Paw Paw's Mattie.

"So what do you think, Joey, start with the interior or the drive train or the body?"

I had to pull myself back to the present. "Sir? Oh, um, I think the drive train, Paw Paw. If we do the interior or the body first we might damage it when we do the mechanic work. And if we do the drive train first, then we can test drive her before we tear the rest down."

"Good thinking, son. But now we've got some decisions to make, what do we want to power her with? A modern computer controlled system with fuel injection and a five speed automatic transmission? Or maybe an older rebuilt Buick nailhead engine with multiple carburetion and a nice five speed manual shift with overdrive?"

We discussed our options, pros and cons for each one and my obvious passion for Mattie inspired Paw Paw to let me make the decisions. And we dived right into our newest project.

A week later we had the ruined Chrysler engine and the mated racing tranny out of the car and we had modified the cross members and motor and transmission mounts to accommodate the 1966 circa 425 cubic inch nailhead engine, which we would rebuild, and the five speed manual tranny which we had ordered.

The rear end gears needed to be changed too. The racing gears Mattie possessed were too low for street use, they'd keep the engine working too hard at cruising speeds. We were not sure what the gear ratios were exactly, so we drew a chalk line on one rear tire and another on the differential yolk where the driveshaft connected before someone removed it to "disable" her. I turned the wheel around and counted out ten rotations while Paw Paw counted the corresponding driveshaft yolk rotations. Then we did the math, or I did the math rather, in my head, at his insistence. Paw Paw was always encouraging me to do math in my head. I didn't understand the importance of it but he seemed to get some kind of pleasure from it so I did it that way. Actually it came pretty easy for me, I could even do Algebra in my head, even long problems, if I'd close my eyes and visualize them.

"4.88" I announced. "She's got 4.88:1 ratio rear gears. Wow, that's low. You going to teach me how to set up the new gears in the housing and set the clearances and everything, Paw Paw?" I was fascinated with anything mechanical and eager to learn. I wanted to someday completely, from the ground up, build my own car.

The widow Ferguson had not reappeared and I dismissed her as the product of an overactive imagination spawned by Frank's spooky warnings. As each day came and went without any mysterious movement inside Mattie, I was able to convince myself to stop thinking about it.

Nearly two weeks had passed since we brought Mattie home, the nailhead engine was now in a machine shop in San Antonio getting bored and milled and fitted with new cam bearings, the new tranny was supposedly being shipped to us from somewhere in California. We made some minor modifications to Mattie's suspension and we were just doing busy work now and waiting for the drive train and other parts to arrive. So with little else to do, we decided to go ahead and remove the racing interior and get that project checked off the list.

Paw Paw retreated to the house to make us some sandwiches which we would eat in the shop, sitting on reproduction bar stools that looked like those used in soda fountain drug stores of long ago. I chose a ratchet and socket set to unbolt the racing seat and harness and returned to Mattie to begin the process of removing what little interior was in her; the seat, harness, and the homemade console.

I was looking for the remote control to open Mattie's door. I thought I had set it on her fender but it was gone. Music came from inside Mattie. How? She had no radio, or any kind of sound system at all. So, she did somehow play that song for me in Frank's garage. Chills covered me as I listened. It was an old song, from the fifties, sixties maybe. I stood and stared through her window, not understanding.

"The night we met I knew I needed you so, and if I had the chance I'd never let you go. So won't you say you love me, I'll make you so proud of me. We'll make them turn their heads, every place we go. So won't you please, be my, be my baby, please be my darlin', be my only baby, be my baby now, wo oh oh oh oh. I'll make you happy baby, just wait and see. For every kiss you give me, I'll give you three. Oh since the day I saw you, I have been waiting for you, you know I will wait for you till eternity. So won't you please, be my, be my baby, please be my darlin', be my only baby, be my baby now, wo oh oh oh oh. Be my little baby..."

The music faded, I saw the remote, right there on her fender. Why hadn't I seen it before? I pushed the button on the remote and the door unlocked and popped open, but as I reached for it, it closed and locked again. I pushed the button again and the same thing happened. "What the heck?"

Every muscle in Sparky's body went tense and his patches of short black, brown, and white hair stood straight out as he went into a furious barking and growling frenzy, looking right at the car window. Instinctively, I ordered him to stop and he did stop barking but still growled and bared his teeth as he walked backward on stiff legs for about five or six feet, never taking his eyes off the car window.

"Joseph."

I heard the whisper, tried not to look but my eyes were drawn against my will. There in the driver side window her face appeared as real as mine. "Joseph McClane." Came the pleading, guttural whisper again.

Sparky yelped as if he'd been hit and he turned and ran full speed out of the shop, feet sliding on the slick concrete like some hilarious Saturday morning television cartoon character. Had the moment not been so frightening I would have found my little dog's antics quite amusing.

My mouth flew open but no sound escaped, eyes wide in fright I dropped the remote and the tools I held and stumbled back tripping over the floor jack I'd left there and fell backwards to the floor. Still frantic to get away, I scrambled away from the coupe on hands and feet in an awkward face up backwards crawl which produced more struggle than actual distance traveled, hands and feet slipping and sliding under me like Sparky's had done with him. Tools rolled out from under me and scattered in all directions.

"Paw Paw!" I yelled frantically, still crawling backwards.

The voice addressed me again. "Joseph. I'm sorry Joseph, please forgive me."

"What do you want from me?" I blurted, my voice cracking like that of a teenager in early stages of puberty. When I realized she wasn't coming out of the car, I calmed down a little and found the courage to get to my feet, but stayed my distance, keeping a suspicious glare on this ghost of an old lady just on the other side of the glass.

"I've been waiting for you, Joseph. I need you to forgive me."

Now I understood but only half believed, hoping to wake up and find that this was only a dream. I responded. "I'm not who you think I am, Mrs. Ferguson. It's my grandfather, you think I'm my grandfather. This is 1990 and I'm only twelve years old, I'm Joseph McClane the third."

Ignoring my declaration, she pleaded again. "Help me, Joseph, please."

Was she helpless? Was this the extent of her power, to merely appear and whisper and plead? I inched closer to the car and her image became clearer, I noticed her features, pretty sky blue eyes but dimmed and reddened with age or maybe fear or unhappiness, deep lines on her face which appeared random like a detailed road map, the unkempt stringy gray hair, and her night gown, the dirty blue night gown I had seen as movement inside the car that first day. What was all over the front of it? It looked nasty, like dried puke or something. Curiosity slowly replaced my fear and I had thoughts of actually trying to help her. But how?

I asked, "What can I do?"

"Talking to the car, Joey?"

Okay, I'm already scared and I'm talking to a ghost and somebody sneaks up behind me. My nerves are already shattered and I don't need another startling surprise. I jumped at the sound of Paw Paw's voice. He had returned with sandwiches and chips and cookies.

I pointed to the car window, wanting him to finally see her. She was gone, completely gone, vanished into thin air, seen only by me, again. I struggled to regain my composure, as if such a thing was possible. "Oh, um, yeah, I fell over that jack and dropped everything. And the remote was acting funny, the door wouldn't stay open, and..."

"The ghost again, Joey? I thought we were over that." He looked a little disgusted.

I couldn't answer, it was all too much to sort out in my twelve year old mind, not that it would have made any sense to me at any age. I needed to change the subject, I couldn't tell him what had just happened. "No, um, it's just, um... The remote was being weird, and I fell. What, uh, what kind of sandwiches did you make,

Paw Paw?"

"Tuna salad. You okay? You didn't hurt yourself when you fell, did you? You seem kind of shook up. Did you hit your head?" He set the paper plates full of food on Mattie's fender, held my shoulder in one hand and brushed me off with the other, as if I were a small child. I could tell he was studying my face, reading me.

I brushed at my clothes too, happy for the distraction. "Paw Paw, why do you think they gave Mattie the number thirteen?"

"Oh, I don't know, maybe she was unlucky for someone. We can take the numbers off though, and repaint the doors." He leaned to Mattie and ran his fingertips over her door, over the thirteen. "This paint job doesn't look very old and somebody did a really nice job on it. I've never seen flames like that, they look like real fire, it'd be a shame to disturb them. Someone was quite an artist." He paused, cocked his head at me and grinned. "You like Mattie painted like this, don't you?"

"Yes sir, I do, I like her just like she is, numbers and all, she's beautiful." Actually I couldn't understand why I liked the flames so much, they looked like Hell Fire, threatening, menacing, evil, ready to leap out at you and consume you. Maybe it was just that they were so real like, so captivating, and definitely not something you were going to see on another car. The number thirteen was just catching fire around the edges and as you watched it you expected the fire to rage out of control and completely engulf the numbers at any second.

We sat on our stools, using Mattie's left front fender, with a protective cover over it, as a table and ate our lunch and drank Dr. Peppers and talked about Mattie. Paw Paw smiled as he listened to my ideas for her and I could tell he was picking up on my love for the coupe. And I made sure the conversation stayed far from ghosts. I had never kept anything from my Paw Paw before, but this time it seemed like the right thing to do, for now anyway.

After that day, Mrs. Ferguson invaded my sleep every night for over a week. All night long I would bear witness to her miserable life from the moment the coupe came into it till her death.

She was a pitiful old woman, alone for the first time in her life and quite sad and lost in her loneliness. In her early seventies and now widowed after being married to Mr. Ferguson since she was seventeen, childless, and with only one nearby neighbor and very few friends. She thought having a car and a way to get around on her own would allow her to start a new life, find a church she liked, get a hobby, go to movies, make some friends, be better able to take care of herself. But driving was harder than it looked and she wasn't able to master it. She couldn't get the car to go with any ease or control, the correct gear was hard to find and it lunged and jerked and threw her around inside. She bruised her ribs against the massive steering wheel and she strained her shoulder trying to hang on.

Mr. Turner, her only close neighbor, tried to give her some driving lessons but quickly gave up, advising her to get rid of the car and go back to using taxis as her mode of transportation. Her determination lasted a little longer though, long enough for her to run the car through the back wall of her garage, doing considerable damage to the right front fender and bumper and knocking a headlamp bucket loose so that it just dangled there by the wires.

On a short, just passing thru visit, Mrs. Ferguson's brother in law, George, attempted to repair the light and he got it to work somewhat, but it looked terrible, a makeshift clamp forced over the stem, with bolts driven thru the fender. The light shook and flopped around when the engine was running. His amateurish attempts at the repair did almost as much damage as the accident had done. I felt so sorry for Mattie.

The following evening Mrs. Ferguson backed right into a huge Pecan tree by her long gravel driveway and bent up the bumper and right rear fender. I watched in horror as the slow destruction of Mattie unfolded in my dreams of the widow's last days on earth. Immediately after hitting the tree, the widow flew out of the car in a rage, cussing like a sailor, screaming profanity at Mattie as if it was all her fault.

"You damned son of a bitch piece of shit car!" She screamed. "How in the hell am I supposed to drive when I can't even see out? Can't see the damned ground from in there or anything.

"Why did I get such a big car? Why didn't Henry teach me how to drive when I was younger? Oh hell! Now look at this! What am I going to do now?" By now she had worked herself up even more and was waving her arms around and stamping her feet and ranting like a crazy person. "Damn it!"

What she did was to call a taxi for her trip to town and she left the coupe sitting right there butted backwards against the tree for all the world to see. And she left it there for days.

I saw, in one of the dreams, my grandfather when he was about my age and that intrigued me, shocked me. Except for the clothes he wore he looked just like me, only slimmer. No wonder the widow thought I was him. No wonder I had been unable to convince her otherwise. He was with his grandfather, his Paw Paw, in the new sedan, Mattie's replacement car, driving past the widow's house and he saw Mattie wrecked against the Pecan tree.

"Stop!" He shouted.

But his Paw Paw didn't stop. "Leave it alone, Joseph. It's her car now."

"No! She ruining it! Paw Paw, please, I love that car! Buy it back from her, keep it for me, I'll pay for it, I'll do anything!"

"Hush up now, son. You're being silly, and disrespectful. You're a child, you can't have a car."

But he didn't "hush up", his protests continued and his tears flowed until his grandfather took him home and his dad gave him a spanking and sent him to bed without supper.

Wow, his Paw Paw wasn't anything like mine. I couldn't imagine my Paw Paw ever hitting me, or denying me anything I was so passionate about. So my first night of dreams in the week plus long series, was one of seeing my grandfather at my age, being denied his precious coupe and watching it being slowly destroyed by an uncaring, incompetent, old woman.

The next day was Saturday and I had a Little League baseball game, next to the last game of the season. But I wasn't in the mood for it and requested permission to stay home and work on Mattie instead. She seemed to be taking over my life, my mind, my time, even when I slept, and I anxiously and totally surrendered.

But permission to skip the game was not given. "Now Joey, you know that would be irresponsible, your team is counting on you and you have an obligation to them. We've got plenty of time to work on that car."

"Yes sir." I went and played but my heart was not in it. Mattie's dreams kept playing in my head and I watched perfect strikes sail right by me without even swinging at them. My performance in the field was poor also and in the third inning, after another error, I was benched for the remainder of the game. It wasn't like I was normally the star of the team or anything like that, but I was always a reliable contributor, just not today. Afterwards I apologized to the coach, and on the way home to Paw Paw. "I'm sorry, I just couldn't get my head in the game. Didn't sleep well last night, just tired I guess."

Paw Paw replied. "Well, nobody is one hundred percent every day, son." I'd heard him use that line before and wondered if he'd gotten it from his Paw Paw or maybe his own Dad. No, I decided, they probably would have spanked him and sent him to bed without supper.

"Paw Paw." I said.

He looked over at me from his side of the car, a 1964 Buick Wildcat convertible, dark blue inside and out except for a canvas colored top, and we had the top down. This was one of the more subtle cars we had restored, a luxury car, not a muscle car or a hot rod, push button everything and as stock as the day it rolled off the assembly line. It was a nice cruiser and got lots of looks everywhere it went. He looked at me and smiled but didn't speak. It occurred to me how well that car fit him, like comfortable clothes.

"I love you." I intended to expand on that, say more about why I appreciated him so much and how he was raising me with such gentleness and understanding, something I had some insight into after the dream of the previous night. But nothing else came out of my mouth, the words wouldn't form.

"I love you too, son, more than life itself."

Before going home from the baseball game we ran a few errands around town; gassed up the car, bought a case of oil at the NAPA auto parts store, shopped for some groceries and Sparky's favorite treats. Then we stopped by our church on the way home to donate a few things to the food pantry there. Paw Paw got into a long conversation, about politics or the economy or something, with the lady who works at the church office. I think she was flirting with him. I became increasingly impatient, I just wanted to go home and work on Mattie. I had even turned down an invitation to go home with a friend from my baseball team, spend the night at his house and play games and watch movies all night. I just wanted to go home and work on Mattie.

But we didn't work on her that evening. Paw Paw said he was tired, I think he just thought I was and instead we just ate supper and watched a movie on TV. The movie was one of our old favorites, Christine, a popular Steven King story about a haunted car and the boy who loved it. And for the first time, that movie scared me. I worried that Mattie might turn evil like the '57 Plymouth in the movie did. I must have fallen asleep watching the movie because the next thing I knew the credits were rolling and Paw Paw was patting me on the shoulder, telling me to go on to bed.

And my dream of Mrs. Ferguson continued. She tried again to navigate the coupe, this time making it onto the road and several blocks into town before having another mishap. Mattie was heavy and her brakes were the old mechanical type, cable brakes without hydraulics, and hard to stop, impossible to stop quickly. She approached a stop sign too fast, people were crossing the intersection and she waited too late to brake and she forgot to push in on the clutch so the car was still pulling forward. The pedestrians scrambled to get out of her way and she was all the way out into the intersection before coming to a complete stop with oncoming traffic braking hard and honking and taking evasive action to avoid a collision with Mattie and each other.

Mrs. Ferguson cursed the car and vowed to sell it for junk. Giving up now, she turned Mattie around, with great effort, still blocking the entire intersection, having to pull forward and then back up three times to reverse her direction, struggling with the hard steering and still confusing the pedals. She had to restart the car twice, and she headed back home. Somehow she made it up her driveway and into the garage without hitting anything else, but she left the back half of the car sticking out, afraid of running into the back wall again. The dream turned vague after that, but continued for what seemed like hours, maybe it just played over and over like bad reruns, I can't remember.

I awoke, not sure where I was at first, dream or reality? But when Sparky whined and nudged me I regained my presence of mind. Sparky needed to go outside so I went with him enjoying the cool dew under my bare feet in the grass and the clear starlit sky overhead. I walked about half way to the shop and stopped, staring, and wondering if I went inside would Mrs. Ferguson appear to me? Sparky scratched on the front door of the house, wanting to go back in, so I followed him back in and to our room. I took a towel from my bathroom and wiped my feet off, then did the same for Sparky and we went back to bed.

Monday morning after a little study time, Paw Paw and I went into town for haircuts, this time taking the little kit car reproduction Cobra, one of my favorites from our collection. Actually it was my favorite, until we got Mattie. It was a true sports car, two passenger, low slung to hug the road, and very pretty, blue and white. Even though it was a replica and not a real Cobra, it had the correct engine, a 427 with two fours and it was worth an easy hundred thousand. The Cobra was such a fun car and we hadn't had it out in a while so we decided to take a little road trip. After haircuts and picking up some shirts at the cleaners, we headed into the Texas Hill Country on a seldom traveled back road to a bar be cue place about twenty miles out. As usual, the Cobra attracted attention, smiles and waves and thumbs up signs, and a small crowd of curious people approached as soon as we arrived in the parking lot.

Paw Paw was always gracious when strangers wanted to admire his toys and took the time to talk and show and explain. He was a happy, friendly man who liked people, a people person, but one without many close friends. He was too absorbed in his private world to hang out at coffee shops or country clubs or bars.

I was sort of like him, I liked people, other kids, but was a little shy and was also very absorbed in our little world of cars and toys and each other. I was homeschooled and Paw Paw pushed me to study hard and long and I never got a break from it, not in the summer or on weekends or holidays. I neither understood nor questioned why, I just did it, and it came easy to me, all of it; the math, reading comprehension, science, history. My mind was a thirsty sponge.

We walked out of the restaurant ahead of another family, a large family that was having some kind of special get together, maybe a birthday or an anniversary or something. They were parked near us and when they saw us going for the Cobra they wanted to see it. I stood back and waited while Paw Paw visited with them and let them see his car, inside and out and under the hood. It tried my patience. I was anxious to get home and back to work on Mattie, I could feel her pulling at me. I also hoped that Mrs. Ferguson would appear.

It was midafternoon when we resumed our project. We decided to work on the running boards, scrape what was left of the old rubber mat off of them, repair a couple of rust holes, and prepare them for paint. With the parts on stands across the shop from Mattie, we began the cleaning process. Every couple of minutes I'd look over at her, watching for the ghost. By now my fear of Mrs. Ferguson was gone and I actually looked forward to seeing her. She disappointed in the shop, but not that night in my sleep.

My first recollection of her in this night's dream was of her ironing clothes. Apparently, Mrs. Ferguson ironed and sewed for other people, in her home, to earn some extra money. A radio was playing in the background but I couldn't see it. A man was talking about the worsening aggression of Germany toward its neighboring countries and how it had to be stopped. Next, the newsman spoke about the depression and the resulting poverty with its soup lines and government work programs. Sunlight shown through the half open curtains but it was unclear to me what the time of day was. She finished ironing a shirt, folded it and laid it on a stack of other clothes.

She walked across the stained Oak living room floor, across a large area rug, to her kitchen and opened the refrigerator which was quite funny looking; short and very square, with a round motor on top. Mrs. Ferguson stood and stared into the little frig for a long moment as if she had forgotten what she wanted from it, then she reached in a retrieved a half gallon glass bottle, half full of milk. She removed the lid and smelled of it and made a face, it was sour, spoiled. She sat down hard in a green vinyl padded metal chair at the little kitchen table, put her face in her hands, and cried.

I felt sorry for her, she seemed so unhappy, but surely the sour milk couldn't have upset her that much. Maybe it just didn't take much anymore to ruin her day.

"Henry," She cried. "Why did you leave me? I can't do anything for myself, I'm lost without you. There is nothing for me to live for anymore."

A car horn blasted out from the garage. Music came from the same direction, jazz I think, loud.

"And that damned car!" She slammed an open hand on the table and winced and shook her hand as if it hurt. "You're not going to beat me, you stupid bucket of bolts!" She jumped up, grabbed her purse from a chair on her way thru the living room and stormed out of the house, across the side yard to the garage. As she neared the car the horn stopped honking and the music faded to silence, she stopped and stared. "No, you're not going to beat me, you are not!" And again, she tried to drive.

Slowly, very slowly, Mrs. Ferguson backed the coupe out of her driveway and onto the street, certainly doing much better this time, remembering the timing with the clutch and brake and gas pedals. She successfully found first gear and the car lunged forward, jerked a few times, and died. "Damn you!" She angrily pounded the steering wheel with the palm of an open hand, several times. She tried again, another jerky start but moving, shift to second, shift to third, doing better, quite a bit better, maybe there's some hope now.

Not more than six blocks down the street, from out of nowhere a dog ran right out in front of her. She felt the car run over the animal as she struggled to get control of the car and stop it. A child was screaming hysterically, calling the dog's name, the dog yelped and went silent, a man came running from a nearby yard, too much was happening too fast. One front wheel hopped the curb, the car came to a rough awkward stop and died. Mrs. Ferguson bailed out and ran around to the back of the car. The little girl was on her knees on the pavement, hugging her little dog and crying, the dog was dead.

"Oh my God, I'm sorry, I'm so sorry, he just came out of nowhere!" She leaned on the car's rear fender, dropped her face to her cupped hands and cried. "Oh my… I'm never going to drive again. It could have been the child. Never, never, never… Never again."

I awoke and cried too, silently, for Mrs. Ferguson, she was such a tormented soul. I cried for the dead dog and the brokenhearted little girl. And I cried for Mattie, so new and so beautiful, and being destroyed piece by piece. I lay on my side, flooding my pillow with tears, slowly stroking Sparky behind his ears. And eventually, I fell back to sleep.

With the little girl still crying over her dog and her daddy trying to sort things out and comfort his daughter and Mrs. Ferguson seemingly in shock over the incident, a policeman showed up. It was unclear to me if someone called him or if he just happened by, but I do remember I liked his car, and old four door Hudson with the bubble gum machine style light on top and the front doors painted white against a black car body, a large silver star painted on each front door.

First the cop spoke to the girl's father then with the little girl. I was impressed with how gentle and caring he was with her. He talked about a dog he had loved when he was younger and hoped to see in Heaven someday, trying to give the girl some kind of comforting thought. He cradled the little dog in his arms, it looked like a Jack Russell Terrier and reminded me of Sparky. The officer carried it out of the street and laid it down on the grass by the concrete sidewalk.

Next the officer talked with Mrs. Ferguson, instructing her to tell him in her words what had happened. And she did. Realizing how upset she was, he opened Mattie's driver side door and invited her to sit down, which she did, tears still streaming down her cheeks. "Could I see your driver's license, Ma'am?"

Oh, well, officer, I uh, don't have one, just yet. You see, my husband passed away recently and I never learned how to drive and I just got this car and thought I'd learn how before, you know…"

"Ma'am, you can't drive on public streets without a license, it's against the law."

"Oh dear, what's going to happen now? Will I be arrested?"

"No ma'am, but you'll have to have someone else drive your car home for you. Is there someone who could do that for you?"

"Well, maybe my neighbor, Mr. Turner, but he isn't here."

A small crowd had gathered and another man offered to help, so he drove the coupe home for Mrs. Ferguson, she riding with him, and afterward the officer gave the man a ride back to his home.

Although it was still daylight, Mrs. Ferguson went to bed soon after getting home. She took some pills and lay down in her bed, fully clothed, and cried herself to sleep. I watched her in her fitful slumber, calling out to her dead husband several times and reliving the dog accident in her dreams. I felt so sorry for the poor lady. I pondered the situation, what could I do to help her? Of course all the events in my dreams of her were things that had happened long ago, but her tortured spirit was still trapped in the coupe and in that long ago time and place. She needed help, release, forgiveness, but what could I do? Paw Paw would never believe any of this was real, and she was appearing to me, thinking I was him. It was up to me but I had no idea how to handle it.

Sunday morning we went to church, our church was a Christian protestant non-denominational church. After the services we headed for the city park for a picnic by the river with several families from our church. While the adults cooked on the brick grills there and set up the concrete tables with table cloths and paper plates and plastic utensils, I played with the kids my age. We enjoyed the playground equipment; swings, see saws, monkey bars, we skipped flat stones on the water and found a soft drink can to use for an awkward soccer ball. A new girl from our church was playing with us, Anita Cantu, she was pretty but tall and skinny and she played rough like a boy. She was Mexican. I had not been around the Mexican kids much because I was home schooled, but I was struck by her pretty, dark features. Her hair was short and so black it shined and her skin was perfect. Her eyes were so dark you couldn't see her pupils and her eyes were big too, and she smiled with her eyes as much as she did with her mouth, more so maybe. I couldn't stop looking at her. I hoped she wouldn't notice. But she did. Our eyes would meet and I'd look away, then quickly back at her and she'd smile and I'd look away again. She knew I was looking at her.

I took a break from the game and walked to a nearby water fountain. Anita followed, staying a few feet back. I got a sip of water and looked up, she was right there. I held the button while she drank.

"Thanks."

"You're welcome."

I was nervous and didn't know what else to say.

"My name's Anita."

"I know."

"And your name is Joey, right?"

"Oh, yeah, sorry, I'm Joey."

She giggled. "I know."

I pulled a candy bar, snickers I think, from my pocket, unwrapped it and offered half of it to her. It was flattened a little and I was embarrassed. She accepted it, thanked me and smiled. Her teeth looked so white against her skin. Dimples, deep black eyes, golden brown skin. She was beautiful. And even though I wasn't really thinking about girls yet, I was struck by her beauty. I was spell bound.

I blurted, "You're pretty." Now why did I say that?

"Thanks." She answered and widened her smile, her dimples deepened. Then she turned and trotted back to the other kids and the aluminum can soccer game.

I stood and watched her. I felt like I had done the wrong thing. I said it all wrong, maybe shouldn't have said anything at all. I had just embarrassed myself.

Arriving home late in the afternoon, we did some yard chores which we both disliked, ate supper, and worked on my studies. Paw Paw was pushing my studies hard and I didn't understand why, after all I was well ahead of where I should be in them. But it seemed important to him and it came easy for me so I just went along with it. Although I was technically in the seventh grade, we were already doing high school math and science courses. But this evening I just wanted to go to bed. I was anxious to get to sleep and back to Mrs. Ferguson and her troubled life.

Mrs. Ferguson was still sleeping and the knock at her front door was growing louder, more frequent, and was now accompanied by a voice. "Annie! Annie! Hey Annie, are you there?"

I heard the door open and the screen door slam shut, a man and a woman entered and crept thru the living room, looking around cautiously. The lady looked a lot like Mrs. Ferguson, a little heavier maybe but same squatty physique, same stringy gray hair, same facial features. They were obviously sisters, and the man was the sister's husband. The lady continued through the house searching for Mrs. Ferguson, her husband carried two large paper grocery sacks thru the living room and dining room, to the kitchen.

It was early in the morning, I suppose, from the light in the windows, and Mrs. Ferguson was still asleep, so much so that she was unaware of her sister and brother in law in her house. On the night stand by her bed were sleeping pills, some kind of pain medicine with Opium in it, and an empty glass that smelled like bourbon. Her sister picked it up and put it to her nose, made a face to her husband. The widow was drugging herself to sleep trying to get some rest and stop her own dreams and thoughts of her dead husband and her loneliness, and also of the coupe which seemed to be tormenting her with increasing ferocity.

With her sister jostling her shoulder and pillow while talking to her, Mrs. Ferguson struggled awake, sat on the edge of her bed, had a short pointless conversation obscured by her own drug induced fuzzy headedness, and went to take a bath.

While she bathed and dressed, her sister and brother in law cleaned her house, it was quite a mess. They took her out to eat and grocery shopping, dropped some clothes off at the cleaners, stopped at the electric company and paid her overdue bill and vowed to keep a closer eye on her. They lived over in the next small town, Guardiola, but it wasn't far away, half an hour maybe. While they ran the errands and ate lunch, Mrs. Ferguson talked about the evil car, she was sure it wanted to kill her.

"Annie," Myrtle told her, "Why don't you come stay with us? You're not taking care of yourself, you have me so worried, I think you're in a depression. And these stories about that car, Annie, they don't make sense. That car is not evil, you just don't know how to drive."

"No, Myrtle, it is evil, and it hates me. The horn goes off, all by itself, at the oddest times, and the radio too, and it stops as soon as I go out to see about it. The lights flash on and off for no reason. Once it backed itself out of the garage, I swear, I heard it running, with nobody in it, I looked out the window and saw the exhaust coming out of the pipe and everything. Then it drove itself back inside and turned itself off. I tell you it wants to kill me. When I try to drive it pulls the steering wheel right out of my hands and does whatever it wants. Sometimes the brakes lock up and other times they don't work at all. I want it out of here, gone, give it to your grandson, he's old enough for a car now, just get it away from me. It killed that poor little dog, and the little girl was so brokenhearted and it could have been her instead of the dog." Mrs. Ferguson sobbed and trembled in her distress.

Myrtle and George looked at each other in disbelief. They were certain Annie had completely lost her mind and was now a danger to herself and others, especially if she continued driving.

"Come stay with us for a while, Annie, let us take care of you, get you away from things that remind you of Henry and keep you sad. Let us help you sis, come on, it'll be fun, we'll go to the movies, play bingo at church, shop together, you'll love my little garden. What do you say?"

"No, no I want to stay home. Just get that car out of here and I'll be fine. Everything was fine till I bought that evil machine."

Myrtle and George gazed at each other, wondering what to do, knowing that Annie was not okay by herself, car or no car. And they certainly did not believe that the coupe had taken on an evil personality and was out to get her. As if they had communicated without speaking they formed a new plan and offered it to her.

"Okay, Annie, tell you what, I'll come stay with you here for a while and George will take the car to our house. How about that? The car will be gone and you and I can do all kinds of fun things together, okay? I'll go home and pack some things and we'll be back tomorrow. George can bring someone to drive your car back to our house and you won't have to worry about that anymore. Sound good?"

"Well, I guess so, Myrtle. But couldn't you take the car today? It does things in the night to scare me, lights flashing, horn blaring, radio playing loud, motor racing..." She shook her head and wiped her eyes. "It's going to kill me, I know it is."

Since Myrtle couldn't drive either, taking the car home was on hold for another day, so George agreed to just drive it a few blocks down the street and leave it parked there to get it away from Annie. But he couldn't get it started, the engine wouldn't turn over at all. He searched for the problem but never figured it out, the battery was not dead, the lights worked, fire was getting to the starter, the tank had plenty of gas and it was pumping to the carburetor, but it would not start.

"Well, I couldn't get it to start, Annie, but it'll be gone tomorrow I promise, even if we have to drag it away."

"Oh no, can't you do something? That thing will start its tricks tonight for sure. I won't get any sleep at all. The lights and horn will be going off..."

So George went back to the garage and disconnected the battery. "There," He declared. "No battery, impossible for anything to work on it now; horns, lights, whatever, it can't start now. It can't do anything. It'll leave you alone tonight, Annie."

"You could still come home with us tonight, and we'll return in the morning after I've had some time to pack some things." Myrtle was afraid to leave her sister alone.

"No, I'll be all right one more night, especially if that car is disabled. I wish you could get it out of here today, George. That car hates me. Maybe I should have let that silly little Joseph McClane have it after all."

Something woke me but I didn't know what, I sat up in bed and listened, nothing. I got up and went to the restroom, checked to see if Sparky wanted to go outside, he did not, just lay on the bed watching me. Restless from my dream, I roamed around our small house without purpose, thinking confusing thoughts, looked at the clock in the kitchen, four twenty a.m., checked the refrigerator but didn't really want anything from it, just stood there staring into it, thought about Mrs. Ferguson's funny little fridge. I ambled back to my room, Sparky at my heels. I peered out a window at the shop, wondering, half wanting to go out there. A light came on in the shop, then another. Was Paw Paw out there? I checked his room, opened his door just a crack. He was asleep in his bed, on his back and snoring. Standing at a window again, this time in the living room, not knowing what to do, I saw the lights go off. Now I worried, someone was out there messing around with our cars and stuff. Should I wake Paw Paw? What if I did and no one was out there?

Sneaking up on the shop, bare feet in the wet grass, avoiding the sidewalk, flashlight in my hand but off, Sparky by my side, I peered into a window. It was dark in there now and I was a little spooked. I shined the light in and around, nothing, no movement, no noise. I found our hidden key, opened the door and crept inside, keeping a hand on the door, ready to make a hasty exit. With the flashlight aimed at the coupe, I saw the blue movement inside. Chills ran up my back.

"Joseph." Came the now familiar whisper.

I looked harder but didn't move any closer, strained my eyes, searched the car windows with the flashlight. Nothing.

A hand touched my shoulder and I jumped so hard I threw the flashlight straight up in the air and I cried out. I turned around to see Paw Paw.

"What are you doing out here, Joey?"

Heart beating hard and fast, it took a moment to gather my composure and answer him. "Oh, uh, I, uh, thought I saw a light on, I worried, someone might be…"

"Well, let's look around. You should have waked me."

He knew more about my reasons than he admitted, he saw my fear. Paw Paw draped his arm around my shoulders and pulled me close, flipped on the light switches with his other hand. I felt safe.

A slow, close inspection of the shop showed that no one was there and nothing had been disturbed.

"Are you okay, Joey?"

"Yes sir." My voice answered shakily in the affirmative, but everything else about me said otherwise.

"Ghosts?"

I was trying to read his look. Accusing? Unhappy? No. Caring, concerned. "No sir."

"Son, you know you can tell me anything."

I just looked at him in silence, wanting to tell him but afraid to. My silent gaze shifted to Mattie. I could feel myself still shaking and wished I could stop it.

He sat on a stool and patted the one beside him, I sat too. He rested a strong hand on my knee and looked me in the eye. "Joey, I don't believe in ghosts because I've never seen one. But I am aware that there are things in this world we don't fully understand, and I do believe we have a spirit that lives on after we die." He moved his hand to my back and rubbed gently between my shoulders, it comforted me. I calmed a little. "Something about this car is eating at you. If you need to talk about it I'll listen, and I'll believe what you tell me because I know you'll tell me the truth." He knew, not everything, not specifics, but he knew.

I hesitated, took a deep breath, in and out, and began. "Paw Paw, I can tell you everything about Mrs. Ferguson; what she looked like, her sky blue eyes, what she wore, what the inside of her house looked like; the black and white checkered floor in her kitchen, her little white refrigerator with the round motor on top, the spoiled milk inside of it, her green kitchen table with small white flowers and chromed edges and matching chairs, four of them, one with a small rip on the seat, the tall wood posts on the corners of her bed, stained wood floors with rugs with flowery patterns on them, how she damaged the coupe each time, the dog she ran over and the little girl the dog belonged to…" I paused but he said nothing. "Mrs. Ferguson's first name was Annie and her sister's name was Myrtle and her husband was George. Mrs. Ferguson's husband's name was Henry and they got married when she was seventeen but never had any children. I watched as you saw Mattie crashed into the big Pecan tree in her driveway and you threw a fit and got into trouble, sent to bed without supper." I stopped and waited for his reaction.

Paw Paw stared at me in silence, realizing I knew too many details to be lying. Finally he swallowed hard, then spoke to me, softly. "How do you know these things, son?"

"She appears to me in Mattie." I swallowed hard, cleared my throat and sniffed, never taking my eyes away from his. "And she whispers to me, and I watch her in my dreams." Even though it felt good to unburden myself, I was close to tears and I didn't know why.

"Should we get rid of the car?"

"No! No, Paw Paw! Please don't do that! I love that car! It's okay, she doesn't scare me, any more. She just wants me to…" I stopped, thinking I'd said too much.

"What? What does she want, Joey?"

"Well, she thinks I'm you, and she wants forgiveness, for not letting you have the car. She thinks it has tormented her all these years because of that. She's trapped, unable to move on, and she thinks forgiveness will free her."

I felt as if I had just told the smartest man in the world the most ridiculous story ever, and expected him to believe it. It was hard for me to believe it myself, but it was really happening, and to me. After a minute or so of somewhat uncomfortable silence, Paw Paw suggested we continue our discussion over breakfast, even though it was only about five in the morning, an hour and a half before we usually got up. And it was a good idea, it wasn't like we could go back to sleep now, either of us. So we retreated to the house and the kitchen, where I sat at the serving bar watching him cook and sip coffee. I told him everything, from the first time I saw the blue movement in the coupe at Frank's shop, to the dream of last night. I finished my story with, "I hope she doesn't quit appearing now that I've told you about her."

Paw Paw glanced over his shoulder at me, grinned and snickered lightly under his breath. "None of this makes any sense, you know that, Joey." He paused, turned back to his cooking. "But there's no other way you could know these things." He hesitated, thinking, obviously had more to say, so I remained silent and waited. He turned the cook top off and scraped the scrambled eggs and fried bacon onto plates, brought them to the kitchen island where I sat opposite him. "Okay, I've got an idea, Joey. Why don't you just tell her that you forgive her?"

"You mean, pretend I'm you?"

"Sure, what could it hurt? You've tried to convince her otherwise and she didn't believe you, right? And if it works and frees her spirit, then you've helped her. And one other thing, son, I don't think you should share this with anyone else. Okay? I mean, I know you're telling the truth, but no one else would believe this. And it would probably give you a reputation you wouldn't appreciate."

I agreed to keep it all between us, I didn't want to be thought of as weird, and I liked Paw Paw's idea and decided to do just what he suggested at her very next appearance which I assumed would be that very day. But our work on the loose parts of the coupe, kept us on the other end of the shop from it, and even though I kept looking over at Mattie, Mrs. Ferguson did not show herself.

That night though, was a totally different story. It felt like the dream began before I was even asleep, as soon as my head hit the pillow I began watching the horrifying end of Mrs. Ferguson.

Once more I saw my Paw Paw as a boy, in his early teens, he was standing on her front porch talking to Mrs. Ferguson who was standing in the doorway holding the screen door open with one hand, looking at him. He was holding up for her to see, a fistful of dollars, and begging her to sell him the car. Not everything was clear to me and I couldn't understand all that was said, but it was certain he was trying to make a deal with her to buy Mattie, and she was not receptive to his offer. He began to cry and plead but she just shook her head and closed the door, leaving him standing there. I saw him walk directly to the coupe which sat half in half out of the rickety looking dirt floor garage, and he talked to it, crying. My Paw Paw, a thirteen year broken hearted kid losing the thing he wanted most, opened the door and sat inside for a long while.

I woke to my own sadness, for my Paw Paw, for his sadness over fifty years ago. Lying there, looking around my room, dim light filtering thru the window from the outside security lights on the shop, eerie silhouettes of tree limbs playing on one wall. Thinking about Mattie and my Paw Paw, I slowly drifted back to sleep, and back to Mrs. Ferguson.

She was sitting at the green table under the window in her little kitchen, eating supper, baked chicken or something that looked like it, and mashed potatoes and rice. The window showed that it was already dark outside, and the old lady looked tired, haggard and stressed. From the garage came the sound of the coupe's horn in short blasts spaced two or three seconds apart.

"No!" She screamed, and stood up so quickly she knocked her plate to the floor. "No, you can't do that! George said he fixed you so you couldn't!" She hurried to another window, in another room, the living room I believe, and peered out into the dark. Mattie was completely out of the garage, sitting in the driveway, horn blasting, lights flashing on and off. "Stop!" She yelled. "I can't stand this anymore!" She ran out in her nightgown but as soon as she reached the porch steps, the noise and lights stopped, and Mattie rolled back into the garage. The widow stood there, face in her hands, crying hysterically. "I've lost my mind, Henry. I've lost my damned mind. Why is this happening to me?"

I watched Mrs. Ferguson return to her house, and to the kitchen. She picked the plate up off the floor and began cleaning the mess. Mattie's horn sounded again. "Damn it!" She screamed and hurled the plate against a wall, broken pieces filling the air, sprinkling down on the table top and the floor, and her. She ran to the bedroom, found her sleeping pills and downed the entire bottle, chased it with the opium medicine and then went back to the kitchen and poured herself a glass of whisky, mixed it with a little water.

She sat in a living room chair, turned on a radio on a stand by her chair, turned it back off and cried, her whole body shaking with the sobbing. Mattie was silent now and Mrs. Ferguson drifted into a fitful sleep. Everything was quiet, but tense, like the proverbial calm before a storm and I was sure something really bad was about to happen. I caught a glimpse of a mouse scurrying across the living room hardwood floor, thin sheer curtains moved lazily in the light breeze coming through the partially open wood framed windows, I heard the motor on top of the little fridge kick on, a clock was ticking somewhere in the background, faint sounds of distant traffic, things you normally do not notice.

Suddenly, Mrs. Ferguson jerked forward in her chair, clutching her stomach and vomiting violently. She jumped to her feet but just as quickly fell forward to her hands and knees, still throwing up, gasping for breath, thrashing around in her own filth, seized by fear and panic.

She struggled to her feet again and shuffled for the front door, frantically fought the lock and handle for a moment before getting it open, and fell out onto the front porch, crashing out through the screen door onto her knees. The screen door banged her back a couple of times. She fought her way off the porch and across the yard to the coupe, trying to run, falling, half crawling half running, falling again, finally reaching it she opened the door and struggled to get herself inside.

"Please, please, I need help, please run, damn you!" She turned the key and floored the gas pedal, nothing. She tried the lights, nothing, the horn, nothing. "Why?!" She grabbed her stomach and in one hard spasm, emptied what was left of its contents all over the front of her blue nightgown. That dirty blue nightgown, that's what I'd been seeing in Mattie. Out of her mind with panic, she beat her fists on the car's wheel and dash, screaming. Her blue eyes bulged and she grabbed the sides of her head with both hands, and slowly, painfully, died, sitting there in Mattie. As life left her body, it gave up the rest of its contents, emptying her bowels and bladder and she sat there in her own stinking mess, slumped against the wheel, hands hanging limp, eyes and mouth wide open still showing her horror.

Terrorized, I leapt from my bed and ran to Paw Paw's room and jumped into his bed with him, crying and gasping and shaking. Sparky came too.

"What's wrong, Joey?" He wrapped me in his strong arms and held me.

"She's dead, Paw Paw. She died in the coupe, she took too much medicine and she got real sick and was throwing up and... She's dead. Now I'll never be able to set her free."

Paw Paw tried to comfort me. "It was just a dream, son, about things that happened a long time ago. There's nothing you can do to change what's already happened. Everything's okay now, Joey, and maybe it's over, maybe the dreams will stop now."

I fell back asleep in my Paw Paw's bed, with Paw Paw's arm around me, and did not dream of Mrs. Ferguson ever again. I did see her ghost one more time though, in Mattie, two days later. She whispered my name thru the window, tears streaming down her face. I told her I forgave her and that I had the car now and everything was okay. She smiled, weakly, but she smiled, perhaps for the first time in over fifty years, and she slowly faded from my sight, forever.

CHAPTER 3

Our progress on Mattie quickened after Mrs. Ferguson left us, a new energy formed around the project and it became more fun. After installing our newly painted running boards and gluing the rubber mats to them, we just sat back and admired our work, sipping Dr. Peppers.

"Yeah, now she's beginning to look a little like the Mattie I knew. You sure you want to leave those numbers on the doors? She looks like she belongs on a race track."

"Yes, Paw Paw, she looks cool like that, see the fire nipping at the edges of the numbers, that's so cool."

He nudged me and winked. "Well, if it's cool, we'd better not change it."

I smiled and gazed at Mattie. "I love this car, Paw Paw. Someday I want her to be mine."

"I thought you wanted the Cobra, Joey."

My gaze still fixed on Mattie, I answered. "Mattie is the most beautiful car in the world. And the leather interior is going to be cool too." I smiled at using the cool word again. "I want a lot of chrome on her too, Paw Paw, okay? Dress up the engine compartment real nice? And can we keep it where the side panels of the hood can be on or off, but with the top of the hood on? I saw that on a coupe at a car show, and they're already separated on Mattie, it couldn't be too hard to do."

He draped one arm around my shoulders and gave me a little tug. "Son, we'll do this one like you want to, since Mattie is yours now." He tightened his hug on my shoulders and gave a couple of more quick tugs.

He said she was mine! I couldn't speak or I'd cry. I sniffed and swallowed, all choked up. Did I hear right? I wanted him to say it again.

He stretched his neck around to look me directly in the eyes, my tear filled eyes. "You really do love this car, don't you?"

Again, I couldn't speak. My heart was in my throat and my eyes about to spill over. I bit my top lip in an effort to control my emotions. After a moment of silence I mustered up enough inner strength to offer, "But, this is your coupe, Paw Paw, the one you've looked for most of your life."

"No, Joey, it's not that same car anymore. That car only lives in my memory. It's very different now, and has a lot of history that doesn't include me. But this is the car that you are passionate about, like I was when I was your age, and this time, the Joseph McClane who loves Mattie will have her." He nodded and smiled. "Old mistakes shouldn't be repeated."

I slid off my stool and shuffled over to Mattie, wiped my eyes with my fingers, and just stood and stared as the reality set in. Paw Paw was giving Mattie to me, right then and there. Walking a circle around her, touching everything; fenders, taillights, glass, numbers, flames, I asked, "You really mean it, Paw Paw?" And without waiting for an answer, I added, "I'll be so good to her. I'll never let her get dirty like old Frank did. I bet she hated him. He was even stacking things on top of her, scratching her."

Still circling and caressing Mattie, I felt something stick my finger, pulled it back and looked, blood. My blood dripped onto Mattie's fender, three large red drops, and just as quickly disappeared like it had been soaked up. I rubbed a different finger over the spot but the blood was completely gone, no trace of it at all, not even a smear. I looked at my injured finger and the small wound disappeared too, while I watched. I tried to find the burr or spot of rust, something that would have pricked me, nothing. This made no sense. Maybe I imagined it.

"What is it, son?"

"Oh, um, nothing. Can I drive her, I mean when we get her finished?" I gave him a pleading look and noticed his eyes were watery too, through a contented smile.

"Well," He drawled, not surprised with my question but careful with his answer. "We'll have to find some back roads with no traffic, but..." He slid off his stool and stood up, stretched his legs and his back, then joined me in circling Mattie. He looked at the spot where my blood had dropped, I wondered how much of that he saw. "You know, Joey, I was afraid we weren't going to be able to keep this car, what with the ghost and the nightmares and all. It was keeping you pretty upset. But that's all over with now, right, Joey?"

Afraid to look him in the eye, I kept my gaze on Mattie. I hadn't seen Mrs. Ferguson for days now, and didn't expect to again but something deep inside of me told me she wasn't Mattie's only haunt. "Yeah, Paw Paw, Mrs. Ferguson is gone now, your idea worked, she even smiled as she faded away. No more dreams either." But his threat of not keeping Mattie scared me. If there were more ghosts, I'd have to keep them to myself, just between me and Mattie. And after all, they couldn't be any scarier than Mrs. Ferguson, whoever they were.

I willed my thoughts away from ghosts and back to Mattie, and my mind went wild with ideas; wire wheels, tan leather, white carpet with deep pile, no shoes allowed inside. Then I thought about the expense. "Paw Paw, I can use my savings to buy things for Mattie, but I don't know how far it will go. Is there something I can do to earn some money?"

"Son, I always planned to pay for your first car, not quite this soon, but... Don't worry about the cost, I was going to invest in her anyway, it's not unexpected. Don't worry about it, just have fun and get her like you want her."

I hugged Paw Paw, and again fought back the tears. This day would surely live on in history as my happiest. We continued to pace around Mattie and make plans. Later we drove into town for lunch then went by the county license office where Paw Paw signed Mattie's title over to me. I signed my name to her title, beaming with pride, later walking out of the building holding the document up in front of me, unable to take my eyes off of it.

The lady who helped us remarked, "You're a little young for a car, aren't you, son?" Looking right at me, she added, "What are you, fourteen?"

"No, ma'am, I'm twelve, and this is my car, Mattie, and she's the most beautiful car in the world. She's a 1934 Buick Coupe and has flames painted on her hood and fenders and racing numbers on her doors and we're putting a new engine in her and wire wheels and chrome and leather interior, all kinds of cool stuff."

"Well, good for you. You'll probably have it finished by the time you get your driver's license. My son restored an older Mustang when he was a teenager and he still loves that car."

Paw Paw and I smiled at each other, we didn't say so but we didn't like Mustangs very much, too common. Later, back at the shop, I framed Mattie's title and hung it on the wall of our little office, which wasn't much more than a cubby hole for a phone, desk, file cabinet, and storage for literature and records.

Over the next few weeks we spent all the time we could working on Mattie, getting her seats cleaned up and repaired and ready for upholstery, preparing the newly rebuilt engine and transmission for installation, ordering more parts and accessories. I became so absorbed in this car, I allowed very little time for anything else. I declined invitations from friends to hang out at the teen club together, ride bikes to the river or play a game of baseball. I just wanted to work on Mattie. Paw Paw still pushed my studies though. I studied the books at night and during our breakfast and Paw Paw would quiz me while we worked on Mattie.

About a month had passed since I had released Mrs. Ferguson and I had all but forgotten about that side of Mattie. And out of nowhere, there it was, movement, unexplained and subtle, and visible to only me. I caught it out of the corner of my eye late one afternoon right after Paw Paw had gone to the house to get supper ready and I stayed in the shop to clean and put away the tools we had been using. Red shop rag in hand, I kept wiping and organizing our tools, keeping one eye on Mattie, unafraid but watching. The movement happened again but it was subtle and colorless, like moving your head around while looking through distorted glass. I walked closer to Mattie and peered in the driver side window, a young man's face materialized, fading in and out, riding invisible ripples. I pulled up a nearby stool and sat on it facing Mattie, two feet away, watching, waiting, wondering if this ghost would appear to me in dreams that night, show me his torment, and plead for release as Mrs. Ferguson had done.

Paw Paw stuck his head thru the open door seventy or seventy five feet away and yelled,

"Supper's ready, Joey. Come on, let's eat, and we need to work on your math lessons some this evening too."

I sat motionless, struggling to break away but not wanting to. I tried to look at Paw Paw and answer him but I couldn't make myself look away from Mattie. I was so anxious to see what she had to show me and so wished for more time alone with her. Paw Paw quietly ambled over to me and touched my shoulder.

"Everything okay, Joey?"

I could hear the suspicion in his voice, and when I looked up I saw it in his expression too. I couldn't tell him about this one, he'd already expressed concerns about keeping Mattie if her haunts continued. I touched his hand still on my shoulder, still staring at Mattie. "Paw Paw, do you think Mattie thinks I'm you?"

He hesitated to answer and I wondered what he was thinking. "Do you?"

"Yes I do, but I don't mind. I think she's happy. I love this car, Paw Paw. I don't know how to thank you for her."

He patted my shoulder and smiled. "Just seeing you enjoy her is thanks enough for me, Joey. I'm happy too, that it turned out this way. Maybe it was always meant to be. Come on now, let's eat before the food gets cold."

I was anxious to get to bed and to sleep that night, expecting a new visitor, and I wasn't disappointed. I saw Mattie, fenders crumpled front and rear on her right side, plus her other scrapes and dents from Mrs. Ferguson's abuse and ignorance. But Mattie was in a strange place now. She sat in a concrete driveway, an old one, one of those that was built as two parallel concrete lanes where the tires roll, with the center remaining dirt and grass. The drive led from a paved asphalt neighborhood street to a small garage, attached to a roof covered walkway about thirty feet long and attached to a white wood frame house. This was where Myrtle and George lived, Mrs. Ferguson's sister and brother in law. They had taken Mattie home, cleaned up all the nastiness in the seat from Mrs. Ferguson's messy death and offered the car to their twenty something year old grandson, Hugh. Hugh and his father were standing there with Annie and George, talking about Mattie.

But Hugh didn't like Mattie and he whined and complained like the spoiled brat he was, even though he was old enough to get a job and buy his own car. "No, that's not what I want. I don't like this car at all, I'm not going to drive this piece of junk."

Mark argued. "But Hugh, it's a coupe, you said you wanted a coupe. And we can fix the damage, it's just a couple of fenders and bumpers, nothing's wrong with the motor. The tires look brand new."

"I want a Ford coupe, with a V8 motor, not this slow, old person's car. It's ugly, what color is that, do do brown? Give it to someone else."

The young man's father was visibly upset with his attitude and grabbed his sleeve and took him aside. "Listen to me, Hugh, there's a depression going on and we're all just trying to survive and hang onto our homes. You're lucky to get a car at all. You should be working and buying your own. I certainly can't afford to buy you a car, and your grandparents are offering you a good car for free. Now you act grateful and take it and you use it to find a job so you can buy your own gas and oil and whatever else the car might need. And if you work hard and save, maybe you can buy the car you want in a year or two, but this is as good as it gets for free. Take it or leave it, and right now the way you're acting, I don't really care which one you do."

Well, Hugh took Mattie, but he didn't act at all grateful, he acted like a spoiled child who didn't get what he wanted for Christmas. I drifted in and out of the dream all night and some parts were vague but I do remember watching Hugh driving Mattie and treating her really bad. He said the most unkind things to her, telling her she was ugly and cumbersome and that he was ashamed to be seen in her. He even hit her with his fist right in the middle of her dash. He had no patience with her, trying to make turns too fast and grinding her gears on purpose, not allowing the clutch time to do its job. He didn't even put her in the garage when he got home, just left her under a tree where the birds pooped all over her.

When I awoke I was angry but not sure why. I was not fun to be around and Paw Paw asked me if I "got up on the wrong side of the bed". His good ol' boy humor, which normally amused me, because that was just the way my best friend was, this time failed to amuse me at all. Paw Paw was the kind of man who could be there for you, or he could just get out of your way if that was what you needed him to do. But he'd still be there for you later if your needs changed. So he just let me work things out myself because that's what my mood was telling him to do and I was grateful for the space. It was about mid-morning when I began to recall the dream with any detail, and the recollection made me aware of why I was so angry. Then knowing why, I had to deal with it.

"Paw Paw, I'm sorry I've been in a bad mood this morning."

We were working on the new wiring system for Mattie and it was a challenge, even for a master mechanic like Paw Paw. He looked up, over his gold wire rimmed glasses, put down his tools and wiped his hands on a shop rag. "Let's take a break, Joey. How about a glass of cold water?"

Paw Paw knew how to fill in gaps of time so that you had a chance to gather your thoughts and relax. While I watched him find our glasses and fill them with ice and water from the door of the shop refrigerator, I gained a little clarity of mind and organized my thoughts. The new ghost and the dreams that went with it had to remain my secret. I was already perched on my usual stool, the one with the blue and white Cobra on the seat cushion, when he handed me my glass and settled onto the stool beside me.

"Well," He drawled. "Some days are just like that, son. No body's a hundred percent every day."

I was thankful for the out, but still was wrestling with my emotions about Hugh's mistreatment of Mattie. Maybe I could talk around it enough to find some comfort but not so much as to reveal the existence of my new visitor. "Paw Paw, you know what? I think Mattie's had some hard times, I mean, maybe not recently, she probably liked racing, but back in the depression, when, if she got damaged they couldn't afford to fix her, or maybe somebody just didn't treat her nice, you know?" I had a feeling I wasn't making any sense and wished I hadn't said anything.

He smiled, that understanding Paw Paw smile, the one that always made me smile too. "I've wondered about that too, Joey. Where all she's been, what she's been through, who has owned her, how she was treated, how she evolved into the state she's in right now? I've thought about that a lot, even before we found her. She's obviously been through some radical changes, look at her. But you know what, Joey? She survived, and she's yours now and everything is up to you; how she looks, how she runs, how clean she is... No matter what is in her past, you've got her now, and as young as you are, I think Mattie is safe for a long time."

I did find comfort in our conversation and, I think, and without tipping my hand about Hugh's ghost in Mattie. Yes, I thought, I can deal with this, it all happened a long time ago, and like Paw Paw said, she survived and I've got her now. But deep in my young mind I was thinking, Mrs. Ferguson was bad to Mattie out of ignorance, but Hugh treated Mattie bad out of spite and hate and his own rotten attitude. Maybe he doesn't deserve forgiveness, if indeed that is what he seeks from me. Maybe Mattie is not finished punishing him yet. How would I know? I'd just have to watch his story play out and then decide. I felt power in my position with Mattie, like I was chosen to mete out judgment for those who had done her wrong. She had held them captive for decades for their sins against her and I was to preside over their judgment, decide their fate, release them or prolong their torture.

We had ordered some reproduction door panels and a headliner, plus some other interior parts, and they had now arrived. The seat frames and springs we had salvaged from Frank's junk pile were right for Mattie, whether they were originally hers or not we didn't know, but they fit so we took them to Gab's upholstery shop for new padding and leather covers. Gab, pronounced Gabe, had a little shop deep in the Mexican barrio of Las Casas, and he was an excellent craftsman. Through the years, he had redone the upholstery on several cars for us, being a classic car owner and restorer himself, he knew the importance of getting the details just right, and Gab was an artist with stitching.

Like most of the cars from her era, Mattie's original interior had been made of Mohair, and though Mohair materials were available, I chose leather, after all, this was not a period perfect restoration. She had come a long way from that, Mattie was a resto-mod in the truest sense. I stood in Gabriel's shop for over an hour, pouring over samples and pictures in catalogues, while Paw Paw and Gab watched me and reminisced about their first cars, agreeing that mine was much nicer than the ones they remembered from their youth. Finally I settled on tan leather, soft calf's skin, with lots of decorative stitching. This was going to look so beautiful in Mattie, and the smell of new leather, I could close my eyes and see it in her already installed and smell the distinctive fragrance of the material. This was something that would be enjoyed over and over, enjoyed anew each time her door was opened, each time a deep breath was inhaled inside of her. I was at peace with my selections.

A delivery truck was waiting at our gate when we returned to the shop. More parts for Mattie, this time the clutch assembly and the new rear end gears, the last items we needed to get her running. She would really start to come together now and with the thought of Mattie running and me driving her I was overwhelmed with excitement.

"How long, Paw Paw, do you think, you know, till she's running and I can drive her?"

"Patience, son, it's not the destination you know, it's the journey. Enjoy the process, when it's over, even though you'll have the enjoyment of a finished car, you'll miss the process, you'll almost be sad when it's over. I know, I've felt those emotions many times."

I countered his ideas. "I can't imagine being sorry when she's finished and ready to drive."

"Yes, well, I guess your first one is like that, but your next one will be different, that's when the patience kicks in. That's when you'll really cherish the process, when you already have a finished hot rod to drive while you work on the next one. I suppose that does help."

A second hot rod? The thought had not occurred to me. Surely Mattie would be enough. What other car could capture my heart like her? What other car would I want to get in and drive while Mattie sat at home?

Teenage hot rod mechanic by day, dreamer by night, and it was all about Mattie. She had taken over my life. I had abandoned my friends, they had all quit stopping by or calling, I was no fun anymore, I just wanted to work on my car. I was glad when Little League baseball season was over, one less diversion. Paw Paw had to stay on me to get me to do my studies, the only way he could get me to keep up the fast pace he had set was to compromise a little.

We'd spend an hour in the morning, during breakfast, going over study materials, take them with us to the shop where he could refer to them while he taught and quizzed me. I turned bolts while reciting presidents in chronological order and states' capitals, soldered wires while spitting out square roots and algebra formulas, defined chemical symbols and properties while gauging gaps and clearances. I was smart like my Paw Paw, math was simple logic to me, like fitting car parts together. If I read something I remembered it, if I heard something I could recall it verbatim days or even weeks later, and I was happy to have inherited his intelligence and received his training.

That night I returned to my secret world of Mattie's past and watched as Hugh deliberately set out to destroy Mattie, thinking that if she were out of the way someone would buy him the Ford coupe with the flathead V8 engine. The things he did, he must have thought he could hurt her without hurting himself, but he underestimated Mattie, and although he did hurt her, each stunt he pulled hurt him too.

Hugh tried to hit a ditch at about forty miles per hour and turn Mattie over. But she didn't flip, she came to a fast sideways stop, threw her door open and flung Hugh onto the ground breaking his left arm, ripping his clothes to shreds and covering him with scrapes and bruises. He lay there crying like a baby, cussing like a sailor and hitting the ground with his right fist in a childish fit of anger. Unable to drive a heavy car in his condition, he waited for someone to come by and help him. It didn't take long, in those days, especially around small towns, people tended to be concerned and helpful. The first car that came by stopped, and gave Hugh a ride home, leaving Mattie in the ditch by the road. Hugh's father took him to the doctor and listened to Hugh spin a lie about the accident.

The next time I saw Hugh he wore a plaster cast on his left arm, had two black eyes and a swollen nose, and walked with a limp. He looked like the most unhappy person in the world, more so than usual. Mattie sat in the driveway idle for weeks. Both hands and both feet were required to navigate the heavy car and the standard transmission.

When he finally did drive Mattie again, Hugh resumed his willful destruction of her. On a lonely open road away from town, Hugh put Mattie in low gear, floored the gas, and ran her wide open till the engine threw a rod, gouging the cylinder wall of the block and ruining the crankshaft. When the engine locked up Mattie screeched to a stop and Hugh was thrown forward, hitting his head hard on the windshield and his ribs on the steering wheel. With one hand on his bleeding forehead and the other holding his rib cage, he left her on the side of the road, smoking and steaming, motor ruined. Hugh hitched a ride back to town and to within a few blocks of home and walked the rest of the way.

I watched while he spun another lie to his dad, he was just driving normally and the engine locked up and he had to walk home. From the look on his dad's face, I don't think he believed Hugh and the conversation heated up.

"Well, Hugh, it looks like you're just out of a car now."

How am I going to get a job without a car? Snake Jones has a Ford for sale, why don't we take a look at it?"

"After the way you've treated this one," Mark replied angrily. "I wouldn't buy you another car, even if I could. You want a car, you fix this one, otherwise walk. You never looked for a job anyway, you lazy brat."

They argued back and forth, called each other names, and Hugh stomped out of the house in a rage, slamming the screen door so hard it bounced against the jamb a couple of times.

During the daytime I watched for Hugh to appear inside of Mattie but he didn't show himself. Perhaps he knew he would get no sympathy from me, I hated him and wanted to tell him so. While working on Mattie, I talked to her and asked what she wanted me to do with Hugh, but of course she didn't tell me.

In the next few dreams I watched Hugh sulk around, argue with his parents, and finally agree to accept his father's help replacing Mattie's blown engine with a new one. They removed her hood, borrowed an engine hoist from a local garage, set it up straddling the car's front end, and bolted the chains to the engine. George and Mark left in an old pickup truck to purchase the used engine they had located a couple of towns away. Hugh crawled under Mattie to unbolt the ruined one, cussing Mattie with every breath. Wrenches in hand, he removed the bolts connecting the engine to the transmission, then the motor mounts. With the engine securely chained to the hoist it should have stayed in place even with all the support bolts removed, but it didn't, it fell, right on Hugh's chest. I could see that one of the chains, though connected to the hoist, was not connected to the engine, but I could have sworn it had been, earlier. I had watched as they checked all of that, and double checked. Hugh was pinned under Mattie, unable to yell for help or to move himself or the weight resting on him. The hoist held the weight just enough to not kill Hugh quickly but cut his breathing to short, small gasps. He pushed and kicked and cried and struggled, and very slowly suffocated.

By the time the men returned with the new engine, Hugh was dead. With quick, desperate efforts, they tried to save him, hoisted the engine up and pulled Hugh out from under the coupe and tried to revive him, but he was gone. The expression on Hugh's face reminded me of that on the face of Mrs. Ferguson the night she died in Mattie, and just like her, I thought he got what he deserved.

CHAPTER 4

The next day in my real world was Sunday, and my thirteenth birthday. We went to church in the morning and I was glad for the quiet time to digest my dreams of Hugh, his abusive experiences with Mattie and his terrible death. I tried to find comfort in Paw Paw's words from when Mrs. Ferguson died (in the dream), that it all happened a long time ago and there was nothing we could do to change things or help them. I believe the thing that bothered me most was that I felt no sorrow for Hugh at all, and I thought I should.

After church services we went home where we entertained several kids my age with a birthday party. Most of our guests were kids from our church and most were home schooled like me; our church encouraged that, observing that public school had become quite anti-Christian. We had also invited some home schoolers with whom we networked for sports and field trips, but who didn't attend our church, and a couple of boys from my Little League baseball team. It was a pretty big party, about a dozen and a half kids and a handful of parents. Most of the parents just dropped their kids off and left, a few stayed. Paw Paw cooked hot dogs and hamburgers on the outside grill while visiting with the other adults. We kids played in the nice shaded yard which stretched across the ninety feet or so between the house and the shop, and then around the back of the house where it was bordered by a Cedar post and net wire ranch type fence covered with Morning Glory vines. My old playground equipment had not been used in a while; swings, an old see saw and a trampoline. I felt like I had outgrown it all but we made good use of it that day. At some point a game of flag football was organized and the girls pretended to be cheerleaders, except for Anita Cantu. Anita was quite a tomboy and preferred to join the football action. Anita was smart and gutsy and fast and she had no trouble keeping up with the boys. She could outrun some of them. I had known her from church for several months now and always thought she was pretty, even told her so once but didn't get much of a reaction from her. Lately though, her tomboy look seemed to be losing a struggle with an emerging beauty which had already become impossible for me to ignore, and for other boys too, I was sure. I guess you could say I had a crush on her but from a distance. My shyness with girls demanded the distance.

Paw Paw called us to eat and we sat around the yard in lawn chairs and at the wooden picnic table, a few kids sat on the brick flower bed borders and some just sat cross legged in the grass, and we devoured the hot dogs and chips, then the birthday cake and ice cream. It was a nice party, fun, and since bringing Mattie home I hadn't had much time for friends or play. We had requested no presents but a few were brought anyway.

Finished eating and ready to play some more, I was taking my trash to a large plastic garbage can placed nearby for our party debris. From several feet away I tossed it in, spun around, and almost crashed into Anita. I was about to apologize for the near collision when she giggled and shoved a small, gift wrapped box at me.

"Oh, um, well thanks, 'nita, but you weren't supposed to bring gifts." Now why did I say that? It sounded rude.

"Yeah, I know, but it's not much. I just saw this and thought, maybe you'd like it. I bought it with my own money and wrapped it myself, Joey."

Unlike me, Anita was anything but bashful, she was full of personality, looked you right in the eye and used a lot of facial expression when she talked. That seemed to intimidate me a little. She had the prettiest smile which shone thru an appealing hint of an overbite of perfectly straight, snow white teeth punctuated by dimples that deepened with her smile. And she also smiled with big, deep, black eyes that gleamed to accent her words. I noticed she was changing, destined to be an early bloomer, she was beautiful, beautiful like a woman, even as a thirteen year old tomboy. She was tall too, almost as tall as me. I found her very presence intimidating. I felt I should look away from her and stop staring, but I couldn't.

Keeping an eye on Anita, I opened the gift, being careful with the wrapping paper since she wrapped it herself, and inside the little box, was Mattie. I did a double take. A scale model car, doors and hood that opened, a rumble seat too, with a continental kit below it, the dash showed all the gauges and the engine compartment was quite detailed. This was not a cheap toy but a nice scale model, the kind collectors buy. This had to have cost at least twenty five dollars, maybe more. It was a 1934 Buick and a coupe, black not yellow, it had flames, not exactly like Mattie's flames, but flames.

"I remember you telling us in Sunday school class one day about your car." She explained. "So I saw this in a store and just had to get it for your birthday, Joey." She reached out and touched my hand, the one holding the car. I flinched and goose bumps covered me.

"Wow, 'nita, this is nice." I looked from the model car to her, her big beautiful black eyes, her perfect soft, dark brown skin, the subtle sprinkle of freckles across her nose, the little silver and blue butterfly earrings in her tiny little pierced earlobes, straight black hair, shining and cut short in sort of a summer style, all messed up from running and playing. And I fell in love. Right then and there I fell head over heels in love. A girl who would rather play football than be a cheerleader, who knew what a hot rod coupe was, with flames, and she was beautiful. She was beautiful and I was speechless, awkwardly at a total loss for words. I just stood and stared and fell deeper in love, mouth open but nothing coming out.

She cocked her head a little and smiled. "You really like it?" Her eyes danced and her smile widened and my heart melted.

"Yeah, I do, and…" I felt so stupid. What was I to do now? I couldn't get another word out.

"And what?" She chirped, cocked her head the other way, smiling, her smile, her teeth, perfect and straight and so white against her pretty complexion. Was she flirting with me or making fun of me? I wasn't sure.

"And… I… I like you too, a lot." Oh, my, gosh! What did I just say? Now she's going to think I'm a total geek. Think of something! But I couldn't. I shuffled my feet, and my hands sweated as I wrung them and twisted my fingers around each other and the model car. I struggled to talk but just stuttered and stammered, unable to get words to form. I looked down at the ground giving up on saying anything intelligent, expecting her to laugh at me and run away.

"I'd like to see your car, Joey, you know, the real one, the one you talk about. She touched my arm and again I flinched and again was covered with goose bumps.

"Oh! Yes! You want to see her? I'd love to show her to you." I looked around, no one was watching, maybe we could sneak away from the party, just the two of us, and I could show her Mattie, impress her, maybe she would fall in love with me too. "Come on, she's in the shop over there, I'll show you."

Anita giggled, "You call your car a she, and a her?"

"Yeah, and her name is Mattie, and she's beautiful." I hesitated, then added, "Like you." I felt the blood rush to my face as I blushed, again sure that I had said the wrong thing, afraid she would laugh at me. Or maybe be insulted, comparing her beauty to a car, what was the matter with me?

Anita smiled. Her eyes sparkled and she stepped closer to me, uncomfortably close, we were almost touching, I could feel her breath on my face. She tilted her face slightly and leaned in, as if to whisper in my ear, reached up and gently placed one very warm hand on my chest and purred, "You think I'm beautiful, Joey?"

I swallowed hard. "Uh, yeah, you are, you're the prettiest girl I've ever seen."

We started for the shop and I thought about what it would be like to hold her hand, but I didn't dare try. I looked at the model car, at her, and around to see if anybody was following. The shop was locked to keep kids from wandering in, and I took the hidden key from its place in the magnetic case under the window and opened the walk thru door, held it open for her and closed it behind us. I thought about locking it but didn't.

When the lights came on she gasped, "Wow, Joey, look at all these cool cars. Are they all yours?"

"Yeah, well, Paw Paw's, but the coupe is mine, the title is in my name and everything." I swerved our path a little to show her the title with my name on it, framed and hanging on the wall. She had to be impressed with that.

We walked past the Cobra and the 38 Dodge pickup and the green Hemi Cuda and the 64 Buick convertible and Anita touched them all and paused at each one and commented on them. She actually knew what a Cobra was and I was impressed with that. I explained the Hemi Head engine and she said I was smart and she touched my arm again. Then we got to Mattie.

"Oh wow, Joey. This is beautiful, and it looks fast, I mean she looks fast, Mattie, right? And those flames are so cool, they look like real fire, like if you put your hand up to them they'd burn you."

I sneaked a candid look at Anita and her awe stricken gaze fixed on Mattie told me her sentiments about my car were sincere. I grabbed the remote control and opened Mattie's door, no interior, I'd forgotten about that. I began to explain. "She's been a drag racer but we're converting her to a street rod. The seats and door panels are in the upholstery shop, I picked out tan leather and white carpet, and we're ready to install the new engine and transmission soon too."

"Electronic door openers." She said. "How cool. So, you do the work on her yourself?"

"Well, yeah, me and Paw Paw. But I know how, I can cut and weld and tune and do lots of stuff myself."

She turned and faced me and moved closer. "You're pretty special, Joey. I like you too, a lot. When you get your coupe finished I want to go for a ride in her, okay?" She grabbed my hand and squeezed. I thought my knees were going to buckle and dump me onto the floor. I was doing pretty well until she did that, showing her my car, talking to her, but now I couldn't even remember what I was saying. She's holding my hand. What do I do now?

There was a bucket seat from another car, sitting in Mattie, a spare, something that had been lying around the shop, and we had temporarily installed it to sit on while working on the dash and steering column. Anita climbed in, it was a climb because Mattie was up on blocks to give us clearance underneath, room to get in and out and to work, and Anita sat there and smiled down at me. "Come on." She motioned with her hand for me to join her.

I slid in beside her on the seat, and we were very close and I was very nervous. There wasn't really room for both of us on the bucket seat and I didn't want to push her off, so I sat at kind of an angle toward her, on the side of one leg, placing one hand on the steering wheel and my other arm behind her on the top of the seat. I was in paradise.

"What about the roll cage, Joey? Are you going to leave it in?"

She knew what a roll cage was! This was a girl who knew about cars, I was impressed. "Uh, well, I'm not sure. Haven't decided yet."

"Well, I like it, I'd leave it. It's very nicely done, and it kind of makes a statement, you know? And I bet, Joey, you're going to want to race Mattie someday."

That was enough for me, the decision was made, the roll cage would stay in Mattie. "Yeah, I guess it does kind of add something, like a statement about her history."

"Mattie is going to be the coolest car in town, Joey, the coolest car in the whole San Antonio area, the entire state." She looked me right in the eye from just inches away, straight on, moved her pretty face closer, and ran the tip of her tongue across her lips. My heart beat so hard I thought it was going to tear through my chest. She was right there, so I kissed her, I didn't even think about it, I just leaned to her and kissed her right on the lips. Never having kissed a girl before, I didn't know how, exactly, so it was little more than a peck, but I did kiss her. She giggled and kissed me back. She was a better kisser than I was, her kiss lasted longer. And she placed her hand on the side of my face, it was warm and felt nice.

Stunned by her return kiss, I blurted out, "You want to be my girlfriend? I'll take you to movies and stuff." I was so awkward and nervous, and downright shocked that this was even happening. I absolutely lacked any grace or finesse, truth be told, I was scared stiff.

But Anita didn't mind, she liked me. "Yeah, Joey, I do! I've liked you for a while but you never even notice me."

"Oh, I've noticed you plenty, 'nita, but you're so pretty, I just didn't think you'd be int..."

"Then why didn't you talk to me? You told me I was pretty once, and I expected you to pay attention to me after that, maybe call me, sit by me at church, but you never did." She hesitated then nodded slowly and thoughtfully. "Joey, you're shy, aren't you?"

I didn't say anything, didn't know what to say. I figured being shy probably wasn't very cool.

She smiled. "That's okay, I don't mind. You going to take me out in your car, like on dates and stuff?" Her eyes flirted and again I wondered if she was just playing with me.

But I answered her question. "Sure, when I get my license." I tried to ignore the fact that I probably wouldn't have a driver's license for another three years. I tried to loosen up, after all, Anita liked me so what was there to be nervous about. It helped that she was so outgoing, she kept the conversation alive and she pulled me into talking about my plans for Mattie and after a few minutes I became aware of how I was going on and on about my car and I found a stopping place. I realized that Anita had worked her arm around my back, it felt nice there. We seemed to have run out of anything to talk about for the moment and the silence was heavy, so I kissed her again. Anita draped her other arm around my shoulders and pulled me tight against her and the kiss seemed to last forever.

While we kissed, Mattie played a song, another girl band from the 50s or 60s. "Going to the chapel and we're going to get married, going to the chapel and we're going to get married. Gee I really love you and we're going to get married, going to the chapel of love. Well, spring is here, the sky is blue, birds all sing as if they knew, today's the day we'll say I do and we'll never be lonely anymore."

It was quite distracting and I worried that Anita might hear it too but I decided that only I could hear Mattie's music without a radio.

A few minutes later Anita and I returned to the party, stopping just outside the shop door for another kiss. This time we were standing up and we held each other in a tight embrace while we kissed and it was very exciting. For my thirteenth birthday I got a beautiful girlfriend who knew cars and liked to kiss. I was so happy. As we walked from the shop, across the yard, holding hands this time, I noticed Paw Paw looking at us. My attempt to avoid his eyes was not successful for very long, and when our eyes did meet, he tilted his head back and smiled and nodded subtly. He was going to tease me about this, I just knew it.

Well, we were back at the party but we didn't actually join it. Anita and I sat by ourselves, across the old sun bleached wood picnic table from each other, leaned on our arms and elbows toward each other, held hands and talked and ignored everyone else. She told me about her school and I told her about my home schooling. She talked about her family; her mom, dad, three brothers and a sister, and I talked about Paw Paw and Sparky. She asked about my mother and I told her about my parents being killed in an accident when I was little. It seemed to sadden her that I had no mother. I admitted that, up to that point, I had never given it much thought, Paw Paw was enough. We discussed favorite music and cars and school subjects.

Anita couldn't believe the math and science courses I was taking. "Joey, that sounds like college work, that's advanced stuff, it's not even offered at our school. Are you that smart?"

"Um, no, um, it's just that, uh, Paw Paw pushes me really hard with the school stuff, seven days a week all year long, holidays and everything. But it's no big deal, it comes easy for me. Just don't ask me to spell anything." The spelling part was not true, but I was embarrassed, I didn't want to look like a nerd.

"Well, I can spell, but math is a real problem for me, especially algebra. I think I just found me a study partner." She squeezed my hand. Then she looked at it. "Joey, look at your fingernails. You're such a grease monkey, my cute, smart, shy, grease monkey." Anita squeezed my hand with both of hers, brought it to her lips, and kissed it, and smiled at me.

The party began to break up and I didn't want it to because that meant Anita would be leaving soon too. Parents were coming back to collect their kids, other parents who had stayed for the party were thanking Paw Paw for the fun time and wishing me a happy birthday one more time and then trailing off. Anita's older brother, who had a rough reputation and was rumored to be a gang member in San Antonio, probably because of his many tattoos, (I found out later when I got to know him, it was a car club, a low rider club, not a street gang at all.) came for her in a 1966 Chevrolet Impala low rider and then I understood her knowledge of hot rods. She seemed a little embarrassed by the low rider and I didn't want her to be so I made a nice comment about it.

"Not exactly my style of car but a very nicely done low rider, 'nita. Look at the paint job, did he do that himself?"

"Um, yeah Joey and I helped him with a lot of it."

"You did? Really? You're really cool, 'nita. I'm glad we… You know… Can I call you later?"

Anita propped her fists on her hips, leaned forward a little and gave me a stern look and replied, "Well, you'd better, you're my boyfriend! I expect you to call me every night, Joey." She told me her phone number and I repeated it several times so I'd remember it. That made her giggle, that made me blush.

Her brother honked for her. We walked holding hands, across the yard, across the driveway to the Impala. I opened the car door for her, spoke a one word greeting to her brother who looked at me without answering, just nodded his head a little. I searched in vain for something else to say, maybe a compliment on his car, I thought. But before I could come up with anything Anita reached her hand around the back of my neck, pulled me to her and kissed me. "Call me about eight tonight." It sounded like an order. I agreed with a nod. Anita slid into the car, I closed the door and they began to back out of the driveway.

I heard Mario ask Anita, "He's the one you've been talking about?"

I couldn't believe she kissed me right there in front of everybody; her brother, Paw Paw, the other kids, their parents. I resisted the urge to look around, certain that everyone was looking at me now. I stood and stared, she waved at me thru the window and smiled, her beautiful smile. My heart was pounding, thirteen years old by one day, and madly in love.

Paw Paw appeared by my side and rested a hand on my shoulder. "Cute girl, Joey."

I looked up at him and back at the disappearing low rider. "Um, yeah, Anita Cantu, she's my girlfriend, now, I guess. She's really pretty Paw Paw, don't you think?"

"Yes, son, she is a pretty girl. Y'all went in the shop, I guess you showed her Mattie, right?"

I was still in a daze. "Yes sir. You know, I think I'd like to leave the roll cage in Mattie."

"Get a little help with that decision, son?"

I glanced up at him, saw his sly smile, quickly refocused my vision down the road even though the low rider carrying my new girlfriend was gone from sight. "Um, yeah, I guess so, a little."

"How old is that girl, Joey?"

"Thirteen, why?"

"Looks fifteen, easy. Sure you can handle an older woman, son?"

He was teasing me now just like I knew he would. "Paw Paw, we're the same age." I whined, blushing.

"What's that you've got there?"

I raised my hand, still holding the model car, which I'd forgotten about. I noticed my hands were sweating and I wiped one on my pants leg, switched hands with the model car and wiped the other. "Oh, uh, a birthday gift, from her, 'nita." I offered him the car.

He took the car from me and examined it. "This is a nice scale model. An older woman buying you expensive gifts, son? I never knew you had such a way with the ladies."

I blushed and turned away, and whined. "Paw Paw… Stop."

He laughed, quietly, under his breath, handed the model car back to me. He draped an arm around my shoulders. "Well, birthday boy, we've got quite a mess to clean up here."

It was a couple of days after the birthday party, and I was so caught up in my life with Mattie, and Anita with whom I talked on the phone for a solid hour every night, as ordered. That was all her dad would allow. I had a car and a girlfriend and they were both beautiful and I had all but forgotten about Hugh. Dreams of him had ended simultaneously with his death and I should have been watching for him in Mattie, begging for forgiveness.

But I wasn't watching, and Hugh took me totally by surprise. Paw Paw and I were finishing the new wiring and were anxious to get started on the drive train installation which would quickly follow, and I saw the movement. I looked at Paw Paw, certain that he didn't see it, certain that he couldn't, and back at Mattie's windshield, and there was Hugh's face, vague, floating, and tortured. I made myself not look again, knowing he was there, knowing that I could not deal with it at the time. I heard a whisper, "Joseph." Again, I looked at Paw Paw, and he was unaware.

I purposely spilled a small cardboard box of electrical connections on the floor and uttered a very mild expletive. "Oh shoot, I made a mess. I'm getting hungry, Paw Paw. Is it time for lunch yet?"

He looked at the clock on the wall, barely eleven a.m. "Yeah, me too, Joey. Close enough, I suppose." He put his tools down and wiped his hand on a shop rag. "Ready? Let's go rustle up some grub."

"Okay, Paw Paw, go ahead, I'll be right there, soon as I pick up all these little connectors I just spilled."

Thankfully, he accepted that and went on ahead of me. The very second he walked out the door, I looked for Hugh and found him, clearer this time. He spoke, a whisper, afraid and pleading. "Joseph, please, help me, I'm sorry, please." His face was the perfect picture of torment, as if he were still feeling the weight of Mattie's engine on his chest, and his brown khaki shirt was covered with a mixture of blood and oil. For the first time, I felt compassion for him.

"Leave." I told him. "Just get out of my car, out of my life, leave. I forgive you, Mattie forgives you. Now leave us." I was not really sure if Mattie or I actually forgave him, but I was certainly anxious to be rid of him. No smile this time, like with Mrs. Ferguson, he just faded and rose, disappeared through Mattie's roof and he was gone forever.

With the absence of the two tortured ghosts, the presence of almost all the parts needed to complete Mattie, and the fact that I was in love with Anita and she was in love with me, life was about as good as it could get for a thirteen year old boy in small town in south Texas in 1991. Anita lived about a five minute bicycle ride away and we took turns making the trip to each other's home. Actually that was across town in our little village of barely five thousand people. Anita enjoyed hanging out in our shop with us which was good because that was where I liked to be, and she helped us work on Mattie. For a thirteen year old girl she had an impressive amount of mechanical knowledge and skill. She explained that she had helped Mario, her older brother, restore and modify his '66 Impala and had been especially active in both the paint job and the engine overhaul.

We went on dates, sort of, Paw Paw would chauffer us wherever we needed to go; the movies, the parks on the little river that ran through town, or Rocky's Den, a teen hangout. Or sometimes we would just ride our bikes. There wasn't really much else to do around Las Casas. I lived for the day when I could take Anita out on a date while driving Mattie. My mind pictured this beautiful girl sitting next to me in my hot rod, cruising, going places. Real dates.

Texas summers were hot so the river was the place we frequented most during the day. Anita wore a bikini and she looked fine with her flawless brown skin shining in the sun, her youthful slim figure, subtle curves. And I was introduced to a new emotion, lust. I took every opportunity to touch her, her back or shoulders or legs, her face while we kissed, sometimes lying on a beach towel on the grassy river bank. I'd roam my anxious hands over her silky skin, wandering as close to her breasts or as far up her legs as I dared and when I'd stray too daringly she'd mutter a closed mouth, "Huh uh." Usually muffled by our kiss. Oh how I wanted to touch her, really touch her. Those moments I'd almost always get an erection and though I'd try to hide the fact, she knew and would sometimes tease me with a funny comment like, "Down boy, we're too young for that." And indeed we were, but that didn't stop me from trying.

Once when we jumped into the water her top came off and she covered her breasts with her hands. "Get it for me, Joey, please." It was drifting down stream and I quickly retrieved it for her. No one was around and when I handed her bikini bra over and she reached for it, now crouching in the water and covering with one hand and arm, I jerked it away.

"Huh uh, I want to see." I told her, hoping but not expecting her to show me. She shook her head no, I nodded yes, no again, yes again. She looked around, grinned mischievously, stood up in the water which was only a little above waist high there, and dropped her hands and gave me a nice long look.

I gasped, stared. I moved the two short steps to her and hugged her like that, naked flesh pressing against naked flesh. I wormed one hand in between us to touch her breast. She let me, but only briefly, then grabbed the bra from my other hand, stepped back and put it on, slowly, while I watched. Anita looked at my crotch and mocked me, "Down boy." She giggled.

We were already lovers, young lovers, to whatever degree virgins can be lovers. And we were friends, such good friends that trust was automatic and being candidly honest with each other felt natural. I know, and I'm sure I realized it even then, it was Anita who held the leadership role in our relationship. She was the outgoing one, the uninhibited one, the one who set the pace and the limits and the very atmosphere. I was the shy one, the one who could be easily embarrassed, the one who would hold back, and I was glad for her assertiveness. But when she got me aroused, and it didn't take much even as young as we were, my immature hormones would rage and my hands and mouth would wander and she'd have to stop me.

By now a couple of months had passed since I had dismissed Hugh from our world and I was becoming convinced that he was the last haunt in the coupe. Mattie was taking shape nicely with her new interior and drive train and reproduction chrome wire wheels with wide white wall tires. We were now busy on details like trying to adapt her old banjo steering wheel to the modern tilt steering column and fitting it with turn signals and a flasher and finding the best locations for her new sound system and speakers. By networking with other Buick restorers, we found body trim pieces and latches and catches for the hood side panels which had been left off for who knew how long and which had missed out on the nice flame paint job.

Finding a painter who could duplicate the flames proved to be the difficult part. After several refusals from paint shops and individuals, Anita suggested we ask her brother. The next day he came, at our invitation, to look at Mattie's unique flames. Mario was quite an artist with an air brush, his '66 Chevy was a rolling mural with a race track background and a sexy bikini clad Mexican woman on the hood and another on the trunk lid. Even the underside of the hood was like a mural. The sides of the car were decorated with mountain scene background with an evolving road race track from front to back. Very impressive work. He agreed to take a shot at extending Mattie's flames onto her hood side panels.

Now our biggest problem in the restoration was solved. Mechanics work was not a problem for us, neither was a normal paint job. But Mattie's flames were one of a kind, created by some mystery painter in her past, and only the most talented of artists could possibly duplicate them. Paw Paw and I both gave sighs of relief at this part of the project being done right.

CHAPTER 5

The very day, the very moment we installed the newly painted hood side panels, Amos appeared to me in Mattie. Paw Paw, Mario, Anita and I were standing back admiring the new addition to the project and it really was a fine finishing touch. I was so proud, and so was Mario. He was quite talented, the flames matched so well that it was hard to see where the sides separated from the top of the hood or from the fenders. But as we were admiring our work, a new face floated into view right inside the driver side window.

Upon seeing it I quickly looked at Paw Paw, then Anita, then Mario and it was clear to me that they were oblivious to the apparition. Encouraging myself to stay calm, I studied the new face. He was a black man, he looked like a big man, fortyish, proudly sporting a goatee with a little gray starting to pop up in it and a New York Yankees baseball cap. He had a gold tooth right in front, front left, his left, and a large gold chain around his neck, and the chain was woven and twisted like a rope but held no pendant.

He was smiling, a big happy smile. Even his eyes smiled. Why was he smiling? Wasn't he another tormented captive of Mattie? He opened his mouth and appeared to laugh but I didn't hear it. In fact I didn't hear anything, including real people talking to me. And Anita was pulling at my arm trying to get my attention and asking me something.

"Huh? What?"

Anita fussed at me. "Joey, didn't you hear anything I just said to you?"

"Oh, um, no, I'm sorry. What?"

Paw Paw gave a little laugh. "Joey gets pretty wrapped up in this car. He was probably thinking about what it'll look like finished, now that we're so close. Right, Joey?"

His suspicious look told me I'd better be careful with my answer. I couldn't take a chance on losing Mattie now just because of another pesky ghost. I laughed it off and shook it off and got myself back in the conversation. But secretly I could not wait to see what this new haunt of Mattie's was all about. I had been warned beforehand about Mrs. Ferguson and Hugh, but this black man, did he own Mattie for a while? Now I seemed to remember Paw Paw mentioning Amos, a black man who did have Mattie for a while, but he had given few details. Yes, Amos was the man who saved Mattie when she had been donated to the war effort. So what was his story? He seemed happy, maybe this part of the puzzle would be different, not so sad or tragic. I hoped. Surely someone in Mattie's history had some fun with her. I had a good feeling about this one.

I expected my new friend to visit me in a dream that night but he failed to show. I watched for him in Mattie when we were in the shop but, nothing. After a few days I wondered if I had really seen him at all. And finally, he returned, in Mattie of course, through the window, his smiling face with the gold tooth in front, his New York Yankees baseball cap, his goatee making his huge face appear even bigger. And he seemed to be really enjoying himself, genuinely happy. I didn't understand. I witnessed his brief and infrequent visits for days, no whisper, no pleading, no tears, no vomit, no blood, always a smile, sometimes a laugh, and no dream.

It was at this exact point in all this madness that I decided to write it all down, a journal of sorts, of a car's life, and its ghosts.

Mattie's entire history was being revealed to me, I was sure of it, I couldn't let it just be lost, it had to be recorded and kept with her. I found an unused spiral notebook among my study materials, a thick one although it wouldn't hold the whole story, not by the time it was all told but it was good for a start. Amos wasn't a very demanding ghost at first so I had some time to start the journal and get it up to date before he added much to the story.

Two months later with Anita and me enjoying a comfortable and fun adolescent romance and Mattie close to finished, lacking only final adjustments and bugs to be worked out, the dreams finally began. So different from the ones before, not scary, not sad or tragic, but fun. Over a period of several months, the pieces of this ghost's story fell into place. The black man's name was Amos Mathew Johnson, and Amos was quite a character. He didn't work, not at a job anyway, he made his living gambling and hustling and he was good enough at it to own his own home on a few acres on the outskirts of town, this town, Las Casas, and live pretty comfortably for the times. As the dreams unfolded, I learned that Amos was single, never married, never held a job, but instead made good money betting on just about everything from his racing pigeons and his greyhounds to dice, cards and horses, plus he bought, fixed up and sold an old car now and then, and was also a small time loan shark in the local Negro community. Amos loved bourbon and cigars and women, especially, it seemed, married women. And he was the happiest, busiest, most conniving person you ever knew.

In the first dream, I saw Mattie sitting in a field, paint chipped and faded, fenders crumpled, bumpers and hood lying on the ground nearby, nice flying lady chrome hood ornament gone, driver side window open, tires flat. Her rear window and surrounding metal showed BB gun damage from kids passing through the field shooting at whatever dared to be within range. She looked rough, abandoned by Hugh's family in their grief, perhaps they couldn't stand to look at her after what happened.

Mattie's replacement engine was sitting in the dirt beside her, never installed. The sight disturbed me so that it shook me half awake and I silently shed my tears on my pillow for Mattie. I drifted back to sleep, and to Mattie's story.

A hundred yards or so away, a car stopped on the road bordering the field, sat there idling a moment, then turned and drove into the field and right up to Mattie. Paw Paw! My Paw Paw in his late teens, thin and straight and young! He brought his late thirties Plymouth sedan to a stop near Mattie, exited his car, walked a circle around Mattie and I swear I saw a tear in his eye. He opened her driver side door, brushed the seat off with his hand a couple of swipes and sat on the seat. He sat in a melancholy silence, caressing the wheel, touching knobs on her dash and the gear shifter, reminiscing. He got out, rolled the open window up and closed the door. He walked around to the back of Mattie, stepped up on the bumper support, then on the step for the rumble seat passengers, turned the handle and pulled the rumble seat hatch open. I watched the young Joseph McClane Sr., sit and look around, to the floor and inside the seat compartment, over the top of Mattie's cab, around the sides of the car, and to the ground below. He slouched down, pretending to be small again, and he spoke.

"Oh my, Mattie, I'm so sorry, girl. Look what they've done to you."

A shout rang out from a nearby farm house, "Hey you! Get the hell out of there! Go on, leave things alone! Git! Now! Sic 'em, Bear! Git 'im!"

A huge black and tan dog with a bobbed tail came barreling out of the yard and charged with evil intent right for my Paw Paw.

Paw Paw spoke to Mattie again. "Hang on, Mattie, I'll come back for you. Don't worry, I'll save you. It may be a while but I'll be back for you, now that I know where you are."

With the angry black and tan dog closing in fast, Paw Paw quickly exited the rumble seat, closed the hatch and sped away in his sedan, bad dog running along beside, growling and barking all the way to the edge of the field.

The next night the dream continued, but it seemed some time had passed, and Mattie was sitting in a different field, by a railroad track with some loading equipment nearby, several other old cars around and lots of activity. They were crushing cars! A huge crane with a big steel weight attached to its cable was raising the weight up and dropping it down on the cars, crushing them! And it was almost Mattie's turn!

Amos appeared, strode over to a man working there, and although I couldn't hear much of the conversation over the crane's noise, I could tell Amos was trying to rescue Mattie but it wasn't going well. He waved his hands around and gestured and argued and stomped his feet. At one point he turned around and marched off fifteen feet or so, only to quickly return and resume the argument. Finally, he pulled some money out of his shirt pocket, counted some off and handed it to the other man. Then Amos left, and Mattie was pulled over to the side of the lot by an old brown, battered, rusty, smoking flatbed truck with a green right front fender that wobbled as if it might just fall off. As I later came to understand, the United States had entered World War II and old cars were being donated to the war effort to be crushed and melted and recycled into guns and tanks and ammunition, things like that.

I awoke from my dream, struggled for a moment to get my brain back in the real time and place, stunned from the things I saw happening to Mattie. Sparky wanted out so I went with him to the front yard. My eyes were drawn to the shop window where I saw a faint light. I knew the light was coming from inside Mattie and I walked over and peered in through the shop window. Amos looked right at me from inside the coupe and he laughed his big toothy laugh with the gold tooth in front. And this time I could hear his laugh. It was not a mocking laugh as I had expected, but a happy laugh, the way one might laugh after hearing news of some unexpected and extremely good fortune. Sparky crept up beside me and he must have seen and heard what I did because he went into a barking fit, legs stiff, hair standing straight out all over him, which seemed to cause Amos to laugh even harder. I grabbed Sparky up in my arms and ran for the house, afraid the noise might wake Paw Paw.

The dream resumed the second my head hit the pillow and Sparky burrowed up close to me under the covers. Amos towed two old beat up cars to the crushing yard to trade for Mattie, plus whatever cash I'd seen him hand over earlier. Somehow he towed both of them at the same time and it looked funny, two big old long rusty sedans, a pipe in between them and also one between the first car and the old truck, inching along in serpentine fashion like some clumsily connected child's toy. Soon he was attaching his tow chain to Mattie's frame under her engine area, the exact same spot where I attached our winch cable when we bought Mattie. Amos was getting ready to pull her home behind his old faded green Dodge pickup. Amos ran the chain thru a long section of steel pipe and worked out all the slack so that they were attached in a way that would stop Mattie when the truck stopped and they wouldn't run together, just like he had done with the other two cars. The crane picked up the engine that was never installed in Mattie by Hugh, and set it in the bed of Amos' pickup. The truck squatted under the weight and the tires appeared to be low on air.

Amos double checked everything; the chain, Mattie's gear shift and handbrake, motor in the truck bed, then he slid into the pickup cab and crept away with his prize, grinning wide, gold tooth displayed. And just like that, Mattie was saved from her fatal appointment with the crusher by this unlikely hero.

As Amos turned into his driveway I got a bird's eye view of his home. It apparently included several acres of land, a house, a barn and several animal pens. His house was small but neat, one story and wood sided and it looked freshly painted, white with bright green trim. And it sat right in the center of the lot, at the end of a long gravel driveway which meandered according to Mother Nature's random tree placement. The large, tall, wood barn with a steep tin roof, surface rust showing on most of the roof panels, was located right behind the house not twenty yards away. The barn dwarfed the house and looked out of proportion. Unlike the house, the barn appeared desperate for a coat or two of paint and some minor repairs. On the other side of the barn, forming an ell shape with the barn and connecting with it by only a small wood gate on the inside corner, I saw dog kennels and runs which housed several Greyhounds and they jumped around in their homes and barked excitedly at the sight of Amos. Five dogs, all females, thin because they were racers, but slick and healthy and happy. Two of his dogs were reddish brown, one white and peppered with small grey freckles, the other two a fine steel gray that looked soft to the touch.

Behind the barn and the dog kennels were at least a couple of dozen old cars in various stages and states of disrepair, parts cars, most of them I figured. Across the drive from the kennels was an old chicken house and its run, but instead of chickens, Amos kept his pretty white racing pigeons there. I was struck by the pigeons' beauty, delicate dove like bodies, graceful lines, snow white, the softest looking creatures I'd ever seen, anxious to stretch their wings and show off the speed for which they had been bred.

Amos pulled Mattie around to the back of the barn, got out of his truck and removed the tow chain and pipe, opened the two large wooden barn doors and pushed Mattie inside by hand. Amos was an extremely large man, I'd guess about six feet eight inches tall and stocky, broad shoulders and big muscular arms and legs, weighed maybe three hundred pounds or more. So pushing Mattie by hand was not a problem for him. He pushed her right up to a long steel ramp, hooked her up to a winch which hauled her up onto the ramp to a platform which would get a car about four feet off the ground. There were walk boards on each side of the ramp and a long narrow pit underneath it. Before disconnecting her from the cable he blocked her wheels so she wouldn't roll off the ramp. Next, Amos drove his pickup into the dirt floor barn and under an engine hoist that looked like it had been made from a large old swing set and its legs were on wheels.

After lifting the engine from the pickup bed he drove the truck out from under the hoisted engine and across the barn, walked back and rolled the hoist over a little ways and set the engine down on a huge steel work bench. Then he positioned the hoist to straddle Mattie's hood so he could finish removing the broken engine that Hugh had started removing when it killed him. While inspecting the engine compartment, Amos noticed Mattie's name on her frame opposite her serial numbers, the name Paw Paw had hand stamped on her with hammer and chisel a few years prior.

And Amos talked to Mattie. "Well, look a' here, whas' dis? M A T T I E." He spelled her name aloud as he underlined the letters with a fingertip. "Mattie, is dat yo' name? Who give you dat name, girl? Well Mattie, purdy lady, you be mine now, and I's gonna fix you up real nice. Oh yeah, I remember you, dat McClane feller bought you brand spankin' new a few years back and you sho' was purdy. So what happened to you, Mattie? You look like hell. Some dumb ass white boy didn't know how to take care of a purdy ting like you? What a shame. Well, I got you now, and everyting gonna be all right. I's sho' glad I saw you sittin' dere in line fo' de crusher, otherwise you be nuttin' but a memory by dis time. Ya' see, I needs me a fast car like you to stop dem crooks from cheatin' me outa' my winnins from de pigeon races. And de women folk, dey always appreciate a nice purdy Buick, especially a coupe, yeah baby, you gonna catch dey eye fo' sho'. We gonna have us a good time, you and me, Mattie girl."

I was so happy that Amos discovered Mattie's name, she deserved at least that. And, as time passed by in the dreams, Mattie liked Amos, after all, he rescued her from the crusher and was promising her a complete makeover. Plus he had a barn for her to live in so she wouldn't have to spend her nights outside anymore. I was happy for Mattie, finally she had an owner who would give her the care she needed.

Over the next few weeks I watched with great personal satisfaction as Amos worked on Mattie. He was a good mechanic and had an adequate shop, he had her engine installed and running in just a few days. During the process of the engine swap, Amos performed some modifications; he split her exhaust manifold and fabricated a dual exhaust system, and he installed a dual carburetor set up from a newer Buick. He was building her for speed, unknowingly setting the stage for what would be her destiny, racing.

When the mechanical projects were all completed, Amos began the body work. He straightened out the damaged front fender, working with special hammers and dies, sometimes heating the metal with a torch to bend and shape it. He replaced the crumpled rear fender with one he had salvaged from another 1934 Buick in a junk yard somewhere.

Amos replaced the damaged headlamp bucket and connecting stem which Mrs. Ferguson had broken when she ran Mattie through her back garage wall several years earlier, and he straightened the bent bumpers and reinstalled them. When all the body work was done, Amos sanded Mattie down and painted her black, five coats of gloss black spray paint, rubbed down and shining. She was beautiful again, maybe even more beautiful than before when she was new and brown.

Amos reupholstered the front seat with a new Mohair seat cover, replaced broken glass, and applied touch up paint in the few interior places that needed it, rubbing them down until they blended and did not look like patches or repairs. Amos' skills were quite admirable; Paw Paw would have liked his work, methodical and exact in every detail, never in a hurry, intent on getting everything just right.

I wished Paw Paw could have seen Mattie painted black. (Actually, I found out later that he did see her black. And he got to know Amos too. And I guessed the reason he never talked about this time was because it was while he was a soldier and he never talked about that.) I wished I could tell him about this part of Mattie's life. I also wanted to tell Anita. But even though I was watching the story in full detail, I couldn't share it, it was just too unbelievable.

By the time Amos had Mattie finished and running, we did too. I was never sure which way I liked her best, black and stock, or yellow with flames and rodded out. And though I thought she was nice in her original brown paint, both the black and the yellow with flames were prettier.

Just a couple of days after finishing Mattie's restoration, Amos put her to the test. I watched as he opened the rumble seat hatch and covered the seat with an old quilt, stretching it out, tucking it in, and carefully insuring that it covered all the upholstery. He selected five pairs of his beautiful, snow white, racing pigeons, inspecting the numbers on their leg bands to make sure he had mated pairs, talking to them as if they were small children, holding each one in turn next to his face and gently stroking them on the neck and behind the head, telling them how special and pretty they were, wishing them a safe and successful race. Then one by one he gently placed them in a cage which he set on the quilt in the rumble seat. I was impressed at the compassion this intimidating giant of a man showed toward his birds and also at the trust they seemed to have in him, allowing him to just pick them up with his huge hands and handle them. Not a one struggled or seemed frightened. In fact they returned his affection, cooing and nibbling at his goatee and lips as he held them close to his face and talked his pigeon baby talk. I wondered if Amos ever allowed anyone to witness this spectacle. I doubted it.

Within minutes two other black men arrived in a late twenties pickup, Ford, and parked near Amos and Mattie. They were in awe of Mattie. And I sure did like their truck. I remember thinking what a cool hot rod it would make.

"Whoa bro, where'd you git dis purty tang?"

Amos puffed up with pride. "Saved her from de crusher over dere at Mary's Field by de tracks few weeks back, gave two cars and forty bucks for her, tought I's gonna have to kick me some butt too. Ol' Buck Malek finally saw tangs my way, once I reminded him of de last time he made me mad."

"Dey was gonna crush sumtin like dis? Go on away from here now."

"Yeah, well, it weren't like dis, exactly, it was purdy sad, but a few weeks o' work and some paint fixed dat. Now boys, let's us synchronize our watches. And we gonna see how dis Buick runs 'cause I plans to beat dem pigeons back here and keep you fellers honest dis time."

The men laughed heartily and pushed at the air, waving their hands around, and one replied, "Oh Amos, you can't beat dem pigeons back here, you gotta go by de roads an' dey fly cross country. Why dey be back home, done had lunch an' be nappin' fo' yo' big black ass git here."

Amos didn't laugh with them, he was serious. "Well, we gonna find out. Don' suppose y'all feel like uppin' de anti a little bit now, do ya'? A little personal side bet, maybe?"

Amos' two friends shot each other a look, let it linger, but said nothing, simultaneously shook their heads no at Amos, no laughter now. Amos slid into Mattie and drove, headed for the starting point for the pigeon race, some fifty miles away. Amos talked to Mattie as he drove.

"Spose I shoulda' test drove ya mo'. But you're okay, ain't ya' girl? Ran ya' in de barn plenty, and up and down de driveway a few times, and down de road couple o' miles and back. Yeah, you be ready. Now look a' here purdy lady, on de way back you jist gobble up all dat high octane fuel you want, see, 'cause I's lookin' to win two races today, one wit my birds against de clock, and de other wit you against my birds. And I done bought up several people's gas rations so fuel ain't no problem fo' us, see. Can't wait to see de faces on dem two when we roll in ahead o' de birds and keep dem boys honest wit dat stop watch. Might as well go ahead and count my money right now. I got de fastest birds in de county, everbody know dat, but dese here niggahs been cheatin' me 'cause I ain't dere to keep em honest. But dat all about to change now, tanks to you. Yes ma'am, I save you from de crusher, you save me from de thieves, we's partners now, you and me."

An hour later, Amos rolled up to the starting point for the race, just an agreed on spot on a lonely back road, correct distance was important, nothing else was. Mattie quickly drew a crowd. "Look but don't touch, boys, fresh paint, don't need no fingerprints in it." Amos was proud of Mattie, it showed all over his big face. He now had the nicest car of anyone in his little network of friends and acquaintances. The fuss over Mattie lasted only a few minutes since the birds had to be released at an exact time, the same time and the same distance from each home, in order for the ultimate timing of the flights to be fair and equal for all. Everything had to stay on schedule, the timers at the finish lines were to start their watches at straight up eleven a.m., not a minute earlier, not a minute later. Decades of racing, timing, measuring distances, checking and rechecking had established their system and it was perfect. One contestant had not yet arrived, but they couldn't wait for him.

Three sets of birds were released from the starting point where Amos was, plus four from a second location and two from a third. The pot contained fifty dollars from each bird owner, the money held by a neutral party, a man with no birds in the race, five hundred dollars total, a lot of money for the time.

I'm certain I gasped, in my sleep, at the beauty of the pigeons as they filled the sky with a sudden burst of speed in flight. I think from the second or third flap of their wings they were flying at full speed. Amos had the only white ones and although the sight of all the birds was an awesome one, his white pigeons were what caught and held my eye. And they held his too, he stood and watched as the flock circled once, a wide sweeping circle, perhaps as a warm up for the race ahead of them, or perhaps to get their bearings, maybe even as a farewell gesture to their owners, I wasn't sure, but it was a beautiful spectacle.

Amos' birds quickly took the lead, all ten of them in a tight pattern, a diamond shape actually, almost touching each other with the tips of their wings, and while still just barely within sight they veered off in their own direction as did each group. Strong instincts quickly and accurately finding the direction home.

Suddenly remembering his plan, Amos roused himself from his bird gazing and bounded toward Mattie. "See y'all on de uder side." He yelled from the car window as he sped away.

"Where ya' goin', man? We got a bottle we need help wit here."

"Gotta go keep somebody honest." His gold tooth caught the sun's reflection and sparkled.

The missing contestant rolled up and Amos greeted him with a quick wave followed by a shift to second gear, unsure and unconcerned whether the late participant would release his birds with the obvious disadvantage or just save his fifty dollars and not even try this time.

Amos was on a mission, convinced that his only chance at a win was to be there when the birds arrived home, thereby keeping the time keepers honest. He weaved and turned and pushed Mattie through intersections and curves on seldom traveled dirt and gravel roads, boiling up dust in his wake, reaching speeds of seventy miles per hour or more on the straight runs, craning his neck looking out the windshield and side windows for his white feathered racers.

He was twenty plus miles down the road and nearly half way home when he spotted them flying high and fast in a tight formation, having found a supportive current at some altitude, and Amos was moved by their beauty.

"Lawd, Lawd, Miz Mattie, look at dem beautiful federed creatures go, dey wanna win as bad as I do. Dey be a special treat o' sunflower seeds fo' dem in tonight's supper, dat's fo' sho'."

Amos and Mattie never did get ahead of the birds. They almost caught up with them a few times, but when the road took a turn or a dip, the birds pulled ahead again, unaffected by conditions on the ground. I watched as the birds circled their home once, and gently, gracefully lit on the tin roof of their house, strutting around cooing and bobbing their heads as if in their own personal celebration. Amos was right behind them, driving Mattie right up to the time keepers not half a minute after the arrival of his pigeons.

"Well boys, let's have a look at dat official watch ya' got dere." Amos baled from the coupe and marched the few feet of distance to the other men, sneaking a glance at his own watch which he had coordinated with theirs just before the race.

"Thirty eight minutes and forty two seconds, Amos, purty darned quick." He held the watch out for Amos to see, and nodded.

"Yeah, well we already knowed I got de fastest birds around, dat shouldn't surprise nobody."

"We knowed dat alright, Amos, ya' got de fastest birds fo' sho', it's dat car I can't believe, musta' sprouted wings itself. Why you had to be travelin' seventy and eighty mile a hour to get back here like dat. Good tang fo' you de sheriff weren't on dem back roads today."

"He couldn't a caught me. Well, let's go to de clubhouse boys, I tank I got me some money comin'."

Amos strutted over to his pigeon house, opened the small wooden door near the roof line and let his racers back inside. He looked them over as they moved to the edge of the roof, peered down, hopped, flapped and glided inside to a perch, joining the others who had sat out this race. Amos silently counted them, making sure all ten had returned, checked their food and water, spoke some kind words thanking them for a race well flown, secured the door and returned to his friends.

The man with the stop watch rode with Amos in Mattie and the other followed in his pickup and they traveled to the bird racing club's meeting place, Tina's Tavern, a Negro bar and dance hall at the edge of town, Las Casas.

Tina's Tavern was a big sprawling place with a massive low slung tin roof, no ceiling, just open rafters with the underside of the tin showing. There was one way in and out, matching full glass double front doors with needy looking screen doors in front of them. The bar was an ancient looking wood structure that had been obviously added onto a few times and had a concrete floor smooth as glass, good for dancing. A makeshift band stage two steps tall, took up one corner of the single huge room and an old Wurlitzer juke box owned the space next the stage. An area about twenty feet square was left vacant in front of the stage, for dancing. Long homemade looking wood tables were arranged in neat symmetrical lines all the way from the left wall to the right with wide separations down the middle and near the walls for people to move about. Several styles of wood chairs, maybe a hundred chairs or more, served the tables. A long plain wood bar with a worn and scarred Formica counter top claimed the corner opposite the band stage. A long mirror took up the entire wall behind the bar and gave the place an even more spacious appearance. Two restroom doors were hung next to each other between the bar and the stage, one marked "men" and the other labeled "women", both said "colored only." Someone's attempt at humor, I supposed.

My dream's view moved inside ahead of Amos and his friends and I saw three men sitting on stools at the bar and a large black lady working behind the bar, Tina, I guessed. They turned and looked as the racing club members entered but they didn't seem to be part of it. The men filtered in, led by Amos, and the place quickly went from quiet to loud as they chattered on about the race and their bird's times and speeds. It became apparent that Amos had indeed won the race easily, by more than three full minutes. And Amos happily collected his five hundred dollars prize money and used some of it to buy a few rounds of drinks for his buddies, about a dozen and a half men.

I awoke with a smile on my face and warmth in my heart, happy for Mattie and Amos too. This smart, fun, giant of a man had won me over with his love for my car. Finally, I had found a time of happiness in Mattie's history.

My smile widened as I shook the sleep from my head and realized what the day was. I was to drive Mattie today for the first time, with Paw Paw and Anita! I had just watched Amos on his maiden voyage in Mattie, and now, five decades later, it was my turn. The irony struck me as funny, and pretty darned cool. The smell of breakfast cooking spurred me on and I leapt from my bed, Sparky in tow, and got myself ready for the special day that awaited me.

By the time I was dressed and ready for breakfast, I heard Anita's knock at the front door. Still as much in love with that beautiful girl as I was several months before on my birthday when we awkwardly spoke our relationship into existence and exchanged first kisses sitting in Mattie, I hurried to the door and she greeted me with that poster perfect smile that melted my heart anew each time she blessed me with it. She stepped thru the door as I held it for her and I glanced to see if Paw Paw was looking before stealing a quick peck on the lips. Of course when I looked again, he was watching, smiling, always knowing.

Anita walked directly to the kitchen, which was visible from the foyer, our small house having a very open layout, and spoke with her own mixture of perfect manners and young girl naivety to Paw Paw. "Good morning, Mr. McClane. What cha cookin'?"

"Oh, hi Anita, how are you today? Just a little breakfast, scrambled eggs and biscuits. Would you care to join us? We've got plenty."

She paused. "Well, okay, if you're sure you've got enough. I had a breakfast taco about an hour or so ago, but I'm still a little hungry. Sure smells good."

The three of us sat together for a quick meal and though I loved breakfast, I could have skipped this one. I was anxious to get Mattie out on the road for her virgin run with me at the wheel. I downed a few bites and began picking at what was left, too impatient for food to hold my interest, my heart and mind already behind Mattie's steering wheel.

"Gonna eat that?" Anita was eyeing the eggs on my plate in which I was no longer interested.

"No, go ahead." I was always amazed at how much she could eat, she was so skinny. Maybe it all had to do with her personality, she was hyper and assertive, and the most uninhibited kid I ever knew, going after whatever she wanted with determination and confidence. I pictured in my mind, the flag football game back at my birthday party, Anita competing against the boys, it brought a smile to my face. Paw Paw was amused with her too, he liked her, I could tell. How could anybody not like Anita, she was so naively pretty and so full of personality.

Finally we went to the shop. It took forever it seemed. I could have skipped breakfast and just gotten on with our cruise. We checked Mattie out, not that we needed to, she had only been in the shop, and we had just rebuilt her and done everything ourselves so there was no danger of her being low on any fluids or pressures or anything, but we checked her out anyway. I was nervous, excited, elated, proud, and beyond ready, thirteen going on fourteen with my first car and about to drive her for the first time.

I started her up, let her idle for a full minute, sat there listening to her purr out that throaty, gutsy, loping rumble that built up hot rods do, watching the gauges, making sure to let her fluids warm up and reach operating pressures before slipping her into gear and setting her into motion. My first moment of driving Mattie was only to back her out of the shop, turn her around in our massive concrete driveway, and roll to where our driveway met the street. I felt her power pulse through my entire body, I sat there and felt it as though we were one. I so wanted to unleash Mattie on the street and turn her loose, feel her plaster me against the seat with her four hundred plus horse power. But I eased her to the gate and stopped.

Paw Paw took over from there, driving Mattie, smiling, happy with the car we had just rebuilt, this car that he once loved but now I loved, this car that had been modified and rebuilt by others in the past to be what they wanted her to be, but now was mine and built by me to be what I wanted her to be.

I saw Amos in the mirror, laughing through his gold tooth and his graying goatee, laughing. I laughed at the sight of him, chuckled, it just slipped out. Paw Paw looked at me and he chuckled too, thinking he knew why I chuckled, excitement over Mattie. He didn't have a clue about Amos. Anita was sitting right next to me, Mattie's front seat was really only supposed to be for two people but we didn't mind, and she moved her hand against my leg and giggled quietly, so I reached over and held her hand. I glanced at her and saw her distracting smile, I wanted to kiss her. I always wanted to kiss her, sure that any face that beautiful must be made for kissing. But what I was really thinking was, only I could see Amos, only I knew there were really four of us going on this maiden voyage in Mattie, and all four of us were smiling and laughing with joy.

We traveled to the outskirts of our little town, choose a lonely country road, coasted a quarter mile or so and stopped.

"You ready, son?"

The question did not need an answer and I didn't give one. Paw Paw got out and walked around behind the car and to the other side. By the time he was getting back in the passenger side I had already moved behind the wheel, stealing a kiss as I maneuvered across Anita leaving her sitting in the middle. Waiting for Paw Paw to close his door and put his seat belt on, I gripped Mattie's wheel with both hands and felt her pulse, that nice antique banjo steering wheel, authentic from 1934, one of the few original parts on her. We were crowded shoulder to shoulder but it had a certain comfort to it, Anita wanted to be here for this and I wanted her to be.

My heart was pumping adrenalin through me at a hectic pace and it required all the self-control I could muster up to stay reasonably calm for this, this highlight of my thirteen years of life. Anita moved the back of her hand against my leg as a subtle gesture of support. A heavy sigh accompanied my perfectly coordinated hand and foot movements, shifter, steering wheel, brake, clutch, clutch slowly released, gas pedal gently engaged, timing precise. Mattie eased forward in response as perfectly as if she and I were one. And indeed I felt we were, having already shared our deepest secrets and most precious moments, our relationship sealed by my personal work on her and her shared history with me, ghosts and all. And Amos smiled at me through Mattie's antique rear view mirror, in obvious support of this special moment.

As if I should have been able to crowd another issue into my thoughts and emotions on that occasion, I had the distinct realization that I would never release Amos from Mattie, not even if he asked. I liked him as much as I had pitied Mrs. Ferguson and as much as I had disliked Hugh. Amos needed to remain with

Mattie.

My shift to second gear came as naturally as breathing and Mattie's response was the same, third gear followed in like manner and by fourth gear we were cruising along at fifty miles per hour, straight and smooth, no shakes or rattles or play in the suspension or steering. It seemed that our work and also previous owners' work on her had all been good and Mattie was indeed road worthy.

Our cruise took us down a narrow hill country road, one of the few the developers had not yet spoiled with their tearing up and paving the countryside and building cheap houses too close to each other. Once in a while we would travel thru areas where the Juniper and Elm and Oak trees lining both sides of the road formed a canopy over us. Eventually the canopy would disappear and we'd ease through the low water crossings, narrow old concrete and wood bridges with water lazily flowing over them just a few inches deep. Farther out, we entered an area of freshly cut hay fields and the aroma coming thru Mattie's open windows was a refreshing treat. Our speed stayed around forty to forty five miles per hour over the hills, through the valleys, around the nice long curves, everything was perfect.

And just as we topped the next hill, a cop passed us going the other way. I tensed up, figuring I'm in big trouble, thirteen years old and driving without a license. Sure that my first cruise in Mattie was about to end with a ticket from a cop. What was he doing anyway on such a lonely road that went nowhere? A glance in the mirror proved my suspicions; he was turning around, blue and red lights flashing.

"He's coming, Paw Paw."

"Well, just pull over. He can't kill you and eat you, you know."

I pulled onto the gravel shoulder and waited, Mattie's strong healthy engine pulsing, wanting to go. I turned the key and killed the engine. I waited, watching thru Mattie's small and perfectly round side mirror.

The officer seemed ten feet tall, very dark sunglasses hid his eyes, he looked quite formal in his starched, clean uniform with a pistol and about a dozen gadgets hanging off of his belt. His presence was imposing as he sauntered up to my window. "License, registration, and insurance, please." He demanded in a robot like voice.

I offered the insurance and registration papers and he took them. I had no license.

"No license, that's what I thought. No inspection sticker either. How old are you, son?"

"Almost fourteen, sir."

"Are you his father?" He looked across Anita at Paw Paw.

"Yes, officer, I am. Uh, we just got this car running, officer, it hasn't been on the street in a long time and we thought we'd check it out a little before trying to get it inspected, you know, to see if everything works right, out here away from traffic."

"Could I see your license, sir?"

Paw Paw leaned forward, pulled his wallet from his back pocket, pulled his license out and handed it across Anita and me to the cop, who looked at the license, looked back at Paw Paw, excused himself and walked back to his car to run the license check.

When he returned, his stiffness seemed to have softened. He handed Paw Paw's license, the insurance card and the registration back to me. I noticed he had nothing else in his hand, no ticket book and I took that as a good sign. "This car is registered to you, isn't it, young man?"

"Yes sir, it's my car." I was still nervous, but was beginning to feel a little better about how this might turn out.

"Driving lessons?"

"Yes, sir."

"This is a beautiful car. Did you do the work on it yourself?"

"Yes sir, except for the paint, I didn't paint it myself."

"What is it? A Buick? What 1932, 33?"

"Yes, sir, 1934 Buick Sports Coupe."

"I don't believe I've ever seen flames like that before." He peered inside. "Nice leather interior. You did a good job on it."

"Thank you, sir. Her name is Mattie. My great great grandfather bought her new in 1934."

He was trying to see Mattie's engine through the open space where I had left her hood side panels off. He obviously wanted to look Mattie over so we all got out and walked around her with Officer Jacobs and showed her off to him, opening her hood and doors and even her rumble seat hatch. I could tell by his interest and the things he noticed that he was a car guy. And I realized what an amusing experience this was, I was walking around my hot rod, on the side of the road, with a cop, showing it off to him, and he was in utter awe of it, just after he pulled me over and discovered I was too young by three years to even have a driver's license.

"Well, you've done an excellent job, young man, it's beautiful." He looked from me to Paw Paw and said, "Mr. McClane, I don't have a problem with driving lessons on these back roads, just keep it slow, okay? To tell ya' the truth, I just wanted to see the car. And I wish more kids could come to us with some actual on the road experience and working knowledge of cars before they apply for their licenses."

We each shook hands with Officer Jacobs and said goodbye. We piled back in Mattie, sat there while Officer Jacobs turned his car around and left in the direction he had been traveling before turning around to come after us. We looked at each other, huge smiles took over our faces, and we laughed, all of us, even Amos, I saw him in the mirror, gold tooth sparkling. Anita patted me on the shoulder.

I drove on, turned down another country road which we explored, then another, and another, never tiring of driving Mattie, getting her feel, perfecting my timing with her gears and her turning ratio and her brakes, nice cruise. And we were lost, and I was happy with that too. The countryside was beautiful, I was driving Mattie for the first time and she was performing so fine, and we were lost, and we didn't care.

We arrived safely back at the shop about an hour and a half after our departure, having had no problems on our road trip except for the cop and getting lost, and it all ended way too quickly for me. Back in the shop, we gave Mattie a thorough checking out, fluids and vital signs, and the worst thing we could find was dirt and road film, especially on her new chrome wire wheels. Well, there was a small run of oil on her left valve cover but a half a turn of the bolt head with a half inch box end wrench and a quick swipe with a shop rag took care of that.

While Anita and I cleaned Mattie and wiped her down, Paw Paw headed for the house to prepare us a quick meal. As soon as he was out the door I grabbed Anita and kissed her, a nice long kiss. She suggested we sit in Mattie and make out and we did, until we were called to lunch. We French kissed, first time, she started it, tongues, it felt strange but it excited me. I wanted to touch her budding breasts but she wouldn't let me, I'd caress her back and neck and her shoulders and face, and try to sneak my hands down or up her shirt.

"Huh uh." She'd say and I'd back off. "We're too young, Joey."

"Yeah, but we're early bloomers." I'd argue.

"No, Joey."

"'nita." I'd whine. "You're so beautiful, I just wanna touch you."

"No!"

And we were too young, way too young. But we were early bloomers, that was certainly true, and we were in love, children in adult bodies, almost, in love and wanting each other.

When my dreams of Amos continued, I watched him fashion a trailer hitch to Mattie's rear bumper. Now I knew what those weld marks were that we had ground off and refinished several weeks ago. Paw Paw and I had wondered about those. Amos attached a dog trailer to Mattie, a single axle, enclosed trailer, small, or short in height at least, with solid wood walls about half way up and then wire mesh from there to the sheet metal roof.

One by one, Amos took his greyhounds from their runs, taking time to pet and praise and kiss each one on the top of the nose before loading her into the trailer. He was always so gentle with his animals, to just look at this man, it would seem out of character for him. His dogs were hyper with excitement, they knew it was race time and they were anxious for it.

Mattie, dog trailer in tow, rolling up to the race track, was a funny sight to me. I wished Paw Paw could see it, he was right when he told me that she had a lot of history that didn't include him. He was more correct that he could imagine. And my feeling was that she was revealing it all to me and that meant it did include me. I felt a sense of pride in it all, like I was chosen. We had a bond, Mattie and I, a secret bond, very personal.

The dog race was a big deal, not just a small club thing like the pigeon racing, hundreds of people were in attendance, maybe a couple of thousand, the stands were full. And of course all the cars were from Mattie's era, hundreds of cars from the 1920s and 30s, filling a huge parking lot, it was an amazing sight to me, a beautiful sight, a page out of automotive history right before my eyes.

Amos opened the trailer door and his dogs spilled out, excited, anticipating, sniffing the air, tails wagging, pacing hurried circles around Amos. He clipped leashes onto their collars and led all five of them at once to the track kennels, concrete and woven wire enclosures built directly under the bleachers. He ushered them into the largest space he could find empty, latched the door and headed for the office to register. As he walked away, one of the dogs, the one he called Lucy, the one who liked to lick him in the face when he talked to her, sat down and howled. That got the others going too, and the dogs in nearby kennels joined in. Amos turned around and faced them, not twenty feet away, held up his hands, palms out and chided. "Now come on girls, y'all hush up." They quieted down, but Lucy got in a couple more yelps.

Moments later, Amos was walking one of his dogs, the one he called Sammie, trotting actually, warming her up, and talking to her the entire time. At the call, he led her to the starting chutes, placed her in the spot reserved for her, slipped her numbered vest on her, unclipped the leash and gave her one last rub down, words of encouragement, and a kiss on the nose.

The gates sprung open with a reverberating clash of metal from a dozen different gates at once, the mechanical rabbit took off along the fence and Sammie lunged forward with the other racers. I watched her jockey for position and work her way to the inside lane. It was a beautiful thing, I had never seen a dog race before and I was amazed at the speed those graceful animals could quickly attain. By the third or fourth stride they were at full speed, must have been doing sixty miles per hour, legs a blur, bodies stretched out in some exaggerated aerodynamic form. Sammie ran in fourth place out of the dozen competitors for about three quarters of the way around the track. Suddenly she really poured it on, stretching her entire body out until it looked like a thin grey line flying just off the ground. It was a close race, half the dogs bunched up in the lead, the others trailed hopelessly behind more and more as the race continued. Sammie seemed to know exactly where the finish line was and with her last step to it she stretched out even more, something that didn't look possible, and won by a nose, literally.

Amos was ecstatic and Sammie rushed to him, fully realizing what she'd done. She jumped right into his arms and he held the big dog and hugged her, burying his huge happy face into her neck and they lavished affectionate congratulations on each other. Amos set Sammie down and made an attempt to slip her leash around her neck but Sammie wouldn't hold still for it so he just let her follow him back to the kennel. Actually she never followed, she ran circles around him and jumped and barked, hyper with excitement. The kennels were under a bank of stands and as Amos and Sammie approached, the crowd cheered and applauded in appreciation of the hard fought win, and also in fun admiration of their relationship. Amos had forgotten about the audience, and suddenly realizing they were cheering for him, he stopped and looked, flashed his gold tooth smile, and tipped his baseball cap in a gesture of gratitude. Sammie jumped up and put her feet on his stomach and he leaned down to her and she kissed him and the fans loved it.

I was constantly amazed in my dreams of him, how Amos could so comfortably maintain two distinctly different personalities, imposing and intimidating with other men, but so kind and gentle with his animals. At the races, right in front of everybody he had no problem showing affection toward his dogs while I never saw that in the other handlers, they were mechanical and cold, not gentle and loving, sometimes even short tempered and cruel, yelling at their dogs and jerking them around, no gentle touches or kind words, no bond, no relationship.

Amos' gentle dog handling tactics paid off, he had a good day at the track, winning two firsts and placing in the money in three other races. His winnings totaled over four hundred dollars, not bad for a time in history when the average person earned only about fifteen dollars in a long work day, and most black men earned less.

After the dog races Amos took his animals back home and walked with them around his place which covered several acres, around twenty five I guessed, we had five acres, and his land looked about five times the size of ours. Amos meandered around leisurely while the dogs ran free, playing and chasing each other, sniffing up trails of rabbits and no telling what else, raccoons and opossums probably, maybe a coyote or a fox. Most of Amos' land was pretty heavily treed with all the native Texas hill country varieties; Live Oak, Ash, Hackberry, Juniper, Native Pecan, a Prickly Pear and a Mountain Laurel thrown in here and there, unspoiled, unworkable rocky soil. A paradise for wildlife, a holiday for dogs. The five greyhounds never got far from each other or from Amos, they'd venture out a ways on their own, look up and around, run back to Amos, one at a time usually, checking in, and back out to run and sniff some more. This was a daily ritual, early afternoon, every day, for a couple of hours, part of Amos routine.

I watched as Amos swept out the dog trailer, then hosed it out, drove Mattie inside the barn and disconnected the trailer. He retreated to his house for about an hour, returned, all dressed up, drove out of the barn and down the driveway and out onto the road, heading in to Tina's to celebrate.

Only one of the double doors was open at Tina's Tavern and Amos' big frame barely fit through it. Most of his buddies were already there and they called out to Amos to join them. Some of them had attended the dog races. Amos settled in at the table, drinking and talking, puffing on a cigar, and he relived each race, bragging on his dogs. Amos' friends were always happy when he won because he would buy several rounds in celebration. They were a fun bunch to watch.

Amos was signaling to the waitress for another round when a stranger entered the place, a white man in uniform, dangerously out of place. The white stranger squinted, trying to get his eyes adjusted to the darkness of the room in contrast to the bright sunlight outside. Everyone looked up at him, every voice went silent, the waitress stopped in mid stride, only the Negro Blues music from the juke box penetrated the sudden silence.

It was Paw Paw! Once again I saw my Paw Paw in a dream, this time a young man in his early twenties and dressed in an Army uniform. He was so handsome, straight and tall and strong, a soldier, an officer with captain's bars. This was exciting, he looked even better than in the photographs I had seen of him in uniform. Later, when I was awake and remembering this I so wished I could tell him about it.

"Who owns that Buick coupe out there?" He asked in a voice meant to be heard by everyone in the room.

Though it seemed impossible things got even quieter; whispers shushed, even subtle movements stopped. Everyone looked back and forth from the soldier to Amos, wondering what was about to happen. Amos was not somebody to mess with, he easily could whip any two men in town at the same time, everyone knew that and some had seen good evidence of it. But now a white man boldly enters a place he shouldn't and seeks Amos out as if he had no fear, or perhaps he just didn't know the danger he might be putting himself in. Amos stood up, set his drink on the old scarred up wood table and pushed his chair out, and it made that noise wood chairs make when scooted across a hard floor. The juke box had just finished its song and the chair noise penetrated the dense silence and everybody flinched in unison.

Amos stretched to his full height of about six feet eight inches, drew in a long breath and expanded his chest and if expecting trouble and about to face a foe. Amos was such a big man, formidable and impressive, intimidating actually. His deep voice roared. "Dat's my car. What be da' problem, soldier?"

I heard other chairs scoot, as if onlookers saw trouble coming and were scurrying to get out of the way.

Paw Paw marched right across the floor, right to Amos, and offered his hand. "I'm Joseph McClane, sir, and there is no problem. I'm just wondering if that might be the coupe my grandfather had several years ago when I was a kid. Someone has sure done a nice job of fixing it up, if it is the same one."

Amos let the soldier's hand hang there for a moment and eyed him suspiciously. "You be little Joseph McClane?"

A smile came across Paw Paw's face. "Yes sir, well, not so little any more, but that's me."

Amos smiled too, slowly, as if in slow motion, his big toothy grin with the gold tooth in front, left front, and his whole body relaxed. He finally accepted the hand shake, vigorously. "Amos Johnson. Last time I saw you, you were little. Look at you now, a soldier. I remember your granddaddy drivin' dat car trew town wit you perched in the rumble seat like you was king o' de' world. Now you out dere fightin' de war. Ya home now? Ya okay? Didn't get shot or nutin' did ya'? And you a officer too, look at dat brass on you, all dem ribbons and medals. You been right in de tick of it, ain't ya'?" Amos paused. " Protectin' my freedom." I heard admiration in Amos' voice.

"I'm fine, thank you, sir. Just home for a few days between assignments. I was passing by and saw that car and had to stop. Mr. Johnson, you have no idea how much I loved that car, and how much I wanted it, but I was just a kid. It makes me happy to see it all fixed up again. I watched Mrs. Ferguson practically destroy it and then some time after that I saw it rotting in a field, when I was on my way out of town, leaving for school. Later, when I was overseas, I was told it had been donated to the war effort and melted down. This is like seeing an old friend that I thought was dead. Would you mind terribly if I had a good look at it, sir?"

"Tell ya what, Joseph, if you stop calling me sir and Mr. Johnson, and jist call me Amos, I'll even take you for a ride in dat car, got her runnin' real good too, you ain't gonna believe how fast she run now. You can even ride in de rumble seat if you like, jist like you used to." Amos offered to buy Paw Paw a drink but the offer was politely declined so Amos gulped down what was left of his, slapped money on the table for the next round and they headed outside to see Mattie. I watched as they walked circles around her, talking, remembering, laughing, touching Mattie with hands and eyes. I saw faces in the windows of the tavern, watching, perhaps disappointed there was no fight.

Mattie's color had changed from brown to black but they both agreed it was an improvement. Amos showed off the engine modifications, dual carburetors, dual exhaust via a split manifold, improved electronics, and he also had converted her to hydraulic brakes and swapped the old artillery style wheels for nice shiny chrome wire wheels, something I also did decades later in my real life. He had redone much of the interior, adding carpet to the wood floors. Mattie was beautiful and fast. She looked to me like a nicely done hot rod coupe, and Amos was very proud. The only old damage still lingering was the missing hood ornament. Paw Paw said he'd try to find one for her. They cruised but Paw Paw declined Amos' invitation to ride in the rumble seat, however he did sit in it briefly just before embarking on the cruise. I could see memories going thru his mind.

I watched the unlikely pair become friends and promise to stay in touch. When Amos called the coupe Mattie I saw gratefulness on Paw Paw's face and he admitted to being the one who gave her that name and talked about when he stamped it on her frame right by her serial numbers with hammer and chisel, and a couple of bruised knuckles. Amos asked why that name, Mattie? And I realized that I didn't know either, and I wanted to know. Mattie was short for Matilda, Paw Paw revealed, who years ago was a very pretty school teacher he had had a boyhood crush on. It was a heartwarming story, I was glad to know that piece of Mattie's history.

The following day, in my real world, I hunted for and found, buried in an old cedar chest, some old photographs of Paw Paw in uniform. I selected two of them and slid one into the journal and set the one in the thin black frame on my chest of drawers in my bedroom. I liked it there and was gazing at it, when Paw Paw stuck his head in the doorway to tell me that breakfast was ready.

"What are you doing with that?" He asked, surprised at seeing the picture.

Pretty much oblivious to the question, I looked at him in silence, seeing in my mind, Paw Paw young and in uniform, shaking hands with Amos in that Negro bar, Tina's Tavern, that day four and a half decades ago, four times my age. Two very different but very impressive men bonding over their love of the same car. And in that instant with him standing there, I wanted so badly to tell him everything. But I did not.

He stepped to the framed photo, picked it up and stared, going back, I was sure, in his mind to that time in his life. He stood there silent for several seconds, slowly set the picture back down, as if returning to the present was difficult, turned and walked out of the room. "Come on Joey, let's eat, 'fore it gets cold."

After breakfast Paw Paw had some errands to run in San Antonio but I stayed home to catch up on school work. I was normally an excellent student, most home schoolers were, in fact in math and science I was several grades ahead of where I was supposed to be. But my good intentions about studying that morning didn't last long as I soon felt Mattie's pull on me and I got out my journal to continue her story. Sitting on the living room couch, enjoying the quiet time, I wrote about the most recent dream. When I couldn't think of anything else to write I laid the journal aside, robbed the refrigerator and headed to the shop.

I hoped to see Amos right away but didn't so I got busy on a project. We had installed a new sound system in the glove box and had it all wired up, but hadn't yet installed speakers. So I opened the doors, unscrewed the sill plates and pulled the carpet up around the edges to run the wiring that would power the rear speakers near the rumble seat.

It was only after I was deeply engrossed in my work on Mattie that I heard the voice, a deep throaty voice with sort of a southern accent speaking slowly with terrible grammar. I looked up and there was Amos, clear and certain, big as life. This was the first time one of Mattie's ghosts had appeared with me inside the car, in full form anyway. Amos had showed only his face in the mirror when I drove Mattie that first time.

Well now, I wasn't really inside the car, not all the way, my feet were on the shop floor but I was leaning my body inside, working with the wires. And Amos was close, close enough to touch, if it's possible to touch a ghost. Surprised by his sudden presence I jumped and dropped my tools and they clattered to the cement floor. He laughed at me. Sparky woke up from his nap on the floor nearby, and seeing Amos he stiffened his body, bristled his hair, and growled.

"You de one!" The big booming voice declared. "You be Joseph McClane. You de one dat crazy ol' bitch Miz Ferguson nagged us all about, over and over. De one Mattie been waitin' fo' all deze years, waitin' fo' you to come fo' her. I sho glad you got dat crazy woman outta here, an' Hugh too, he jist as crazy as her. We sho got tired o' dey cryin' an' complainin' all de time. Good riddance to boof of 'em. Now maybe we can have some fun, like old times."

Amos opened his big mouth wide and gave a hearty laugh through his gold tooth and his kinky salt and pepper goatee, then he began to fade away, his laugh slowly faded too.

"No! Wait! Amos, wait! I have some questions for you! You said 'us' and 'we.' How many more ghosts are there? Who's still here in Mattie? Amos! Damn it!"

He was gone, for the moment, and my questions went unanswered, most of them unasked. They would be answered though, in time, whether asked or not. One thing I've learned about ghosts, they can't be hurried, they act on their own schedules. I suppose that time is all they have and they have plenty of it.

I heard the diesel pickup outside and knew that Paw Paw had returned, maybe that was why Amos didn't stay longer. He stuck his head thru the open shop door, asked if I'd finished my studies and said he'd be in the house "getting us some lunch whipped up", he'd call when it was ready. I picked up my tools and continued where I'd left off with the speaker wiring project and hoped, in vain, for Amos to return.

After what seemed like way more time than was needed to prepare lunch, hunger drove me to the house without being summoned. What I saw upon entering was not Paw Paw preparing a meal for us, but Paw Paw sitting on the couch reading my journal about Mattie. I had forgotten about it and left it out. A silent panic swept through me and I froze in my tracks, barely two steps inside the door.

Paw Paw looked up at me, a serious look. "We need to talk, Joey." He motioned with one hand for me to come to the couch, patted the space beside him for me to sit. After looking into each other's eyes for several long torturous seconds, he spoke again. "It never stopped, did it?"

I slowly shook my head. My eyes were glued to his. "No sir, it didn't, not for long anyway. And... And Amos just appeared in Mattie, just now, and he spoke to me." I figured I might as well be completely honest with him, if he'd read the journal he knew everything anyway.

Another moment of piercing eyes and uncomfortable silence. "What did he say?"

I swallowed hard. "That he was glad to be rid of Mrs. Ferguson and Hugh."

"That's all?"

"Yes, sir."

He hesitated, looked at the journal, held it up with one hand and looked back at me, slowly shaking his head, and he sighed. "Why, Joey?"

"He said they were crazy and not fun to be around."

"No, not that!" Paw Paw sounded aggravated. "I mean why have you been keeping this all to yourself? Why haven't you told me?"

"Well, um..." I squirmed in my seat, uneasy, afraid of the consequences of Paw Paw knowing everything. It wasn't that I was afraid of getting spanked or anything like that, he never hit me, even when I was smaller, but I loved and admired him so much, just to know he was disappointed in me was punishment enough. "Well, I was afraid you'd get rid of Mattie if you knew. You said, maybe, we, if they kept it up, we might have to..." Tears rolled down my cheeks and I lost my voice, but didn't know what else to say anyway. I felt terrible about keeping things from Paw Paw, but I felt worse about the danger of losing Mattie.

"Don't you trust me, Joey?"

I struggled to regain my composure. "Paw Paw, yes, of course, but... It, it's like this can't be happening, you know, it's just not right, not normal, not even possible. But it is happening and I don't know how to handle it. So I just keep it to myself. And I was afraid you'd get rid of Mattie if you knew. This isn't hurting anything, Paw Paw. It's like a secret little world and it doesn't hurt anything. It's something that belongs to Mattie and she wants to share it with me, her life, her history. Except..." I stopped, drew in a breath, let it out, afraid I'd said too much.

"What Joey, except what?"

I looked down, and back up, slowly, into his eyes, pleading my case.

"Except, she thinks I'm you, come back for her. They all do, they all think I'm you. I'm sorry Paw Paw, I didn't mean to be dishonest with you. But how do you tell someone you're seeing ghosts, in your car, and that they talk to you, and come to you in dreams? How do you do that?"

He offered no answer to my question, just a worried look. "Does the car talk to you?"

I grinned and almost laughed, almost, just a little snicker. "No, Paw Paw, Mattie doesn't talk, just the ghosts, and they don't say much, it's not like we have a conversation or anything. They just reveal things to me, show me their story. They tell me what they need from me."

Our eyes were locked onto each other's again, and the short silence that followed my answer was quite uncomfortable. "Yes, you're right, it is hard to believe, it's something that shouldn't be. But you know too much, too many details, the evidence is all here and there's no way to doubt it." He held up the journal again as if to emphasize his point. "You certainly had no other way of knowing these things, I mean yes I've given you bits and pieces over the years, but not the details, not word for word conversations. It has got to be happening just like you say." He hesitated. "Are you okay, son?" He draped his arm around me and I immediately felt better, I released a sigh of relief and moved closer to him looping one arm around his back, grateful for the hug.

I wiped my teary eyes with my fingers and sniffed. "Paw Paw, am I crazy? I mean, I've heard about people who hear voices, and..."

He breathed a quiet laugh. "No son, you're not crazy. Somehow you've managed to experience something from another dimension of time, but you still keep your feet planted in the present. I don't think I could do it. I'd be avoiding sleep, and the car."

"You're not going to make me get rid of Mattie?"

Another low chuckle. "No, but please, promise me something, son. If this gets out of hand, you know, frightening or threatening, tell me, let me be there for you. Okay?"

I agreed with a nod.

"And another thing, very important Joey, don't tell anyone else about this. Believe me, no one would understand and it would just reflect badly on you." He hesitated, thinking. "You haven't told anyone, have you?"

"No, Paw Paw, I haven't."

"Not even Anita?"

"No, not even 'nita. Wanted to, lots of times, but didn't. Wanted to tell you too, Paw Paw, especially the parts where I saw you, young and in uniform, you looked very impressive, Paw Paw. That's why I found that old Army picture of you and put it in my room, and the other one in the journal. Were you a war hero, Paw Paw?"

He handed the journal to me and looked away, stiffened his back a little, drew in a deep breath and let it out slowly. His mind seemed to drift and he took his time answering my question. "No, just another soldier." Another long pause. "Here, put this where Anita won't see it."

He had already gotten up from the couch and was already walking away and added without looking back. "You know I don't like to talk about that, Joey."

After that day I faithfully kept up the journal but didn't hide it from Paw Paw anymore. I could tell that he read it from time to time but he seldom asked questions. At times I would voluntarily share parts of the ongoing story with him. What had been my secret was now our secret and it felt good to be open about it with him.

CHAPTER 6

The summer of '92 was now in full swing and Anita was out of school for a few weeks but Paw Paw refused to allow me a break from my home school studies, as usual. Like me, Anita had all but deserted her friends, preferring to hang around with me. We rode our bikes together and swam in the river, went to movies, and spent quite a bit of time in the shop with whatever projects were going on there. We were always ready to go for a cruise in Mattie and we went for a lot of cruises, Paw Paw chaperoning, of course.

In June, a couple of months before my birthday, Anita turned fourteen but looked seventeen. She had spent the last year blooming like crazy, not quite as skinny anymore and a lot more curvy. But she was still that playful tomboy I fell in love with, maybe even more so. She liked to wrestle with me and she was aggressive and strong, probably from growing up with older brothers. I was reluctant to use all my strength with her, I didn't want to hurt her and she took full advantage of that. I hated it when she pinned me to the floor but she always made it okay by ending it with a kiss, and she was rough even with the kiss. However, when I was about to pin her down, she would bite me.

I had the whole day planned, I wanted to give my girlfriend a very special birthday. Just before noon, Paw Paw dropped us off at a nice restaurant in town and after eating we walked from there to a movie theater and later from there to Rocky's Den where the kids our age hung out. Las Casas was such a small town it would require only a few minutes to walk from one end of it to the other and the business district consisted of just a few blocks that wrapped around the square, a nice park like area with huge Pecan trees surrounding city offices. Rocky's was in an old converted furniture store nestled between a drug store and a little mom and pop store that specialized in homemade ice cream and baked goods. Rocky's was on the outside perimeter of the square, across the street, opposite a statue of one of the town's founding fathers.

We were dancing, they had a nice wood dance floor and played continuous music that was popular with the kids. With a slow song playing, we were enjoying dancing close when trouble started. Billy Davis, a redneck bully and known trouble maker a couple of years older than me (but probably several grades lower in school) was sitting at a table at the edge of the dance floor. When we danced nearby he stuck his foot out and tried to trip us. Although his attempt didn't succeed, I knew what he did and I stopped and looked at him, which was probably a mistake.

"Well, there's Joey McClane and his wetback girlfriend!" He loudly proclaimed to his friends and they all laughed.

I turned and faced him. "You better shut up, Davis."

He jumped to his feet and crowded me, anxious to make a scene. He was towering over me and looking down at me and his breath stunk. "You gonna make me? Huh? Come on tough guy, make me shut up." He shoved me in the chest with both hands but didn't knock me off balance and I pushed his hands away. He was a lanky kid with a mean reputation and he stood at least three inches taller than me and used that to his advantage now, looking down on me as he inched even closer and we were almost touching but I wouldn't back up. I wasn't afraid, just angry. He glared at me, fist cocked back, daring me to make a move or say something else.

Now I was not a small kid myself, I was pretty tall for my age, stocky and strong and plenty gutsy and not about to let him get away with insulting Anita. I was ready for this. My Paw Paw had boxed in college and had been a soldier in the war, and he taught me a few things about how to defend myself and his advice immediately filled my thoughts. "Try to avoid fighting, but if you know you are in a situation where you are going to have to fight, get the first punch in and make it count, then do your best to just overwhelm him. Most fights are won or lost in the first few seconds. Aggression counts a lot more than size." And he showed me some moves, where to land a punch, how to stand, how to put your shoulder into the punch and judge the distance for the most effectiveness, punching through the target, not at it.

Anita tried to avoid the trouble. "Come on Joey, let's just go."

"Yeah, Joey, just take your Meskin pussy and run away like the Meskin lovin' coward you are."

I turned to Anita, keeping Billy in the corner of my eye. "'nita, move back." My look said it all and she backed up a few steps without an argument but she looked worried, almost in tears. In one swift motion I turned to Billy Davis and slugged him with every ounce of strength in me, right in the nose. That first punch broke his nose and you could hear the crack and blood poured out. Stunned and hurt, he stumbled back and fell backwards across a table and I laid into him with a flurry of punches that went on till he rolled off the table and fell to the floor. Billy went down covering his face with both hands and blood streamed out between his fingers. He was thrashing around on the floor in a panic and I swear he was crying. I looked around, expecting to have to take on Billy's redneck friends next but they had all scrambled out of the way. I positioned myself to deliver a hard kick to Billy's crotch but Anita grabbed my arm and pulled.

"No! Joey, stop!"

A crowd had formed around us and the man working there was pushing his way though, ordering kids to "Get out of the way!"

Anita was still trying to restrain me and I was still trying to get into position to kick the crap out of Billy when the man reached us and stepped in front of me, hands up, palms out. "Whoa, wait, stop, hold it! I saw and heard the whole thing, Joey. You two go on home now, I'll handle this. This troublemaker got what he deserved and he won't be back in here, ever."

We found a pay phone down the street and called Paw Paw to come get us. Anita wasn't ready to go home yet so she went home with me. On our way there we told Paw Paw about the incident. He was sorry that I got into a fight but proud of the way I handled it and agreed that it was justified. Anita was clinging to me like never before. The entire ride home she kept both arms wrapped around my left arm and her head on my shoulder.

My left thumb was swelling and throbbing, so the first thing we did after getting home was to put an ice pack on it. When we calmed down, emotion wise, Anita said she wanted to hear Mattie's new sound system so after taking care of my hurt thumb she and I went to the shop. Once inside Mattie we closed the door and wrapped ourselves up in each other and kissed. She was especially passionate that evening with her hugs and kisses and caresses. Defending her honor certainly seemed to have its rewards.

Between kisses she whispered softly in my ear, "Joey, it didn't bother me what that boy said about me. I know who I am and it doesn't matter what anyone else thinks. But you, Joey, you fought for me, you kicked his butt for me, and he was a lot bigger than you. I love you, Joey. I feel so safe when I'm with you."

Between more passionate kisses I tried to answer. "I'm in love with you, 'nita. I love you so much. You're the nicest, prettiest, most fun girl in the whole world. You're like a best friend that I can make out with and wrestle with." I suppose I wasn't that good at love talk.

She laughed at what I'd said. "You're sweet." She held my face with both hands and kissed me hard.

"Oh, wait, I forgot your birthday present." I fumbled around in my pants pocket and pulled out a very small box and handed it to her. It was a ring, a small gold band, in fact it looked a lot like a wedding ring. I hadn't thought about that when I bought it, I just liked the petite style and the patterns etched in the yellow gold, but now watching her unwrap it...

In the box with the ring was a thin gold chain. I explained that I had intended to give it to her at Rocky's but the fight happened first and then we had to leave and I forgot about it.

"Oh Joey, this is beautiful." She threaded the chain thru the ring and then around her neck, checking it in Mattie's mirror. Man, that gold looked good against her dark complexion. I always thought she had the prettiest skin. She looped her arms around my neck and pulled me close, touching her forehead to mine. Her beautiful face, right there, her black eyes burning holes in my soul. "Does this mean we're going steady?"

"Well, yeah sure, if you want it to." In fact, it could have meant anything she wanted it to, I was, as usual, completely under her spell.

We got back to our making out, forgetting all about the sound system we had come to hear and the next thing I knew we were laying down on the seat, me on top of her, kissing and running our hands all over each other. I lost my head in the passion and my left hand, my hurt hand, went to her breasts, down the neck of her shirt and right inside her bra. I had so been wanting to touch her there again, having so far been granted only that quick look and feel at the river that day when her top floated away. I had dreamed of the moment when my hands might be allowed to stray and linger and explore.

Anita let out a surprised gasp and she grabbed me by the wrist. It was my hand with the swollen thumb, and she gripped it tight and it hurt. She moved my hand away but she didn't loosen her grip. She stared into my eyes but said nothing. I was afraid I had really messed up and she might break up with me, or at least slap me and go home mad, maybe give the ring back. Seconds passed but it seemed like forever. I nervously searched her eyes but her glare gave no hint of what she was thinking.

Heart pounding and hands shaking, I made an awkward attempt at an apology. "Oh, I sorry, 'nita. Please don't be mad at me. I won't do it again."

She continued to glare at me, still hurting my hand with her tight grip. She looked furious. And like the old adage, she was beautiful when she was angry, her pouting lips, her breath heaving, black eyes unreadable and a mile deep, damn she was beautiful.

"'nita... Please..." I whined and pulled against her grip, but she wouldn't let go.

Finally, Anita spoke to me, still glaring. "We're too young, you know, for that, for touching like that." She hesitated, long enough for me to get even more uncomfortable with worry. I still had no idea what she was going to do about me touching her and what she did surprised the hell out of me.

"But I love you, Joey. This is as far as you can go. Okay?" She then slowly placed my quivering hand back on her breast, ran her arms around my shoulders, closed her eyes and pulled my face to hers.

Wow, I had permission! Making out again, I managed to get her top three buttons undone and work my trembling hand inside her bra and explore. I couldn't believe she was letting me do this and I was totally consumed with passion. Or was it lust? So was Anita. She unbuttoned my shirt and pulled my shirt tail out of my pants and ran her hands all over me. Anita squirmed under my weight and moaned my name, one hand around my shoulders, the other on the back of my head keeping my face buried in her breasts. I wanted to explore more of her body so I unbuttoned the rest of her blouse. Slowly running my hands around her rib cage, I could feel every rib, then around her back, and she arched her back a little for me, around front again and over her nice skinny stomach. I kept moving down and let my fingertips slip just under the belt line of her shorts.

I unbuttoned her shorts, tugged at the zipper and slid my hand inside. She whispered a breathless and unconvincing, "Joey, no, we can't." But she kept her arms around me and made no effort to stop me.

That's when we heard the shop door opening and we quickly sat up. Anita straightened her bra and buttoned her blouse and shorts. I looked around thru Mattie's rear window and saw Paw Paw in the front of the shop, only thirty or so feet away, opening the overhead roll up door. My heart was pounding and I felt busted and nervous and didn't know what to do. Anita reached over and turned Mattie's key on and then the radio. Music played but I don't remember what it was. Paw Paw walked back out, through the door he had just opened, and walked down the driveway about a hundred feet to the street to get the mail before coming inside the shop again.

A little later, back in the house, we were playing a video game when Anita's mother called to tell her to come home. Her family had a birthday cake and some gifts for her. I asked Paw Paw if I could drive her home, just Anita and me. He didn't say no immediately, the question caught him off guard. I argued that I had driven Mattie at least a hundred times and promised to go just to Anita's house and back home. It was less than a mile and I wouldn't even need to go through any of the business section of town. To my surprise, he allowed it. Wow, what a day! I had whipped the town bully defending my girlfriend's honor, touched a woman, and now was driving without an adult. Suddenly, thirteen going on fourteen felt more like twenty going on twenty one.

Driving Anita home, she sat close to me and she shifted the gears so I could keep my arm around her. She was quiet and I knew something was on her mind, and I knew what it was. I parked Mattie along the curb in front of her house and we sat there for a few minutes talking.

She was thinking about what we did earlier in Mattie. "Joey, are you sure you love me? I mean, I liked what we did earlier, but…"

I kissed her. "'nita, I am sure I love you, I am so in love with you. I'm sorry I went too far. I just couldn't stop myself. How could I? You're so beautiful and I love you so much."

Her dad appeared at the front door and waved for her to come inside, and he went back in and closed the door. I got out and held the car door for Anita. Her little brother and sister were playing in the front yard with a couple of neighborhood friends. We walked past them to the front porch, up the steps to the door and I was about to get my goodbye kiss when her father opened the door again. We moved over so he could step out onto the porch.

A stern look was followed by, "I guess you're Joey."

"Yes sir, Joey McClane." I offered my hand and we shook but he didn't say his name.

His eyes moved to Mattie. "Is there someone else in your car?"

"No sir."

He looked back at me and raised his eyebrows. "You drove here?"

"Yes sir, that's my car."

He shot back an angry sounding, "You got a driver's license to go with that car?"

"No sir, not yet." Now this was becoming really uncomfortable.

"How old are you, Joey?"

"Almost fourteen, sir."

"Does your father know you're driving?"

"Yes sir, he gave me permission."

He breathed in and out heavily and studied me. "Well, this doesn't seem like a good idea to me, Joey. You go on home now and I'm going to have a talk with your father. Come on in the house, Anita." I saw him point to the ring and chain around her neck and ask, "What's this? You're too young for all of this, Anita. Come in here and sit down, young lady, we need to talk." He looked past me as if I was not there and yelled at the younger kids in the yard. "Yolanda, Armando, y'all come in now and get washed up, your mother's getting the cake and ice cream ready." I was glad he didn't invite me to stay and I hoped he wasn't about to ruin Anita's birthday.

As they disappeared into the house, Anita shot me a weak smile and waved with her fingers. "Thanks for the nice birthday, Joey, it was really special. Call me later, okay?"

Paw Paw was on the phone when I walked through the front door and I knew who he was talking with. I sat in a nearby chair and listened to our side of the conversation and speculated about the other side.

"Yes, Mr. Cantu, I should have cleared it with you, I understand your concerns. But let me assure you, Joey is as good a driver as most adults, he and I restored that car and he has put hundreds of miles on it, with my supervision, of course. He's a safe, capable driver. But this was his first time without me and if you are uncomfortable with it, I'll not let it happen again. I promise."

Paw Paw listened to John Cantu for a moment, looking at me for the first time since I'd arrived. His worried expression caused me serious concern. I had not made a good impression on Anita's father and now I was worried.

"Oh, I don't think so, these kids aren't likely to get into any trouble. I think they're good for each other. I think it's a very healthy relationship. They're best friends."

He listened again.

"Well, no, I didn't know he gave her a ring."

Listening.

"Yes, they are very young. I have to admit, I too thought the puppy love would burn itself out long before now. But they're buddies, they get along like best friends."

Listening.

"Okay, yes, we can certainly agree on that. I'll make sure they are never in our house alone and you do the same. And, uh, Mr. Cantu, if you ever get a chance to really get to know Joey, I think you'll like him. He's really a good kid, and very smart, he's more than two years ahead in his schooling, technically he's now skipped two entire grades. Joey is a nice, hardworking, well mannered, young man. I never have any trouble with him. And I've gotten to know Anita over the past few months and she's a great kid too. I can't imagine these two giving us any trouble.

Listening.

"His mother? Uh, well, Joey is actually my grandson. His parents were killed in an accident when he was an infant. I've raised Joey by myself. My wife was killed in the same accident so it's just the two of us, and I'm retired so I'm home all the time and Joey has constant supervision. I have taken raising him very seriously, and he has taken my training very well, I can assure you of that."

Listening.

"Well good, Mr. Cantu, it was nice talking with you too, we should have done this months ago. Call anytime, or come by, come over with Anita sometime, come see our shop and cars and things, hang around and visit. And please, don't worry about Anita when she's over here. Next to her own home, this is probably the safest place she could be."

Listening.

"Okay, John, and call me Joseph, please."

Hearing this, I felt the tension in my shoulders relax a little, Paw Paw had won John Cantu over. They were not breaking us up as I feared they might.

Listening.

"Yes, John, they told me about the fight with the Davis boy. Sounded to me like he got what he deserved. I know who that boy is and he's nothing but a bully and a trouble maker."

Listening.

"No, Joey doesn't like to fight. In fact, that was Joey's first fight ever."

Listening.

"Well, I'm probably to blame for that. I've taught him some self-defense moves. But I think he had some extra motivation today, Billy said some pretty nasty things to Anita. I don't blame Joey at all for what he did, I admire it actually. I don't think he went too far at all. And I seriously doubt if Billy will bother either of them again after taking a whipping like that."

Listening.

"Okay, John, thank you for calling, I appreciate your concerns. Call anytime, please. Bye now."

Paw Paw hung up the phone, walked over and sat in the chair next to me, leaned forward and rested his elbows on his knees. I knew we were about to have one of those talks and I waited for him to organize his thoughts.

"Son, it looks like I messed up letting you drive Anita home. Her father didn't like it at all. And he was right, if the tables were turned, I wouldn't have liked it either. And he's got some other concerns about the two of you. Y'all have been an item for nearly a year now, and you seem to be getting closer all the time. Most kids your age are in and out of these little relationships in a few weeks, or even days." He stopped talking.

It seemed that I was expected to say something at this point but I didn't know what, so I just nodded.

"Did you give Anita a ring?"

"Yes, but it was just a birthday present, a necklace too, it's just jewelry Paw Paw. Not like we're engaged or something." I was getting defensive now.

He smirked and chuckled but then quickly turned serious again. "Joey, you are quite mature for your age, but Anita is a little girl. She may not look like one anymore but she is, mentally and emotionally. It would be a big mistake to let your relationship get too physical. She is at a very vulnerable age, son, very impressionable. She's a little girl in a woman's body. One thing can easily lead to another and before you know it you're doing things you shouldn't and you can't stop. Then you set yourself up for trouble that could ruin Anita's life. Do you understand what I'm trying to tell you, son?"

"We just kiss, that's all." I was a terrible liar but I was in a corner and had to try.

He looked down his nose at me and I knew I wasn't getting off that easy. "When I went into the shop earlier, when you two were in your car, were y'all lying down on the seat?"

Busted! I'm sure my shocked reaction gave him his answer but I worked at quickly regaining my composure. "Well, no, not really, just playing. Um, Anita started wrestling with me, you know, like she does, she thinks it's funny 'cause she can get me down sometimes. That's all it was." I felt like he was reading me like a book in spite of my explanation. I was paying for my sin, but at least he wasn't trying to break us up.

That suspicious look again. "Just make sure you keep your hands to yourself, okay? Anita loves you and trusts you, Joey, and I'm sure you're very much her hero now since you've given her a ring and fought for her. It would be a terrible thing for you to do something that would end up hurting her." He reached over and patted my back. "And I know you son, you're not that kind of a person."

"How do I do that, Paw Paw?"

"How do you do what, son?"

"Keep my hands off someone that beautiful, and that I love, and want to be close to?" I was shocked at my own honesty, but he had always told me I could come to him with anything. And I knew that keeping my hands off Anita was going to be tough now.

He rested his hand on my shoulder. "Self-discipline, son, and it'll set you apart from most other people. All your life you're going to be tempted to do things you shouldn't, but the rewards of giving in are very short term, and the damage sometimes lasts forever. And the hurt spreads to those you care for the most."

Paw Paw's words echoed through my head all evening and shamed me. I wouldn't intentionally do anything to hurt Anita, I loved her. We were going to have to tone down the making out. I intended to call Anita about nine that evening but she called me about a half hour or so before that.

"I thought you were going to call me." It sounded like an accusation, one with hurt feelings.

"Yeah, I was going to wait till about nine, figured you were celebrating your birthday with your family."

"Oh… That's all?"

"Yeah."

"You sure?"

"What's up, 'nita? Something wrong?"

"Something wrong! Yeah! Our dads talked, and mine talked to me, and said yours was going to talk to you. They think we're getting too serious, Joey. I was afraid you'd break up with me now, especially after, you know, like maybe you wouldn't respect me anymore."

"'nita! I love you! I'll never break up with you. Anyway, I listened to their conversation and everything's okay. We're okay, 'nita. Look, they see us as teenagers in love and they're probably going to be watching us. But who cares? We're not going to do anything wrong anyway. But we should talk about that later, when we're alone together. 'nita, I would never do anything that would hurt you, I'm sorry, earlier, you know, I wasn't thinking, I wasn't being fair to you, I…" I hesitated, hoping she would help me, say something, but she didn't. "You still love me?"

"Of course! I can't wait to see you. I wish I could be with you right now. Hey, know what? While my dad and I were talking, I told him you beat Billy Davis bloody for calling me a wetback and saying something nasty about me. He really liked that, Joey, that you did that for me. And he asked if you were really two years ahead in school, and he wants to look at your car. I think Dad might treat you a little nicer next time he sees you. And he said it might be okay for you to bring me home in your car, just from your house, like today. No car dates for a long time though, he made that clear."

"He didn't like the ring, did he? He said something to Paw Paw about it."

"It's okay. I told him it was just a birthday present." She paused.

"But it's more than that, isn't it, Joey?"

"Yeah, 'nita, it is, the ring is more than just a birthday present, much more."

I was sprawled out on the living room couch talking to Anita, Paw Paw was sitting at the computer across the room. He didn't act like he was listening but I knew he was and for some reason I didn't mind. After I sat up and hung up the phone he walked over and patted me on the shoulder. "I'm proud of you, son. I knew you'd do what was right."

I touched his hand on my shoulder. "I was wondering, I've been thinking, and, well, Paw Paw sounds kind of childish." I looked up at him. "I'm not a child anymore. Do you think it would be all right if I called you Dad?"

I stood up and faced him, not quite as tall as him yet, but getting there. I'd been thinking about this for a while, and even though the moment was caught up in something else, the time seemed right.

His eyes teared up, he bit his lower lip, grabbed me and hugged me, patted my back. "Sure, son, I'd like that." We stood there like that, hugging, for at least a full minute.

As if I needed more to deal with, Amos visited me that night and every night thereafter for a while. By day I'd see his laughing face in Mattie, but he didn't speak to me. In dreams I watched his pigeon races and his dog races and his skirt chasing and his gambling. His life intrigued me, he was the freest spirit I'd ever known. Amos was both intimidating and gentle at the same time, and he had more fun than the law allowed. He was so enjoyable to watch it made me look back on the two former ghosts with disgust.

And I am sure there is a lesson in there somewhere, Dad said it was about enjoying life in spite of hard times. And thinking about it, I guess Dad knew something about that, he grew up in the

Great Depression and fought in a long brutal war, after which, he got busy building a good life for himself. Then his mate and only son died and he was saddled with me. His reaction to that was to retire early from a very successful career and devote himself to raising this infant that was thrust on him in what must have been the bleakest time of his life. Yes, he knew something about enjoying life in spite of hard times.

With Mattie finished, Dad decided to start a new project. He had acquired a little shell of a 1932 Ford coupe body, nothing more than the body, no frame or drive train or interior at all, and more rust than I would have thought he would have been interested in repairing. But he got the car almost free, traded a few small block Chevrolet engine parts for it. It was a cute car, looked like a 50s hot rod in the making, looked like fun. We put it up on jack stands and began to disassemble it. There wasn't much to disassemble, just doors, fenders and running boards, seat rails, a little trim and some window mechanics and glass.

Dad had talked for years about building an old school 50s hot rod and now he was doing it. He said most of the old steel car bodies were already in collections or had been destroyed and everyone was using fiberglass reproductions now. "The last of the steel bodies." He declared with pride as he stood back and admired his new project car.

The dreams kept coming. Amos ambled down his long meandering gravel driveway with his five greyhounds playfully running circles around him and each other. The cigar in his mouth was no longer lit and having forgotten to stick a few matches in his pocket like he usually did, he just chewed on what was left of the stogie. When he reached his mailbox where his drive met the, as yet, unnamed gravel road, it was just route 49, he spit the cigar butt out and pulled open the mailbox door. Along with something that looked like an electric bill, there was a small package in the mail box. Amos stuck the envelope in his shirt pocket without opening it, then he opened the package with his pocket knife.

Something was wrapped up in newspaper, Mattie's flying lady hood ornament! Amos laughed as he held it up and viewed it against the clear blue sky and he yelled, "All right! Mattie's got her hood ornament back!"

Checking the box again he found a tightly folded letter. It was from Dad, he had a three day layover in New York, he explained in the note, on his way back to Europe and so with time on his hands, he toured junk yards hunting a flying lady hood ornament for Mattie and Amos.

"Well, look a here, little Joseph McClane de soldier boy done sent Mattie a present.

Amos wasted no time in getting the new prize installed and Mattie sure looked fine wearing it, it was that finishing touch she had lacked.

In the next night's dream I saw Amos sitting on his front porch reading a newspaper, sipping from a steaming white ceramic mug full of coffee, and smoking a very large cigar. This was the way he began most mornings. This particular morning Amos seemed to be quite absorbed in a front page article and when my view of it cleared a little I saw why it had captured his attention. LOCAL WAR HERO DECORATED FOR BRAVERY! I knew it! Dad was a war hero! Although I was unable to read anything but the head line, Amos reading aloud to himself gave me plenty of information. Dad was an officer in the Army and the leader of a platoon of infantry soldiers somewhere in Northern Africa. They were pinned down under heavy fire and taking casualties. Dad ran out several times under fire and carried wounded men to safety, sometimes carrying one while dragging another. Then he rushed the machine gun bunker and tossed in a grenade.

He had been shot twice and received a concussion from the grenade blast. The incident earned him his third Purple Heart medal plus another citation for bravery, a silver star I think. Now I knew why his hearing in his left ear was weak, often he'd turn his head to hear with his right ear, but never said why. And I wondered where the medals were. I'd never seen them, except in old pictures. I wanted to search for them.

Sparky was having a dream of his own and was running in his sleep, or digging or something, and he scratched my leg and woke me up. I tucked some of the sheet and blanket in between myself and Sparky, turned over in the bed, and looked at Dad's Army picture on my chest of drawers. Yes, he certainly did have a lot of medals. I tried to imagine him in the war, in situations that called for bravery, and disregard for his own safety. I always knew he was a good man, and an accomplished man, but lately, with these dreams and what they've shown me... And the way he talked to me about my conduct with Anita, when he knew, and right after he had bragged on me and defended me to Anita's father... I was just beginning to understand what a special person he really was. I wanted to be just like him.

First thing the next morning, with mixed emotions because of Dad's quietness about his time as a soldier, I wrote in my journal about Amos' newspaper story. I knew Dad was reading my journal and would see it, and I hoped that it would not upset him. But it was a part of the history that the journal was recording, something Mattie revealed to me for some reason, and it needed to be included. Dad never said anything to me about it. It puzzled me how he could repress something he should be so proud of, maybe there were just too many painful memories of the violence and death, maybe he saw too many of his old army buddies die, maybe he came too close to death himself for the memories to be welcome, even after all these years. But Dad was a hero, of that I was certain.

Amos sent Dad a thank you letter and he wrote and spelled about like he spoke, but it was from the heart and that was what counted. The letter accompanied a box of gifts, a care package of sorts; cookies, magazines, writing pads and envelopes and stamps, and a photograph of Mattie sporting her new chrome flying lady hood ornament. Something else that Dad never told me about.

One night after the dog races I watched Amos with his friends at Tina's Tavern when the subject of car racing came up. Amos had tuned Mattie to be fast enough to keep up with his pigeons, well almost, and one of his buddies suggested entering Mattie in the local races.

"Ya' know, Amos, dat car a' yorn be mighty fast. I was tankin', you might jist win some money wit it over to San Antone at de races."

"Oh no, Will, dat dirt track is too dangerous, dem cars gets smashed up all de time. I'd never put my car in dat kind a' danger, she be much too nice fo' dat kinda foolishness."

Another friend joined in. "Well, how 'bout de drag races, Amos? Quarter mile straight away, dey don' crash dem cars. Jist run 'em down de track, den drive 'em back to de parkin' lot."

They kept talking about it through several rounds of drinks and I could tell Amos was getting interested. He smiled thru his gold tooth, and his cigar in the right corner of his mouth, and got that look in his eyes. The wheels in his big head were turning. Amos made no decision about racing Mattie that night but might have if not for a certain distraction.

A lady walked in, a black lady of course, tall and slim, dressed in a nice long silky white gown, heals and all, hair all done up. She went straight to the bar and claimed a stool, shot Amos a very brief but purposeful glance, and ordered a drink.

Amos slid his chair back from the table. "And I tell ya sumpin else dat coupe be good fo' boys, de ladies loves it. Jis maybe I oughta go see what Miss Janine over dere is up to."

"Amos," Will said. "Ya know Miss Janine ain't Miss no mo', she be a married woman now."

"Yeah, I do know dat." Amos was already on his feet, his eyes on Miss Janine across the cavernous room. "But her husband be in de Army now and he bin gone a while. Po' girl, she must be awful lonesome, probably need somebody to talk to, a kind ear to listen to her troubles."

Amos pulled at his belt line, took his New York Yankees baseball cap off with one hand and brushed the other across his hair, wrestled the cap back into its comfortable position, and strutted over to the bar.

"Well, hello dere, Miss Janine, you lookin' mighty purty tonight. What brings you out on a night like dis? Mind if I sit here? I'd be honored if I could buy you a drink, anytang you like." As he talked, Amos settled onto the stool next to Miss Janine, never taking his eyes off of hers, flashing his signature smile. Half an hour later they were dancing together, half an hour even later they were leaving together.

I dreamed of Mattie at the San Antonio drag races in 1944. It was a beautiful thing to see. There were so many coupes and roadsters from the twenties and thirties, some street cars and others built strictly for drag racing. Mattie ran in a stock class, I guess they didn't realize that her dual carburetors were not original equipment. Several of Amos' buddies accompanied him and helped him get Mattie ready to race. They disconnected the exhaust pipes and mufflers and removed them, lightened Mattie's weight what little they could by taking out the spare tire and the rumble seat, the jack and stuff, and added some kind of wide rear tires for traction.

Amos made a few practice runs and it was a good thing that he did. The first time down the track he did not get off the line well and Mattie jerked and lunged. He corrected that on the next run but missed second gear trying to shift too fast with that old style poorly synchronized three speed manual transmission. By the time the competition racing began, lessons were learned and adjustments were made and Amos and Mattie were doing the quarter mile like pros, well, almost.

Five races later, Mattie won her class with a time of 19.59 seconds and a speed of 83 mph. For the first race in the run offs they were pitted against a '34 Ford roadster with a newer souped up flathead V8, a four speed transmission built for racing and a low geared positraction rear end. Now we were out of our class. The Ford left the starting line hard, I was impressed, and he quickly led by several car lengths. By midway down the track Mattie began to close the huge gap but ran out of track way before she could become a real threat. I was still proud of her though, she looked so cool speeding down the track with her shiny black paint job.

Amos collected his class champion trophy and he and his friends started putting Mattie back together for the drive home. They seemed happy about the evening of racing and were, as always, ready to go celebrate. Just as they were ready to drive out of the track parking lot, a white man approached.

"Excuse me, sir." He called to Amos. He walked up to Mattie's open window with outstretched hand and introduced himself. "My name is Royce Benson, and I was just wondering... Would you be interested in selling this car? I could make a real drag racer out of it, those straight eights build up real nice and your car is perfect for this."

Amos refused the offer without even discussing price but took Royce's business card and promised to call if he changed his mind. Amos loved Mattie and didn't need money, the racing was just for fun, and a onetime thing. But it certainly was fun, and Mattie had a trophy, the first of many to come, years later.

August 23, 1992 I celebrated my fourteenth birthday. Like my girlfriend, I had done a lot of growing and maturing over the past year. Changes in both of us had seemed gradual and slow through the months, but thinking back they now seemed sudden, like we had entered a new stage while we weren't paying attention. I had hit a growth spurt and added nearly three inches to my height and now stood six feet tall, if I stood real straight. I would be tall like my grandfather but stocky and not slim like he was, I already weighed nearly one ninety. And I was shaving now, mostly just peach fuzz but shaving and proud of it. Anita liked to rub my whiskers with the back of her hand, but she didn't like razor burn on her face.

Instead of a party at home with kids running around the yard like my last birthday, we led a caravan of cars to the outskirts of San Antonio and celebrated my turning fourteen at a pizza restaurant with a game room. Dad treated of course, and about a dozen and a half friends showed up, mostly kids from church, a couple of Anita's friends from her school, and three boys from my home school sports network. The game room, an arcade in the rear of the restaurant was where we spent most of the time while Dad and John Cantu, and a couple of other parents visited and sipped draft beer.

John hadn't had many opportunities to watch Anita and me together, we almost never hung out at the Cantu house. We were aware that he was watching us now, so we kept it fun and casual, acting like best friends and not like the young lovers we had become. We were sitting, playing a video game, competing with each other, and both of our dads were watching us, standing right behind us. I was winning and Anita threw a shoulder into me to mess me up with my controls and it worked and she won, she shot my guy down.

"'nita." I whined and heard the laugh behind us.

"Anita, you're so mean to Joey." Her Dad fussed. "I don't see how he puts up with you."

"Well, I can't just let him win." She replied with a surprised glance back.

John turned to Dad, shaking his head. "Growing up with big brothers has made her such a tomboy. Victor was the one who really made her that way, Mario too, he made a grease monkey out of her but Victor was the one who got her to wrestling on the floor all the time. But you're right Joseph, this is the way she gets along with her brothers, these two do act like buddies."

"Well, the tomboy thing is what first attracted Joey to her." Dad agreed. "He brags that his girlfriend likes hot rods and she would rather play football than be a cheerleader."

I whispered to Anita, "Doesn't hurt that you're the prettiest girl in town either."

She started to kiss me but stopped herself, remembering who was behind us, she whispered, "Let's go do something later where we can be alone, okay Joey?"

I whispered back, "Sure, what do ya' wanna do?"

She giggled and I thought her whisper got too loud when she said, "I'm gonna hold you down and feel you up like you did me on my birthday." Then she laughed out loud and covered her mouth with her hand but kept on laughing.

"Shhhh!" I warned with a stern look, it wouldn't be funny if our dads heard it, especially hers. I tried to look at them without really turning and looking. They gave no reaction, they didn't hear what she said, I could tell. I looked back at Anita and frowned and shook my head.

Anita laughed again and slapped me on the back and it stung.

"Ow, 'nita." I whined. She laughed.

John and Dad looked at each other, shook their heads, walked away, back to the serving area for another beer.

After the party Anita and I accepted a ride from Dad to the only movie theater in Las Casas where we sat far away from everybody else and held hands and kissed and saw little of the film. Afterward, instead of calling one of our dads to come and give us a ride home we walked to my house by way of the city river park where we hung around a while and skipped flat rocks on the water and sat on the concrete bank with our bare feet dangling in the water and watched the ducks who hoped in vain for us to toss them something to eat.

"You know, Joey, Billy Davis is telling everyone at school that you hit him when he wasn't looking."

"Yeah," I laughed. "How do you hit someone in the nose when they aren't looking?"

"Well, anyway, enough people were there to see it and get the truth circulating; he's lost some status over that fight. He didn't come to school for an entire week and when he did he had two black eyes and a very swollen nose. Everyone knows how you beat his butt, and why too."

"'nita, you let me know if he says anything to you and I'll take care of him again." I tingled with pride at my role as her protector.

She wrapped both her arms around my left arm and held my hand between both of hers. After a few minutes of sitting there snuggling we got up and put our socks and shoes back on and headed for my house, about a fifteen minute walk. By then we were wishing for our bikes.

My Dad was waiting for us, he was all excited about something. "Oh Joey, good, y'all are back, I've got something to show you, son." He was all charged up, hurried us thru the door and into the living room, grabbing a handful of papers on his way by the computer. "Okay, look, there's this foundation that grants scholarships for college courses to gifted students. No age limit at all, and they have some very young kids in the program. You'd have to test into the program but I'm sure you'd have no problem with that, you're already doing college level work in Math and Science. What do you say, son, you want to give it a shot?"

"What, Dad? What are you talking about? College? I'm only

fourteen, I'm in the eighth grade." I glanced over the top page, scanning the heading and the first few lines and paragraph headings. "Dad, this program is for geniuses."

"Yeah, I know. Listen, courses get double credit for high school and college. By the time you get your high school diploma, you could already be a sophomore or a junior in college. This is a real opportunity, son. I think we should try it."

"Dad..." I whined, rolling my eyes, shook my head, sighed. "Oh man, this sounds like something that's going to be a lot of hard work."

Anita giggled. "And I'll be dating a college boy."

I could tell Dad wasn't going to be dissuaded from this, he was acting like it was already a done deal, mapping out my progress thru the program, and we hadn't even applied yet. He pushed hard enough with my home studies, now this. "Dad, why is this important?"

"Everyone should work to their potential, son."

Amos had been quiet for a while and I had a gut feeling it was not a good sign. I was struck by the sudden realization that his ghost was in Mattie because he had died. I mean, I already knew that, but I had never really thought about it. Amos was not that much older than Dad, well maybe twelve or thirteen years, but they were the same generation, and Dad was still alive. Now, thinking about it, I wondered how Amos died. The first thing that popped into my mind was that he was probably shot by a jealous husband. Finally, after nearly a three week silence, Amos appeared to me in Mattie, and he was not smiling. For the very first time he looked at me and did not smile or laugh. His face was simply expressionless. I spoke to him and asked him what was wrong, not that I expected that to work, but it was worth a try. Amos just faded away.

The next day I asked Dad if he'd like to go for a cruise, and we did. I drove Mattie in a new direction this time, one we never traveled. We usually cruised through the hill country west of town because it still had many of the beautiful ranches that used to dominate the landscape before the developers found it. But this time we went east and into a flatter and poorer, traditionally nonwhite, part of the county.

"Taking a different route, son?"

I looked Dad in the eye, "Where was Amos' place, Dad? I'd like to see it. I know it's out this way somewhere."

He seemed to read my mind. "Trouble?"

"No, not really, he's changed though, not happy anymore. How did he die? You've never mentioned that."

Dad pointed. "Take a right on fm 1115 up here and then a left on the next little gravel road. Haven't been by there in a long time, son, may not be anything left of it by now, or more likely, there's something completely different built in place of his old house and barn. Don't expect much, okay?"

I followed his instructions, turned onto farm road 1115, then left on the gravel road which was aptly named Johnson lane, and without further directions I drove on about another half mile and stopped right in front of Amos' driveway. And there it was, though badly deteriorated, I recognized it immediately. The big old wooden barn had been kept up pretty well, it had a several years old paint job, ugly brown, and a fairly new tin roof, but there it was. Probably the paint job and the new roof had been done at the same time, a little remodel project for a new owner maybe. But Amos' little house had not been kept up and the roof was sagging badly in the middle with shingles missing and the wood decking exposed and rotting in spots. The front porch roof had already collapsed in one corner, rotten rafter ends touching the ground. Vandals had sprayed graffiti on the exterior walls and broken out all the windows leaving only small jagged pieces of glass hanging on around the frames. I sat and stared, unable to speak or even organize a clear thought. Dad's hand on my shoulder brought me back to the present with a start.

"Seen enough, son? Maybe we should go."

I answered slowly, my mind divided between the past and the present. "No, I want to look around, Dad, just a little." I turned to him. "You never said, how'd Amos die?"

He looked down, back at me, and out the car window, drew in a deep breath. "The sign says, 'no trespassing', we should just go on."

"Tell me, Dad, what happened?"

"Amos died in a fire, Joey. He died a hero, he saved a lot of kids from a fire but it killed him. I wasn't back home yet, at the time, from the Army, but I have a feeling you'll be able to tell me the details soon." He sighed and looked away. Peering out the window, he added, "Son, keep in mind, it was a long time ago."

Without further protests from Dad, I turned Mattie onto Amos' driveway and slowly rolled down the long gravel path to the house and barn. The badly pitted driveway still meandered around trees like in my dreams and I felt like I was in familiar territory. We stopped near the house and got out of Mattie. Dad stayed back and watched me. I stood and stared at the front porch, imagining Amos sitting there, feet propped up on the bottom porch rail, big smile on his huge face, large brown cigar sticking out of his mouth, steaming coffee cup perched on the top rail that was now laying rotted on the ground, and a newspaper in his hands.

Dad cleared his throat and shook me back to the present. I walked a slow circle around the house peering through the broken windows at the inside of Amos' old home in its last stages of deterioration, almost ready to fall. I wanted to go in and look around but knew it wasn't safe so I didn't. Wouldn't be any point to it anyway, others had lived there since him and nothing of him would remain in the house. Still though, just to walk through Amos' house…

We made our way around to the barn and discovered that it was locked. I so wanted to go inside. I found a lone window to look in and saw Amos' old car ramp that I had watched him winch Mattie up on when he first rescued her from the crusher. Now there was a '57 Chevy two door hardtop sitting on it with its hood off and its engine hanging from a hoist. That made me smile. I looked back at Mattie and imagined her tripping down memory lane too. Did her lights just flash? No, I decided, I must have imagined it, a reflection from the sun maybe. The old dog pens were gone and the pigeon coop too but I knew where they had sat and I surveyed the old layout of things in my mind.

Through all of this, Dad stayed silent and about twenty feet back as if to give me room to explore without any interruptions to my thoughts, deep and secret thoughts. And I was grateful. Looking out over the field, I imagined Amos out there with his beautiful greyhounds running circles around him and chasing rabbits, noses to the ground. I looked to the clear blue sky and envisioned his petite white racing pigeons circling overhead, as graceful in flight as angels. Whether he realized it or not, Amos had contributed a lot of beauty to this world. With this thought I glanced back again at Mattie and for a moment, I saw her shiny black with all her chrome intact, door handles shining like mirrors in the sun. She doesn't have door handles, she's shaved! But she did have them, and she looked so beautiful. I did a double take on her. She was black! I looked at Dad, he didn't see what I saw. I looked at Mattie again, she was yellow with flames. I decided I needed to pull myself back into reality again.

"What happened to his animals, Dad, the greyhounds and the racing pigeons?"

"I don't know, son. I don't think I ever heard anything about them, never really thought about that."

Driving back home without even thinking about our cruise anymore, I was lost in Amos' past and in kind of a trance. And I knew Amos was about to show me everything. I felt his pull, was aware of a gentle puff of wind across my face, something like an invisible feather brushed my left hand on the steering wheel, and looking at the rear view mirror I saw his face. Amos smiled, slightly, just a hint of a smile, his eyes watery, and he silently mouthed, "Thank you, Joey." He lingered for a moment, smiling, gold tooth, then he faded. I had taken him home, and he was grateful, even if the visit was brief. And I wondered what had taken me so long to do this.

"It's okay, Amos, we'll do it again."

Realizing I had spoken out loud to someone visible to only me, I nervously looked over at Dad. He didn't return my look but I did see the corners of his mouth turn up and the crow's feet appear at the corners of his eyes.

I was anxious for the rest of Amos' story to play out, but I guess he needed more time. Nights rolled by with no dreams, days without seeing him, and I waited, knowing it was coming, just not knowing when. I updated the journal, recording the visit to Amos' home along with all my thoughts during and after. And of witnessing Mattie change to black, and then back to yellow. And again, I slipped up and left the journal laying out in the living room.

Anita called and said she was coming over on her bike. I was at the computer in the corner of the living room, filling out forms online from the scholarship foundation, when Anita walked in. She knocked once and let herself in and I stood up and kissed her. I asked her to find something to do while I finished the questionnaire and she plopped down on the couch and hit the TV remote. Completing the forms took longer than I thought it would, maybe another twenty minutes, and when I looked around Anita was reading Mattie's journal! I jumped up and ran over to her and tried to grab it but she was too quick for me, as usual.

"What is this, Joey? You writing a novel or something?"

"You can't see that!" I objected.

"Why, what is it?" She turned a half circle one way, then the other, keeping the notebook out of my reach and looking at it at arms' length, reading what she could while fighting me off.

"'nita, please. Let me have it." I tried to reach around her again.

"This is good, Joey, I didn't know you could write like this." She looked at me and back to the book. "It's about your car, isn't it? Is this stuff true or do you just have a good imagination? How would you know these things?"

I stopped trying to grab the book, it was too late. My hands went limp by my sides. I thought about Dad and how he warned me to keep the story to myself. Our eyes met and she read me like the story I had written. She must have gotten to a part about a ghost because the expression that took over her pretty face was almost frightening. Anita's body went limp and she plopped down hard on the couch and thumbed through several pages scanning as she went. She looked up at me and stared. "Joey?" Our eyes locked and I couldn't speak.

Anita shivered from chills traveling up her spine, eyes wide in a spooky realization. "Joey, this is real, isn't it? Oh Joey, why didn't you tell me about this?"

I didn't answer and she asked again.

I shook my head and looked away, sighed. "It's just too, unbelievable, 'nita. It's something that shouldn't be."

"Wow." She shook her head, slowly, and turned another page. "You see them and everything. I knew there was something about that car, but..."

"Oh my gosh, 'nita, nobody's supposed to know about this. My dad said it would just make me look like a weirdo or something.

Please, you can't tell anyone, okay?"

She just kept on reading and scanning and turning pages. Finally she spoke again. "So, he knows, right? Your dad knows?"

"Yeah, he does, and he knows it's true, 'cause otherwise I wouldn't have any way to know the details and conversations and stuff." Now I wondered if the girl I loved thought I was crazy, if she would feel the same way about me as she did before she knew I was seeing ghosts.

She was still trying to get a perspective. "So, like, when I'm with you, you know, around Mattie, you see these ghosts, and I don't, I mean, I'm not even aware they are there and you're looking at them?"

"Yeah, sometimes, not all the time. Not even much of the time. They choose when." I felt self-conscious and worried about what she was thinking. "'nita, what do you... I mean, do you think, I'm, like, weird, or something, now? You still like me?"

She sat the journal down, wrapped her arms around me and kissed me hard. She bumped her forehead to mine, like she always did, and looked me in the eyes from two inches away, that look that melts me into a puddle, quickly, as if I were a chocolate candy bar left in the sun on the roof of a black car. "You're so special, Joey. The more I know you, the more I love you."

I sighed, relieved, and pleaded, a little calmer now. "Please, 'nita, nobody can know about this, okay?"

"Don't worry, I won't tell anyone." She turned to the journal again, flipped a few pages, shook her head and smiled. "I guess I understand why you didn't tell me, but I wish you had."

"It doesn't have anything to do with trust, 'nita. It's just, how do you tell someone you're seeing ghosts in your car, without making yourself look crazy?"

"What was your dad's reaction when you told him?"

"I didn't tell him. He found out the same way you did, he found the journal. He read the whole thing before I knew it, and some of the story he had lived, you know, so he had to believe it. And you know what, 'nita? I found out my dad was a war hero, a real honest to goodness hero, newspaper headlines and everything. He put himself in danger to save a lot of people. And he got wounded too. And he never told me about that, not any of it. I found out from Amos, one of the ghosts, he was reading it in the newspaper in one of my dreams. I think Mattie wanted me to know that."

Anita and I talked about Mattie's secrets for the rest of the day. She wished she could see the ghosts but that was never going to happen. We spent time in the shop talking about it, near Mattie, inside of Mattie much of the time, hoping Amos would appear. But he did not.

Later that evening I told Dad about Anita finding the journal. I expected him to be upset but he just said he figured she would find it sooner or later. And the saga continued, just with the addition of Anita into the small club of those of us aware of it.

That very night I saw Amos again in a dream. He was sitting in Tina's Tavern, with friends, sipping bourbon, puffing on a cigar. Someone burst through the front door yelling that the colored elementary school was on fire with children trapped inside. Amos jumped up and ran out to Mattie. The next thing I saw was Mattie screeching to a stop in front of an old wooden school building with flames leaping from a corner of the roof and out of a front window near the door. A large crowd of people; black, white and Mexican, parents, neighbors, cops, some who had just happened on the scene, others who had heard and came to see, a growing crowd, bunching up around between the road and the schoolhouse. But nobody was doing anything. I could hear screams from kids inside and from frantic mothers outside, crying, wringing their hands and pleading for someone to help the kids.

Amos bailed out of Mattie and charged down the dirt path leading to the school's front door. Two white cops were pushing on the front door and yelling for the panicked kids to get back away from the door so they could open it. As Amos approached one cop grabbed Amos by the arm and ordered him to stay back. Amos drew back a massive fist and punched the cop in the face knocking him down, out probably, shoved the other cop out of the way and rushed the door.

Amos ducked his head and threw his shoulder into that door with his huge three hundred twenty pound body and the door shattered. Amos went down with the broken door and kids spilled out, seven of them, little black boys and girls who looked to be about eight or nine years old, one with what seemed to be a broken arm from Amos and the door crashing in on him.

Screaming and crying, they ran for their mothers. One little girl's skirt had caught fire and her running fanned the flames. Someone stopped her and ripped the skirt off and stomped the fire out, leaving the little girl in her shirt and panties, frantically climbing up her mom's leg, her mom leaning over grasping for her. Mothers were grabbing their sons and daughters in a sobbing panic, hugging them, checking them from head to toe for burns and injuries.

I saw Amos get back to his feet, a little stunned and just inside the building, and just as he disappeared from sight I heard the crash of another door being demolished. Almost instantly Amos emerged again, stepping over the front door he had destroyed, and he came running out with kids all over him. He had two in each arm and one hanging from his neck with one more being dragged along, his arms locked around Amos' waist. Frantic parents raced to get their children from him.

"How many were in there?" Amos shouted.

"Forty seven kids and three teachers." Came the reply.

Amos did some quick math in his head and ran back into the burning building. The next thing I knew, Amos was going from window to window kicking out the glass and tossing children out. A teacher struggled out of a window cutting her arm badly on the broken glass and she collapsed onto the ground, overcome from the smoke and panic. Men were grabbing the teachers and kids and dragging them away from the burning building. Amos emerged again carrying five more terrified kids. I heard sirens, fire trucks were on the way, but too late.

"How many is that? How many still in there?" Amos looked bad now, skin on his face and arms was blistering from the intense heat, his hair was singed, and his eyes were just slits blinking wildly from the smoke, desperate to see well enough to finish his mission.

There was too much confusion for anybody to know for sure who might still be in the school house, so no answer came and Amos turned back to the burning building. Now the attic and roof were totally engulfed in flames and I wished I could stop Amos from going back inside. Just seconds after he did, the building collapsed, first with a mournful groan and then an explosion as fire and smoke and burning particles were blown out in all directions from the crash. Everyone, even those at a safe distance, turned away and shielded their faces with arms and hands and felt the sudden rush of heat overtake them.

A hush came over the crowd and they began to look back at the fire, everybody knew, Amos wasn't coming out again.

Someone thought to take a count of the kids and teachers. Along with Amos, two seven year old boys and a lady teacher died. When the fire was finally out and the charred, flattened structure gone through, Amos' body was found with the teacher and two kids in his arms, just a dozen feet from the doorway. He had willingly, eagerly, given his life to save two teachers and forty five children from a horrible and certain death.

I awoke from my dream in a sobbing fit of grief, it was too much. Unable to control my emotions, I trudged to the living room, Sparky following, and I sat on the couch and cried my eyes out. Sparky crawled up on my lap and licked my hand. Dad came in and sat beside me and put his arm around me. He knew.

"I feel like a good friend just died, Paw Paw, Dad."

"I'm sorry, son." Was all he could think to say.

We didn't go back to bed that night, it was already about four thirty in the morning. After I calmed down some Dad started cooking breakfast. He poured me a glass of orange juice and set it on the end table by the couch. I picked up the journal and recorded it all, spilling tears on the paper as I wrote. I waited till about eight o'clock and called Anita and choked on tears while I told her about the fire and how Amos died saving the school children.

Anita came over within the hour and the three of us went to the shop. They hung back while I approached Mattie, slowly, hoping to see Amos, wanting to tell him how sorry I was, afraid of what he might look like now. But what I saw in Mattie surprised me, shocked me, and cheered me up. I saw Amos, through the driver side window, smiling. The smile grew and his gold tooth sparkled through his salt and pepper goatee, then he laughed, loud and happy. He tipped his New York Yankees baseball cap to me and nodded, and he yelled at me. "Wha's de' matter wi' chew, boy? Quit cha cryin'. Let's go take Mattie out for a cruise!"

I laughed, loud like Amos. I turned to Dad and Anita and laughed again. "He wants to go for a cruise!" I announced, almost unable to get the words out for my laughing. We all laughed, and then we went for a cruise, all four of us.

I thought it was finished, Amos' history, but one more dream came to me and answered my questions about the fate of his animals. It also revealed how Mattie eluded Dad's grasp again.

Amos left a will, I was somewhat surprised at this. I guess I just thought that he wouldn't because of the way he lived, and the times, and his lack of family, but he did leave one.

His pigeons went to his slow witted friend Billy Latham who was always around for the pigeon club meetings, always anxious to help with the races, but had no pigeons of his own. Billy had always admired Amos' birds and talked about when he got his birds he wanted them to be just like Amos'. He had already built a nice pigeon coop for the birds he didn't have, might never have. Billy once found an injured pigeon and nursed it back to health and let it go. The others laughed at him and said he should just "wring its neck and be done with it." But Amos silently admired the way Billy had cared for that poor helpless bird. So Bill inherited Amos' beautiful, petite, white, racing champions.

The dogs got split up, except for two that went to the same home, but they all got good homes and they all retired from racing. Amos left instructions for who would get which dog.

Mattie and Amos' home were willed to Amos' only child. It seemed that although never married, Amos had a son, a son he had never been a dad to and now the twenty year old man hated Amos for that. Larry Johnson looked like Amos, a young Amos. He was tall and stocky but appeared bitter, not happy like his father. I watched Larry walk around Amos' place a few times, ignoring two of Amos' friends who were hanging around to make sure the animals went with the right people. He ambled thru the house looking at photos and things, hurled a picture of his father across the room, shattering the frame and glass against the wall. He strolled around the barn noticing tools and unfinished car repair projects. He scoffed, and he spit, his hatred of Amos not letting him get too deep into thought about Amos' life as he trudged along around the estate. Larry wasn't there when Bill came to claim the pigeons, or when two of the four new dog owners came. The other two dog heirs did come by when Larry was around but he hardly acknowledged their presence. While in the barn, he looked Mattie over, found Amos' whiskey bottle under the seat, and his .38 caliber revolver in the glove box. Larry laid the bottle on the seat and slid the gun in his belt, just after swinging the cylinder open and seeing that it was indeed loaded. He went through the glove box again and found Mattie's title and a business card that advertised B & D Custom Racers on the front and on the back read, "Call when you want to sell the '34 coupe, Royce Benson."

The next day a sale sign went up in front of the property and Royce Benson came to buy Mattie and haul her off to Tulsa, Oklahoma.

CHAPTER 7

School would start soon and Anita would not be around during the day, on weekdays anyway and I knew I'd miss her. Amos still smiled at me occasionally but did not send me any more dreams, and I wondered if Royce Benson would supply Mattie's next haunt. Till now I'd had some previous knowledge of each ghost from Dad's stories of Mattie back when he was young. But with Amos' passing, and Mattie disappearing from the area, Dad unable to find her after returning home at the end of WWII, I was entering forty five years of the unknown. Everything that Mattie would reveal to me from this point on would be news, old news, but news, to me, and to Dad.

I would lay awake in my bed at night, Sparky curled up in a ball beside me, and stare at the shadows on the walls created by the shop's security lights filtering in through the Elm and Oak trees in the front yard and the curtains on my bedroom windows, and wonder. I would sit on my favorite stool, the one with the Cobra image on it, and stare at Mattie and wait. I would peer into her rear view mirror while driving her or working on her, expecting to see the next chapter of her story. What was coming? What would be next? Memories of Mrs. Ferguson and Hugh caused me to worry about the character of Mattie's other owners. And how many of them were there? How many ghosts did Mattie still have to show me? Would there be sad ones like Mrs. Ferguson, lost souls with no hope, and no relationship with Mattie? Would there be abusive ones, stupid and angering like Hugh?

According to his business card, Royce Benson built race cars, and he had wanted Mattie for a while. What would he do with her? Did he die while he still owned her and leave his spirit in her, or just keep her a while and sell her to someone else? Was he the one who painted her yellow with the burning number thirteen on her doors? Probably not, that paint job was still too nice to be that old. Maybe he left her in the shiny black finish that Amos had given her.

One thing was for sure, in my mind, I would get the answers to my questions. Mattie would give them to me, in her own time.

Dad and I took the '69 Cuda, with him driving, into San Antonio and to the University of Texas campus. We followed our map to the correct building, checked in at the guard shack, parked in the nearly empty parking lot, and walked up the wide red brick sidewalk. The building looked more like an office building, a government one maybe, than part of a college campus, ugly 1960s architecture, a shapeless concrete block with a glass front. We climbed the wide concrete steps, eight of them, I counted, and entered through the double glass doors marked, 'Alice Warhead Foundation for Advanced Academic Achievement'. Such a long name. Alice Warhead must have donated a fortune for this, whoever she was. I later found out that the foundation was a front of sorts for an engineering firm that developed space travel and communication technology. I guess this was their way of recruiting young geniuses to later work in their research and development companies.

We stopped at the front desk and spoke with a very attractive middle aged Hispanic lady, mid-forties I guessed. Secretly I wondered if Anita would keep her beauty through life like this lady was doing. Dad told her that we were there for the testing that was scheduled for the entire week. She found my name on a list and directed us to a large room on the second floor, room 211. Three other kids were already there. Seated around a large oval shaped Mahogany table were two girls and one boy. Two more boys arrived soon after I did. I was the youngest kid, I observed, by at least couple of years.

After a brief introduction to the program by a man named Dr. Larson, but who looked to me like a young Albert Einstein, the parents were dismissed. Dad stood up, leaned to me and gave me a silent kiss on the forehead, patted my back, and walked away without a word. I was the only kid who got a kiss goodbye and although I felt I should have been embarrassed, I wasn't. Other kids' parents offered last minute admonishments to do well and one sounded almost like a threat. It occurred to me that Dr. Larson was noticing the interactions, not just mine with my dad, but those of all of us. I could tell he was smart and he was already reading us.

Right away pencils and written tests were distributed around the table, it was four sheets of paper, blank except for numbers, one thru ten on the first sheet, one thru fifteen on the second, one thru twenty on the third and one thru twenty five on the last one. We were instructed to listen carefully as he read a sequence of statements and when he finished and gave us the go ahead we were to write them down in the order in which he had read them.

The sequence of statements for the first page made sense; they were instructions for opening and using a computer program. I closed my eyes while he read them and I visualized them. I wrote them on the paper pretty much word for word just as he had voiced them. The second set turned out to be the solving of a calculus problem, step by step. That one was easy. The third set of statements, twenty of them, made no sense at all, they sounded like sentences taken at random from some mystery novel but unrelated to each other. Again, I closed my eyes while he read them, stored them in my head, and then wrote them down, word for word. The fourth set was more difficult, it had to do with placement of moons around the planets of our galaxy, twenty five of them all mixed up, no order to them. By the time I wrote the nineteenth one on my paper I was having trouble. I closed my eyes, separated myself from the present, and ran his words back through my memory. I think I did pretty well with them despite my temporary memory glitch. When I looked up, Dr. Larson was looking directly at me, so were the other students. It unnerved me, they were all finished and waiting on me. Then I noticed their papers, none of them had finished that page. Most got less than half way through the list or had skips in sequence. I wondered how they had done on the first three pages.

Dr. Larson took our papers and started a film. I didn't understand the significance of the little movie, it was about family life in the fifties. But I did like the cars in it. After we watched it he asked questions, mostly about the technology of that time. Dr. Larson was taking notes about our comments so I was careful with what I said.

We watched another film and took another test, this one about geometric shapes, resistance of the elements to forward motion, and how shape and design effects and is effected by various modes of travel. This sparked my interest to the point of excitement and I feared I may have gotten too elaborate with my answers. I was the last to finish, and again they were all sitting there waiting for me.

We broke for lunch, modest meals of sandwiches and chips and bottled water were brought in for us and we ate at the testing table. We were given a few minutes to go to the restroom and stretch our legs a little before testing resumed. I noticed that Dr. Larson silently and thoughtfully looked over our tests while he nibbled at his meal. Once in a while he would look from the papers to me and let his look linger. It made me so nervous that I left the room and visited with another boy in the hall till we were called back in.

More films and discussion filled the afternoon but no more written tests. One film was quite comical; it was about space travel bloopers and mistakes. Another was a completely absurd science fiction film from the fifties about invaders from outer space.

Before dismissing us for the day, Dr. Larson asked each of us about our schools. Only one kid attended public school, one of the boys, and only because he was an athlete and needed the sports program offered there. Two attended religious schools and the other boy and I were home schooled. He talked to me last and it could have been my imagination but I thought he spent more time with me than the others, a little anyway. When I told him that my Dad was my only teacher he asked about my Dad's career. I explained that he was a retired petroleum engineer. Dr. Larson stared at me for a moment longer, nodding, looked at the papers in his hand. He nodded at me again in silence, and told us to be back at eight in the morning.

As we filed out, Theresa, one of the two girls, whispered to me, "He likes you." I didn't reply. I was afraid the opposite was true, he had made me extremely nervous all day long with his pointed questions and his scrutinizing looks. I felt singled out, like I didn't fit in. I couldn't tell Dad this, he'd be so disappointed. I'd do better the next day, work faster and keep my head down and watch what I said.

Dad let me skip my studies that night, something he never ever did. We tinkered with Mattie some in the shop and Dad watched my quietness. He tried a couple of times to pry my thoughts from me but all I would tell him was that Dr. Larson made me nervous and I was worried about how I had done, especially with my spoken answers. And also about being last to finish the written tests and everybody having to wait for me.

"Hey, we'll just give it our best shot and go on. Okay? This does not define your life, Joey. Your life is going to be so full of opportunities, someday you'll look back on this and laugh." He patted me on the back and smiled.

I felt better, relaxed a little. "I just want to make you proud of me, Dad."

"You do that every day, son."

The second and final day of testing at the Alice Warhead Foundation for Advanced Academic Achievement was similar to the first. We assembled in the same room, at the same table, with the same instructor in charge. The sequence of events was the same too, written test, film, written test, film, lunch break, and more tests and films. Tests the second day were more of a science nature; chemistry, electronic and mechanical technology, and physics. I found none of it difficult in the least. I had expected this to be hard and wondered if maybe I was missing something, some important point to it all.

One of the films we saw was mainly of World War II. I couldn't watch the explosive battle scenes, I closed my eyes and my mind and daydreamed about Dad when he was a soldier. I was afraid I wasn't going to be able to properly answer questions now. But Einstein's questions were mainly about weapons technology, a subject about which none of us had any knowledge or interest. When asked my opinion I replied that I felt it was a shame so much research and development went into methods of harming people rather than helping them. Einstein made a long note on his paper about that and I was sure I had hurt myself with that answer. When he looked back at me he volunteered the fact that some of the people who had worked on the development of and in the delivery of the atom bombs that were used on Japan to end the war, had committed suicide. I felt better about my comment, a little.

When we were shown the film clips from several car manufacturing plants I perked up. The scenes began in the early twenties and ran on into the early nineties, which is where we were at the time, and mostly of assembly line work and technology. But it also included the building and testing of a few experimental models which certainly captured my interest.

Dr. Larson noticed my increased attention and questioned me first after the film. When he asked me what I thought was the most significant point, I expressed my concern that the auto manufacturers' body styles and drive trains all followed the same basic patterns from year to year, and even when they would create a concept car that was out of the norm they would end up destroying it instead of producing it.

"So, Joseph," He looked at his papers as if for confirmation of my name. "Joseph McClane, you arrived at that deduction from that film?"

"Well, no sir, not completely from that film, but it sure did give strong evidence to what I already thought."

"You know a lot about automobiles, Joseph?"

Here was my chance to impress him, or so I thought. "Um, yes sir, I guess so. My Dad and I have restored several classics, and I own a 1934 Buick coupe hot rod that I built myself."

"You own a 1934 Buick? And you built it yourself?" He dropped the hand holding the papers to his side and stroked his chin with the thumb and forefinger of his other hand. His look was one of skepticism and doubt.

"Yes, sir." I wished I could show Mattie to him. Why didn't we come in her?

His hand left his face and went to his pants pocket where it jingled his keys. His other hand set the papers it was holding on the table. "You have those skills at your age?"

"Yes, sir." I wondered what he would think if he knew about the ghosts in my car. The thought brought a smile to my face.

He picked up the small stack of papers from the table and rifled thru them. "Uh, how old are you, Joseph?"

"I'm fourteen, sir."

"Fourteen, you're an early bloomer, I would have guessed

sixteen, at least." He stared at me for a moment and so did the kids and it made me really uncomfortable. I squirmed in my seat. He turned to the computer controls and started another film, a documentation of alternative fuel development over the last very few years. That would be our final film and none of the subsequent questions were directed to me. He didn't even look at me. I was sure I had blown it, I had said too much. And I had been determined to not do that this time. What was the matter with me? Stupid! Now he probably thought of me as a mechanic, a grease monkey, not a whiz kid ripe for his program. I was sure my big mouth had gotten me eliminated. Dad would be so disappointed. I felt like crying.

When Einstein dismissed the class he called out three names, mine among them, the losers I thought. But then he asked us to report immediately to room 221 down the hall. The others should go home and wait to be called, something I figured probably wasn't going to happen.

I sat in a room with the two others who were asked to stay, one girl and a boy, the athlete. Two adult men were present also, one of which was Mr. Einstein, the other a much more mainstream appearing man about my Dad's age, I guessed, maybe a little younger. We were introduced to him, one at a time, with a brief statement of personal information; age, schooling, test results. The other man didn't say much, not even his name, just nodded as we were introduced by Dr. Larson. I noticed his name on a tag which hung from a ribbon around his neck, Dr. Gregory Halstead.

Dr. Larson pointed out to Dr. Halstead some things on one of the test papers and he took a minute to read, then looked at me and nodded in silence. I felt like crawling under the table. They whispered to each other and agreed on something and Halstead left the room.

Einstein spoke to us. "Each of you has been selected to continue the testing for admittance into the scholarship program. Be here at eight tomorrow morning, this room, 221, to begin the math section of the tests. Bring nothing with you, we'll have computers and calculators set up for you; paper, pencils, everything you need will be provided. You'll be tested on your knowledge and abilities with emphasis on the ability to quickly work thru difficult situations in algebra, geometry, calculus, and open ended formulas. You may leave now, except for, uh, Mr. McClane." He looked at me, a determined look, a concerned look, took a couple of deep breaths without breaking his stare, and it worried me. "Could you stay a moment longer, please?"

"Um, sure, sir, but my Dad is probably waiting for me in the lobby by now."

"No, we sent for him, he'll be here in a second."

The girl, Susan I think was her name, walked behind me on her way out and touched my shoulder and whispered. "They like you."

I didn't reply. I wished I could be so sure.

With my Dad sitting next to me, Dr. Larson and Dr. Halstead sitting across the table, I wondered what this was all about. Clearly the ones already deemed not right for the program had been dismissed. Those of us who would be allowed to continue had been given our instructions for tomorrow. What was going on here? Did they still have doubts about me fitting in? I worried.

Dr. Larson began. "Mr. McClane, your son's test scores are quite impressive, as is the speed with which he has worked through entire high school and college courses, according to his records. We are looking for a certain type of young man or young woman here, to possibly move on into the industry, you understand. Among other things, a good mechanical aptitude is a big plus for this program. So we'd just like for you to confirm something that Joseph mentioned in class. Has your son here, at fourteen years of age," He glanced at his paper as if to reassure himself of my age. "Built, uh, a car?" The skepticism was obvious in his voice and I wished I hadn't said anything about Mattie back in the classroom.

Dad gave a little chuckle. "Yes, yes he has. He's helped me with several car restoration projects, since, oh, since he was big enough to hold a tool in his hand. In fact, most of his home schooling has been done orally in our shop while working on our cars. A little over a year ago, he started on his dream car, a '34 Buick Coupe that had been used in drag racing for many years. He rebuilt it for street use but it's still quite a powerful performer. He removed and replaced the entire drive train, the interior, and the electrical system. The body and paint were fine except for a little freshening up. And he is still performing modifications on it."

"Just a minute, sir." Einstein crossed his arms, rested them on the table, leaned forward and looked at my Dad very pointedly. "What do you mean, 'home schooled orally?' Did you not have the state required literature and study materials?"

"Well yes, of course, and we would go over them initially and from time to time thereafter, but with our hands occupied with our work in the shop, we conducted most of his studies orally."

"Like, algebra, orally?" His eyes showed disbelief and his question sounded skeptical.

"Yes, and spelling and history and chemistry, geography, all of it, whatever was possible to do that way."

Dr. Larson took in a deep breath and let it out. "That's pretty hard to believe. Could you give us an example, say, of working an algebra problem, orally?" He emphasized orally, as if he doubted I could do it.

"Sure. Joey, let's see, how would you answer the problem of," Dad paused, looked directly at me and spoke slowly. "X plus, t over y, minus x squared, if x equals 3.3, y equals .5 and t equals 4?"

I repeated the problem and the values, closed my eyes and

mentally worked thru the problem, first figuring what 3.3 squared was. I opened my eyes and gave the answer. ".41"

The two men jerked their heads around and looked at each other in surprise. Einstein reached for one of my forms and turned it over, pulled a pen from his shirt pocket and worked the problem on the back of the paper, but he had to have Dad confirm what the values were first. He wasn't sure he remembered correctly and that made me smile. The other man watched. They looked at each other again, a shocked look.

"Let me give you one, Joseph." He wrote out another problem while he told it to me, as if he thought Dad's had been rehearsed. I answered it quickly, before he had it worked out on his paper. For the first time, the men smiled.

The other man, Dr. Halstead, wanted a turn at me and I worked his algebra problem quickly too. He asked me for the chemistry symbols for several substances and I readily gave them to him. He asked some geometric formulas and I knew them too. He asked who invented the car, "Since you're a car buff."

I told him that a Frenchman invented a steam powered car in 1769, but Benz made the first internal combustion engine car in 1888 in Germany. He asked if I understood how a turbine engine worked and I explained that to him.

Halstead turned his attention to my Dad. "Just curious, Mr. McClane, are you an educated man?"

"I have a bachelor's degree from UT in Chemistry, a master's in Petroleum Engineering."

The men looked at each other in silence for a short moment and turned back to Dad. "And you are his biological father, right? What about his mother, what about her education?"

"Actually, I'm Joey's grandfather. After his parents and my wife were killed in an accident, I retired from work to devote my time to raising Joey. He was an infant when it happened, he's never known his parents. But yes, they were well educated. My son was still working toward his PHD in Chemistry when he died."

"Would you excuse us for a moment?"

The men whispered while they scurried out to the hall, quickly returned and sat back down. "Mr. McClane, would you consent to an IQ test for Joseph?"

"I kind of thought that's what you were doing here anyway."

"Well, no, not exactly. We're looking for students who can excel in certain areas. But we'd like to run some additional testing on Joseph, mostly for IQ placement. Of course he fits the scholarship program too, that's not going to be a problem."

"You mean he's in?"

"Oh, yes! Well, we'll go ahead and run him through the remainder of the testing, just for the record, but from what I've already seen... Let's just say, I think Joseph is precisely what we're looking for."

Dr. Larson, aka Einstein to me, asked me, "Joseph, do you know your IQ level? Have you ever been tested for that?"

"No sir, I've never even thought about it."

"Do you know what Albert Einstein's IQ was?"

"Yes sir, it was 165." The irony of him asking me about Einstein struck me as funny and I struggled to not laugh. He must have wondered about the smirk on my face as he had to make himself look away, or maybe he knew.

I was tested over the next couple of weeks, but never told what my IQ score was. I didn't much care, but Dad did. When he pressed Dr. Larson about it, days later, he was told that the tests were inconclusive and they had just assigned me an IQ of 175.

The drive home was joyous. Dad was so proud of me, he just beamed. We talked about the testing, I told him about the films and about my Mr. Einstein, and the questions he asked us. Dad reached over with one hand and messed up my hair and laughed.

"Well, your Mr. Einstein is a smart man." Dad explained. "He was exposing the whole person in each of you and he was looking for certain things, not just intellect but social skills and personality and genes and interests, discipline maybe."

"I think he must be a car guy."

"Why do you say that?"

"That's where we connected, the car manufacturing films, I saw it in his eyes, for the first time he locked into eye contact with me. I was trying to read him, like you taught me, you know, when you are negotiating a car purchase, or sale? We had a nice exchange going and I tried to use it and I mentioned my coupe, but he pulled back then and I was afraid I'd overdone it. Turned out he just didn't believe me, I guess."

"Overdone it? Didn't believe you? Joey, you're going to college at fourteen years old! Do you have any idea how impressed they are with you, son?"

As soon as we got home I called Anita and told her everything. She was happy for me and was so confident I would get into the program she had already bragged to her parents about it. Dad and I were so pumped we didn't go to bed until after midnight.

What happened later that night answered a question that had plagued me from the beginning. Did Mattie have powers of her own or was it just the ghosts revealing things to me? Things that happened that contributed to the fates of Mrs. Ferguson and Hugh had me convinced that Mattie had powers. But nothing, not a single incident in Amos' story indicated that she did. Maybe she's quiet when she's content. Or maybe she saw Amos as the savior he was for her and hoped he'd eventually sell her back to Dad. That night the question was answered, to me anyway. I dreamed about Dad coming home at the end of the war and searching for Mattie. It was too accurate and detailed to be only a dream, it was part of Mattie's story, with no ghost attached.

The headlines read, "WAR OVER!" World War II had ended and the entire nation was caught up in the celebration. I dreamed of a parade in downtown San Antonio, Texas. Soldiers in uniform were riding on parade floats, in convertible cars with the tops down, in backs of pickups, and others were marching to high school band music and following flags held high. There were even soldiers in wheelchairs being pushed down the street by other soldiers.

Hundreds of people, maybe thousands, as far as I could see. Spectators lined each side of the street, kids on parents' shoulders, everybody waving flags and cheering, confetti flying through the air.

And there was Dad, quietly standing on the sidelines, just part of the crowd. Why? He was a hero, a real war hero, he had saved the lives of fellow soldiers, risked his life to do so, gotten wounded, had been decorated for bravery. Why was he so reluctant to accept his hero's welcome home that was being so enthusiastically offered by an entire city, an entire nation? He wasn't even in uniform, his beautiful dress blue uniform with so many medals and ribbons on it, decorations for his service and bravery. I couldn't understand it.

I awoke; my dream had turned sad and disturbing enough to wake me. I stroked Sparky and he stretched beside me in the bed. Then he stood up and jumped to the floor. I followed him to the front door and he scratched it wanting out. I walked outside with Sparky. I walked to the shop while he sniffed around in the landscaping near the house. Standing looking at Mattie, lost in thought, I searched for answers. Amos appeared. He looked directly at me, stared expressionless for a moment, then he smiled, slightly, no gold tooth exposed, just subtle upturned corners of his large mouth. He licked his lips, and he spoke to me, his big booming voice. "Leave it alone, boy. You don't have to understand. Jist write it down, and walk away from it." And that is what I did.

But it occurred to me, just at that moment, that Amos' ghost knew who I was, he knew I was not Dad. Why then, were things being revealed to me? It must have been Mattie's decision. So she knew too. And she had chosen me. Why? She had Dad back, after all those years. Why me then?

Dad was waiting at the front door. It shocked me to see him, it was the middle of the night. I walked in and closed the door. Sparky headed for our bedroom, anxious to get back in bed. I looked at Dad, wanting to ask him questions but remembering Amos' advise to "leave it alone".

"You okay?" Dad asked, his hand on my shoulder.

I hugged him, tight. "Thanks, Dad."

"For what, son?"

"Everything, just, everything."

My dream continued as soon as my head hit the pillow, it seemed I was watching the familiar shadows on my walls and getting lost in a dream at the same time. Dad was searching for Mattie. He was there at Amos' place, but Amos was not, he was dead. New owners, a young couple with one small child, they were black, of course, and not very friendly.

"What you want?"

"Hi, sorry to bother you. Do you live here now?"

"Yeah, what you want?"

"Uh, well, I was wondering, Mr. Johnson, the man who used to live here..."

"He be dead. This be our place now."

"Yes, I know. But he had a car I was interested in, a Buick coupe, 1934. It wouldn't still be around, would it?"

"No, no cars left here, they took 'em all, even the junk ones in the field."

"Yes, okay, you don't know where they went do you, who got them? It was a black coupe, fixed up real nice. I'd pay well for it. I'll even pay you something for information about where it is, if you know."

The young man turned his back and walked away, dismissing Dad with a wave of his hand. "No, don't know nothin' 'bout it."

Dad got back in his car and drove away, to Tina's Tavern. I hated to see him go inside, I didn't think it was safe for a white man in there. But he did. A couple of Amos' old friends were there and they remembered Dad from the time he went there and talked to Amos. They remembered how the two had hit it off and they were willing to be helpful. Dad sat down at their table, at their invitation, and bought a round of drinks, then another, to keep them talking. They didn't know the name of the man who had bought Mattie or where he had taken her, but they thought he was the same man that Amos met at the drag races that time, the man who wanted to buy Mattie that night. A white guy, they said, he had a race car there that night, a professional racer, and he won a trophy. Sure seemed interested in Amos' car, tried to buy it on the spot. Left his name and number, they thought, with Amos, on a business card. Maybe someone working at the race track knew who he was.

So Dad's search for Mattie took him to the race track. No one knew anything or seemed very concerned. But they did allow Dad to post a note on the bulletin board about it. After that, he tried the county office where you register the title when you buy a car or sell one and sign it over to the new owner. No records of Mattie's sale there, could have been done in any county, or even out of state.

Dad learned of Amos' son and looked him up. The boy became angry at the very mention of his father. He cussed and bitched and declared that he hoped Amos was "rotting in Hell" and he "didn't give a shit about the damned car or what happened to it".

"But you sold it, you know who bought it. Please, it was my grandfather's car. I'd really like to find it."

"Some race car builder from out of state, Benton or Benson, something like that, out of Louisiana or Oklahoma, somewhere like that. I didn't care, I just wanted it gone. Wanted all of that son of a bitches' shit gone." He had the man's card but threw it away, found it in the glove box and called the guy. "He came and got the car the next day. It's gone, forget it." Larry spat on the ground and walked away, permanently angry.

It felt like Dad's search for Mattie was over, right then in 1945, unsuccessful and hopeless. But it wasn't. He would search for decades; watch the magazine ads, the internet, newspapers, drag racing publications. He would travel hundreds of miles over the years to look at '34 coupes, time and time again, only to be disappointed. He would go on with his life, but never really give up the search for Mattie. And he would find her, so many years later, just to give her to me.

At the end of the week, the testing for the foundation program finished, the three of us plus family members met again with Mr. Einstein and Dr. Halstead. We were all accepted into the program but at different levels. I tested out of several freshman and sophomore courses such as entry level college algebra and chemistry, and some of the basic courses like English and History. The Foundation was affiliated with The University of Texas at San Antonio and credits earned would transfer to any state school and most private colleges. I tested out of and got credit for forty two hours. I was now officially a freshman in high school and a sophomore in college at the same time.

My first college courses would be at the sophomore and junior levels. The plan was to find the starting point right for me and go from there so it was possible I would test out of more courses as we went along. Though I never did, I was allowed to actually attend classes on the UT campus, just sort of sit it on them. But studying at home I moved at a much faster pace. It was required that I turn in all work and be tested at the Foundation building. Dad persuaded them to authorize a form for me to get a hardship driver's license, two years early. That was a good thing, since I was already driving Mattie around town anyway.

Anita's parents gave her permission to go on car dates with me as soon as I received my license so we were counting the days. They had learned to like me, especially her mother. But I still caught those suspicious looks from her father now and then, like he wondered what I did with his daughter when we were alone. He always insisted on knowing where we were going, who we would be with, when I would have her back home, and she had early curfews; ten on school nights, eleven on weekends. For something very special, and safe, I was able to talk them into midnight, like a school dance. Her school, of course, I didn't have one. Well, we were still just fourteen years old, and looking back, I guess we did have a lot of freedom for our age.

I once asked Anita if she ever wanted to go out with other boys, she was in high school now, you know, and there was a whole society there, one that I was not a part of. That never bothered me before our relationship. But now I wondered, would it become a problem with Anita, that I wasn't a part of her school crowd.

She answered my insecure question with a sarcastic snicker and a quick and definite, "Who would I go out with? There's no one who compares with you. And besides, I love you, Joey. I'm going to marry you someday." And she kissed me, and bumped her forehead to mine, gave me that look through the top of her eyes, her beautiful black eyes, that look that melted my heart, and she said, "I'll show you off at the school dances and stuff. I'm in high school now. Even the upper classmen girls will be jealous. And don't you be looking around either, boy. You're mine."

That summer, the summer of 1992, in Las Casas, Texas, things began to change for me. Anita and I both turned fourteen years old, we were both early bloomers and could pass for sixteen or seventeen, easy. Our relationship was a year old now and we were best friends, never tiring of each other, and we were lovers, virgin lovers, but lovers. Soon after my birthday, school started for both of us. Actually, mine never had a summer break, Dad wouldn't allow it, especially now that I had been accepted into The Foundation. But now the courses with the Foundation were starting and I think Dad was more nervous about it than I was.

On my birthday, Dad gave me a cell phone. The day after my fourteenth birthday Dad took me to the DPS office, presented them with the hardship certificate authorized by The Foundation, and other paper work showing my age and his age and reasons why I should get a driver's license two years earlier than normally possible by law. An officer looked over everything, gave me study material and scheduled me for testing, both written and driving. A few days later we showed up at the same place in Mattie. I aced the written test, then I drove with an officer in Mattie with me. Officer Martinez gave Mattie a very critical visual inspection before finally getting into her passenger seat.

"How long you been drivin', young man?" The officer asked when he saw the ease and confidence with which I drove. "You shift that stick like an experienced driver." He was checking things off the list as I followed his instructions; turns, parking, backing up, proper signals and lane changes.

"About a year, sir."

"Yeah, that's what I thought. I've seen this car around town. I guess you got away with it 'cause you look older than you are. Is this your car?"

"Yes sir, I built it in our shop at home."

"Yeah, I knew you were a hot rodder when I first saw this car. Well, don't let me catch you racing it on the street, ya' hear? Says on your paper work here, you need your license early 'cause you're startin' college, your parents are deceased, and you live with your grandfather. Is that right?"

"Yes sir, it is."

"Fourteen and starting college?" He shook his head and sighed, as if he did not believe it. He signed my paper as we pulled back into the DPS parking lot and settled into a parking space. "Here ya' go. You know how to drive, all right." He handed the completion certificate to me. "Good luck, young man."

It was sometime in 1946, autumn I think, early fall, September if the pages on the calendar had been changed when they should have. Dreams of this time in Mattie's life were vague, spotty, just short glimpses of passing time. But the page on the calendar, the September page did not look too fresh, so I wasn't sure. Tractors, I saw tractors on the calendar, John Deere, pretty and green, Massey Harris red, and Case yellow. The rest of the shop slowly spun around in a semi-blur. Race cars, V8 Fords, flatheads, a Hudson dirt track racer with a flathead inline six, engines on stands, engine parts, body parts, this was a real race car shop, in 1946. And there sat Mattie, over in a corner, gathering dust. Why? Why wasn't someone getting her ready to race?

Dreams, and without a ghost. I dreamed of Mattie by night, but by day I saw no new spirit in her. "Come on, baby. Show me something. I know there are more in there, Amos said so." At times I'd see Amos in Mattie. His presence was less frequent, blessing me with very short visits, just a glimpse, or a quick smile or a laugh. He liked to visit with me while I worked on Mattie, I'd feel something like a feather gently passing across my cheek or my hand, a wisp of a breeze against my face. At first I'd stop what I was doing and look around but I soon realized it was just a subtle greeting from my invisible friend and my response would only be to grin, or maybe to whisper, "Hi, Amos."

I was looking for Royce Benson, or rather his ghost. But he never came. I decided he must not have had a significant place in Mattie's history except to take her far away from Las Casas, and Dad. She sat in his shop, in an out of the way corner, while other cars were worked on and readied for action. Mattie gathered dust and eventually became a fixture that stuff was stacked on top of. And this went on for nearly four years. A mechanic tore three pages off the calendar and suddenly it was Christmas 1946. The holidays came and went and it was spring 1947. World War II was now a memory, albeit a horrible one, and something to try to just get beyond for most people. Both an economic boom and a baby boom were in full swing and everyone was busy. Royce Benson's wife gave birth to twin girls and they needed money, so in the spring of 1949, he sold Mattie to his friend, Jimmy Cox. Jimmy had wanted her since he first saw her, the day after she was delivered to Royce's shop. Deciding that Royce was not ever going to get around to Mattie, Jimmy stepped up the pressure for Royce to sell her to him, and his timing was perfect.

Jimmy Cox showed up in a Ford pickup, a 1934 model which was as beautiful as if it were brand new. The flathead V8 purred through dual exhaust and drank fuel through three Webber carburetors. I liked him right away. But, still no ghost. Royce, it turned out, was just passing through Mattie's life, was Jimmy doing that too?

Mattie's engine was started for Jimmy Cox. It took some effort, she'd been sitting for four years. But she did fire up, coughing and sputtering as dry seals and gaskets struggled to hold pressure, blowing smoke from unburned gas out her dual exhaust pipes under her rear bumper until things inside her engine smoothed out, and then she purred and Jimmy smiled.

Mattie was driven up onto the trailer behind Jimmy's truck, strapped down, money was exchanged, papers signed, and she and I anxiously awaited our introduction to her new home and owner and life. Jimmy, as would unfold over the next few months, was good for Mattie and he loved her. He had no shop, no barn, no car lift or ramp, no elaborate facilities, but he did have a nice roomy garage with four stalls, each with its own eight foot wide, wooden, pull up door. Mattie was given the stall on the end away from the house which was nice because it had windows on two walls and a regular walk thru door in the back wall leading to the yard outside. The three other spaces belonged to the '34 pickup and Jimmy's and his wife's personal cars, which were both four door Chevrolet sedans a couple of years old.

For the first few months, Jimmy drove Mattie around without changing anything about her. He tuned and adjusted and tweaked, he changed all her fluids and she rewarded him by running very smoothly and trouble free. He loved showing her off and used her to run errands and even to just go to work a few times, jumped on opportunities to show her to friends and coworkers and even strangers, anyone who would take a moment to gaze at his new found treasure. I liked Jimmy and enjoyed watching his relationship with Mattie develop. But he was accumulating parts and making plans. Mattie was about to undergo some radical changes.

By the fall of 1950 Mattie was in a thousand pieces, spread out over the floor of her garage, hanging on the walls and from the ceiling, on stands and work benches, parts of her everywhere, even spilling out the door and into the driveway and yard. Dismantling a car requires a lot of space. So her body was all apart, her interior out, and her entire drive train removed and discarded. She looked sad.

Jimmy Cox was a good mechanic and he worked on Mattie by himself, except for the times when he needed help lifting or moving something large and heavy. Friends would stop by evenings and weekends while he was working on her and they would drink a beer or two together and look over his work and talk about it, but Mattie was Jimmy's project, a very personal project it seemed.

A noticeable absence in all of this was Jimmy's wife. Jean was not supportive of this project, she would visit only briefly usually only in passing, on her way from her car to the house or vice versa, and her comments were never complimentary. She didn't understand the attraction to an old car or the justification of the time and money invested, especially the money.

The next ghost appeared. But he was neither Royce nor Jimmy. He was a white man, in his mid-fifties I guessed, medium height, maybe five feet nine or ten, and he was bald, completely bald. And very slim, as if maybe he was not well. But he was happy, he smiled. I was rubbing a leather treatment into Mattie's upholstery, I was alone and sitting on the passenger side of the seat, and he showed up right beside me in full body view, and he smiled at me, then promptly vanished. I started, not out of fear, I'd been expecting someone's spirit sooner or later, just not at that moment and maybe not quite that close.

"Hey!" I yelled, and I jumped. His smile widened, and he was gone. Immediately, Amos materialized and spoke to me, smiling, "Meet, Shawn." He said. His gold tooth sparkled and he was gone too.

"Wait! Wait a minute!" I demanded. But ghosts are an independent bunch, they do what they want. They're terrible listeners and even worse team players, and they have no sense of whose property they are on, or in. Anyway, they never listen to me or do what I say. So I figured I had some waiting to do. Meanwhile, I realized Jimmy, like Royce, must just be passing through without leaving anything of himself behind and all I could do was watch his part of the story play out and wait for Shawn, whom I guessed would be Mattie's next owner.

The dreams of Jimmy's reconstruction of Mattie went on for months. He kept her in Amos' beautiful black color, but he wet sanded her and added more coats of paint, rubbed her down nicely and got her real shiny and there wasn't a scratch on her. Jimmy didn't know Mattie's name so he gave her one, BAD COMPANY. He taped top and bottom borders and wrote the words out in pencil, which was barely visible on the jet black paint, and in a very fancy, eight inch tall, extremely slanted, longhand style, gold color, he painted BAD COMPANY. The letters slanted toward the back of Mattie so they appeared to be blown back by her speed. It was a nice finishing touch and she was beautiful.

Before reassembling her body, he fitted her with many new mechanical parts. The hydraulic brake system that Amos had converted her to, he upgraded with larger, finned drums and better shoes, a dual compartment master cylinder and it was chrome. New stainless steel lines, and top of the line brake fluid finished off the project in fine fashion. This guy did things right, like Mattie deserved.

I got the impression that Jimmy was not planning on putting the same engine back in Mattie, the first clue was when he started cutting her motor mounts off of her frame. And when Royce came by and bought the old straight eight mill and the three speed manual transmission, I knew for sure something new was coming. But what would it be? The good American high performance, overhead valve V8s did not yet exist, not in 1951. From the limited options I could think of, I couldn't imagine what kind of new engine Mattie was going to receive. Surely Jimmy wouldn't put a Ford flathead in a Buick! That'd be an insult to Mattie.

Saturday morning a box truck backed up Jimmy's driveway to Mattie's door. Jimmy had everything ready, a portable engine hoist and couple of friends to help; Jake, a neighbor and Royce. The back door of the truck rolled up, the driver dollied an obviously heavy wood crate onto the truck's power tailgate and lowered it to the ground, moved it clear of the tailgate, raised the tailgate, hung his dolly on a hook on the side of the truck, handed Jimmy some papers and drove away.

The three men, with hammers in hands, fought the top off of the crate, connected the engine hoist to a very strange looking engine and lifted it out of the box. With the engine dangling from chains as if it were a toy, they circled and inspected. From Jimmy's description I learned that it was a 1931, one thousand horsepower Mercer aircraft flathead V-12 gasoline engine. For Mattie? A one thousand horsepower motor for Mattie? It was big and long and impressive. Would it fit? Would it run? Something told me we were about to have some fun.

Over the next few weeks Jimmy Cox mated a four speed manual racing transmission to the back of the V-12 and installed them in Mattie, or Bad Company, as he called her. More alterations were necessary to her frame and motor and transmission mounts but Jimmy methodically and carefully fabricated and fit each part just right. I watched as he would slide the power train into place in Mattie, run back and forth from side to side checking clearances and fit and alignment, just to slide it back out, cut and weld some more on the frame and slide the engine into place again and repeat the whole process several times before finally getting the perfect fit he wanted.

When you alter something on a car the domino effect comes into play every time. So the new engine was in but it was so long the radiator would have to be moved forward so new mounts for it would have to be made and then hoses and lines wouldn't fit, and now it needed a custom fan. He had somehow lowered the huge engine on the frame to buy clearance on top but it still looked too big to me for the hood fit back on. But none of it was a problem, Jimmy was good at this and Mattie wasn't his first hot rod, that much was apparent. And this was just one in Mattie's long history of modifications, she would never again be the 1934 Buick coupe that Dad and Amos once knew. But man, did Mattie look fine with that V-12 power plant!

She was up on blocks and had no differential under her yet. But Jimmy had one ready for her, a Ford rear end that used an open style driveshaft. Installing her new rear end was a tough job too, mounts and suspension parts didn't match up and all had to be moved and rebuilt. She needed traction bars too for racing and they had to be custom made. So for the remainder of the month Jimmy spent his spare time underneath Mattie cutting and welding. The garage walls flashed, reflecting bursts of light from the welder and red hot spray from the cutting torch peppered the floor all around, molten particles bouncing across the garage in all directions. It looked to me like a mechanical version of Dr. Frankenstein's Monster being created in some mad mechanic's shop. And indeed, this was going to change Mattie drastically and launch her into a different world.

Exactly two years and three months to the day after Jimmy acquired Mattie from Royce Benson, he trailered her behind his '34 Ford pickup to the race track.   Mattie looked fine in her new gloss black finish, chrome all polished and reflecting light like mirrors. And her new name BAD COMPANY, in fancy gold writing on both doors. Jimmy took some teasing about that, his friends asked if it referred to him or his car, but he just laughed with them.

Mattie's hood was altered so that the side panels were off, exposing just a glimpse of her V-12 from each side, but the top section of the hood was in place and I liked that look on her. Her nice sweeping fenders were in place but Jimmy had removed her running boards, to reduce body weight and clutter I suppose. That, I didn't like, and I would, forty one years later, reinstall her running boards.

Mattie sat up in the rear and looked like a serious drag racing coupe with a menacing attitude, huge slicks perched under her, she looked like she would just jump up and jerk her front wheels off the ground and speed out of sight in a cloud of burning rubber.

It was Tech and Tune night, not an actual race night, time to run down the track and see if your car was ready, make adjustments and run down the track again and repeat the process until it was ready for the Saturday night races. I was as anxious as Jimmy and his friends to find out how Mattie would run with her V-12, 1000 horsepower aircraft engine.

Mattie was on the line, a Ford roadster sat ready in the lane beside her, and the flag went down. Mattie eased off the line, Jimmy was being careful. When she was rolling well he floored her and her rear tires broke loose and boiled out smoke. Her right front tire raised off of the pavement just a little, maybe three or four inches, and lowered back down and she tried to get squirrelly but Jimmy held her straight. Mattie sped along burning up her slicks, unable to get traction. Jimmy let off the gas back to about half throttle and shifted to second. When engine rpms hit four thousand he floored it again and took off like a rocket. The roadster had taken Mattie off the line by several car lengths but now Mattie ran that Ford down and by the eighth of a mile marker put worlds of distance between them. Mattie flew over the finish line and the sign lit up, 11.8 seconds and 122 mph! And she did it after taking forever to get off the line!

The excitement was everywhere. The new car on the drag scene had made a big first impression. Other racers and crew members hurried to Mattie's pit space to see what she was and how she was powered. Royce Benson was there with a couple of his race cars and he came over to congratulate Jimmy on how well he had built this car. While Royce and the others were admiring Mattie and her V-12 aircraft engine, a track official paid Jimmy a visit.

"Uh, excuse me, please." He cleared his throat. "But, uh, James Cox?" Jimmy was sitting on a portable air tank and he raised one hand high. "Present."

"Yes, uh, Mr. Cox, you can't run anymore tonight. If you turn times under twelve seconds, you must have a roll cage in the car."

"What? I never heard of that before. I thought it was required for under eleven seconds."

"New rules, sorry, if you've raced here before you should have gotten a mail out about it. We had a death here last year and this rule would have prevented it, you know."

So Mattie's first race as a professional, off street, track only, drag racer, was to get kicked out after her first run because she was too fast. I thought that was great and so did Jimmy Cox. He and his racing buddies there at the track that night had a big laugh about it. Well, that was okay, he found out from his one and only run down the track, what he needed to know. Traction was the problem to overcome. Power was there and was efficiently delivered to the rear wheels, but the rear wheels couldn't handle the power. Jimmy and Royce talked it over, after the night of racing had ended and guys were just sitting around in the parking lot drinking beer and telling slight exaggerations and discussing race car dilemmas.

What was the solution to Mattie's traction problem? Lower gears? Bigger slicks? Wider slicks? Different kind of rubber? Would bigger slicks fit under the fenders or would Jimmy need to cut the wheel wells and fenders? I didn't like that idea, but I was a fly on the wall, a spectator only, unable to even offer input. And if you got the traction you needed, someone asked, would it then be too much power and just start breaking things? Twist the driveshaft in two, or break a rear axle? I recognized their questions as some of the same things racers still deal with today.

But Mattie ran an eleven second quarter mile and did sort of a little wheelie, in 1951, twenty seven years before I was born, but still, I got to watch it happen.

I awoke from this dream in the middle of the night and felt my mood turn sour. I lay there on my bed, Sparky's back up against me under the sheet, shadows playing on the walls, and my mind drifted moodily over the dream. I felt I should have been happy for Mattie, but I was not. It became clear to me that I was jealous of Jimmy Cox. He was a great guy, and did really special things with Mattie, but I had a problem with it. Amos, I didn't mind, he didn't change her that much, he saved her. But Jimmy transformed Mattie, made her into his own personal custom car. It was like I had found out another guy had kissed my girlfriend and I was pissed off. And now I was working myself up about it and getting angrier.

In too rotten of a mood to just go back to sleep, I got out the journal and read. As if my hand was guided, as if Mattie wanted me to get over what I was feeling, I opened the book right to the time when Dad told me, whatever Mattie had been through, she survived, and she was mine now, and she would be whatever I wanted her to be. I laid the open notebook across my chest and stared at the ceiling, going over that good advice in my mind, feeling a little better. And I fell asleep.

School was in full swing for Anita, and for me too. She was now a freshman at Las Casas High School, home of the fighting Badgers, their 2A sports mascot. I was now a fourteen year old college student. Mr. Einstein, aka Dr. Larson, was my guidance counselor and we hit it off pretty well. Actually, he sort of took me under his wing. He mapped out my academic career as if it were of personal importance to him.

So, I was driving into the Foundation parking lot in Mattie one morning. (Looking back, I can't believe how Dad just turned me loose in Mattie.) Anyway, I pulled into the parking lot and Mr. Einstein was getting out of a 1957 Ford Thunderbird. We stayed out there in the parking lot and looked at and talked about our cars and how we got them and how we built them, until we were both quite late for the testing session we were going to, which made several other people have to wait for us. So it turned out that I did connect with him about the cars back in that first testing session. Maybe I even reminded him of himself, at an earlier age.

Anita's parents were strict but they always allowed her go to school related activities and I believe we went together to every social function and event her school had; pep rallies and games (they really did have a good sports program), plays, dances, band concerts. At first one of our Dads would chauffeur us, but before the start of the second semester we were going by ourselves in Mattie to the school events, not anywhere else, but it was good. Anita's friends were impressed that as a freshman she already had a boyfriend with a car. I think she really enjoyed that, that feeling of being at that point already, that point of freedom and independence. And to tell the truth, I did too, I was just as proud of it as she was.

Before she was given that freedom though, I had to endure a heart to heart with her dad. We both sat on the very edge of the same couch, half facing each other, in his living room, with Anita eavesdropping around the corner. John Cantu informed me that he was young once too and he knew what kids did in cars and if he ever found out I was taking his daughter parking he would see to it that she never laid eyes on me again plus he would beat the crap out of me. Wow! He was protective of her.

I replied that I cared very much for his daughter and I would never do anything disrespectful with her and besides my Dad had already talked to me about this. He said that he was glad we had this talk and he thought we understood each other. I looked him right in the eye, the way my Dad always did when making an important deal, and he stuck his hand out and we shook. The thought that was going through my mind though, was how I couldn't wait to get Anita alone with me in my car and hold her close and kiss her and let my hands wander and I felt a little guilty for that thought, but only a little.

With both high school and college courses keeping me busy there was no time for me to participate in little league or any of the youth sports that were organized for the home schooled kids. Dad became concerned that I'd get out of shape so he bought me a membership at the one and only privately owned gym in Las Casas, it was a little hole in the wall kind of place right on the square.

The gym was long and narrow, probably not more than thirty feet across and sandwiched between a pizza restaurant and an ice cream place and I saw the irony of that right away. A large wood paneled door painted red, flanked on each side by huge plate glass windows with a clear view of the tread mills, led to a tunnel of a one room weight lifting club with mirrored walls facing rows of benches and weight stands and cable machines.

Several ceiling fans formed a perfect dividing row down the middle of the ceiling from front to back and were always on and twisting slowly at the ends of their long pipe rods. Inspiring posters of male and female bodybuilders filled every bit of wall space not taken by mirrors.

Personal training and instruction were available for a fee but I wasn't going to get into it that much. Robbie Jordon, the owner, a man in his mid-thirties and with a very impressive build, helped me get started, recommended a workout routine and helped me to understand proper technique. He gave me his full attention for my first couple of workouts and after that would now and then offer suggestions and advice.

I was a tall, stocky kid and maybe a little too heavy and my body responded quickly to the weight training and began to tone up within a few weeks. Anita liked that, as my arms and chest and back and shoulders became more defined she would stroke and caress them when we made out in my car. She'd whisper to me between kisses about how nice my muscles felt and how sexy I was and it fueled her passion for me. With her hands all over me and her mouth kissing and biting, my passion was aroused as well. Her father was giving us a little more freedom and occasionally I could talk him into letting us take my car to the movies or to friends' houses, if he knew exactly where we were going and exactly when I would have her back home. But frequently we would sneak away from the movies or school dances early and go parking and our making out got progressively more intense and our hands grew braver and explored each other more and more. It occurred to me that we might be headed for trouble and I worried about her father. If he caught us, he'd kill me.

I had a little bit of an edge with John, I was the kind of boy he wanted Anita to be interested in, just not quite this serious this young. But he liked me, in spite of his protective nature, he liked me and he would ask questions about my college courses and my future plans. When I told him I wanted to build custom cars and race cars for a living, he laughed. I didn't have the heart to tell him I was serious.

"You'll find what you are meant for." He replied. "I have a feeling a lot of doors are going to open for you, Joey."

While school and relationships and my car filled my days, Mattie's history continued to dominate my nights. I lived in two parallel worlds that had nothing to do with each other, except for Mattie's involvement in them.

Dad really enjoyed reading the journal now, since it was a part of Mattie's history he didn't know, and he was intrigued with her V-12 engine. I could see the wheels turning in his head. He was restoring another car, a '32 Ford coupe, deuce coupe as car guys call it, and he had not yet decided on an engine for it. It was a similar body style to Mattie but was somewhat smaller and was just a shell of a car, missing fenders and running boards and any hint of an interior. But the V-12 engine made him want something special for his new project car.

I'd help him when I could but didn't have a lot of spare time any more. But one such afternoon when he and I were repairing some rust holes in the floor, we discussed Mattie's unfolding history and I silently realized how we would do that now, talk about the story with its dreams and ghosts as if it was all quite normal and not her history being revealed to us through some supernatural means. All the fear and anxiety that initially came with it all was so far from us now, we just accepted what was happening and watched it with curious pleasure.

But secretly, I wondered about Mattie's powers. What was she really capable of? Had she really killed Mrs. Ferguson and Hugh? Did she possess a conscious love for Amos and acquire her love for racing while chasing his pigeons, then later take his spirit captive in order to hold onto him. Did she willingly choose me over Dad? How did she behave with other owners? Had she killed anyone else?

The one thing I knew for sure, in the deepest part of my mind, was that eventually I would know all of these things, in time I would come to know all of Mattie's history and the extent of her powers. That thought was always with me. I was not afraid of her, she was no threat to me, of that I was certain, but could I control her or would she control me? What was in our future together? Would she reveal things to some future owner decades from now about her life with me, show him my ghost? How would she choose him? Maybe he would be my son, or grandson and call me Paw Paw. That thought brought a smile to my face.

I thought of Stephen King's novel, "Christine" and how she turned on all of Arnie's friends and family and his girlfriend, eventually even Arnie. Mattie wasn't like that. Dad was her first love. And Anita was supportive of my relationship with Mattie, even knowing about the ghosts and dreams. Anita loved Mattie just like I did, enjoyed our time in her, bragged about her, touched her with affection. No, Mattie was not a threat to me, not in that way at least. But I wondered, if I ever pulled away from her… No, I would never do that.

A couple of weeks or so passed before I dreamed about Jimmy and Mattie again, maybe because of my jealousy, maybe to give me time to get over that. But when I did dream of them again he was changing her even more and my anger returned. He removed her interior. Since she was a coupe she didn't have a huge interior like the old sedans, but there she was pretty much bare inside. And he started cutting holes in her floor to get tubing down to the frame. I have to admit, Jimmy was good at fabricating parts, cutting and fitting, he had the patience to stay with a tedious job until he got it just right.

He worked at his real estate sales job weekdays nine to five, came straight home and spent an hour or two on Mattie's roll cage, and was able to spend a little more time with in on the weekends.

Jimmy's welding skills were remarkable, his welds were so even and pretty, his bends with the tubing so perfect and symmetrical, it was hard to believe his vocation was office work. Over a period of about three weeks Mattie's new custom built roll cage evolved right inside of her. Jimmy papered and masked off everything in Mattie except the roll cage, and he spray painted the new metal with sealer, primer, and three coats of black, to match her body paint. With her interior installed, the roll cage actually added to her appeal. Something about it gave her a serious look. Mattie was a serious drag racer now, officially, she had a roll cage.

As Jimmy reinstalled Mattie's seat he added a seat belt harness, one made for race cars, but he had to modify it and adapt it to her bench seat.

His wife complained about both the time and the money he was spending on "that old car". On occasion, she would storm into the garage and angrily question Jimmy about what things cost. He would get defensive and they would argue, which made him want to stay out in the garage even more and avoid more confrontations. I guess they had problems with their relationship before Mattie, but now they had problems with Mattie. I hated to see this, it looked bad enough to me to be a threat to Mattie.

Mattie was now ready to return to the drag races. This time is was the Saturday night races, the serious ones. Jimmy had changed the slicks to larger diameter and width, and softer rubber for better traction. They made her sit up in such an impressive stance, like she had an attitude. Friends came over to help unload her, they set up the ramps and Jimmy backed her off the trailer. The sound of her exhaust flowing through the custom headers was captivating, powerful and deep. The excitement built with anticipation over how she'd run this time.

The new roll cage had passed inspection at the check in gate and also with Jimmy's friends. One fellow racer asked what he'd charge to make one for his car.

"No, I don't have time, this one took several weeks of my spare time and my wife bitched about it every minute. I wish she'd come out sometime and watch, maybe she'd get the fever. Of course, if she actually had a good time it'd probably kill her."

"Guess I'm lucky." Royce offered. "My wife likes the cars and the races. Maybe you ought to build Jean a car, Jim. That's what turned my wife around on the whole car thing. Now her little red '40 Ford Roadster is her prized possession and she understands all of this. Watching just wasn't enough, she needed to be part of it."

The small talk was short lived as racers began lining up in the staging lanes for practice runs, which were only allowed until seven p.m. after which the competition racing would begin. A few minutes later, Mattie was on the line. Man, she looked fine. Jimmy took her through three practice runs, mainly working on getting off the line with as little tire spin as possible. But each time he let off the gas after he got thru the gears, not wanting to reveal everything to his competitors.

Back in the pits, last minute adjustments were made, pressures, levels, and mixtures were checked, Jimmy was nervous, Mattie was ready. Back on the line again, the flag went down and Mattie shot out like a bullet, both front wheels raised off the pavement at least a foot as the slicks hooked up and sent her flying down the track, leaving the Willys coupe in the next lane to just fall farther behind as the seconds ticked off.

10.2 seconds! Mattie ran the quarter mile in ten and two tenths seconds and at the speed of one hundred twenty nine miles per hour! By the end of the night she had made seven runs for seven wins with a best time of 9.8 seconds and had captured the championship trophy for the Modified Class. I'll never forget how she looked pulling those front wheels off the ground, it was a thing of pure beauty. I still get chills just thinking about it.

I watched Mattie perform for Jimmy Cox Saturday night after Saturday night and she won regularly with all her beauty and style and grace and her big V-12 engine, she was something very special now and soon trophies began to line new shelves in the garage. I wished there was a way to record dreams, I mean like videotaped so you could watch them over and over. I wished I could share this with Dad, in some better way than just words spoken or on paper, I wished he could see what I was seeing.

Problems between Jimmy and his wife grew worse, they fought and yelled and threatened. Jean complained about money problems in general but mostly about his hobby and what it cost in both time and money. He tried to persuade her to go along with him to the races, just try it, other wives went, she could visit with them and watch him race. But she was not going to do it.

She found something else to do, though. If he could play she could too. He'd return home from the Saturday night races to find her not at home. When she returned it was very late and she wouldn't say where she'd been but she sure was dressed nice, and she smelled like cigarette smoke and alcohol. And the fights grew worse.

It seems that people can live in bad situations for a long time before they are motivated to do anything about it. And the war between them raged for another year, a little longer actually. One Saturday night Jimmy towed Mattie to the races, unloaded her, unhitched the trailer and left. He drove back home, parked down the street, and waited for Jean to leave. When she did he followed her at a distance to a bar where he sat and waited across the street in a parking lot. A couple of hours later he watched her leave the bar with another man, someone he didn't know. They drove away together in his car. Jimmy followed them to a motel. He watched them check in and go into a room. He parked his truck right in front of the door and waited.

An hour and a half later the door opened and Jean appeared and saw him sitting there waiting. It really startled her, her eyes and mouth flew wide open and she froze. Jimmy pulled out a camera and snapped a photo of his wife and the other man standing in the motel room doorway. He drove away.

Back at the track, Jimmy hitched up his trailer and loaded Mattie. Royce walked over to help and find out why he didn't race, and he saw on Jimmy's face that something was very wrong. He was concerned for his friend, he'd seen Jimmy's marriage problems growing worse and wondered when they would hit the breaking point.

"Want to talk, old friend?"

Jimmy didn't look his friend in the eye, just kept his gaze to the ground. "Got a spare beer?"

"Yeah, sure." Royce stepped to his tow truck, opened an ice chest, and pulled out four beers. "Let's walk." He handed Jimmy two cans of beer and they began a slow stroll. Jimmy walked in silence for a couple of minutes till they were off on the other side of the parking lot by themselves. Royce stayed quiet too and gave him the time he needed.

Jimmy told his story about finally needing to see what Jean was up to and what he found out. "How do I go home now, Royce? How do I even look at her again? What do I say? Get out?" He shook his head and fought the tears that already burned his eyes. "Why didn't she just tell me, why did she do it this way? She must really hate me, and now I hate her too." They walked in silence again, dropped their empties and opened the other beers. Jimmy added another thought, "Thank God we don't have any kids."

"Look Jim, you're welcome to stay at my place tonight, you know, to give yourself some time, before having to deal with all this, time to think."

Jimmy stopped, Royce did too. They looked at each other. "Think it'd be alright with Karen?"

"Sure, no problem at all. We've got plenty of room, especially since the kids are all grown and gone."

Not much else was said. They finished the beer and returned to the pits and their cars. Some of the other racers asked Jimmy why he didn't run and he just replied that he had some personal business to take care of and didn't make it back in time to race. Jimmy and Royce did not hang around for the usual bull session after the racing was over, just headed for Royce's place.

I awoke sad for Jimmy and my sadness put me in a solemn mood for the rest of the day. I thought about Jimmy and Jean and about relationships in general. I had never known a bad relationship, but I had not known many relationships at all, to be quite honest. I talked to Dad about it and he said that sometimes people just grow apart, or maybe are just mismatched from the start. He talked to me about mutual relationships and how to keep them healthy, each person giving the other what they need. I asked if he thought Anita and I were well matched and he thought we were, but added that young people sometimes change as they mature and explore new interests.

"If you stay together," He said. "You'll have to give each other room and support to grow, Joey. Like she is doing with you now in your college studies. Someday she'll find something to pursue and you'll need to be supportive of her then." I thought a lot about that.

There were no more dreams for nearly two weeks and no ghosts either. I hoped that Amos would come around but he didn't, perhaps he was just minding his own business. I waited, and I talked to Mattie.

I started a new project on Mattie, an air conditioner. South Texas summers were brutally hot. Dad helped me, I knew nothing about air conditioning systems, till we finished, then I knew a lot about them. And Mattie had her very first ac. We had to cut holes in her dash, trying to think like architects and engineers and place the holes in just the right spots for proper air circulation, and fit vents to them and chrome trim. We had to run duct work behind the dash and a new electrical harness. The fit was tight and the process tedious. It was a much more involved modification than I had bargained for. But Mattie was cool with a/c, pun intended. Anita liked it too, cruising was much more comfortable now, and parking was too. And Mattie's new ac looked like a factory original unit, not some aftermarket under the dash thing. That was funny, a factory a/c in a 1934 Buick.

Looking back, I think the thing I liked most about installing an air conditioning system in Mattie was that I had done a unique modification on her. I had grown jealous watching Jimmy transform her into his custom machine and I needed to do something with her that no one else had ever done, just to put my signature on her. But in the coming months and years of dreams and ghosts of former owners, I would see many more modifications to Mattie. I knew that. I had acquired her in a chopped and shaved with yellow paint and flames condition, and with no interior except a racing seat and harness, all things that Jimmy and his predecessors did not do to her. Someone else did. But who? Only Mattie knew, but in time she would tell me everything.

Jimmy took Mattie home just a little before noon the next day, which was Sunday. He had killed time over coffee and breakfast with Royce and Karen and then piddled around with Royce in his home shop, procrastinating. When he did go home his wife was not there and he was glad, emotionally not ready for the final battle. He unloaded Mattie and drove her into her garage space and checked her out. It was just busy work, quiet time, he had not driven her the night before except to take her off the trailer and put her back on. But still he checked things over and wiped her down, getting the road dust off of her. Then Jimmy drove his pickup into town to find some lunch.

My dream did not follow Jimmy into town, it showed me the wrath of an angry woman. Almost as soon as Jimmy drove away, Jean returned home, parked her car, got out, and carried a five pound bag of sugar directly to Mattie and poured it into her gas tank. I was horrified, I wanted to reach out and stop her! My emotions woke me. I sat straight up in bed and gasped, heart beating hard, looking around in confusion, trying to find reality. And there it was on my dresser, the clock. I saw that it was time to get up and start the day. I was already emotionally drained by what I had just witnessed.

I lay back down and let my mind wander. Poor Mattie. If Jimmy didn't discover what Jean had done, Mattie's beautiful V-12 engine would be ruined. I smelled bacon frying and realized that Dad was up and cooking breakfast. I drifted back into a fitful half sleep just long enough to watch Jean throw some clothes and bags of stuff into her car and drive away. Dad knocked on my door and announced the time and the fact that breakfast was ready. I got up, splashed some water on my face and brushed my teeth. This was going to be a long day. I had to go in for testing at the Foundation today and though I was ready knowledge wise, I worried if I'd be able to concentrate.

I arrived at The Foundation about five minutes late. I'd never been late before, anywhere. I was the only student testing that day and it was a very important chemistry exam, if I scored above ninety percent on it I would be finished with my underclassman science courses. Dr. Larson sat next to me at the table and explained some things to me about the test. I didn't react and he asked if I understood. Yes, I did.

"Are you okay, Joey? You seem distracted."

I glanced at him and looked back down at the papers. "Yes sir, I'm okay, just in a weird mood, that's all, just some trouble about my car."

"Your coupe? What's wrong with it?" He sounded genuinely concerned.

Okay, now how do I tell my college councilor about problems with a former owner of my car, back in the nineteen fifties, decades before I was even born? Why did I even start this conversation?

"Um, well, it's nothing really, actually it was just a bad dream about something that happened a long time ago, before I was even born. I mean, I'm not even sure if it's true. It's nothing, I'm just being weird." I was sure I sounded really stupid.

Dr. Larson straightened his back and his eyes widened and he smiled. "Hey, know what? That's happened to me too. When I first started restoring my T-bird, I dreamed about it when it was new, every night, vivid dreams, conversations and everything. After a while of having those dreams, I did some research and found out some of the car's actual history and guess what? It was like I had seen into the past, I even dreamed the original owner's first name correctly! It was the strangest thing, I wrote down some of the dreams but I never told anybody about them, till now."

Oh boy! Now what do I do? What I did was to take the conversation a little farther. I told Dr. Larson a little about my dreams, holding back enough to not let the story sound too supernatural, and I was careful to not mention the ghosts at all. I explained that Mattie first belonged to my grandfather's grandfather and that Dad had confirmed some of my dreams as having really happened. We exchanged stories for nearly an hour, and my mood improved.

"Joey, you know what? You should really try to research that car's history, your dreams may be more accurate than you think. This might sound funny coming from a scientist but, there simply are some things in this world that science cannot explain, you know?" He looked at his watch. "Hey, tell you what, let's reschedule this exam for another day, when you're more up to it. And let's you and me go cruising. What do ya' say? Let's go have some fun."

And we did. He told his secretary we had to go on a field trip and it would probably take the rest of the morning. It ended up taking the afternoon too, and he didn't even call in, he was much more of a rebel than he appeared to be. First we cruised around San Antonio in Mattie and then in his '57 T-bird. We stopped at a

Sonic and ate lunch in his car. We cruised out country roads and ended up in Las Casas and I took him to our shop where Dad and I showed him all our cars. Dad thought it was hilarious that my teacher and I were playing hooky together and playing with cars. We went back and got in Mattie again and picked up Anita at her school. We had to go by her house and get permission for her to go cruising. I think Dr. Larson fell in love with Anita, he told me later that I had the prettiest girlfriend in town and I agreed.

I took that chemistry exam two days later and aced it.

That night I went back to 1954 and Jimmy Cox. He had discovered that Jean had moved out, sort of. Jim was sitting in Mattie in the garage, drinking a Jax beer from a tin can. He seemed to be deep in thought but unaware of what Jean had done to his car. Jimmy startled at a sudden knock on the garage door frame.

"Jim Bob, what's going on, man?"

It was Royce, checking on his friend. He walked over to Mattie's window and they made small talk for a few minutes. Royce started admiring Mattie's trophies lining new shelves placed up high along the garage walls. He walked around reading the plaques and remembering specific races, trying to draw Jimmy into an enjoyable conversation to cheer him up a little. When he walked behind the car he noticed granules of white powder sprinkled on the floor, not much, but enough to catch his eye.

"What's this?" Royce reached down and ran his finger across the powder and smelled it. He looked closely at Mattie, around her rear fenders and saw a few granules, wiped a finger around the gas tank cap and tasted it. "Jim, this is sugar. What's goin' on here? Looks like somebody's put sugar in your gas tank."

Jimmy sprang from the car seat in a panic and was at Royce's side in two strides, investigating the evidence. He unscrewed the gas cap and saw more sugar on the inside of the filler neck. "Son of a bitch! That whore! She's tried to ruin my race car, damn it!"

"Hold on now, Jim. The important thing is, is the car okay? Have you started it, you know, since bringing it home from the races?"

He had not started her since putting her back in the garage so if Jean didn't start her after pouring the sugar in the tank, Mattie was out of danger. To know for sure, they disconnected the coil wire so she wouldn't fire, then the fuel line from the carburetor and turned the key to run the electric fuel pump. Aiming the fuel line into a coffee can they collected the gas and inspected it; looking, smelling, feeling it between their fingers, they decided the sugar had not reached the engine yet, she hadn't been started since the sugar had been added to the gas.

"Royce, my cars aren't safe here, can I keep them in your shop for a few days?"

"Yeah man, let's get 'em on over there."

I watched this part of Mattie's life play out over several nights' dreams. Though relieved that Jean's sabotage effort had been thwarted, I still had this feeling of impending doom. Jimmy and Royce siphoned the tainted gasoline out of the tank and then removed the tank itself. They hitched Jimmy's trailer to Royce's pickup, loaded Jimmy's '34 Ford pickup onto the trailer, and placed Mattie's gas tank in the back of the '34. They would flush the tank out at Royce's shop and return for Mattie.

As if she had been hiding down the street waiting for them to go, Jean returned quickly after they left. She loaded her car again with clothes and things and then walked over to Mattie. Where the filler neck for the gas tank normally protruded thru the body panel, there was only a hole. "Shit!" She yelled. "He found it! Damn!" She walked a circle around Mattie, trying to think of something else to do to her. "I know, I'll drop a nut down the carburetor, that'll fix that damned motor he's so proud of. Wish I could be here to watch when it drops down onto a piston." Jean saw a nut on the floor right in front of the coupe and bent over to pick it up.

Mattie's engine roared to life with an angry rev, then another, and another, adding rpms each time. Her headlights flashed on and off in angry rapid succession and her horn blasted. Jean straightened up quickly and I don't think I'll ever forget the look on her face; it was like she knew what was coming but couldn't make her legs move to get out of the way. Mattie revved to about four thousand rpms, slipped into gear and drove Jean all the way thru the back garage wall, crushing her and snapping her spine in several places, killing her instantly.

Mattie's engine died and she sat there, front end protruding thru the wall, Jean's mangled and lifeless body lying in front of Mattie in a bloody tangled mess of sheetrock, broken two by fours and siding. Mattie was badly damaged, her nice chrome grill was shattered and pushed into the radiator and both fenders and her hood were crumpled.

Within seconds, neighbors responded, running to see what the commotion was. Someone called the police.

Jimmy and Royce unloaded the pickup and parked it in the shop, cleaned out the gas tank and hurried back to rescue Mattie. Turning onto Jimmy's street, they saw the crowd that had gathered, punctuated by police cars, an ambulance and a fire truck.

"What the heck's going on here?" Jimmy queried.

Unable to drive anywhere near Jimmy's house, they parked several houses down the block and walked. The entire yard had been roped off and an officer stopped them when they tried to slip under the ropes. Jimmy explained that he lived there and wanted to know what was happening. The officer checked his driver's license for the name and address and allowed them in, signaling for another officer to come and escort them. The medics were just moving Jean's bloody, mangled body to a stretcher as Jimmy walked up. She was so broken up that her head and arms and legs just flopped around like those of a worn out rag doll, as hands slid her over onto the stretcher. Jimmy turned away from the sight in horror, doubled over and threw up.

When he'd had a minute to regain some composure he asked, "Oh my God! How did this happen?"

An officer replied, "Why don't you tell me, sir?"

"What? Look, I just got here. My friend and I were moving cars and we just got back. This isn't even possible! Look officer, this car doesn't even have a gas tank in it. It can't run like this!"

Jimmy was in shock, he couldn't make sense of it. And now it seemed the cops thought he had murdered his wife. It was all too much. His knees were weak and he needed to sit down. Two cops ushered him to a police car and put him in the back seat. They talked to him, accusing him of running over his wife and then removing the gas tank and leaving the scene. They cuffed him and took him to the police station. Royce stood and stared, first at Mattie and the mess, then at the police cruiser disappearing down the street with Jimmy's terrified face peering thru the rear window.

I woke up in the middle of the night in a cold sweat, trembling, my mind racing with confusing thoughts. I couldn't write this in the journal, Dad and Anita would read it and it would look bad for Mattie. I had to protect Mattie, I'd have to make up something else for the journal. Dad and Anita had dismissed Mrs. Ferguson's torment and death as her own doing, resulting largely from her own craziness and drug and whisky induced confusion. Hugh's death must have been brought on by his own carelessness with attaching the engine hoist improperly. They attributed no blame or suspicion to Mattie. But I knew better. Mattie killed Mrs. Ferguson because she wouldn't let Dad have her, she killed Hugh for abusing her, just like she had now killed Jean. But it was much more obvious with Jean.

A fearful thought entered my mind, what if Jean's ghost appeared in Mattie? It would almost surely show her mangled body and horrified face. My gut feeling was that Jean's spirit was not in Mattie but if it was I'd not let Dad or Anita know, I'd not record it in the journal. I'd simply dismiss her to wherever she was to go to next and get rid of her, get her out of my car.

Sparky followed me to the shop and I sat in Mattie, intending to talk to her, but I could not speak. Her dash lights flickered a few times which was her way of reaching out to me, it was intended to soften me up but it didn't work this time. I caressed her nice banjo steering wheel, tracing the chrome bands with the tip of one finger. "Oh, Mattie… Why?" Her radio clicked on.

"You know I can be found, sitting home all alone. If you can't come around, at least please telephone. Don't be cruel, to a heart that's true. Baby if I made you mad for something that I might have said, please let's forget the past, the future looks bright ahead. Don't be cruel, to a heart that's true. I don't want no other love, baby it's just you I'm thinking of. Don't stop thinking of me, don't make me feel this way, come on over here and love me, you know what I want to say. Don't be cruel, to a heart that's true. Why should we be apart? I really love you baby, cross my heart. Let's walk up to the preacher and let us say I do. Then you'll know you'll have me and I'll know that I'll have you, don't be cruel, to a heart that's true. I don't want no other love, baby it's just you I'm thinking of. Don't be cruel, to a heart that's true."

I tried to talk to her again, I whispered dolefully. "I understand, Mattie, but why did you have to kill her, why couldn't you just scare her?" Her dash lights flickered again and she played another song for me, Anita's favorite old song by Peter Frampton. "Ooh baby I love your way, every day, wanna be with you night and day…" She finished her song, flickered her dash lights at me again, and turned her radio off. I rested my head on her steering wheel and sighed heavily. My mind went blank.

I must have fallen asleep in Mattie, or maybe I was just under her spell, and the rest of Jimmy's story played out in my head. He was arrested and charged with murder. The cops had had time at his house to go through things and they saw plenty of evidence that Jean was moving out; her belongings in her car and a paid receipt for an apartment across town. And the most damning thing of all was something they confiscated from Jimmy himself, the Polaroid photo of Jean and her boyfriend obviously surprised by Jimmy while they were coming out of their motel room.

Jimmy got out on bail the next day and Royce gave a statement. So did the neighbors who all said they heard the crash and ran over immediately and saw no one else around, no one leaving the scene. Even the police had to realize it would require some time to commit the murder, remove the gas tank, and get away unseen. The murder charge was dropped a few days later because nothing made any sense, Jimmy had witnesses who swore he was not there when Jean was killed, and the prosecuting attorney could not put together a case he could logically present to a judge or jury. Jimmy quit his job, sold Jean's car, put his house on the market, sold Mattie back to Royce, loaded his car on his trailer and drove away with it hitched to his pickup. Where he went, I never knew.

Royce parked Mattie back in the corner of his shop and she sat there quietly in her wrecked condition for two years. I was sad for her. Why had Jean tried to hurt her? It could have all been worked out, they could have just gone their separate ways and everyone would have been just fine. And now, I felt that I knew the extent of Mattie's power. But I was wrong. I did not know the extent of Mattie's power, not yet.

CHAPTER 8

It had been nearly a year since my first vision of Shawn, and Jimmy was gone, but I really didn't expect Mattie to show me the next chapter very soon. I thought that she, like me, needed a little break in the action, a chance to let emotions calm down, a chance to get back to daily life. But I was wrong. Maybe she was just holding so much inside she needed to get it out, maybe there was something she needed me to know, something still to come, something it's all leading up to.

The dreams didn't start right away but the sightings did, Shawn appeared in Mattie, just briefly, but with increasing frequency over the next couple of weeks. He never spoke but he smiled and seemed happy like Amos, but not well. From his appearance I decided he must be battling cancer. And in 1956 a battle with cancer was fatal more often than not.

And then the dreams began. Royce hoped that Jimmy Cox might change his mind and want Mattie back, maybe after he got settled in somewhere new and had time to get over how things had ended here. But two years went by with not even a call or a card from Jimmy. Royce worried about his old friend, it was as though he had just dropped off the face of the earth. The truth was, I was sure, that Jimmy realized Mattie had willfully killed Jean, and that fact frightened him so deeply he would spend the rest of his life hiding from Mattie. I was no longer jealous.

So finally, Royce put Mattie up for sale. The day the ad came out in the Tulsa newspaper, Shawn called and asked about the coupe, and he came to look at her the same afternoon. She looked bad, her entire front end severely damaged, sitting in a slump because of one flat front tire cowering under the wreckage, and she was covered with two years' worth of dust. Shawn saw beyond all of that though, I could tell by the wide grin and the look in his eyes as he circled the crippled racer, and when he saw her V-12 engine, his mouth flew open and he gasped.

He spoke slowly and without taking his eyes off of Mattie. "Oh, my, goodness. What, a, beauty." He looked over quickly at Royce as if he'd forgotten he was there. "I can fix this, you know." He nodded toward the damage. He rubbed one hand over his chin as if to smooth out a goatee that wasn't there. "Tell you what, Mr. Benson, if we can get that engine started, I'll buy this car from you."

Royce called another mechanic over and with Shawn's help, he was so excited they couldn't have stopped him from helping if they'd wanted to, the three of them worked to get Mattie running. They removed all twelve spark plugs, squirted some kind of lubricant down the cylinders, and screwed the plugs back in. They poured a couple of gallons of gas in the tank and primed the carburetor, put a jumper on the battery and Shawn sat inside Mattie and turned the key. Mattie's engine turned over a few times, fired, sputtered, died, fired again, and roared to life like a lion awakened from a nap. They couldn't let her run very long because the radiator was ruined so there was no coolant. But she ran long enough for Shawn to fall in love.

Shawn said a few kind words to Mattie, BAD COMPANY was still painted on her doors but he didn't like that and vowed to find her a new name. He patted her fender and left. Early the next morning he returned with a trailer and twenty five hundred dollars in cash, and took Mattie to his home in nearby Indian Hills, Oklahoma.

I quickly learned to like Shawn Remington and felt that Mattie did too. He appeared very Irish with green eyes and sandy hair, except on his head, it was completely bald. A slim frame that could have, and probably did at one time, supported a stocky build. Mid-sixties and recently retired, and as I suspected, fighting cancer, a brain tumor, slow growing but deemed inoperable. And Mattie turned out to be just the diversion he needed to get his mind off his health problems. Shawn knew nothing of Mattie's history and didn't seem curious; he hadn't even asked Royce how or why she was wrecked. And Royce certainly didn't volunteer the information. He had thought about how to answer the question and had a little story prepared about the parking brake not holding and the car hitting a wall. But thankfully, no explanation was requested. Possibly, he thought, because the car had been stored for a while and the damage was not recent.

Shawn had a wonderful attitude and a very supportive family and I was glad for that, not wanting a repeat performance of Mrs. Ferguson or Hugh. He and his wife, Rita, had been married since their early twenties and were now sixty five and sixty four years old. They had two sons and a daughter, all grown and on their own, several grandchildren, and they all lived within an hour of each other.

When Shawn announced his purchase of the coupe and his intentions of racing her, his whole family showed up to see his new hobby. As though they were all planning to be active participants in the project, they began suggesting possible paint colors, ideas on the interior, maybe different wheels, and names to replace BAD COMPANY. Lots of ideas on that, but Shawn just couldn't make that decision yet. "Maybe she'll earn a name." He told them.

Watching the Remington family rally around Shawn and his newfound hot rod, I was convinced that they were simply happy that Shawn was going on with his life rather than letting his illness get him down and make him give up.

Okay, there was one in the family who was skeptical of Shawn's new endeavor, Charlene, or Charlie as they called her. Charlene pulled her mother aside and asked her if she was "really going along with this race car thing." She argued that her Dad was too old and sick and should find a safer hobby, stamp collecting, she suggested, or photography. Her mother laughed and answered that if this would take Shawn's mind off the tumor and give him something to enjoy and look forward to, she was all for it. Besides, she added, she thought this coupe was absolutely beautiful and she knew how creative and talented her husband was, he would immerse himself in this and do something he would be really proud of.

Shawn didn't delay getting started on Mattie. Having just retired from his teaching job at a local community college where he taught diesel mechanics, he had time for the rebuild and he had the necessary skills. He also had a nice garage and Mattie got a comfortable space in it.

For several days Shawn worked at removing the damaged front end; fenders, grill, hood, and radiator. With the V-12 engine exposed, he cleaned and painted it. That's when he discovered Mattie's name where Dad had hand stamped it twenty something years earlier. "M A T T I E." He read the letters aloud while running a fingertip under them, and it reminded me of when Amos first read them. "Now that's not a factory stamp." He pulled his head back a little, adjusting his glasses, and looked closely at her name, pulled his yellow baseball cap off and rubbed his bald head. "Now why would somebody stamp MATTIE on you, and right by your serial numbers? This is somebody's name. Is it the name of someone who loved you? Or is it your name? It's a girl's name, I bet it's yours." He chuckled as he pondered the moment, wondering about the origin of this strange find on his car. "Well, it's your name now, baby, whether it was before or not."

I was happy. Mattie had her name back, BAD COMPANY may have been flattering, in a race car sense, but I never liked it. I knew now for certain Shawn would rebuild Mattie with the love and care she deserved. She would be happy again too. And my mood was better now. Lately my state of mind seemed to follow Mattie's mood in the dreams, something I failed to get the significance of right away.

These new dreams of Shawn were quiet ones, and usually just quick glimpses of the restoration process in his garage. Even though his illness was potentially fatal, he never hurried his work, he worked as though he had all the time in the world. I think Mattie was good therapy for him.

Shawn was able to repair one front fender, the same one Amos had repaired, and as Shawn worked with it I flashed back to Amos' big capable hands performing the same repair years earlier. The other fender and the grill were a total loss. Mattie was only twenty two or twenty three years old at the time so replacement parts were still available. Shawn bought a new fender, a new grill, and a new radiator, and started prepping everything for paint. I had taken it for granted he'd leave her black, even though he had had inconclusive discussions with family members about color possibilities. But he picked a deep blood red color for Mattie.

I would have never imagined Mattie red. She came to me yellow with flames but started life brown, was changed to black by Amos, and now Shawn was making her red. Blue and yellow flames covering her front end and her name on her doors in gold would also be part of her new color scheme.

And for the first time since Jean's death, I returned to the journal. I sat in quiet solitude pondering what to write. Finally, unable to come up with a suitable story, I simply wrote that Jimmy and Jean divorced and their financial problems caused Jimmy to have to sell Mattie. Of course, I then had to skip the part about Shawn repairing the damage but there would be plenty to say about his repaint in the new color. It was really difficult for me to do this, and having to leave out part of the story caused me to do a poor job of what I wrote instead of the truth. Right away, Anita picked up on it. She questioned it, saying it seemed as though I didn't have my heart in that part. Our eyes met and she knew.

"It didn't happen that way, did it?" She knew me well.

I answered that I didn't want to talk about it and I changed the subject. She allowed me the luxury of handling it that way. But I was certain I would someday have to rewrite it truthfully. It was Mattie's history and whatever happened, did happen, right or wrong. So I left a few pages blank for possible future use.

In the summer of 1993, my world changed a little more. We celebrated our fifteenth birthdays. Anita completed her freshman year of high school with extra credits toward her sophomore year and signed up for summer school to earn more credits. I tested out of high school altogether with the guidance of Dad and Dr. Larson. Dad seemed more determined than ever for me to keep up a fast pace through my studies, even when Dr. Larson suggested a break for at least part of the summer. Of course, I was on Dr. Larson's side of this issue. Dad, Dr. Larson and I had a meeting about this and it went well, we argued a little but no one got angry. Dr. Larson voiced a concern about the possibility of burn out if I didn't get a break once in a while. He argued that I was a teenage boy with a car and a girlfriend.

Dad explained to Dr. Larson that by my second birthday I was able to spell, and print a couple of dozen words, and I could do simple addition. It was at that precise point in my life, he admitted, that he decided he would push me to my potential, whatever that might turn out to be.

This was the first time I had ever heard Dad explain why he had always pushed me so hard and it was very thought provoking. In the few seconds I could manage to mentally check out from the three way conversation, years of thoughts and memories rushed through my head. For example; memories of my Paw Paw asking me, as a small child, to go to the tool box and get him a 5/16 inch 3/8 drive socket and a four inch extension with a swivel, and in the same breath asking me what the chemical symbol for sulfur was. Or insisting I do hard math problems orally, mentally really, or teaching me self-defense, or telling me I was a better person than to do something that could hurt Anita. No wonder I loved him so much, he was an incredibly accomplished man and he had devoted the last fifteen years of his life to training me. I decided that I would do whatever he said I should.

That summer I simultaneously received my high school diploma and an associate college degree, and both of them through the Alice Warhead Foundation, about two months before my fifteenth birthday. And the pace was wearing me down. So, to create a compromise, I was sure, Dr. Larson used his influence to generate an offer for me from NASA to participate in a student work program in Houston. It was a six week program and I would be working with space scientists on experimental things like synthetic fuels, lubricants and coolants. I'd probably just be a grunt in a laboratory, recording tests results and measuring mixture amounts but I'd be where I could see what goes on behind the scene in new product developments.

When I voiced concern about leaving Anita and Mattie for six weeks, I was told that I could drive Mattie there, half was across Texas, and I could come home for a couple of three day weekends. I still wasn't sold on it but when Dad found out that the work program would be worth five hours of advanced college credits for me, credits that could even be later applied to graduate work, he insisted.

Anita and I had two weeks to spend with each other before I was to leave for Houston. I would be gone two weeks, and then home for a three day weekend, back to Houston for two weeks, home for three days, and back to Houston for the final two weeks. The two weeks part sounded like an eternity to us. By eight each morning we were meeting somewhere, usually at my house or hers, and I kept her out till her ten p.m. curfew every night. Then we'd hang out at her house playing video games or watching movies till her Dad made me go home, usually sometime before midnight.

By now Anita's dad had grown to like me quite a bit, he was

sure I had a future. Anita told me she heard him tell her mother that I was the best mannered and most ambitious fifteen year old he had ever known. Plus I did what I was told, never once had I brought Anita home even one minute later than her curfew. I knew he hadn't liked me at first, he would have not liked any boy interested in his daughter, but the turning point was the time I beat Billy Davis up for calling Anita a wetback. He knew then that I cared for her. I knew in my heart though, there would be real trouble with John if he ever found out that Anita and I went parking all the time and that we would get nearly naked and have our hands and mouths all over each other.

And the last night before I had to leave for Houston, we went all the way. We had been to the movies but decided to leave before the show ended. We didn't see the end of very many movies in those days. I drove Mattie to our favorite parking place, a little clearing just beyond a cul-de-sac in a remote subdivision that for some reason never had many houses built in it. With lights off and radio on, while kissing and groping, we removed each other's shirts and lay down on the seat.

"Ooh baby I love your way, everyday..." Mattie's radio played Anita's favorite oldie almost as soon as we were horizontal.

Anita pulled her mouth back from mine and giggled, "Mattie always plays that for me."

She didn't know how right she was.

When my hands had thoroughly explored the upper half of her body, they wandered down, unbuttoning her blue jean shorts, unzipping her zipper, exploring further. Anita unfastened my belt and pants button and zipper and did some exploring of her own. We had been here before, often lately, at this point in our making out, but not beyond. Dad's words usually stopped me as they rang in my memory telling me that I shouldn't take a chance on hurting Anita with careless passion. But this time I shoved those words aside, I wanted this beautiful girl so bad, this time I didn't stop. With both hands I slid her shorts and panties over her slender legs and she kicked her feet clear of them, they dropped to the floor. She tugged at my pants and looked me in the eye; we both knew it was time. I took my pants off and moved myself up between her legs.

"Joey," She whispered. "Be careful, please. Joey, I love you."

And together, we went to paradise. That first time, I don't know if it was the passion or the fact that we'd waited so long for this, or if it was simply genuine and pure love, but that first time with Anita was the most unspeakable, on top of the world, moment in my whole life. And I forgot to be careful, actually I'm not sure I forgot, maybe I just couldn't leave her, couldn't make myself disconnect our bodies at a moment like that. But I was definitely not careful. And even after the climax, I rested there on top of her, unmoving, our breath heaving and hearts racing, arms around each other, cheek to cheek, clinging, mingling our sweat in silence.

It took us a few minutes to get our hearts and breathing back to normal, in a quick moment of silent panic I wondered if I might not be able to calm my heart down and I'd just die right then and there. But no sooner did we settle down into normal breathing and heartbeats, we started kissing again, and that led to roving hands, and moving around, and we made love again. This time we loved slower and took longer and again, I was not careful. But what good would it do to be careful now?

Her voice shook me from my mental paradise. "Joey, you weren't careful, were you?"

"What? Oh, no, I wasn't. I'm sorry. What was I thinking?"

She was silent for a minute. "It's probably okay this time, I mean with my cycle and everything, but we can't take that chance again. Okay?"

"Okay, yeah. 'nita?"

"Yeah."

"You alright?"

'Yeah, why?"

We were still laying down, my head buried in her tangled hair, the side of my face resting on Mattie's seat.

"Uh, well, I've heard it hurts the first time, for a girl, you know."

"Yeah, it did at first, for a while, I'm okay. We made love, Joey. I feel so close to you, like we're part of each other."

Lights! Headlights shined thru Mattie's windows! I shot upright and looked out the rear window, imagining John Cantu finding us naked together, making love! But it was not him.

"Just more parkers." I said, but I was shaking like a leaf on a tree and my heart was beating as hard as before.

We sat up and put our clothes on and then we talked, kissed, hugged, and stayed as long as we could. Anita talked about her decision to go to summer school, this and next summer and take extra courses in the regular semesters, then she would graduate a year early. I asked why she wanted to do that and she said so she could get on with her life.

It took a minute for that to sink in. "Get on with your life?"

She bumped her forehead to mine and stared into my eyes at point blank range. "Get, married." She said, very slowly.

"Oh! Oh, then we can get married! Yeah, when you finish high school we can get married."

She hugged me really tight and whispered in my ear, "Think we can stay out of trouble that long?"

We had gotten permission to extend our curfew till eleven and I got her back home four or five minutes early, keeping my perfect record intact, even tonight, the most special of all nights. Her parents had already gone to bed and we were glad, imagining we must look guilty, we had to, look what we just did. We sat on her front porch, the concrete steps leading to the porch actually, and talked, avoiding her younger brother and sister who were in the living room watching Little Mermaid or Sponge Bob or something equally silly on TV. Shows like that never interested me even as a small child. I had to leave for Houston early the next morning and we were already missing each other.

About twenty or so minutes later a sleepy eyed John stepped into the living room in his robe and ordered the kids to brush their teeth and go to bed and they scrambled to do so, he was a strict dad and his kids knew better than to argue with him. Then he came out on the front porch where we were. I stood up and shook his hand and greeted him and assured him we had arrived before the curfew time. He replied that he knew, he had heard us drive up but added that he didn't worry about us, we were never late. We talked briefly about my Houston job and then he went back to bed, giving us permission as he turned to go, to stay up till midnight.

Evidently, he hadn't detected my nervous guilt. I just knew it showed on our faces that we were no longer virgins. And I was sure that we smelled like sex. Even my handshake must have given me away. And I must say, Anita handled it much better than I did. She just sat there and smiled and didn't say a thing. But her hair was really a mess and I couldn't believe he didn't pick up on that.

The next day was Monday and I was due in Houston at eleven in the morning for orientation. Dad and I hit the road at four a.m., leaving his pickup at the airport in San Antonio, then continuing the trip to Houston with me driving Mattie. Dad would fly back home from Houston later that evening and his truck would be there waiting at the airport. We arrived in Houston more than an hour early and ate a late breakfast at a Mexican food restaurant which, as Dad said, "...wouldn't know real Mexican food if they sat on it." But how bad can you mess up huevos rancheros anyway? Dad made a phone call to get directions and we drove to our NASA appointment.

We were to meet Mr. Fletcher at an office building on the outskirts of the Houston NASA facility. A uniformed guard at the gate stopped us, took my license and called someone to confirm our right to enter, after which he returned my driver's license, raised the barricade and waved us in. I was overwhelmed even with what little of the place I could see, and the feeling of deep apprehension struck me dead silent. I was frozen with a feeling that I was way over my head.

Dad looked at me and smiled, "Son, this is what people like you are meant for."

"Huh, what? What do you mean, Dad?"

"People like you, people with genius mentality; good, smart, disciplined people."

I snickered, "Genius, you think I'm a genius?"

"You are, Joey. I've known that since you were two years old. You're destined for greatness, son."

The things he told Dr. Larson came back to me. "Dad, whatever I am, whatever abilities or potential I may have, whatever I achieve, I owe to you."

"No." He shook his head. "You'd have done it anyway. I just got you started early."

I thought for a moment. "Dad, if my real daddy had lived, do you think he would have raised me like you have?" We had never talked about my parents much, and not at all in the last several years. Like his time as a soldier in WW II, it was something he did not like to talk about. And my question caught him off guard.

After a brief hesitation, he answered without looking at me.

"Well, I'm sure he would have done his best with you. I had the luxury of time. Joey, your daddy got cheated out of not only most of his life, but also out of the best thing this world had to offer him."

I naively asked, "What was that?"

"You. And although my life has been full and richly rewarded, you are the best thing that has ever happened to me."

I looked straight thru Mattie's windshield, afraid to look Dad in the eye or I'd not be able to stop the tears. If he thought I was the best thing that ever happened to him, he had it backwards. Look where he'd brought me, fifteen years old, almost fifteen, half way through college and invited to work at NASA, even if it was only for the summer.

Mr. Fletcher was a small thin man with thick glasses and kinky sandy hair with a little gray starting to show around the temples, early fifties I guessed, but he possessed a firm handshake and a strong clear voice. He stood up behind his desk as we entered his office, and he walked around and toward us with outstretched hand. He shook hands with Dad and exchanged names, then turned to me.

"And you must be Joseph McClane III." He reached for my hand and gave me an enthusiastic handshake. You've made quite an impression on the people at the Warhead Foundation, Joseph. Dr. Larson sang your praises to me for nearly an hour on the phone the other day."

I looked him right in the eye and read what I could from the handshake, his eyes, and his voice, just as Dad had taught me to do. "Thank you, sir. Please, call me Joey. Yes, I consider Dr. Larson a good friend as well as my councilor."

At his invitation, we sat across the desk from Mr. Fletcher and talked casually for a few minutes. The discussion was obviously intended to help him decide the proper work station for me there, or perhaps to confirm the one he'd already chosen. He asked a lot of questions, some of which he had to have already had the answers to, but he was building on information about me and making notes and decisions as he went. He established that I was fourteen, almost fifteen, a home schooled high school graduate, and had amassed over eighty hours of college credits.

"Have you chosen a college major yet, Joey?"

"Well, almost, sir, I'm trying to decide between automotive engineering and alternative fuels technology. Cars are my passion, but I feel that a lot of new discoveries in fuels and lubricants are about to be developed and I'd like to be a part of that. My Dad here, is a petroleum engineer."

He nodded. "Yes, I know he is." Mr. Fletcher removed his glasses and his eyes looked much smaller. He squinted at me and turned the interview to more personal things. Thumbing thru his folder of papers on me, he continued. "Okay, let's see." He put his glasses back on and turned a page. "I think maybe Dr. Larson was right on the money about you, Joey." He took a few seconds to read something then looked up at me. "It looks like you're an early bloomer, pretty much about everything, you are already driving, in fact, Dr. Larson has a note in here that you have already restored a classic car."

"Yes sir, Mattie, she's a '34 Buick coupe, Paw Paw, (Now why did I slip and say that?) uh, Dad and I took her off the drag strip and made a street rod out of her. She was once my grandfather's grandfather's car, when she was new, and we found her and rebuilt her." He wanted to hear more so I told him the whole story in as condensed a version as I could manage, without ghosts and dreams of course, and he listened intently, as though genuinely interested. Could he be a car guy too? I wondered. When I told him I drove my car there, he wanted to see her so we went outside to look at Mattie. He walked around her several times and seemed quite impressed and made a comment about my attention to detail.

We began a tour of a nearby laboratory building, and the interview continued as he pointed out things of interest and occasionally introduced me to people working there. As if testing my attention span or maybe my memory, he mixed my orientation with more questions, questions about my hobbies and pastimes and other interests, and relationships. I answered his queries truthfully and told him about Anita. "I have a steady girlfriend, Anita Cantu, we've been going together for over two years and plan to get married as soon as she finishes high school."

"Cantu, that's Hispanic, right?"

I wasn't sure why he made that distinction. "Yes, sir. And she's the prettiest girl in town and she's going to graduate a year early."

"Oh, so she's smart too, huh? You're quite young for a relationship that serious. Is she the only girl you've dated?"

"Yes sir."

"Is she older than you?"

"Uh, well, just a little, a couple of months."

"Yes, well it all fits your profile all right; quick decisions, few but strong relationships, stable, and the ability to read people and situations quickly and clearly. You've probably been reading me while I've been reading you. And confidence, you fully expect to succeed at whatever you attempt, don't you, Joey?"

My only reply was a smile. I had never thought about myself like that before, but couldn't argue with any of it. Dad beamed with pride. He had been working with me all these years to bring me to this point.

We toured a couple of large buildings full of offices, work rooms, and laboratories with busy people dressed in white lab robes. We were chauffeured around in a golf cart and toured a section of the grounds and I saw, at not too great a distance, a rocket on a launch pad. Now it finally sunk in, I was at NASA in Houston, Texas by invitation to work alongside scientists in top secret, high tech space exploration. Of course this was just a summer student job, but look where I was! Thoughts and emotions went racing through my inner consciousness at a blinding rate. Was I up to this? Was I good enough, smart enough, mature enough? I wanted to talk to Anita, I don't know why but I wanted to hear her voice, to hear her tell me she knew I could live up to what was being thrown at me, help me have confidence.

As if he could read my mind, Dad placed his hand on my shoulder and when I looked at him he winked at me. "This is right down your alley, son. You're going to do fine here."

We entered another building, Mr. Fletcher flashed his security card at the electronic eye to gain entry. This one had a couple of public rooms in the very front, one of which was lined with computers along one wall and file cabinets lined the other. 'Information Storage' the sign by the door said. The other room was a lounge; couches and chairs, a couple of round steel tables, a refrigerator and some vending machines. I was struck by the cleanliness of everything there, you could eat off the floor.

Dad and I were invited to have a seat while Mr. Fletcher walked down the hall and summoned one of the researchers, Sam Garza. The four of us sat at a table and talked. I was to be Sam's assistant, working with experimental material composites for improved heat shields. Sam was Cuban, medium height and build, with a full but short cropped, jet black beard and shoulder length hair. He spoke with a heavy Spanish accent but was very articulate. Mr. Fletcher told us that Sam had escaped from Cuba to Florida with his family when he was a small child. They had spent several days on a homemade raft and his youngest sister died from dehydration during the trip. Sam was educated at the University of Florida where he earned a master's degree in chemistry.

Sam was a quiet man and Mr. Fletcher led the conversation. Because of Sam's solemn manner, I worried that Sam didn't want a helper and I might just be unneeded responsibility. And he was hard to read, never revealing any thoughts with his eyes or facial expressions. I'd probably need to be a quiet worker as well as a quick learner. After a somewhat lengthy conversation which got us properly introduced and a little familiar with each other, we walked together down the hall to Sam's work station, all four of us. We were given a brief overview of Sam's project and then Dad and I accompanied Mr. Fletcher back to his office where I was given the necessary paper work and vouchers and a security badge so I could enter secured areas. We were given directions to a nearby motel where a room had already been reserved for me. Dad thanked Mr. Fletcher and they exchanged contact information and we left to get me settled into my motel room.

After getting my stuff put away in my room, Dad and I sat in the motel restaurant, ate lunch and talked about the coming six weeks. He went down a mental list to make sure I had all the things I would need for the next two weeks, and handed me a few hundred dollars cash and a credit card for gas. I offered to drive him to the airport but he declined the offer, not wanting me to drive in Houston traffic any more than necessary. We waited outside for his taxi and when it arrived we hugged and said our goodbyes. I stood and watched as the cab disappeared down the busy street.

Now I felt really alone, for the first time in my life, I think. It was a deep empty feeling and I didn't like it at all. I had an overwhelming desire to just go home. I could do it, just get in my car and drive home. I looked over at Mattie in the parking lot, I didn't like that either, it was not an appropriate setting for her. I'll cover her up here at night, and when I'm at work too, I told myself.

I sat in Mattie and called Anita on my cell phone. Mrs. Cantu answered and asked me questions about where I was and what I was doing. The Cantu family had become very supportive of me. I had to work at it to not be irritable with her, I wanted to talk to Anita. Finally she called Anita to the phone. Anita was happy to hear from me so soon and we talked for nearly a half hour and I felt better. I was expected back at NASA to start work or I'd have kept her on the phone longer. Without saying it, we talked about when we made love. She said she felt different and more in love with me than ever. And I so wished I could touch her, kiss her, be near her.

I went back to my room but wasn't sure why. I brushed my teeth and looked at myself in the mirror. My peach fuzz beard had grown thicker and darker, freckles had disappeared. I tightened my chest and arm muscles, I would miss six weeks of working out. I turned around and looked over the room. I missed Sparky, he'd not be snuggling up to me under the covers here, and he'd miss me too. I walked back outside and to Mattie and drove the short distance to my new temporary job.

Most of the afternoon was used to get me acquainted with my new work area and associates. Sam turned out to be a pleasant, helpful person who seemed to love his job and get along well with others but I detected a bit of territorialism in him. I wondered if he and I would become friends.

Sam's work was very susceptible to outside interferences and the room had to be kept at a constant temperature and free of any possible contaminants. We wore protective suits over our clothes, paper slippers over our very clean shoes, and latex gloves at all times inside his laboratory.

Still though, with all the precautions, something was having a negative effect on Sam's work. One of the ingredients in the composite material he was working with would not adhere to the other materials for long, it kept trying to separate from the rest. The composite performed fine in very small amounts and in small enclosed test tube type situations, but when tried on a larger scale, out in the open, it failed. If he could just get past this one problem he would be on his way to developing a new product for space travel heat shields which would in turn save huge amounts of energy needed to not only power a craft but also to keep inside temperatures regulated and stable and reduce stress. Sam had been working on this project for months, nearly a year, and now at this stage it seemed to be at an impasse. The room was kept clean to the point of sterilization, and Sam's work had been relocated to different labs twice, but the problem persisted. Maybe it was something simple, I thought, so simple that Sam could not bring his thought process down to such a basic level.

For the first week I worked as an ignorant helper, fetching things, learning names and procedures, measuring and mixing and watching and recording data on forms in a computer. And the first week came and went. Over the weekend I had little to do and spent most of my time in boredom. Exploring the hotel, I discovered it had a gym for guests to use and I did use it, that day and every day for the rest of my stay there. Anita and I had long conversations and I worried about my phone bill, a little. I had a long talk with Dad about Sam's problem in the lab and he sent me in a direction with it. He suggested that maybe a chemical mutation caused by mixing techniques with the composite, or with a catalyst in the procedure.

Sam invited me to his home Sunday evening for supper and introduced me to his young family. His wife was also a Cuban refugee but they had not known each other in Cuba. Her name was Andrea and she was quite pretty but beginning to grow a little pudgy. I hoped Anita wouldn't do that, she sure did like to eat. And I liked her skinny. They had one child, a daughter, Mercedes, three years old. She was a pretty child, dark features, alert eyes, happy.

After supper, Sam and I sat in his living room and sipped Mexican beer, my first beer, I drank two of them and it made me a little light headed. We discussed my Dad's idea. I didn't know how Sam would react to me trying to contribute at his level but he was graciously receptive.

Monday back at work we poured over the chemical makeup of all the ingredients used and how they might interact with each other but came up with no suspect. We kept digging but by Wednesday we felt we had eliminated the idea as a possible cause of the problem. It was worth a try and Mr. Fletcher complimented me on the thought, even though it wasn't really my thought originally.

By Thursday I could think of nothing but going home. I missed Dad and Anita and Sparky and just home in general. I decided that I wanted to stay a kid a while longer and was not ready to join the work force of the world. The thought occurred to me that I might even slow down the pace of my education and spend more time in the shop and with Anita.

I suppose that Mr. Fletcher read my homesick mood, to some extent, because let me off work at noon so I could miss most of the rush hour traffic trying to get out of the city. He sent a letter with me to Dad which was full of praise. I peeked at it. I left a few things in my motel room since I had it rented for the full six weeks, threw my dirty clothes and a few necessities in my car and hit the road. As soon as I found I-10, the highway that would take me all the way to San Antonio, Amos appeared in the rearview mirror, his big face smiling right at me.

"Amos!" I yelled as if I had just seen a long lost friend. And indeed I had forgotten all about him, in fact my new situation had pushed that whole part of my life to the back of my brain. Since arriving in Houston there had been no ghosts or dreams and I had not even noticed. And I now realized that I had missed them, I had missed my secret world of Mattie's history. Mattie's dash lights flashed three times in quick succession at me and her radio changed its own channel and played, "Ooh baby I love your way…" Chills ran up and down my spine and I patted her dash and smiled. "I've missed you too, Mattie. Even though you've been with me the whole time, I've missed you."

Amos told me, "Listen to Shawn, he smart."

Shawn appeared in full body form in the seat beside me, looking right at me, and for the first time he spoke to me. "Look to the cleaning solutions, Joey."

"What?" I asked.

But he just faded away. Now what in the world was that supposed to mean? Had I been cleaning Mattie with something that was bad for her paint or maybe her leather? I looked around me at Mattie's surfaces and the thought bothered me all the way home.

I missed the worst of the Houston rush hour traffic but hit San Antonio just in time to catch it there and it took almost as long to get thru the city as it did to drive the hundred and fifty miles or so to get to it. I sure was glad I had added the air conditioning to Mattie, at least I was comfortable. Rolling into Las Casas a few minutes before six p.m., I headed straight for Anita's house. We had talked on the phone just minutes before and she was sitting on the porch waiting for me. As I was parking Mattie along the curb in front, Anita came running down the sidewalk. We met behind Mattie and fell into each other's arms and enjoyed a long passionate kiss and hug with her entire family watching from the porch and I didn't care. She was mine, I could kiss her if I wanted to. I drew back and held her by the shoulders at arm's length, she looked more like a mature woman than I remembered, a tall, slim, classy, beautiful woman. The two weeks we had spent apart had done something.

"You've gotten even more beautiful, if that's possible, and I can't wait to get you alone." I muttered, and I was aching to touch her.

She pulled me close again and bumped her forehead to mine and tattooed my eyes with hers point blank and countered. "No, I can't wait to get you alone. And you better have some protection this time."

Oh crap, I'd forgotten about that. "I'll get some." I replied, sheepishly.

She teased me. "For a genius, you're not very smart."

Well, we went into her house and sat with the entire family, except for Mario who wasn't there, in the living room and after a few minutes of visiting with her family about NASA and what all I was doing there, I mentioned that I hadn't seen my Dad yet. So Anita and I left for my house. I so wanted to go parking but it was still daylight and I needed to go see Dad and Sparky, so after stealing a long kiss at each and every stop sign, Las Casas had no traffic lights, we finally turned into my driveway and rolled right up to the open shop door.

Dad was in the shop tinkering with his new project car and he stopped what he was doing, wiped his hands on a red shop rag and walked in eager steps toward us while we got out of the car. Dad had installed a doggy door in the front door of the house so he wouldn't have to get up at night to let Sparky out and Sparky crashed through the doggy door and came running full speed to me. When he reached me he leaped and I caught him and hugged him. He squirmed and cried and licked me in the face. Dad ran his arm around me, kissed me on the cheek, laughed at Sparky and said he wasn't going to try to compete with him. Dad draped his other arm around Anita's shoulders and greeted her and we walked together into the shop.

"This little girl sure missed you." He told me. "She even came over a few times and helped me some with my rat rod."

"Yeah, I missed her too, a lot. Hey, you're not trying to steal my girlfriend while I'm out of town, are you?"

Anita laughed at what I'd said. "Well, at least summer school helps keep me occupied."

Dad gave us the grand tour of his '32 coupe and talked about what he'd done to it and what he planned to do. He had found a 1952 Mercury flathead V-8 engine in running condition, plus a few pieces of performance parts for it, a three-two barrel carburetor set up and some chrome dress up trim pieces and he was excited about it. The little car was in gray primer and ready for paint but he said he might just leave it in primer. He liked the way that looked, it reminded him of younger days when he had more know-how than money.

Dad retrieved three Dr. Peppers from the shop refrigerator and we sat on stools to visit. He wanted to hear all about my NASA experience, even though I had kept him pretty well caught up on the phone each evening.

Monday would be Anita's fifteenth birthday and I would be back in Houston, so Dad took us out for an early birthday dinner celebration at a nice seafood restaurant at the edge of San Antonio. Anita loved seafood and Dad told her to order anything and everything she wanted. It was embarrassing, she had two lobsters, oysters cooked three different ways, and I lost track of how many fried shrimp when I ran out of fingers to count on. I told her she wasn't going to stay skinny for long eating like that and she stuck her tongue out at me. Finally, soon after supper, we were alone.

Having been separated almost immediately after our first time to make love, Anita and I were anxious to pick up where we had left off, and it was getting dark now.

The local Wal Mart had a drug store and we stopped there to buy some condoms. I went in by myself and it was embarrassing because everybody pretty much knew everybody else in Las Casas and I was elated to discover that I did not know the lady who checked me out and I refused to let my eyes meet her suspicious look. Under my guidance Mattie took us to the cul-de-sac where we liked to park and we wasted no time in getting each other aroused and undressed.

Lying on top of Anita, kissing and fondling, I entered her and then lay still for a moment. I was so aroused I was afraid I'd climax before having time to enjoy the act and I needed to calm down. I tried to think of something else as a diversion, Dad's new coupe, NASA, Sam, anything, but I could not keep a thought in my head, except about this beautiful young woman lying under my body, willing to let me do whatever I wished.

Lights from another car flashed through the back window and that old fear of John Cantu catching us shot thru me and provided the distraction I needed. Of course, it was just kids looking for a parking place so my fears subsided and my attention returned to Anita. And we made glorious, unhurried, passionate love. Man, I loved that girl.

"I wish we were already married, 'nita, and we could make love in our own home in our own bed anytime we liked."

"Yeah, Joey. We'll get there, we'll get there."

After a short silence, Anita said to me. "Joey, I need to tell you something."

"What?!" The seriousness of her tone worried me. "Something wrong?" Oh God, please don't let her be pregnant.

"No. But, well, your dad confided in me, something he will probably not tell you. He's built his whole world around you, Joey, for the last fifteen years. And now he thinks he sees you slipping away from him, you know, with you moving through school so fast and leaving most of the summer to work in Houston, and with you and me spending all our free time together. I don't think he thought about anything but you the whole time you were gone, and he seemed lost. You need to spend some of this weekend with him, Joey, just the two of you, let him know he's not losing you. Why don't y'all go to that car show in San Antonio tomorrow?"

Anita's words captured my mind, she was right, I had felt it too. When Dad left me in Houston, that last long hug, that last look, he wanted to cry, I knew it even then. I could almost read his mind. While he pushed me from the nest, he feared losing me. To see that his job of raising me was nearing the end was breaking his heart.

My mind wandered and I rambled. Anita let me, lying there beneath me, naked and beautiful in the dim moon light, she listened while I poured my heart out. "You know 'nita, at a time in his life when he had accomplished all he was supposed to, just when he was planning his retirement from a very successful but demanding career, ready to spend the rest of his life with his wife, traveling and doing things together, things they had wanted for years to do, enjoying some leisure time and a break from all the responsibility, at just that point in his life, his family was taken from him. I can just imagine that knock on the door, 'Mr. Mc Clane, I'm sorry to have to tell you this, but there's been an accident...'

"And then the other untimely change in his life, which I'm sure came close behind, without even giving him time to grieve. This, weeks old, dirty diapered, crying, hungry, demanding infant, was thrust on him, insisting he start over and raise another kid, this time by himself. He simply accepted the challenge with the same disciplined, unselfish, enthusiastic energy with which he had accepted all of life's challenges, of being a soldier in a war, an engineer, a mate and provider, and a father.

"And now he's almost finished raising me, and he's preparing me to take on the world, but what will Dad do? Live alone? Tinker with his cars in solitude? Grow old by himself? Go down to the country club and hope someone will play a round of golf with him before he goes back home to be alone some more?"

"You won't let that happen, Joey. I know you. You'll take care of him. You'll always be there, close by for him. He knows it too, he just needs you to reassure him." She reached up with one hand and stroked the side of my face. "I handpicked you, Joey. We were just children, but I could see how special you were even then."

"You're pretty special too, 'nita. You're unselfish is what you are. We just have a little time to spend together and I'm gone again for two more weeks, and you tell me I need to spend some of this time with my Dad."

We stopped talking, and shared comfortable silence. We just stared into each other's eyes for what seemed like a long time. We kissed. And we made love again.

While I was home for the weekend, dreams of Shawn and Mattie filled my sleep as if they felt a need to make up for lost time. I could tell that a little time in the story had been skipped over because in my next dream Mattie's restoration was almost finished. Shawn had repaired the body damage done when Mattie rammed Jean thru the garage wall. The candy apple red paint job had been sprayed and rubbed to a shine, and yellow and blue flames adorned my car. Mattie was beautiful, the color shined like a polished apple and made her look fresh and new and young. Shawn had painted her right there in his garage and it was every bit as nice as the paint job Amos had given her years earlier in his old barn, deep rich color that reflected like a red mirror. The new flames were symmetrical, they started on the very front around the grill and fanned out in yellow, turned to a deep golden as they traveled back over the hood and fenders, then the colors mingled to blue as they reached the back of the fenders and on to the doors. Hints of red and green swam with the other colors and the flames were outlined by a very thin white border. Mattie was absolutely beautiful.

I remembered how jealous I had grown while watching Jimmy Cox customize Mattie and I expected that emotion to creep in now, but it did not. I was happy for Mattie and remembered Dad's words about how she survived previous owners just to become mine. As I recorded these things in the journal, I decided to include Shawn's repair of the damage, and maybe someday I would go back and write the truth about how the damage occurred. Dad and Anita would see this and have questions, but they would not pressure me to answer until I was ready to do so. I wondered how the people at NASA would feel if they knew this part of my life, but I knew better than to even mention it.

Over Saturday morning's breakfast, I asked Dad if he'd like to go with me to the car show in San Antonio. He reacted with a half hidden joy as he suggested I take Anita instead, but I made up some excuse about her having to help her mother do something. I knew that look, he could always read me, but he agreed to go and he couldn't hide his happiness about it. I could read him too, he taught me how.

Maybe I'll get some ideas for my coupe too, son. I still haven't decided on how to finish out the interior, and I'd like to see some really well done ghost flames too, in case I decide to paint it. Hey, you think Anita's brother can do ghost flames?"

We hadn't been to a car show in a while, actually we had not done much together at all since I started driving by myself. And I realized that I missed our time together, this was a good idea. I was excited. I could tell Dad was too.

By seven in the morning we were on the road, hoping to beat some of the Texas heat. We roamed around the car show and swap meet till about three in the afternoon, admiring other car guys' customs and hot rods. The slow pace of the day allowed us to enjoy unhurried conversations about Mattie, and about his coupe project, and my summer job at NASA, and about the rest of my education. We paused at a concession stand for a quick lunch and sat at one of the wood picnic tables and downed hot dogs and Dr. Peppers. Dad turned the subject of our discussion to my relationship with Anita.

After the first time Anita and I made love I was afraid her parents could tell, that they would read that in us somehow. I can't say just how it changed us but it did, it was like we entered a new stage in our relationship and our maturing, and I just knew it would be obvious to them. It wasn't with them, but with Dad, well that was another thing. He knew me too well.

Not wanting to ruin our day together, but needing to make a point, he mentioned what was on his mind without actually starting a conversation about it. He simply told me that it was apparent that Anita and I had grown more mature and more intimate, and we should be very careful to not get into trouble. Then he pointed out something on the paint job on a T-bucket and mentioned that if he decided to paint his coupe and not just leave it in primer he'd do something like that.

Dad was always making his point without causing me to get defensive. It was like he was on my side, looking out for me. I gave him a quick one arm hug and we talked about his coupe. But I knew that he knew. He always knew.

The time with Dad was great, like a nice day spent with a best friend you haven't had much time for lately, and it picked both our moods up considerably. But things were about to turn serious. On our way home we stopped at our favorite Mexican food restaurant on the edge of the city, we had snacked on junk food at the car show but now welcomed a good meal. It was midafternoon and we were among very few other diners, which gave us an opportunity for the serious, private conversation that was to come. We sat at a booth in a corner, away from traffic patterns of servers and other customers. Dad had something to tell me. I never saw this coming.

"Son, there are some things I need to tell you, and I guess it is time, since you're a man now, in spite of your young age. Joey, when your parents died nearly fifteen years ago, they each had five hundred thousand dollar life insurance policies. You are the sole beneficiary."

"The policies paid double for accidental death, and now, after a decade and a half of earnings from interest and investments, you have a trust fund of over five million dollars."

"What? Dad, what are you saying? I've got five million dollars in the bank?"

"Yes. You have a pretty incredible inheritance waiting for you, but it's set up to allow you to draw out a maximum of only one hundred thousand dollars per year, starting when you graduate from college with at least a bachelor's degree, or when you turn thirty, whichever comes first."

I was stunned, I had never even thought about an inheritance. In some ways I was a pretty naïve kid. I sat in an open mouth speechless stupor and just shook my head.

"I didn't tell you before, son, because I didn't want you to think you didn't need to be as productive as you could be. Does that make sense to you, Joey? I didn't want it to keep you from reaching your potential, from making your own life, and a contribution to the world."

"Dad, I'll have a bachelor's degree in, maybe a year from now. I'll just be sixteen years old."

"Yeah, that's why I'm telling you this now. And I hope it doesn't hurt your ambition. You need to think of it as security, son, not as all you need. Make it spur you on to your goals, use it as backup, that way you can pursue things without always having to worry about the salary. Don't let this change you, Joey, stay the person you are."

I was remembering things from a business finance course I took and my wheels were turning. "What kind of interest is it earning?"

He knew what I was thinking. "It varies, right now, about four percent."

I did some quick math in my head, the way I'd been trained to do, calculating interest and growth and interest on growth. "It will earn more than it pays. It'll never run out, will it?"

He hesitated, our eyes were locked, "No, it won't. However, certain types of limited investments can also be paid for out of it. And Joey, I don't think you should tell anyone about this, not even Anita. If you two do get married when she graduates high school, tell her then, but not until. I just don't think it would be healthy for your relationship to throw this in on it. She loves you for you, let it stay that way."

So he knew we were planning to marry as soon as Anita graduates. I guess we had been pretty open about that, but it felt odd to hear him say it.

Five million dollars! I couldn't even imagine that much money. I would get a check for one hundred thousand dollars per year for as long as I lived, and then there would be money left over for whoever my heirs would be. Perpetual wealth.

But Dad wasn't through. Giving me news like this ought to be a happy thing, but Dad didn't seem happy, and he still had more to tell me. I had never seen exactly this mood in him before, it was almost like he was grieving. Maybe talking about the inheritance made him think about when his wife and my parents died and that made him sad. He had always avoided talking about my parents at all, as though there were no happy memories to tell. I never understood, but I never pressed him on it.

"Son, I need to tell you something else, I'm not sure why, maybe I just need to get it off my chest, or maybe it's just time to be honest with you. And I hope this doesn't change the way you feel about me. Joey, I was not a good daddy to your father. And I was not a good husband to my wife, your grandmother. I was married to my career, I was gone most of the time, and when I was not gone, I was planning to be gone soon. I was somewhere on the other side of the world when little Joseph hit his first little league home run, and when he brought home his first report card. Hell, I wasn't even there when he was born, or took his first step, or said his first word. And when I was home, I was hard on him. Nothing was ever good enough, why didn't you make a hundred instead of ninety eight, why didn't you catch the ball, you ruined the game for everybody, when I was your age... And on and on, and I was quick to punish, spanking, grounding, chewing him out about things that certainly were not that important."

Dad choked up and had to stop and regain his composure, it took a minute. I couldn't believe what I was hearing. My Paw Paw was not the perfect man, the man who taught me people skills, how to get along, show love, be helpful and gracious. This was the man who dedicated his life to me, and raised me with affection and gentleness, always there, always patient, always teaching and encouraging. How could he have been someone else with my father? I didn't speak. I reached across the table and placed my hand over his and squeezed, softly.

He continued. "I'm sure it didn't take long before he didn't even want me home. We were never close and he grew up hating me. We were supposed to go to a concert together that night, Dora, Joseph, and Nan, your mother. He and I had an argument, it got emotional, Dora stepped in to defend him, and I said some horrible things, to both of them. I stayed home and they went on without me. Three hours later, the police were knocking on my door with news of the accident, an eighteen wheeler jackknifed out of control. They were all killed.

"You were with a baby sitter. I had to go and get you, then, that night, with all that on my mind. You were eleven weeks old, Joey. I remember sitting there in that rocking chair, feeding you with a bottle, looking at you. And I saw your father in you. I cried, hard and deep, my body shook with grief, not only for my lost family, but also for how I'd lived my life, the relationships I'd wasted. And I saw myself, I mean I really took a good long look at myself, my flaws were exposed like open wounds, and I begged God to help me do it right this time."

He went silent, he wiped away a tear with his free hand, and looked down. I wasn't sure he was finished so I didn't speak right away. He looked up, and back down. I squeezed his hand again.

"You did." He looked at me and I smiled at him. "Dad, you did do it right this time."

"God, I love you, son. You're my second chance." He said, almost under his breath. He was fighting back tears, and losing the fight.

I had to say something but it was hard to know what, so I just spoke my mind. "Well Dad, you know, it's hard to know my hero wasn't always perfect, but nothing could change how much I love you." I remembered Anita telling me I needed to spend some time with my Dad, something she had read in how he was missing me, afraid of losing me. Boy, was she right. "Dad, you'll never lose me. I'll always be near you, I promise."

Since he was baring his soul to me, I wanted to ask about his military service and why he always refused to talk about it, why he stood on the sidelines of the welcome home parade for the veterans, but I didn't think I should. Maybe I was afraid of what the answer might be. But it was impossible to get around this man's perceptiveness, he knew a question was perched on the edge of my mind.

"What, son?"

"No, it's nothing."

"Go ahead, while I'm in a confessing mood, ask."

I hesitated, made eye contact, looked across the dining room for a diversion. "Well, Dad, if this is inappropriate just say so and I'll drop it." Again, I hesitated, unsure and apprehensive. "It's just that, well, I know a few things about your war experiences, I know you were a hero at times, but, why…" I didn't know how to continue, I couldn't form the question, but I'd said enough for him to get my point.

"It's really nothing personal, Joey, no hidden skeletons or shameful acts…"

He was having difficulty with this and I was sorry I had asked. I started to retract my question but he waved me off and continued.

"Joey, war is about death, it's about which side can kill the most people on the other side. And it is a shameful way for governments to settle their differences. I can't remember any good times from that war. I remember only death, the sight of death all around, young men, all so pointless, the smell of death, that awful smell of gunpowder and blood and spilled intestines... And the sounds of death; guns and bombs, and the screaming and crying... Even the young men who were the enemy, just young men doing what their government told them to do, young men with homes and families and lives. War is not something to celebrate, even in victory; it is something to get behind you, to forget about, to get over. And the dreams, Joey, the dreams, as if the whole terrible experience wasn't enough, I've relived the horror a thousand times in dreams; the death, the screams, the bombs, the devastation. Joey, I hope you never go to war. There is nothing right about it, it makes evil men rich and powerful, and it makes innocent people dead. You needed to know and that's okay, but that's the last time I'll speak of it."

"I'm sorry, Dad. I shouldn't have..."

"No, don't, it's okay son, really."

The drive home started out quiet and a little uncomfortable. Amos showed up in the rear view mirror and spoke to me. "Talk to him, Joey. He needs you now more than ever." I had no idea what to say, but once I got started, it flowed.

"Dad, you know, I've seen you in my dreams, young, and at different stages in your life. I know that you grew up in the depression when life was about survival, and I know that your own grandfather and father were strict and quick to discipline. And I know that a lot of history goes into making someone who they turn out to be, much of it early history that's hard to overcome later in life. And I know that you were thrown right into some of the worst of the World War II battles. I know that left lasting scars on you. Who knows why things happen like they do? How could you have been expected to turn out perfect and all-knowing? But when you accepted the challenge of raising me, Dad, you became that perfect and all-knowing father. That's who you'll always be to me, that's why I'll always love you, just as you are."

Dad shot me a weak smile mixed with watery eyes, and he looked away again, out the side window. After a short silence he looked over at me and touched my shoulder.

"When it came to you, son, I had good material to work with, and a lot of hard lessons already under my belt. Joey, for the past fifteen years you've been my whole reason..." He choked up and looked away again.

Amos smiled and nodded, and faded away. I knew we had said all we needed to, all we ever needed to say on that subject. "Well Dad, did you get some good ideas for your coupe? I saw you looking at ghost flames and paint jobs and custom interiors."

He seized the opportunity to move to a light hearted subject. "Some good ideas, yes, but no real decisions yet. I still like a black primer finish but maybe go a little fancy on the interior. I'll be glad when you're back from Houston and can help me more with it."

"I'm glad you went with the Mercury flathead engine, that's the right engine for that car, and they dress up real nice too."

"Yeah Joey, a lot of parts are being remanufactured for them now. I've got a set of high compression chromed heads ordered and chrome water pipes and Laker style headers, I've always wanted to build a hot rod, just a raw 50s style hot rod."

Things that needed to be said, had been said, and now they needed to be put to rest. We had done all of that and now moved to happier things with no damage done.

When we neared Las Casas I called Anita to let her know we were on our way. We picked her up at her house and drove on to mine. Dad went in to take a nap and Anita and I headed for the river to go tubing, tubes hanging out of Mattie's rumble seat. We took Sparky too, he loved the river, and he loved riding in my lap floating down the cool water in the summer sun, jumping in once in a while to cool off, then climbing back onto my lap. I had to help him back up or he'd scratch me. We went to a movie that night and later made love in my car.

Saturday night brought dreams of Shawn and Mattie. Shawn was hand painting Mattie's name on her doors in tall gold lettering and it was striking against the bright red finish. He was almost finished with one side when he dropped his paint brush to the garage floor and fell to his knees clutching the right side of his head. His tumor was back. I watched as he struggled to his feet and sat on Mattie's running board, still cradling his head.

"No, not now, please." He pleaded with God to not let this be what he feared it was.

As the pain eased a little, Shawn retrieved his brush, cleaned it with a rag, and moved around to the other door to continue his lettering. He was talented like an artist, printing Mattie's name freehand style in large script. It looked professional. He finished up the second door, put his tools and supplies away and sat inside his car. I could tell pain was still shooting thru his head, but the real pain was in his heart as his mind went through the treatments and sickness he knew were coming. He'd been through this before, and gone into remission, or so they thought. Now it was back. He would keep this to himself for now, at least until it got worse, there was nothing they could do about it anyway, surgery was not an option and the treatments had made him so sick.

Sunday I shared a nice home cooked breakfast with Dad, I'd been missing that tradition in Houston, and a friend from church had given us some deer sausage so Dad scrambled it in with the eggs. It was a good diversion from our usual meal of bacon and fried or scrambled eggs. We sat and talked a while but not about the money or other things he had revealed to me the day before. Our conversation was mostly about NASA and my job there. What we talked about wasn't important at all, the time together was, starting our day together, and I realized how I'd missed that. He felt the same way, I could tell.

I spent the rest of the day with Anita, and we were sunburned from the previous day at the river so we stayed inside most of the day. We played video games, she helped me clean Mattie out in the shop and later we went to see a movie where we gorged on hot dogs and buttered popcorn. By late Sunday afternoon it was time for me to hit the road for Houston and I didn't want to go. I told Dad I thought I could make the trip each weekend without a problem but he didn't want me on the road after dark and added that half my weekend would be taken up driving. So I said my goodbyes to Dad and Anita for two weeks. This time I took the journal with me and this time I dreamed of Mattie while in Houston. I don't know if those two things had anything to do with each other or not but I suspect they did.

Monday morning I was back at work with Sam Garza. Coffee cups in hands, we made small talk about the weekend for a few minutes and then got right to work. I was measuring our precise amounts of liquid materials for Sam to try again to get his composite to bond and stay bonded. I held a beaker up to the light and Shawn's words came to me like a voice from the clouds. "Look to the cleaning solutions." I could see faint streaks on the glass. Now, how would Shawn know?

"Sam," I asked, still peering thru the beaker. "Do you think something they clean these with could be causing our problems? Maybe in the heating or blending stage or something?"

Sam walked over to me, took the beaker to see what I saw. "Oh, well, I don't think so, Joey. Our people who clean for us use only approved solutions. Still though, he examined the glass closely in the light of the overhead fluorescents.

"What about when we get these new, though? Do we clean them before we use them?"

Sam hesitated in thought for a moment. "Well, they're supposed to be sterile but, let's get some of these tested, just to make sure."

Sam called Mr. Fletcher in and shared my suspicion with him and all the new glassware was sent for testing. Later in the day we were advised that trace amounts of ammonia and lye were detected and were indeed suspected for the cause of Sam's problems. A new policy was implemented and new glassware was to be cleaned in house before being used.

I was given credit for the discovery and though it felt good, I knew I wasn't the one who first realized the source of the contamination. The praise and recognition were nice though, and I couldn't wait for evening when I could call Dad and tell him.

That night I dreamed about Shawn, hiding his pain from his family, and preparing Mattie for the races. He was anxious to see how she would perform with her V-12 engine and I had forgotten he had never seen her race. Shawn was in for a surprise. My alarm clock ended the dream with Mattie loaded on a trailer, ready to go racing.

The next day the bonding of Sam's concoction held and we felt that the problem was solved. He and Mr. Fletcher mused at what a fresh perspective could do to solve a dilemma. It had been so simple but they had been looking for a complicated answer. After that, Sam's project moved ahead, and it could have been my imagination, but it sure seemed to me that from that point on I was trusted with more complex tasks.

That night after talking on the phone to Anita for an hour and Dad for a half an hour, and tired of TV, I dug the journal out of my still packed suitcase and wrote about Shawn giving me the solution to Sam's laboratory problem. With the book across my chest, I drifted off to sleep, and I dreamed. Though Shawn's headaches became more frequent and painful, he said nothing to his family about them. He was so nearly finished with Mattie he didn't want to stop or even think about the interruption or perhaps even the end to his life that might be coming soon. He had her V-12 in place and detailed and running smooth, her deep red paint job and new interior were finished and beautiful, and MATTIE painted in gold letters on her doors was the perfect finishing touch.

Mattie was on her way to the races with Shawn's entire family in tow, he had his own cheering section. I enjoyed the closeness of the Remington family, the way they always did things together, and the appreciation they all showed for Mattie. She was like a family pet to them, when any of them came to visit, the first thing they wanted to do was to run to the garage and see what was new or different about Mattie.

His oldest son, Jay, and Jay's son, Ian, rode with and accompanied Shawn and Mattie to the pits to help. They were new to this and it showed. When asked to give a dial in time, Shawn had no idea what to declare, so he guessed he might turn around thirteen seconds, realizing from the roll cage the car was probably pretty fast or at least had been at one time.

The burn out scared him, he'd never felt raw power like that before, and he had trouble keeping Mattie straight on the track. Traction was the issue to deal with, but then it usually is, many drag races are won or lost at the starting line.

At the green light he eased out, riding the clutch a little, while his opponent, a '28 Ford roadster with a V-8 flathead, shot off the line to take the lead by several lengths. But the roadster's lead didn't last long because Mattie finally got traction and took off like a cannon shot. Mattie's overwhelming power frightened Shawn all the way down the track and he missed third gear which slowed him down some but he still won the race by four car lengths with a time of 13.88 seconds and a speed of 107.22 mph. I believe that particular run down the track still holds the distinction of being the worst executed one I've ever witnessed.

The second run was a little better with Shawn doing a longer and more controlled burn out which got the slicks hot and sticky which let Mattie come off the line stronger and she actually pulled her front wheels off the pavement by a foot or more. This run Shawn shifted quicker and with more accuracy and they turned a time of 12.1 seconds and a speed of 118.21 mph.

Back at the pits, a crowd gathered around Mattie as other racers wanted to know what powered this car and a track official came over to warn Shawn that he had exceeded his dial in time and if he cut anymore time off his next run he'd be disqualified. It appeared that Mattie was in the wrong class for a fair competition. Shawn explained that is was his first time out with the car and he didn't know what to expect from it, he'd just run all out and accept the consequences, he'd know better the next race night. And in the next race, Shawn gained a feel for the car and Mattie just flat screamed, turning an eleven point three second time at one hundred twenty six miles per hour. It was a beautiful sight.

Mattie and Shawn were disqualified for the night, but happily so. For the second time, I had witnessed Mattie get disqualified for being too fast. The irony amused me, a race car being thrown out of the races for being too fast.

For the remainder of the night, Shawn and his family were spectators, sitting around Mattie in the pits, watching the races. Other racers and crew members came by to look and talk and satisfy their curiosity about this candy apple red, with yellow and gold and blue flames, '34 Buick coupe that ran like a dragster. An offer to buy was made but Shawn was hopelessly in love with Mattie and refused to even discuss price. Amos came to my mind, his night with Mattie at the races when Royce wanted to buy her.

I awoke happy for Mattie, she had her name back and a nice owner and was doing what she loved, drag racing. I glanced at my alarm clock on the table by my bed and saw that it was a few minutes before four in the morning, too early to get up yet, by a couple of hours. I thought about breakfast, I thought about the restaurant downstairs, and I missed Dad's breakfast. I wished I was lying in my bed at home with Sparky beside me under the covers and smelling and hearing Dad in the kitchen cooking eggs and bacon, and maybe some whole wheat biscuits.

The journal was lying beside me on the bed where it had slid off my chest earlier when I fell asleep and I realized how often that happened, falling asleep while writing Mattie's history and drifting into more of the continuing story only to awake and repeat the cycle. So I started to write what I had just seen, and again, I fell asleep, and back into the dreams about my car.

Only this time, the dream was not of Shawn, it was of me, driving Mattie really fast in some strange place; country roads, flat country, not hilly like around home. Anita sat beside me wide eyed and scared. Police were chasing us, a helicopter was hovering and buzzing. The helicopter dipped low beside us, the wind from it was making it hard to keep Mattie straight on the road. I looked at the speedometer and we were going 92 mph. I looked over at the helicopter keeping pace with us and flying almost at ground level and the man on the passenger side looked at us through binoculars. He looked right at me, shook his head, talked into the microphone built into his helmet. Then the chopper quickly rose straight up and hurried away off to one side and the police cars behind us slowed and fell back, eventually taking another road and disappearing in some other direction.

"What's going on, Joey? Why did they stop?" Anita's frightened voice pleaded for an explanation.

Amos' face appeared in the rear view mirror and he threw his head back and gave a hearty laugh and his gold tooth sparkled.

"I don't know, 'nita. Maybe they're going to set up a road block up ahead somewhere, we'd better change roads as soon as we can."

I awoke with a jump that threatened to dump me off the edge of the bed. What the heck was that? It didn't make any sense at all. The dream didn't fit Shawn's story and it didn't reflect anything in my life either. It troubled me. I got up and went to the rest room, looked at myself in the mirror. The dream meant something, I was sure, but I had no clue what. I threw on pants and a tee shirt and made my way down to the parking lot, rounded the corner just in time to see Mattie's cover slide off of her onto the pavement. Was somebody bothering her? I trotted over to inspect, my bare feet hurting on loose pieces of gravel. No one was around, it was still dark and only dim light shone from the few very tall lamps in the parking lot.

"What is it, girl?" I asked, as I pushed the unlock button on my remote control. Mattie's horn sounded two quick toots, her lights flashed on and off twice, and her door popped open for me. "Shhh." I cautioned as I slid onto her seat.

Amos appeared in the mirror and he smiled and spoke. "Trust in Mattie, Joey. She'll take care o' ya when ya needs her to."

"What? What do you mean? Wait! No, wait, Amos! Aw man, why do you do that?"

Amos faded. Mattie's dash lights flashed and her radio played, quite loudly, an old Elvis Presley song. "The warden threw a party in the county jail. The prison band was there and they began to wail. The band was jumpin' and the joint began to swing. You should have heard the knocked out jailbirds sing. Let's rock, everybody let's rock, everybody in the whole cell block, was dancin' to the jailhouse rock. Spider Murphy played the tenor saxophone. Little Joe was blowin' on the slide trombone. The drummer boy from Illinois went crash, boom, bang. The whole rhythm section was a purple gang. Let's rock, everybody..."

I tried to turn the volume down but it wouldn't cooperate. "Mattie, you're going to wake everybody up!" The music stopped. I slumped forward and rested my head on her steering wheel. "What's going on, Mattie? Am I going to get into some kind of trouble with the police?" It was all very disturbing. I covered her up and returned to my room, sure that I couldn't go back to sleep, afraid to, actually. But I was wrong. I immediately fell asleep and back into Shawn's world. Shawn had a rough night too, actually mine was nothing compared to his. His head was pounding and he got up in the night to take something for the pain, and he fell, out cold, hitting his head on the bathroom door knob on his way down. The noise woke his wife and she hurried to him. She couldn't wake him, she couldn't move him, and she was terrified. Minutes later an ambulance sped away with Shawn, still unconscious.

My work dragged on through Thursday and nights brought vague pieces of dreams and I grew homesick. I saw Mattie sitting in the garage in quiet solitude, at least she got to go to the races before Shawn's health problems took over. And Shawn, I saw Shawn lying in a hospital bed, his wife and others from his family hovering over him, all looking very worried. He was awake now, barely, head bandaged, tubes running in and out of him, and they were begging him to go through the treatments the doctor was recommending but he was refusing to do it.

The year was 1958 in Shawn's world, and I wondered just how effective cancer treatments were then. It didn't matter though, he wasn't going to take them. He'd tried all that before and all it accomplished, as far as he was concerned, was to make him very sick. If he was going to die, he reasoned, he should die doing things that make him happy and "not lying in a hospital bed sick as shit trying to stop the inevitable." He did agree to some oral medications for the symptoms and the next day he went home. Shawn was not home ten minutes before he was in the garage tinkering with Mattie.

"Why don't you come in and rest, dear?" His wife pleaded through the screen door.

"No, that's all I've been doing for a week. I've got to get Mattie ready for the races this weekend."

"The races this weekend? Shawn! No! The doctor told you not to drive. What if you pass out going down the track a hundred miles per hour?"

Shawn looked his worried wife right in the eye and smiled. "Honey, I've got a feeling this car knows its way down the track, and besides, it only takes a few seconds to go from one end to the other."

Disgust and worry written across her face, she frowned hard at him and turned around for a hasty exit. Shawn hummed an old Buddy Holley tune, maybe it wasn't that old then, and he turned back to his work on Mattie.

I was allowed to leave work a couple of hours early Thursday afternoon. They were so nice to me there, probably because I was so young. I had thrown the journal and my dirty laundry in my car that morning when I left the motel for work, so now I was ready to just hit the road. I was anxious to get home, anxious to see Anita and to touch her and to make love with her, anxious to see my Dad and my dog and to sleep in my own bed and work in our shop. I wanted to be home and I wanted to stay there and not go back to Houston or anywhere else.

If I was to learn anything from this experience, it was that I loved my home and that was where I wanted to be. I did not want to live in the city, any city, I did not want to work for NASA or anyone else, I wanted to live at home and build cars. At that moment I didn't even want to continue my education, but I was sure that I would. Anyway, if I did not earn a degree I would not start collecting my inheritance till I turned thirty, and I planned to marry Anita in a little more than a year, so I needed to stay on plan, for now.

On my way out of Houston I spotted a helicopter overhead, it was one of those that report traffic conditions on the radio and television, but it reminded me of that strange dream of being chased by the cops. And every time I saw a police officer on the road I thought about it. But I could never make any kind of connection, it didn't make any sense.

By the time I pulled up in front of Anita's house it was nearly eight p.m. and she was sitting on the front steps waiting for me. I had called her from my cell phone when I had battled through the heavy San Antonio traffic and was on our side of the city. I bailed out of Mattie and I met Anita in a hug on the sidewalk, halfway between her house and the street. We went inside and visited with her parents briefly and then headed for my house. Sparky jumped into my arms, licking and whining and Dad and I hugged with Sparky between us.

Anita and I had planned to take in a movie that night but Dad was ready to install his freshly overhauled Mercury flathead V-8 engine in his coupe so we offered to help him. That turned out to be more fun than a movie anyway. Anita was good at operating the electronically controlled engine hoist, and indeed it required an operator with a soft touch, sometimes the heavy cumbersome engine hanging from chains needed to be moved just a quarter of an inch in some direction for the bolt to line up with a hole, or a line with a fitting, and the movement needed to be slow and controlled, not jerky and not producing a swinging back and forth motion. So Anita ran the hoist while Dad and I bolted things together and we had the engine installed in the car by around ten thirty that night. That's all we planned to do with the car that night. Connecting fuel lines and vacuum hoses and electrical harnesses would be time consuming and require long term concentration, tasks better left till the next day when we would be fresh.

We stood back and admired our work and the little hot rod was indeed coming together nicely. The engine we had just installed looked like it belonged there, it was right for the car. Dad had added a nice chrome dress up kit to the old style power plant and it was a work of art.

Anita was supposed to be home by eleven and she called and told her Dad what we had been doing and begged him for another hour. We declined an invitation from Dad to let him "whip up a late night supper" for us. We had something else on our minds. Before leaving the shop in Mattie, we scrubbed the mechanic's grime off our hands and arms in the big shop sink. Anita had a grease smear across her right cheek and another on her forehead and I liked the way she looked with it so I didn't tell her.

Later, after making love, lying there together naked on the car seat, I just stared at her face, thinking she was the sexiest grease monkey I'd ever seen. We talked. Unimportant stuff at first, things that had happened with each of us for the past two weeks. I told her about Shawn in the dreams, his brain cancer returning, Mattie's success at the races and getting disqualified that time for going too fast, but I didn't tell her about the dream with the cops chasing us. I confessed to Anita that I was sure I didn't want to work at NASA after college, or anywhere else away from home. She asked what I'd do to make a living then. I was tempted to tell her about the inheritance but I remembered Dad's warning about that so I didn't mention it. I told her that I wanted to build custom cars, maybe race cars, for a living.

Anita bumped her forehead to mine and whispered, "I'm sure whatever you do, you'll be a success at it."

She talked about summer school and her classes and grades. She told me about her little sister who wanted to start dating at thirteen years old and her daddy wouldn't allow it, and the fights those two were having about it. Sarah was strong willed like her daddy and the two butted heads often. Sarah pointed out to her dad that Anita had a boyfriend at twelve (although it was actually thirteen by a few weeks), and according to Anita, John told Sarah if she could find another boy like Joey she could date him. That brought a smile to my already contented face.

We made love again.

We arrived at Anita's house eight minutes before her curfew, sat on the front steps and talked for another hour. Within seconds after we sat down, John turned on the porch light but he did not come outside.

Dreams that night were calm but spotty, Shawn rubbed down Mattie's new paint job since it now had had a few days to cure, and he waxed her paint and chrome and she shined so pretty. I began to wonder where her old discarded parts were, her hood side skirts and bumpers, her continental kit spare tire holder, all left behind, perhaps laying around outside someone's shop with them wondering what they belonged to. Maybe the ones we took from Frank's junk pile didn't really belong to Mattie.

Shawn worked on Mattie but sat down to take a break every few minutes, held his hurting head, but never complained to anyone. I wondered just how bad the pain was. I admired him, going on with his life on a day to day basis, determined to enjoy, in spite of the fact that his ailment was sure to be fatal.

Saturday morning I awoke to that smell of breakfast cooking that I had missed so much while in Houston and I leapt from bed, startling Sparky with the sudden motion, and got myself to the kitchen as quickly as I could. I sat at the serving bar and sipped coffee, a new habit I'd picked up at work, and enjoyed a relaxed chat with Dad about his little deuce coupe and the work that it still needed. And except for making love with Anita, I do believe that was the most enjoyable moment of my weekend. Dad was having a lot of fun with this project, and listening to him talk about it, I thought about what he'd always said about restoring a car - that it was about the journey, not the destination, like life itself. It is amazing to me, how one misses the little things, like this, this unhurried moment that would give the day such a nice beginning, things that become half noticed rituals in everyday life, but things that are pulled away when life changes. I decided I did not like change.

While Dad verbally lined out for me his agenda and time line for the coupe, I half listened and my mind wandered back to his admission that day in the Mexican food restaurant that he'd not been a good daddy to my father or a good husband to his wife, and I decided that he was not entirely correct about it all. One of his favorite old sayings came to my mind, "Things are never quite as good or as bad as they seem at the time." No one could change that much, to be completely one way for that many years and then just change to the opposite kind of person. He had always been that perfect man I knew for all my life, he just didn't realize it himself. That was what I decided anyway. I slipped off my stool, walked around to his side of the island and hugged him, his side turned to me, spatula in hand, standing over the cook top.

"What was that for?"

"I've missed you, Dad."

From beginning to end, the entire weekend was great. Anita and I, and Sparky, spent lots of time at the river. We helped Dad with his coupe project both days. I took Anita for a cruise out to Amos' old place, just to show it to her, but someone was doing something in the old barn so we just drove down the meandering driveway and back out to the road before they noticed us. I felt Amos' presence but didn't see him.

And all too soon, it was time to return to Houston for the last two weeks of my summer job. Sunday evening I packed my car, said my goodbyes and hit the road. Sparky saw me packing and he knew I was leaving again and he stuck by me like a shadow. If I sat down he jumped in my lap. If I walked from one room to another he was right there under foot. I gave him a nice long goodbye, stroking him and talking to him and assured him I'd be back. Dad said something about how old Sparky was getting and for the first time I noticed it in his face and coat, a little gray creeping in, especially around his muzzle. I believe Sparky was about ten at the time.

I had picked Sparky out of a litter at a neighbor's house when I was five or six years old. I was riding bicycles with a friend, and there were all these puppies in a short round wire pen in a front yard, a lady sitting in one of those fold up aluminum and nylon yard chairs, a sign that said, "Free Puppies". I stepped over the wire into the pen and the runt chose me immediately, he was all over me. I picked him up, he licked me in the face and squirmed and whined. I put him down and he tried to climb up my leg. I stepped back out of the pen and he sat down and howled at me. I pleaded with the lady to hold him for me and I peddled home as fast as I could. I hurriedly drug Paw Paw by the hand down three blocks and begged for the puppy I'd already picked out.

I arrived at my motel about sunset, covered Mattie and took my things to my room. After settling in I called, first Dad, and then Anita, to let them know I had completed the trip with no problems. I had not slept much through the weekend and it was catching up to me now.

Though it was only about eight thirty and not quite dark outside yet, I changed into my pajamas and settled in under the covers, missing Sparky next to me there. After just a few minutes of trying to catch up with my writing in the journal, I fell asleep, and dreams of Shawn wasted no time in taking over my slumber.

Shawn and Mattie were at the races, his personal cheering section in place in the stands, two sons in the pits with him. Shawn was hurting but doing a decent job of concealing it. Now Mattie was perched on the starting line, dialed in this time at eleven seconds flat to avoid another disqualification. As the lights gave the green signal for the racers, Shawn's head rolled forward and he passed out. Mattie lunged ahead, jerking her front wheels off the pavement by a foot and a half, her best wheel stand yet and as she sat them back down she power shifted to second gear and jerked her right front wheel up again clearing the ground by several inches, shifted to third and gained momentum. Mattie shifted to fourth gear and promptly crossed the finish line several lengths ahead of her opponent. And she stopped. Her engine slowed to a throaty idle and she sat motionless, just beyond the end of the quarter mile mark.

The lighted sign flashed 9.8 seconds, 131.7 mph and cheers rose from the stands and pits. I immediately realized that this equaled Jim Cox's best time in Mattie years prior. But the excitement died down as it became apparent something was wrong. Mattie didn't move. She didn't continue on thru the turn around and back down the return lane. She just sat there. Shawn's sons took off running down the track and were quickly picked up by the track tow truck and taken to Mattie. Shawn was unconscious, still strapped into the seat, head laying over to one side, arms and hands hanging limp. No one but me realized it but Mattie made that run without Shawn's help, he was out for the entire ride.

Minutes later Shawn was on his way to the hospital in a screaming, speeding ambulance followed by two cars containing his family. Mattie sat in the pits behind her trailer, having been driven there by another racer who was willing to help. Mattie was to be disqualified again for outrunning her dial in time by more than a second, but that was not important at the moment. It would be after midnight before anyone would return to load Mattie up and take her home, by then she was alone in the lot. I was afraid somebody would mess with her, and a little afraid of what she might do to them if they tried, but they didn't, and she looked lonely.

For my last two weeks at NASA work was robotic and repetitive and through most of it my mind turned to my dreams which filled each night. Shawn had to have the surgery which would probably kill him, because without it now, there was no probably, he would die, the pressure on his brain was too great. The surgery was only a partial success, the doctors were only able to remove part of the mass without damaging brain tissue and after the operation Shawn went into a coma for several days and hope for recovery faded.

Family members constantly in and out, always a couple of them there with him, but Charley, his daughter hovered day and night, praying, crying, and reading to her father though she didn't have a clue if he heard any of it. Once in a while Shawn would stir a little or move an arm or leg or his eyes might flutter as if trying to open, but he slept. The surgeon said if he didn't regain consciousness soon, he might never.

Jay, the oldest son, discussed an idea with Charley. It seemed farfetched but anything was worth a try. An hour later she heard the agreed signal of three quick horn honks followed by a pause and one more honk and she moved over to the window and opened it. Mattie was right outside and her engine raced several times, loudly, and with Jay at the controls. She did one hell of a burn out right there in the hospital parking lot. Jay took Mattie out onto the street and ran her thru the gears hard, making all the noise he could. Angry hospital staff poured out the front doors to see who was uncaring enough to raise such a commotion in a quiet hospital zone. Mattie turned back into the parking lot and settled into a parking space, her nice throaty exhaust rumbling out a fast idle that filtered in thru Shawn's open window.

Shawn's eyes opened to a squint, blinked, and he muttered, "Mattie! I hear Mattie! How'd we do?"

Tears burst from Charlie's eyes. "Nine point eight seconds, Daddy. You got disqualified for going too fast again."

Shawn mustered a weak smile and his head rolled to one side. Charley ran to the hall to call for help.

The last weekend I had to stay in Houston turned out to be the best. I had struck up a few casual friendships around work, mostly from break times in the coffee room, as it was called, and Bill Jordon had mentioned a car museum so he and I toured it Saturday. We spent hours there enjoying antique cars, factory muscle cars and retired racers. Sunday, Sam threw a going away party for me at his house with the back yard full of people from work, and their families.   It was a little early, I still had another week of work, but they knew it was now or never since I'd certainly not stick around after next Friday.

So that weekend didn't drag on like the others with me hanging around my motel room wishing I was home. Mr. Fletcher announced to the small crowd of NASA employees who were at the party, about my discovery of the contamination source and I received a round of applause. Sam admitted that at first he was sure this was just going to be a pain in the ass six week babysitting session that he didn't have time for but that as it quickly turned out, I became a very welcome and competent contributor to his project and he wished I could stay and work with him longer. I was flattered and embarrassed with the praise.

Shawn remained conscious, made steady improvement, graduated to rehab within a few days and went home a couple of weeks later. "Now go home and rest." The doctor warned. "Take it easy, do your therapy exercises but not much else. You need to stay calm and not exert yourself too much." When he added, "And don't try to drive for at least a month." Shawn's wife laughed out loud. "Now, why is that funny?" The doctor queried.

"He'll be in his race car at the drag races Saturday night, if I know this stubborn man."

"Is that right?" The doctor shot an irritated glare at Shawn, but all he got from Shawn was a sheepish smile and a slight nod and the doctor left the room shaking his head. But what did he know? What I knew, and what Shawn knew, at least deep down inside, was that Mattie contained more healing power than that entire hospital. And indeed she had worked her magic on Shawn. By his next checkup, three weeks after leaving the hospital, Shawn had been to the races twice and won trophies in Mattie and he had made the most remarkable recovery the doctors had ever seen. Shawn refused further tests and treatments.

My last week at work dragged on, Sam and I put his heat shield concoction through the torture tests. It held together now and was ready for production, at least in an amount sufficient to use in a real live situation. And finally my last day at work was over and I was on my way home. I may have been able to work and study and even interact at a higher level, but I was a fifteen year old kid with a hot rod and a girlfriend, and a wonderful life in a small town. The Houston NASA experience provided a lot of lessons for me, not the least of which was the reality of how much I loved my life just as it was. But along with that reality, I think, came a certain naïve assumption that at home in Las Casas things would be immune to change, just because I wanted them to be.

Anita and I finished out the summer spending our time swimming and tubing in the local river, and helping Dad with his deuce coupe. In late August I turned fifteen and Anita resumed her high school education at Las Casas High School with enough credits to put her deep into her junior year instead of just beginning her sophomore year as was supposed to be the case. I returned to the Alice Warhead Foundation for Advanced Academic Achievement to continue my pursuit of a college degree in Chemistry. It was good to get back, it felt right, normal, and I was anxious to relate my NASA experience to Dr. Larson with whom I had had only brief telephone conversations during the six weeks. However, I could not tell him that I had discovered in myself a profound dislike for the city, and large crowds of people, and time clocks, and deadlines. The Foundation was investing in me with every expectation that I would seek a career in their industry.

Dreams began to come with less frequency but somehow passed thru time at a quicker pace. I watched Shawn recover his health and stamina, and race Mattie on a regular basis and I recorded it all in the journal.

For several days after I returned home for the final time from Houston, Sparky was a little shadow, following and being all clingy and watching suspiciously for signs of another departure.

And I have to admit, to sleep in my own bed in my own room with my little dog all snuggled up under the covers next to me was something old for which I had found a new appreciation.

NASA had paid me some sort of union scale wage, and I had

three – two week paychecks which I had not cashed and which amounted to a little over four thousand dollars after taxes. My normal allowance from my Dad was one hundred dollars per week and from that I bought my own gas and paid for whatever Anita and I wanted to do around town like movies and snacks and things. Somehow I managed to spend it all, but now I had a nice lump sum that would buy something special. To deposit the four thousand in my savings seemed silly since I now knew I had millions in some kind of an account somewhere, and saving for college any more was pointless since I was already more than half way through that and it was free anyway, so I decided to do something for Mattie with my summer job money.

My announcement to Dad that I wanted to buy Mattie a set of racing slicks, lower rear gears and a hotter ignition so I could take her to the drag races in San Antonio was met with a mischievous smile. He started to speak, but changed his mind. He walked over to the stack of catalogues on a shelf in a corner of the shop and grabbed a couple of them to begin our hunt for racing equipment for Mattie. I had not been sure what his reaction would be to my racing idea or to spending the money and I was quite relieved that he was in favor of this little adventure I proposed. His only negative input at all was to warn me of the disadvantage my manual four speed would suffer in getting off the line against cars with built up automatic transmissions with trans-brakes. I was so excited I wasn't about to let anything discourage me. After having watched Mattie storm down the track, setting records and taking trophies in decade's worth of dreams, I was ready to take my place on the list of racers she had thrilled.

And something else, I had watched every one of Mattie's former owners, well the ones who loved her anyway, customize her in some way; Amos had changed her paint color from brown to black and installed dual carburetors and dual exhaust and hydraulic brakes, Jim Cox had given her a custom drive train from front to rear, Shawn had changed her entire color scheme and added flames, and ghosts that I had not yet met had chopped and shaved her body and painted it yellow with Hell Flames.

I wanted to do something for Mattie that would be my signature on her, I wanted to suicide her doors, turn them around so that they hinged on the back side and opened from the front. Again, Dad was supportive but warned that such an endeavor done correctly would challenge my skills and possibly take them to another level. That thought only fueled my excitement about customizing Mattie with my own two hands.

Later, when I was alone with Mattie, I asked her what she thought about my plans. Of course I was just actually talking to myself, not expecting a reaction from her. But she answered immediately by blaring out an old song on her radio, an old Beatles song. "Baby you can drive my car, yes I'm gonna be a star, Baby you can drive my car, 'cause Baby I love you, beep beep n beep beep yeah, beep beep n beep beep yeah." She switched her radio off and flashed her lights. I laughed, happy with her acceptance of my customizing plans.

Later that day, I realized that for the first time, Dad and I were working in the shop on different projects. When that fact first occurred to me, I stopped what I was doing and stood up straight, I was over six feet tall now, and I gazed at Dad.

He felt my eyes on him and returned my look. "Let me know if you need help with something, son."

"Sure Dad, in a couple of minutes here, when I get the hinge bolts out, I'll need help moving the door to the stands." It was difficult to pull my eyes away from him. It was just one of those moments.

Reversing the opening direction of Mattie's doors involved cutting and welding and fabricating and even patching. Electrical work was necessary too; since the wiring for the automatic door controls came from the front, the wiring had to be redirected to enter the door cavity from the rear, where the new hinges would be mounted. I had to remove some of the interior to do that, well okay, just about all of it, the seat and the carpet, there's not much more to Mattie's interior than that.

The first cut was the most difficult, I would have rather cut myself. I was bent over the door which was resting on the parts stands, safety goggles and gloves on, I knew how to do this, I had done body work before, but when the cutting wheel touched the metal, sparks flew and paint burned and I dropped the drill and jumped back. "Shit!" That was the first time I had used any swear word in the presence of Dad and I quickly looked for his reaction.

He was sanding his coupe, readying it for paint, he looked up and pulled his dust mask off, walked over and picked up my drill. "You're not causing Mattie any physical pain, Joey." He laughed and handed the drill to me.

I felt awkward. "No, it's uh, it's just, it's going to damage the paint more than I figured it would. Look, it gets so hot, so quick."

Dad reminded me that we knew the cutting and welding was going to do some damage and also that we knew how to paint and we knew someone who could match the flames.

We took a break, at his suggestion, and sat on our stools and sipped on Dr. Peppers. Dad advised me to place a wet towel on the door near my cutting, to stop the flow of heat. When I got back to work I tried his idea and it helped a lot.

While I modified Mattie in my world in late 1994, Shawn raced Mattie in 1959 and on through the early sixties. I was busy making her my custom car and she was busy showing me more of her history. Royce called Shawn and told him that he had acquired, from Jim's estate, dozens of Mattie's racing trophies and some old original body parts. Shawn was eager to keep all of it with Mattie and he retrieved a trailer load. During the brief meeting, Shawn described for Royce his new color scheme for Mattie and joyfully related his racing experiences with her. Royce seemed happy to hear that Mattie was doing well, and staying out of trouble, but I could see troubling memories in his eyes.

Nearly three dozen racing trophies were reunited with Mattie, including the one Amos had won. That was a nice surprise, Amos must have left it in her and it just stayed there when his son sold her to Royce. Those boxes of trophies that had come from Frank's, now I wanted to go through them, don't know why I had not done that already. I was especially interested in the one from Amos' night of racing her and when I found it I just sat and stared at it. The brass plaque was engraved, "C-2 STOCK CHAMPION, 1934 Buick, San Antonio Drag Raceway, 8-11-42". I cleaned it with a damp rag and carefully placed it in Mattie right behind the seat, in the floor of the rumble seat, where I intended for it to remain forever.

Now I had both of Mattie's doors off and laying on work stands, one almost finished except for the necessary paint touch ups, the other I had not yet started. I hated to have Mattie not running, or at least in a non-drivable state, that was the worst part of the project. But the thrill of customizing her myself overrode all that. And she would be down for a while, the body and electrical work would take weeks.

Two weeks into the door project I had the driver side door installed and adjusted. I was connecting the wiring harness for the electric door opener, when a new ghost appeared. A woman! What? My first reaction was, oh no not another Mrs. Ferguson. However, as it turned out, this one was anything but another Mrs. Ferguson. Kim, nickname for Kimberly, was a pretty Irish looking lady with very appropriate flaming red hair, freckles, green eyes, and a strong build. Her long red hair trailed below a maroon racing helmet and she wore a fireproof racing suit, red of course. A woman raced my car! I was dumb founded, couldn't say a word. She smiled at me, a pretty smile with full red lips and straight white teeth, and she vaporized.

"No, wait!" But she was gone. I knew she'd be back, just not when. And I also knew the end of Shawn was near. That thought bothered me. Did his cancer return and kill him this time? I decided Shawn needed to remain in Mattie, I'd not let him go, even if he asked.

And Amos appeared. "Meet, Kim." He told me with a throaty chuckle. His gold tooth sparkled a reflection off the shop lights, then Amos quickly disappeared.

"Come on, Amos." I whined. "Don't just leave me hanging like that." But he did.

Dreams of the following several nights showed me Shawn's last days of racing Mattie. The year was 1965 in his world and he must have been about Dad's age, in my world. His cancer had been in remission for five or six years, but now the headaches and dizzy spells were back. And he kept it to himself, not telling his family or even his doctor. Shawn was losing weight and his wife became concerned, but he waved it off as nothing more than the result of hot summer weather.

An August Saturday night at the drag races, I was never sure where these races were, the track was not in town but out in the country away from any houses or neighborhoods. It was near Oklahoma City and not more than a twenty minute drive from Shawn's home town of Indian Hills, anyway Shawn had won each of his six races that night and was ready for the last one, and this one was for the class championship. A very low nine second time would yield a trophy. But he was hurting badly, it was all he could do to stay alert.

Shawn buckled himself in and spoke to Mattie, "One more, Mattie, give me just one more good run. And then I think it's time for me to go see Jesus." His voice was weak, he strained to speak to Mattie as he eased her to the starting line. His pain was so bad he was shaking and sweat poured from his forehead.

At the green light Mattie exploded off the line, front wheels in the air, and I saw Shawn's head fall to one side. Mattie ate up the track, pulling ahead of her opponent steadily as she slashed through her gears and flew past the finish line out front by several car lengths. 8.81 seconds, 139.52 mph, the sign flashed! Mattie rounded the turn around and cruised proudly down the return lane approaching a wild victory celebration in her pit space. But the celebration was cut short when Mattie slowed to a stop near them and popped her door open. Shawn was dead, and Mattie's engine had a loud knock, she had ruined her beautiful V-12 Rolls Royce aircraft engine, giving Shawn his last victory in record time. Her engine sputtered, hissed, and died, never to run again.

I awoke and grieved silently, for Shawn, and for Mattie. I reached one hand under the sheet and stroked Sparky as he stretched, crawled out from under the covers and jumped to the floor. I got up too and followed Sparky to the front door. While he hiked his leg on the bushes near the house I trudged mournfully to the shop, opened the door and went inside. Mattie's driver side door popped open, from the front this time, and her radio played a quick verse from an old car song. "My daddy said son, you're going to drive me to drinkin' if you don't stop drivin' that hot rod Lincoln." The guitar in the song twanged and the radio switched off and Shawn appeared, smiling, and he asked me, "How'd ya' like that last run, Joey? Do I know how to go out with a bang, or what? I'll be a legend at that track forever." He disappeared. I smiled.

Mattie was winched onto a trailer, taken home and stored in her usual space in the garage, and there she sat for nearly three years. She seemed at a dead end; engine blown, Shawn gone, not in anybody's way and nobody interested. It wasn't the first time I'd watched her sit; in a driveway, in a garage, in a field, in a shop. Sooner or later, she'd get into someone's head and they'd get to work on her. I knew it was about to happen again.

In my world, Mattie got quiet, maybe she was just enjoying life with me, enjoying the modifications I was doing to her now, but

I had no dreams of her past and saw no ghosts for a couple of weeks. At this point I had both of her doors turned around in suicide fashion and the electronic controls upgraded somewhat and working, plus I had added push button window controls. I was so proud of what I had done with her and Dad and Anita made sure to sufficiently praise my mechanical genius. So I was waiting for Mario to come and repaint the flames on the doors where I had damaged her paint with my cutting and welding. That night the dreams began.

CHAPTER 9

Roy. What? No. It was supposed to be Kim. Okay, we've got another owner that did not become one of Mattie's captives. Roy Castillo worked with Lee, Shawn's youngest son, in a downtown Houston mechanic garage, a specialty shop that built performance equipment for race cars and hot rods. Roy and Lee were good friends. Roy was a car guy, of course, an old school hot rod builder, so when Lee told him about Mattie, he wanted to see her.

One weekend Roy accompanied Lee on a visit home, back to Indian Hills, Oklahoma. Roy stepped into the garage, and it was love at first sight, and he begged Mrs. Remington to sell Mattie to him. She had thought about selling the coupe, a few times, but just couldn't do it. But now, listening to Roy talk about how much he could love a car like that, and as he went into detail about what all he would do with it while walking circles around Mattie, touching her, praising her beauty, she decided that maybe this might be an opportunity to move Shawn's prized possession to a loving new home. The very next weekend, Roy returned with a trailer and took Mattie home to Houston, Texas.

Roy's wife, Olivia, a petite and pretty Mexican lady, maybe early thirties, made no comment to him upon seeing Mattie for the first time when Roy arrived home with her on the trailer, she just shook her head and turned back to the house, muttering something to herself about another money pit. And with that introduction out of the way, Roy towed Mattie to the shop where he worked and began a two year long rebuild.

Mattie's V-12 engine was such a beautiful thing, and Roy tried hard to find parts for it. He did locate a few of the parts needed to rebuild it, but others were no longer available. If it had been possible to fix that motor, I honestly do believe that Roy would have gotten it done. And if the internet had been in use at that time he probably would have found what he needed. The technology of the machine was just too old and too obsolete and too foreign and no one would dare try to reproduce it. It was a death sentence for the V-12.

The hunt for a new power plant began and in 1968 there were finally some really great options. It was the age of factory muscle cars, and engines producing in excess of four hundred horse power were being cranked out by literally every car manufacturer in the nation. Roy was young and I did not yet know much of his life story, but so far I had gathered that he was in his very early thirties, married, and worked as a mechanic in a shop in Houston, Texas. Roy was smart, equipped with that God given mechanical aptitude that allowed him to quickly understand whatever machine was placed before him. And he wanted something special for Mattie.

So while she sat engineless, Roy upgraded other things like wiring and brakes and he installed a power steering unit on her. For many mechanics, that would be a tough project, Roy had to make many of the parts, like mounting brackets and pressure hoses, but he breezed right thru it, and it fit together like pieces of a puzzle. Now I realized that Roy was converting Mattie back to a street machine, he intended for her to be his daily driver and that was fine with me, but he did have in mind a few radical modifications that would be hard for me to watch.

Roy rented a small corner of his employer's shop and there Mattie would sit while Roy spent the better part of two years customizing her. The corner became a shrine with her years' of trophy accumulation lining high shelves, and body and mechanical parts taking up nearly all of the wall and floor space. I watched in almost nightly dreams for months as Roy turned Mattie into a very different car. Some of the shop's customers watched it too, sneaking back there when they came by, to see what was new on this rare coupe.

Most weekday mornings Roy would show up an hour or so early and sip coffee while tinkering with Mattie till time to start his job. He was a person with a high level of energy but it was not nervous energy; Roy used energy driven movements that were methodical and determined, energy that motivated him to show up early at the shop, stay busy, and leave late, but never appear tired or discouraged. I wished Dad could see what I saw, he would have appreciated the way Roy worked on Mattie. After work Roy would spend another hour to an hour and a half on her, reasoning that he'd just be sitting in rush hour traffic anyway. Most Saturdays Roy came in and gave Mattie a half a day worth of attention, careful to not spend so much time on her that he neglected his wife. I liked Roy, he was smart and quiet and I could tell he was happy with his life. But some of the things he did to Mattie caused me inner pain, sort of like when I first touched the cutting wheel to her door.

Roy stripped and gutted Mattie; he removed Mattie's interior including her headliner, all of her glass and interior trim, plus some exterior body trim. I knew he was preparing to chop her top but I was so unprepared for the destructiveness of the process. And Roy cut Mattie's roof all the way off, and with help from two coworkers laid it over to one side. The frightful sight caused me to jump in my sleep which woke me. Not wanting to fall back asleep and face that horrible sight again, I glanced at the clock and saw it was nearly six a.m. so I decided to stay up. Within a few minutes I was dressed and ready for the day, most of which would be spent at the Foundation. I heard Dad up and getting ready and knew he'd be in the kitchen making breakfast soon, so to kill a few minutes I ventured to the shop. Sitting on a stool, not more than six feet from my car, I stared, shook my head and I whined a sad apology for what I'd just witnessed.

Mattie responded by blaring out an old Beech Boys song on her radio, "Two girls for every boy. I've got a '34 wagon and we call it a woody, Surf City here we come. You know it ain't very cherry it's an oldie but a goodie, surf city here we come. Ah well it ain't got a back seat or a rear window, but it still gets me where I wanna go. You know we're goin' to surf city where it's two to one, you know we're goin' to surf city gonna have some fun…" I laughed and patted her front fender and returned to the house for breakfast.

My reliving the chop top experience in my dream didn't seem to bother Mattie so I got through the day without much more stress about it. But that night, as if determined to make me watch every painful detail in the process, my dream was a replay of the last one, and again, I was a silent observer as Roy neatly and methodically cut the top right off of Mattie. He had welded temporary braces inside of her in several different directions so nothing would warp out of shape when the top was separated from the rest of the body. So that's what those strange weld marks were that I saw when I installed her new interior a year or so earlier. After the final cut, two other mechanics came over and helped lift the top and lay it over to one side on a work table and set it up on blocks and spacers. Roy would stand back and eye Mattie's roof, while Mattie sat topless behind it, then he'd adjust a spacer under it, inspect again, adjust again, and again, he wanted to see it positioned exactly as it would be when reinstalled.

I wondered if I was supposed to learn something from having to watch the grizzly top chop process twice, in detail. Roy took a lot of care and spent the necessary time to get this laid out perfectly. Now he had to make another series of cuts that, when the top was welded back on, would lower the front at the windshield by two inches and the rear by less than one inch, giving her roof a subtle frontward sloping effect. This was a tricky procedure because it involved structural support and window casings in the doors and if one cut was off any at all, even an eighth of an inch, it would be difficult to make the roof fit and appear correct. Plus, the door tops might not fit into the openings perfectly. For a fleeting moment I feared Roy had ruined my car, but then I remembered; no, I had her now, years later, and she was fine.

While the top was off, Roy also removed the large soft insert at the roof's center with its wood frame and mohair insulation, and replaced it all with a sheet metal filler. The filler piece had been cut from a 1955 Pontiac station wagon and it had raised ridges running front to back about five inches apart, they were for strength but added to the style too. He made and attached metal bows to which he would affix a new headliner when the whole process was completed, several months later. It all seemed useless to me, Mattie's top had come from the factory already low enough, it didn't stick up tall like some of the other coupes I'd seen, but when the chop job was finished, she did look custom.

Roy removed the little triangle vent windows, the door handles and other chrome trim, and filled the holes. He welded, ground, filled and sanded, seemingly forever. Finally, Mattie was chopped and shaved. He unbolted her chrome flying lady hood ornament, stepped back and stared, deep in thought. He put it back on and stared some more, took it off, put it on, and left it on, and I was glad. It was the same hood ornament Dad had found in New York and sent to Amos during World War II.

While Roy Castillo chopped and shaved my car in 1969, I reversed her doors and prepared her for the drag races in 1994 and 1995. Anita and I and studied our way through another year of school and another summer. We turned sixteen, one more year to go.

I watched as my dream world and my real world inched closer together in time, and while I so enjoyed witnessing Mattie's history, I longed for the rest of it and the answers to many questions.

Among my most unforgettable dreams was of the day Roy's new power plant for Mattie arrived, a box truck backed up to the shop and unloaded a large wood crate. Roy had sold a 1967 Pontiac Firebird, a beautiful car, blue, with the Firebird painted in gold on the hood, to buy a brand new 426 cid Chrysler Hemi Head engine, possibly the most sought after race car motor of the time. Roy made modifications to Mattie's frame and motor mounts to accommodate the new hemi. Her new transmission also arrived, and it was something special too, a four speed, race modified automatic, already set up with switch pitch and trans brake. This engine and tranny set came as close as possible to making up for the loss of the old V-12 Rolls Royce engine. And she looked so fine with it, chrome valve covers with plug wires protruding thru the middle, big gutsy looking engine. If she didn't love Roy before this, she had to love him now. I wondered what could possibly break them up, but something did, and maybe it wasn't tragic since his ghost never appeared to me.

With Mattie's hood completely off, and with the help of a couple of friends, Roy installed his new hemi in her. But later, when he tried to bolt the hood back in place it no longer fit, the new engine was just a tad too wide, maybe two inches, maybe even less, the top fit but not the side skirts. And now I knew how Mattie lost the sides to her hood. And that, in turn, interrupted the pattern of Shawn's flames. Now what would Roy do? This was a lesson Dad and I had learned and relearned, when you modify something on a car, it affects something else, and it can sometimes be quite difficult to stop the domino effect.

But, in the same manner Roy did everything, he modified the hood to look so street roddish that I think his mistake actually became a positive thing.

The two top halves remained but the chrome center hinge which divided them was welded stationary, and the hood now hinged in front near the radiator and opened from the back, up and forward. When open it rested on two chrome rods that folded down and locked into place and held it up. And there sat Mattie, with a serious drag race stance; ass end up in the air via her huge rear drag racing tires, new lowered front end suspension, roof line sloping forward and screaming attitude, enough of the engine exposed thru the sideless hood to flaunt her 500 horse power hemi and show the world she was one serious hot rod.

And except for her paint color and style of flames, that was what Mattie looked like when I first met her. I kept thinking about how my two worlds were continually moving closer together, or maybe my world of Mattie's history was just catching up with my world of the present. And I became quite concerned, I had questions. What will happen when the two worlds collide, when I know everything? Will Mattie go silent? Will I continue to see Amos and Shawn and whoever else is in there that I haven't yet met? Will the dreams be over, for the rest of my life? Or will they maybe start over and run for me a second time?

Saturday, mid-morning, I believe it had to have been in December of '95, I know it was near the end of the school semester; Anita and I were studying together in my living room. Anita was a good student, smart and disciplined in her studies, and very motivated to do well, partially because that's just the way she was, but also to some extent because she was anxious to finish high school and marry me. But a senior math course, calculus I believe, was giving her trouble and I was helping her try to understand it.

Dad had broken his promise to John about not leaving us alone in the house but I don't think that by that point in time anyone even remembered that anymore. Anyway, Dad was gone to San Antonio on a parts hunting venture for his deuce coupe and we were doing our homework.

"Joey, do you realize how close we are now to finishing school? Have you thought about what's next?"

"I think about it all the time." I dropped the paper and the mechanical pencil I was using and reached up to touch Anita on the side of her pretty face.

She grabbed my wrist, wanting to make her point without a distraction. "No, I mean really think about it, the how and when of everything. Maybe we should start making some definite plans."

Actually I had thought about "the how and when of everything", some, but the seriousness of it all had always made me move on to other thoughts.

"You mean like, where we will live, and how we will make a living, stuff like that?"

"Yeah." She also abandoned the math problem we had been working on and swung one leg over me and sat on my lap facing me. I reached for her and she threw her hands to my shoulders and locked her elbows to keep me at a distance. "Do you think we'll live around here somewhere?"

"We'll be okay, I've got some savings." I came dangerously close to telling her about my inheritance, wanted to, just to ease her seemingly new worries, but Dad's advice stopped me.

"But what about earning a living, paying rent and bills and stuff? Even though you'll have a college degree, who's going to give you a good job when you're still a teenager? Do you think NASA will offer you something, or Professor Larson will help you find something?"

"Job? I'm not going to get a job, I'm not going to work for somebody else."

"No? Well, what will we do?"

"You know what I want to do, 'nita. I'm going to build custom cars for people, maybe build some to sell."

"Well, yeah, later, when we can afford to start a business like that, but what about when we're just starting out? Are you counting on your Dad to help you? We're not going to live with him, are we?"

Difficult questions, how would I answer them? "No, we'll have our own place, around here somewhere, I don't want to move away." I paused and she stared at me, right there sitting on my lap, inches away. Her questions made me uncomfortable. I looked across the room, thinking. How do I keep my promise to Dad but put her mind at ease about this?

"Hey Joey, I don't mean to put you on the spot, but we need to start thinking about these things. Don't you think?"

"'nita, I need to tell you something, something Dad made me promise to not tell anyone, except you, but only after we marry." I fidgeted, I pulled her close and hugged her, she let me. I held her face in my hands and kissed her. "So, I'm just going to give you the general idea, not any details, okay?" She nodded, looking into my eyes, wondering. "I have an inheritance, 'nita, a good one, real good, not all immediately at my disposal, but doled out annually, a good safety net, but only after I finish school, I have to earn a degree first, then it starts. Okay?"

She gave a little nasal snort and a giggle, her dimples deepened and she gently bumped her forehead to mine. "I should know better than to think you don't have everything all figured out. No wonder I love you. You're so special, Joey." Her smile turned mischievous. "Let's talk about having a baby."

"No!"

She laughed. "Just kidding."

"Don't do that, 'nita!"

The wonderful year of 1995, Anita and I both turned sixteen years old. I was six feet two inches tall and still growing, shaving a fairly mature set of whiskers, and thirty two credit hours away from a bachelor's degree in Chemical Engineering which pretty much had to be accompanied by a master's degree to be very marketable. But then I wasn't very interested in marketing it anyway. Anita was a beautiful five feet ten inches tall and slim and built with curves that turned heads everywhere she went. She had grown her silky black hair out to about shoulder length, was sporting quite a dark complexion from adding a deep summer tan to her already naturally brown skin tone. And Anita was less than two regular school semesters away from high school graduation a full year early. Though we were still technically children, our love had matured us beyond our years and nothing could interfere with our plans for a life together, or so we thought.

And that very night, as if being warned of some impending doom, I dreamed again that frightful dream of Anita and me in Mattie in some strange area running from the police. The landscape was drab and flat with short Mesquite trees, very unlike where we lived. Anita was hugging her door and her face bore an expression of fear, maybe even desperation, and tears, tears were streaming down her cheeks. I looked in the rear view mirror and saw the same expression on my face only perhaps slightly more controlled and minus the tears. Amos appeared, not smiling, and again he told me, "Trust in Mattie, Joey."

We were traveling at a little over ninety miles per hour and as we passed through a wooded area into a clearing along the road, a cop shot out from a ranch entrance, siren blaring and red and blue lights flashing. The sheriff's car contained two deputies and they quickly gave chase as if they had been waiting for us. My first reaction was to accelerate even more, try to outrun them. Then the helicopter came into view from somewhere to our left, and another sheriff's car merged from a small side road. It was hopeless and I began to slow down. Anita and I looked at each other and she pleaded, "Joey, don't let them separate us again, please."

The police car behind us backed off a little and the helicopter closed in on my side. Our speed was down to about sixty now and the chopper was pacing us and lowering to our level. Wind generated by the rotors was creating turbulence and I was fighting the wheel to stay on the road. Looking over I saw a uniformed passenger in the chopper eyeing me with binoculars and talking into a head set. Suddenly the flying police veered away and up and headed for who knows where and the two police cars turned down another narrow farm road and left us. Amos, still in the mirror, caught my eye and gave me a hearty laugh, I could even hear it.

"What just happened, Joey?" Anita wiped the tears from her eyes with her fingertips and looked around for the cops. "Why did they quit? They had us."

"I don't know, 'nita. But I think Mattie had something to do with it."

Sparky woke me, he wanted out. I slipped out of bed and followed him to the front door. He had a doggy door now that Dad had installed when I worked in Houston, so he could have gone out by himself but he seemed to want me to come along. Once out the door I noticed a faint light coming from the shop. Realizing I was being summoned, I obediently entered the shop and approached Mattie. Her driver side door popped open and she played a song for me, an old Deep Purple song, hard seventies rock and roll, "Nobody gonna take my car I'm gonna race it to the ground, nobody gonna take my car I'm gonna break the speed of sound, oooh it's a killer machine and got everything, like drivin' power, big fat tires and everything, I love her, I need her, I feel her, yeah she turns me on, all right, hold tight, I'm a highway star, I'm a highway star..."

The music faded and Amos appeared and spoke, "Everyting gonna be all right, boy. Jist let Mattie take care of you." He faded. I would have felt better if he had laughed and showed me his gold tooth, but he didn't, he was serious this time. I returned to the house, and to bed, and to my dream.

We were traveling in another area now and I recognized it, we were nearing Houston. Why? Though we were staying on the back roads, we were getting into a more populated area with more traffic. A cop quickly pulled in behind us from a side road, he came up fast and turned on his red and blue lights. I wanted to run, thought about it, but with all the other cars on the road it would have been dangerous. I looked out over Mattie's hood, it was red with symmetrical flames, not yellow with Hell Fire. I saw a red haired woman in the mirror looking more like a reflection than a spirit. The officer pulled right up beside us, glared at me while talking on his radio, and faded back, killing the lights.

Within five minutes we were at Sam's house, my friend from NASA. He was outside waiting for us and waved us into his garage through the already open overhead door, and closed the door behind us. The dream made no sense at all but it disturbed me deeply, and I neither wrote about it in the journal nor mentioned it, to anybody.

By the summer of 1970 Roy Castillo's two year modification of Mattie was finally complete and he was ready to introduce her to the streets of Houston. I knew all along, he was very clear in his goal, he was making her into a street rod, not the professional drag racer she had been. For the next four years Roy drove Mattie to work, to cruise nights, to run errands, to take his wife out to eat, or dance, or visit family and friends.

Occasionally, they would get into a street race and that is where Mattie was at her best, never losing, always outclassing and outdistancing her unfortunate opponent. She was entered in a few local classic car shows and won some plaques and trophies, and even ran at the local drag strip a few times but not often. It was fun watching her race again and though she didn't turn quite the quarter mile times she had with her V-12 engine, she was a fire breathing terror charging down the track and she did break into the high nine second times if she was properly tuned and if Roy got off the line just right.

This was a unique and fun time in Mattie's history and I enjoyed what she shared with me, but the dreams came fast and random and covered the years quickly. I wished Mattie had allowed me more time with this part of her life but the closer her story got to when she and I met, the more anxious she seemed to get through it. By now I had gotten the distinct impression that Mattie had a purpose in showing me her history and it was all leading up to something she wanted me to know, maybe something I needed to know.

So just when she appeared to be comfortably settled into a nice situation, things changed, again. Roy and Olivia had always wanted children, but for their twelve years of marriage they had been unable to conceive. Well, now they were pregnant, and with twins. Olivia was ecstatic, this is what she most wanted, and she insisted that she would quit her job and be a full time stay at home mother. But it'd be hard to make it on just Roy's salary.

It was not an easy decision or something he wanted to do, but Roy agreed to sell Mattie and use the money to pay off the house and eliminate that monthly payment.

CHAPTER 10

Kimberley O'Keefe was the red haired ghost I got a brief glance of back in Shawn's time with Mattie. As usual, I got to know Kim through dreams and as her story unfolded I learned that she was forty eight years old, mother of two young men who were in their mid-twenties and out on their own, she worked part time for a dentist, and had been married to Brian since she was twenty one years old. She was a pretty lady, aging gracefully, naturally happy and friendly, and shared her husband's love for old cars.

Brian bought Mattie for Kim, realizing she had already fallen in love with the coupe after watching it run at the drag races one night. Brian ran his modified car there every Saturday night, a '40 Willys coupe which also sported a Chrysler hemi head engine. Kim rattled on and on to her husband about this modified Buick coupe that "just had to be the most beautiful hot rod in the city." She talked so much about it that Brian approached Roy and asked if he'd sell, but at the time he did not want to. Now with the twins on the way, Roy needed to sell, and he contacted Brian first and they worked out a deal. Mattie sold for twenty thousand dollars and in 1975 that was a lot of money for a car, even a custom car as nice as Mattie. But that was what Roy needed to pay off his home and Kim wanted Mattie that much and Brian didn't want to wait and take the chance of losing her to another buyer. Mattie became Kim's car.

Brian hid Mattie for a couple of weeks in a friend's garage which added to the suspense because when Kim looked for the coupe at the races those two Saturday nights it wasn't there. Mattie was to be a surprise for Kim on their wedding anniversary. So the next Friday evening, Kim and Brian, planning on a night of dining and dancing in celebration of their marriage, walked out of their house and into the garage, and there sat Mattie, with a big red bow on her hood. Kim broke down and cried, she covered her face with open hands and cried like a baby, tears peppering the floor beneath her, all the while pacing circles around Mattie and going on and on about how beautiful she was.

Needless to say, they did not go to a restaurant or a dance, they cruised the city streets with Kim driving of course. They ate at a drive in, stopped by friends' homes to show off her new hot rod, and even got into a street race from a stop light with a Cobra Mustang which Mattie promptly and mercilessly thrashed. Someone new was now in love with Mattie, and boy was she in love. You'd think her husband had given her a Duisenberg or some other million dollar car. And with Mattie's name still painted on her doors, thanks to Shawn for putting it there and Roy for leaving it, Kim knew Mattie's name, and I was grateful for that.

I wondered what Kim would do with Mattie, race car or driver or a little of each? Brian had a nice shop behind their house, where he worked on his race car and that became Mattie's new home. For the first year and a half or so, Kim was content with Mattie as a driver. Two or three times a week she'd pull the car cover off and take her out, sometimes to run errands and sometimes just to cruise, and always to the drag races on Saturday nights to park in the pits and watch Brian run his Willys. One Wednesday night at the weekly tech and tune event at the drags, Kim decided she wanted to run Mattie down the track, just for fun.

Running Mattie down the track was supposed to be a one night, just for the fun of it event, but I knew better. Kim was a regular at the races but only to help her husband and to socialize with other racer's wives. This time she would be behind the wheel. Her first three runs netted slow times, twelves and one thirteen second pass, but she finally figured out how to come off the line, first with a hard burn out to heat up the slicks, and then with the right rpms to hook up. And Mattie's times began to dip into the ten second range. And when Kim got a taste of ten second quarter miles, achieving speeds of around one hundred thirty miles per hour, she was hooked. That brute force that plasters you to the seat, that feel of unleashed power, the adrenalin, the thrill, the satisfaction, even the sounds, it all got to her, and she knew, and Brain knew, and Mattie knew, and I knew this was not going to be a one night just for the fun of it thing.

Over a period of several months, as time in Mattie's world passed from 1975 thru 1976 and into 1977, my fly on the wall observation through dreams saw Kim slowly change Mattie from street rod back to drag racer. Shawn's roll cage was left in place but Roy's nice interior began to come out, rumble seat first, bench seat later, bumpers, stereo and other things over time, to lighten her weight. With Brian's help, a fuel injection system replaced the carburetor and a ram air induction system was custom fitted. Mattie's entire rear end was swapped for a performance differential and special racing wheels took the place of her beautiful chrome wire spoke wheels. That was the change I didn't like, the wheels. The new ones were chrome too and nice, but not the period correct style like the wire wheels.

You'd think that after nearly five years of being jerked back and forth through time, I'd be somewhat accustomed to it but when I woke up on a March 1995 morning, it took me several minutes to figure out just what this day was and what I was supposed to do with it. And when I did accomplish that mental task, I was consumed with dread, and for a fleeting moment, I considered staying in bed all day. Silly thought. But the smell of Dad's breakfast cooking in the kitchen and the sound of the phone ringing, and I knew it was Anita, demanded I get up and take on the day. This was the day Anita and I agreed we would tell our parents of our wedding plans.

In my mind, several times, I had gone over how the conversations would probably play out. Dad would know he could not discourage us, he knew this was coming, we had been pretty candid around him about our intentions to be married soon after Anita's graduation. Dad would talk about practical things like; where and how we would live, what we would do for a living, and the importance of continuing our education, both of us. And he would offer his help and support. He was far too perceptive, and he knew us too well, to think he could stop us.

Anita's parents would be a different story; they would act surprised, they would object, offer later curfews and more relaxed rules, demand Anita attend college first. They would, especially her Dad, throw up objections like our ages and how hard it is to make a living these days, how the struggle would hurt our relationship. They might even worry that Anita was pregnant, might even ask. The conversation would probably get a little emotional, if I knew her father, and end with his passionate forbidding of the marriage till some more appropriate time in our young lives.

And we would leave it at that, for the moment. But we'd continue our plans, find a house to rent, set a date, and try to convince them we were right about this. And even if we failed to gain their approval, we would marry anyway. The problem was of course, we were both underage, by a full year, and needed our parents written consent to marry. The possibility of eloping in Mexico had occurred to us, but we didn't really think it'd come to that.

Shuffling into the living room, sleepy headed still, I heard Dad's end of the last of a short phone conversation, and I knew it was Anita saying she was on her way over. Dad cheerfully offered to cook breakfast for her too, if she'd hurry. She did, within ten minutes she was at our door, opened it and entered without knocking. I met her with a kiss just a few feet inside the door, she smiled, I loved her smile, full lips, pretty mouth, little girl dimples - the only things keeping her from looking like a mature woman.

"You ready?" I asked nervously.

"Sure." She chirped, as if she felt no tension at all with what we were about to do. "This is the easy one, you know."

Yes, she was right about that, telling Dad was going to be the easy one for sure. But I was still on edge about it and if it hadn't been for my dreams of Mattie and Kim pulling me in so deep all night, I'd have gotten very little sleep.

I just picked at my eggs and sausage and toast, eating little of it, and Anita began to steal food from my plate, as usual. The meal finished, Dad pushed his chair out with his feet and reached for some of the dirty dishes. "Dad, um, uh, wait, we need to, uh…"

"Okay." He said, settling back into the straight backed wooden chair. "What's going on? I can tell you kids have something on your minds."

I looked at Anita, looked at my plate, began to stammer again, and Anita blurted out the news. "Mr. McClane, Joey and I are going to get married this summer, right after I graduate."

I couldn't believe it, she sat straight up and looked him right in the eye and informed him of this, no apologies, no request for his blessings, no qualifying or convincing, nothing, just a plain bold proclamation of what we were going to do.

Dad picked up a napkin and wiped his hands, more of nervous necessity to occupy his hands than a need to actually clean them. Body language, I thought, the kind he taught me to notice. Gathering his thoughts he looked at me, then at Anita, and back to me again. He drew in a deep breath and let it back out. "Well, sounds to me like the decision has been made. Can't say I'm at all surprised. It's been pretty obvious why you were rushing to an early graduation, Anita." He stood up, refilled his coffee cup from the pot on the bar top, and started for the living room. "Let's sit over here, in more comfortable chairs, kids, and talk about this."

We talked for nearly two hours, he had to make another pot of coffee, and I had a couple of cups too. Dad briefly touched on the advantages of waiting; to gain more maturity, continue our education, figure out how and where we will live, etc. But I could tell by his body language and the tone of his voice he knew these arguments would have no effect on our plans. His eyes were silently asking me if I had mentioned my inheritance to Anita and I dropped subtle hints throughout the conversation that she knew something but not much. Thankfully, Anita said nothing about it at all. Then came what I knew ultimately would, offers to help.

"You know, Joey, we have five acres here, and we've left the back four pretty much to the wild animals. We could clear out a building site and put up a small house for y'all back there. Then you'd still be near the shop and Mattie could stay there, until you finish school, get your master's degree, or maybe your PHD." He was hinting, wondering if I planned to stay in school.

Anita and I smiled at each other, it was a nice idea, we liked it, the house part, not the school part.

"But," He continued, not giving up on the school thing. "You should both attend college. I'll help you any way I can. And Joey, the Foundation is counting on you to go for your master's degree, and you know after that they'll offer you a job somewhere. I'd hate to see you turn down such a once in a lifetime opportunity."

Then came the part I knew he wouldn't like. I explained to him that I never wanted to move away or live in any city or work for anyone else. I wanted to build cars for a living. He advised that that needed to be an avocation, something on the side, part time, for fun, not a career. But he couldn't argue about money, because of what we both knew. I was too smart to just be a grease monkey, he did argue that, I was destined, created to be an engineer like him; successful in my own right, earn tons of money, and make some important contribution to the world. But, knowing he wasn't going to win the argument, he reconciled himself to what was, and the idea that I was young enough and educated enough and smart enough to take a detour and a little later in life pick back up where I'd left off. In a way I'd broken his heart; I was not following the grand plan. But in another way I had warmed his heart; he wasn't going to lose me to some distant city where a new life would surely separate us forever except for occasional visits.

Then Dad popped our happy little bubble with one question. "What do your parents think about this, Anita?"

The three of us, plus Sparky, retreated to the shop where Anita and I helped Dad mount the new radiator in his deuce coupe project car. By the time we finished it was noon and Dad treated us to a lunch of hamburgers and onion rings at the only drive in café in Las Casas. We went in our '64 Buick Electra convertible, top down. And after returning home, Anita and I left in Mattie for the dreaded meeting with her parents.

When we pulled up to the curb out front, John was mowing the front lawn and Anita walked right up to him and told him we needed to talk. Minutes later, seated in the dining room since the living room was occupied by Anita's younger cartoon watching siblings, we faced her parents across the table. Anita touched my leg under the table, her signal to hold hands, and I reached for her. John must have suspected our intentions as his expression was grim, serious, and not happy.

Thinking that Anita's head-on approach with my dad was the way to handle this too, I just came out with it. "Mr. and Mrs. Cantu, Anita and I want to get married this summer, after we graduate."

John slammed the table hard with an open hand, upsetting everything on it and knocking over the salt shaker, fine white sand pouring out in spasms. "Absolutely not!" The combination of the noise from the table hit and his loud vocal reaction caused me to jump in shocked surprise. I knew he would object but didn't expect such a course reaction from him. "Not no, but hell no!

No child of mine is going to get married at sixteen years old!" He turned his angry look from me to Anita. "Are you pregnant? Is that what this is all about, little girl? Son of a bitch! I knew you two were getting too much freedom and spending too much time alone, especially in that damned car of his! That's where it happened, isn't it?"

I wanted to get up and run out of there, but of course I couldn't. I was trying to figure out how to answer his accusations and objections when Anita answered him. With a glare just as pointed as his and shaking a little from anger, Anita spoke to her father as if she were his equal, perhaps for the first time in her life. "Daddy, I'll be seventeen then, and we are not in any kind of trouble, we are in love, and we are going to get married and you can't stop us. We have waited, Daddy, but our love won't let us wait anymore, we are ready for this and we will make it work, with or without your consent."

He stood up, bumping the table hard with one leg, and he leaned down and hit the table again, with the bottom of his fist this time. "Over my dead body! You are underage, little girl, and I'm not signing anything! The matter is closed!" He stomped off, exited the house through the back door, slamming it so hard I thought it'd fall off its hinges. In a moment I heard the lawnmower start again.

I looked across the table at Mrs. Cantu, her right elbow was resting on the table and her hand was shielding her eyes, as if the light were too bright. Her shoulders and head were shaking, trembling sort of, she was crying but making no sound. Anita stood up, leaned over her mother from behind and hugged her around the shoulders.

"Anita, give him some time, he just gets so angry. We knew this was coming, we were talking about it just the other day. You're so young, both of you. We just don't want you to make a mistake." She got up from her chair, excused herself, and hurried off to a back room, probably her bedroom, to cry some more.

Moments later, Anita and I already in Mattie and ready to go, John killed the lawn mower engine and glared at us, opened his mouth to speak but didn't. I saw him out of the corner of my eye but intentionally did not make eye contact with him, and we drove off, no destination in mind, just needing to be somewhere else, anywhere but there.

Just like she did with Roy, Mattie was hurrying my dreams of Kim's time with her, which disappointed me. It seemed like so much was skipped between dreams, everyday things left out of the story, maybe not anything monumental, but enough to cause new things to be hard to accept or understand when thrust upon me without the connecting details.

In what seemed no time at all to me, Mattie was changed from a custom street car to a full blown dragster with little interior and no sound system, even her power steering was disconnected and removed to lighten her weight and lessen wasted horsepower. New headers, transmission modifications, new ignition, new rear gears, and other changes happened without my being able to watch much of the process.

Kim and Mattie had, almost overnight, no pun intended, become a drag racing force to be feared by the men who competed with them. With quarter mile times in the low nine second ranges now, and speeds in excess of one hundred thirty miles per hour, Mattie was at her best again, just like in Shawn's time. Trophies stacked up and time flew by and traces of gray showed up under Kim's racing helmet. I caught a glimpse of a calendar on the shop wall and it was June 1983, Kim had owned Mattie for eight years, but to me it was the blink of an eye.

Dr. Larson began questioning me about my plans after receiving my bachelor's degree and I assured him I would stay and work on my master's. When he spoke of career plans I lied and told him I had none just yet. But he was smart and perceptive like my dad and he had become somewhat familiar with my life and he knew Anita and I wanted to get married soon. We had lunch together and talked about it and he advised me, regardless of what happened in my personal life, to "leave the career doors open, Joey, we want to be there for you".

Anita's father was not softening up toward our plans and I could tell he was harboring a lot of malice toward me. I was so uncomfortable around him that I avoided him and even avoided being around his house anymore. He and Anita weren't talking much either but she was handling it better than I was which was good because she had to live there, for a while anyway. For much of my life I had lived in a perfect world; unaffected by outside forces, home schooled by my retired grandfather, attended a small church, and had only a small group of friends. I didn't like it when things were not perfect, such as this new tension with the Cantu family. And Mattie was bringing something to a head which was also unsettling.

And one unsuspecting night it happened, I saw the end of Kim. She was on her way to a race, driving a Chevrolet Suburban and towing Mattie on a trailer. She was following Brian who was driving his pickup and towing his race car. They were traveling south on Interstate 35 when a north bound eighteen wheeler semi, driver asleep, came barreling across the median.

The semi slammed into the side of Kim's Suburban and the force knocked her all the way off the road and completely thru a guard rail and down a grassy slope. Mattie's trailer jackknifed, blew out the tires of one side of the trailer and dumped her over onto her passenger side, still strapped to the trailer. When the smoke and dust cleared; the Suburban was almost cut in two, Kim was dead and a bloody mess, still strapped in her seat belt, air bags now deflated but having failed to save her. Mattie rested on her side, trailer wheels sideways in the air. The semi was blocking all three lanes of traffic and several cars that had braked hard to miss it had begun a chain reaction of continuous rear ending.

The next thing I saw was ambulance personnel placing Kim's bloody, broken, lifeless body on a stretcher and Brian sitting on the grass, arms hugging his knees, rocking, crying. Someone was touching his shoulder, offering assistance, but he wasn't even aware of their voice, he was in shock.

I awoke with a jump and a gasp. I must have startled Sparky because he hurried out from under the covers, looked at me and whined. "Oh crap, Sparky! I didn't see that one coming." I grabbed my flashlight and headed for the shop. As I knew it would be, Mattie's dome light was glowing and I approached her slowly. Her driver side door opened slowly and she played a song for me, an old song, of course, an Everly Brothers tune I believe, from the fifties, I had heard it somewhere before. "When I want you, in my arms, when I want you, with all your charms, whenever I want you all I have to do is dream. Dream, dream, dream, all I have to do is dream. I can make you mine, any place or time, any time night or day, only trouble is, gee whiz, I'm dreamin' my life away..."

I touched Mattie's door and looked in. "Oh Mattie, I'm so sorry. I know you loved her. I know because she loved you, and you kept her with you. Kim appeared, I knew she would. She looked good and that was a relief, she looked young and pretty, in her red racing helmet with her flaming red hair flowing from under it. And she smiled at me. Mattie played another song, by the Chiffons, I think. "He's so fine, do lang, do lang, do lang, wish he was mine, do lang, do lang, do lang, and I'm gonna make him mine, if it takes me forever, I'm gonna love him forever." Drums. "He's so fine, oh yeah, gotta be mine, oh yeah, sooner or later, oh yeah, I hope it's not later, oh yeah. Gotta get together, oh yeah, the sooner the better, oh yeah. I just can't wait, I just can't wait, to be held in his arms..." Kim spoke to me. "You Joey, she loves you. We all got to enjoy her for a while, but it's you she loves. All she ever wanted was to get back to you." Kim faded.

I protested. "But, I'm not... I'm Joey. It was my grandfather... Oh, I don't understand."

Though I could no longer see her, I heard a reply in Kim's voice, not much more than a whisper, I had to listen carefully. "But she changed too much for him, Joey, and he changed, got old, and when she saw you that night at the races, she thought you were... Well, you'll see. And the way you fell in love with her, so quick, so hard, and you looked just like... You'll see, Joey, you'll see."

"What? What night at the races? What are you talking about?"

But she was gone, for the time being. And I wondered.

Back in bed, dreaming again, a huge wrecker pulled Mattie upright, still strapped to the trailer. She hit the ground with a violent crash and bounced from side to side a couple of times before settling. Mattie's entire passenger side was badly damaged, shattered glass and bent and twisted metal had displaced perfection. The wreck had jolted everything about her and her engine was broken off it mounts and her racing interior was in loose pieces, much of the suspension system under her was ruined. It was more than I could stand and I got out of bed and trudged to the living room. I tried to write in Mattie's journal but I could not transfer one word from my mind to the paper. I was in shock, unprepared for what I'd been shown and unable to handle it. Sparky jumped up on the couch beside me, turned a circle, settled down against my leg and buried his head under his back legs. I stroked him.

Dad walked into the room, rubbed his eyes, looked at me, then at the journal. "Rough night?"

I nodded.

"Want to talk?"

I nodded again and he sat near me. I told him of the latest dreams, the death of Kim, and the destruction of Mattie. "I know someone put her back together, fixed her, 'cause she's here now and she's okay. But it was so bad. I never would have imagined this. Poor Mattie, she was so torn up."

Dad patted my shoulder. "Well, that's the life of race cars son, fast and dangerous. Yes, someone fixed her. But you know what I think? You haven't seen the last of the damage done to her yet. Remember when we got her; the hole blown thru the floor, the damage to her grill and fenders? It didn't tear her body up but it did look like something violent happened. And Frank's reluctance to answer questions about it? You've got at least one more episode to go through, son. And things happen for a reason, Joey. If Jimmy Cox hadn't built her roll cage, she might not have survived this incident. She might not have been repairable, she would have never found her way back to us."

The next night I saw Mattie back in Kim and Brian's shop, just sitting there, all broken up and sad. The Willys was there too. The dreams were surreal, floating and pointless, more so than most dreams are, and Brian was never around, he didn't come to the shop for a long time. Nearly a year passed by and finally Brian started coming back into his shop. He tinkered with the Willys as if getting it ready to race again. He puttered around the shop, cleaning and organizing, alone and quiet. Weeks, maybe months passed quietly like that, and then one of his friends came to help him and they spent all weekend getting the Willys ready to race. Brian was slowly putting his life back together, but he was not putting Mattie back together. She sat there in her wrecked and twisted condition for three years. The dreams were spotty and meaningless, as far as Mattie was concerned, and I was sad for her.

One September day in 1987, Brian approached Mattie, it was the first time since the wreck that I had seen him go near her. He paced circles around her, touching, examining, and muttering to himself. "Kim would want you fixed, Mattie. She wouldn't want you left like this. I just haven't been able to do it, to face you, not with the memory still fresh in my mind. But maybe now..." He opened her good door, on her driver side, and cried, he covered his face with his hands and sobbed. Inside, on the floor, was Kim's red racing helmet.

Repair work began almost immediately but progressed quite slowly. Brian was back to racing his Willys coupe every weekend and keeping it up required some of his shop time. But he spent at least a couple of hours on Mattie three or four days each week. A year or so later most of the body work was done, lots of cutting and welding, sanding and filling, straightening and aligning. Mattie was taking shape and looking like herself again. But Shawn's red paint job with symmetrical flames was ruined. And surely the yellow paint with Hell Flames with which she came to me had to be next. After all, in just two more years, she and I would meet, and that is how she was adorned then. What about the hole in the floor from the blown engine, did that happen to Brian? Soon I would know. Soon I would know everything Mattie wanted me to know.

Dad and I found two seats together near the front of the Las Casas High School auditorium to watch Anita's graduation ceremony. Had things been different we might have sat with her family, but John had called several times to bitch Dad out about his support of our plans, so both our relationships with John were quite strained now. We would not even celebrate together this evening after graduation. I was sorry things had gone this way and worried about what was to soon come when we attempted to put our plans into action.

She was beautiful, walking across the stage, accepting her diploma, and her smile beamed. As the principal handed the document to her, the speaker at the podium announced Anita's high school accomplishments which included a 3.6 grade point average, participation in several school functions and organizations and several awards, ending with her graduation a full year early.

After the ceremony her father whisked her away claiming reservations at a nice restaurant demanded a hurried departure. "I'll call you later." She told me. When she did call it was after eleven that evening and she was in a quiet panic, whispering. "Listen, Joey, something's going on, I don't know what, but we're packing, we're going to my grandmother's house in Laredo. I don't like this, Joey. My dad is trying to separate us. He thinks you and I are going to run off and elope."

In the background John yelled for Anita to "Get off the damned phone, right now!" She tried to stall him but he took the receiver away from her and slammed it down. I knew she had family in Laredo. Was he going to leave her there? I'd go get her, but where, what address, how would I find her? She'd call again.

I talked to Dad and he tried to calm me down and make me feel better. He suggested that maybe a short separation would be good for Anita and me, and John too. He urged me to be patient, keep my head, wait for Anita to call, and finish the last few days of my school work and get my degree. So that is what I did, but I grew more restless every day. I drove by the Cantu house often but saw no one there. I made a decision, when I found out where Anita was, I would go and get her.

A slow tortuous week went by; I finished my studies and prepared for finals, I watched the mail and listened for the phone, and hoped to hear from Anita. Anita's seventeenth birthday came and went and I felt totally empty. Mattie filled my nights with visions of her becoming the yellow coupe with Hell Flames that I now knew. I grew more restless and angry with each passing day.

Finally the call came, Anita had sneaked out from under her grandmother's careful watch, jogged a few blocks and found a pay phone. She had scrounged up a few dollars in change, sufficient to pay for phone time to tell me what I needed to know, her grandmother's address, 1021 Nueces Street. Her family had just headed back for Las Casas and we set up a rendezvous for Sunday afternoon when she and her grandmother would be just back from mass, had lunch, and the old lady would be down for a nap. I'd drive up to the front of the house at exactly one thirty p.m. and Anita would run for the car and we'd speed over into Mexico and get married. Beyond that we had no plans, maybe just find a place to hide out for a while.

I didn't dare tell Dad. When he'd ask if I'd heard from Anita yet I'd lie and tell him no, not yet. But I could tell he read something in my eyes and he cautioned me. "Joey, don't do anything foolish. I know you're hurting, but just give it a little more time."

My next cruise by the Cantu residence assured me they were back, without Anita of course. And I didn't drive by there anymore. But just to throw John off, I called. I angrily demanded to know where she was and he responded by telling me she had decided to break it off with me and attend college in another state. I pretended to believe him and to be broken hearted over the news. I tearfully asked him to tell her that I still loved her and he hung up on me. The stage was set and I had John off guard. But I didn't tell Dad about any of this.

Somehow I found new energy and readied myself for the college finals, motivated by the fact that I needed the degree in order to start my inheritance so I could support Anita and myself in our new life, whatever that would turn out to be. I took my last exam on Friday and was congratulated by Dr. Larson who quickly volunteered to get my post grad courses lined out for me. Not sure if I would ever take the courses, I graciously accepted his offer and hoped that that would keep Dad's suspicions at bay.

As if Mattie sensed the urgency and the time growing short, she filled my few remaining nights at home with the rest of her story. Brian had her ready for paint but wanted a professional job. Why he chose the color scheme he did I'll probably never know but he picked a bright yellow and showed the painter flames in a magazine, Hell Flames they were described as in the article. I had been calling them that for the past five years and never knew why. Maybe Mattie had whispered it to me via one of her ghosts.

A few days later the painter called Brian to let him know she was finished, shiny and pretty, all rubbed down and polished. He took her home and she sat in the shop for days, he couldn't bring himself to get behind the wheel and drive her. He talked to Kim while standing there looking at Mattie. "Well, baby, I put her back together for you. I thought if she went back a little different I might be able to keep her here, but it's just too painful. I'm going to find her a new home. I hope you don't mind, Kim."

CHAPTER 11

I don't know how much time had passed, in Mattie's world, but I watched the money and title exchange, and I watched Mattie's new owner load her onto an open car hauler trailer and take her away. There was something about this man I didn't like but I couldn't quite put my finger on it. I feared Brian had made a poor choice of who to sell Mattie to. The man, Phillip, did not have a gentle nature, and Mattie was just another car to him, beautiful and fast, but not special to him, he did not fall in love with her like Kim did, or Amos, or Shawn, or Roy, or me. It was not right.

Mattie didn't like Phillip either, and she resisted him. Out on the open highway, a tie down strap broke and she rolled back on the trailer. Before Phillip realized the problem and got his truck stopped, she had dropped her rear wheels off the back of the trailer and broke an axle and bent a wheel. When he got her to the city he took her to Frank's garage for repairs. Frank, so this was the start of his nightmare with my car. And I knew if Phillip was not capable of doing his own mechanic work on Mattie he didn't deserve her. As soon as she was road worthy again Phillip took her to the drag races, with a for sale sign on her. So that was it, he thought he could make a quick profit on her, he never really wanted her for himself. He was just a cheap hustler. I hated him.

It wasn't Phillip but another man, Mark, a friend of his, or a business associate maybe, that raced her that night and he was rough with her, didn't let her warm up and she broke her clutch the first time down the track. Back to Frank's but Phillip was out of money and promised to pay within a few days.

Mattie ran well the next time out, maybe she was trying to show Phillip something, or the goon he had driving for him. She turned several consecutive low nine second runs and won her class and on through the finals for several rounds before being edged out by another car because of driver error. Mattie gave them two more good and trouble free nights at the drags and won trophies and prize money. But Phillip was greedy and offered a challenge for a grudge match for a thousand dollars against the winner of another class. This time Mark screwed up on his shifting and tore the guts out of Mattie's transmission, losing the bet and generating another very expensive repair.

Back at Frank's the next day, Phillip couldn't afford the transmission change out but to get it done, he signed a note against Mattie for the cost. If he did not pay the bill within thirty days Frank would own the car. It was do or die time for Phillip.

I saw myself and Dad in 1990. I was twelve years old. We were in attendance at a car show in Houston, Texas. It was an outside show being held in a field next to the drag races, the drag races where Mattie was! We walked around looking at cars, admiring, criticizing, getting ideas, munching on the junk food sold in booths there, and looking for the restrooms. We were given directions to a wide hallway that led to the races, the restrooms were in that hallway. Dad needed to go but I didn't, so while I waited for him I slipped over to the railing by the concrete stairs and looked out over the aluminum bleachers to the track. There was Mattie, in the staging lane, in line for the next race. I had heard Dad's stories about Mattie but of course I had never seen her, not even a picture, and never would have expected to see her there and looking like she did. But she saw me, and I looked just like my grandfather fifty something years earlier.

Dad called, I looked around. "Come on, Joey, we haven't seen all the cars yet, and then I want to go to the swap meet." I turned around and followed him but looked back at the races one more time, unaware of Mattie.

And Mattie threw a big fit. Just as the cars in front of her got the green light and left the line, Mattie floored her own accelerator. This time Phillip was driving and he desperately tried to get her under control. He hammered the brakes but Mattie gulped down more gas and air and jerked her front wheels up, slicks and exhaust screaming, trying to get my attention. The man whose job it was to line the cars up at the starting line jumped out of the way, cussing Phillip for his antics. Phillip fought the transmission out of gear but Mattie forced it back and pulled another wheelie. Phillip turned the key off but Mattie turned it back on, hauled down the track a ways and shifted to second, slicks and engine still screaming, she was desperate to get my attention. Confused and terrified, Phillip jerked the key from the slot and threw it on the floor on the other side of the car but Mattie kept running. He pushed the brake pedal as hard as he could with both feet and Mattie turned two complete rubber burning doughnuts right there on the track, barely missing the concrete wall separating her from the spectators. Spectators retreated in fright and racers and officials rushed toward Mattie. Semitransparent faces in rapid succession showed themselves to Phillip; Mrs. Ferguson, Amos, Shawn and Kim, they flashed at him over and over through the windshield and in the mirror and near him in the car and Phillip lost it. He screamed like a woman and fought to get free of his racing harness to get out of the car but he could not do it. Mattie revved her engine tighter than she should have, threw herself into gear and charged back toward the starting line scattering people out of her path. There was a loud bang and smoke and steam poured out of Mattie's engine compartment. Her engine blew apart and sent a piston and connecting rod through the floor tearing into Phillip's leg and severing an artery. Mattie stopped, her horn blasted, and her lights flashed, and I was unaware, already back at the car show. Would be rescuers tried to free Phillip from inside Mattie but he had the remote control for her doors inside with him.

Someone raised a steel bar to break the window glass and Mattie started up again and spun around threatening anyone foolish enough to come near her. Two large tow trucks sped onto the track and hemmed Mattie in against the concrete wall. Phillip's tortured face looked through the glass and he exhaled his last breath of air. Mattie popped her door open and her engine died again, this time with a loud backfire and everybody jumped for cover. Phillip slumped partially through the open door, head and one shoulder, arm dangling, held in the seat by the harness, and blood spilled from the floor onto the pavement. Moments later Phillip was in an ambulance but it departed slowly and quietly.

Those in the immediate area exchanged quiet looks of horror in reaction to what they had just witnessed but only half believed and did not understand at all. Eventually, Frank came forward to claim the car. One of the tow trucks started up and began backing out of the way and Mattie's engine turned over in another attempt to start. The panic began anew. Someone shouted orders, "Get that tow truck back in here! Get the battery out of this damned thing! Get it disabled before it hurts someone else!"

A man with bolt cutters approached and severed the positive battery cable thru the open space under the hood. But as soon as he pulled back, the cut ends touched together again and the engine turned. He cut it again a little farther up and the disconnected piece fell to the ground. A brave soul slid under the coupe with a half inch open end wrench and removed the driveshaft. The tow trucks were moved away and racers and crew members and track officials breathed easier. They milled around discussing the frightful event, trying to figure just what happened and why. And I was back at the car show, unaware that Mattie had just gone on a murderous rampage for the sole and futile purpose of getting my attention.

Frank was afraid of the coupe after seeing what she did that night. He took her home, she was rightfully his, but he did not want her, did not even want her around. And late that night she woke him up blasting her horn and flashing her lights. He wasn't happy about being woke and when he went to his shop to investigate, Mattie had moved herself to the other side of the shop.

"Damn you, you murdering piece of shit! You can't move or do anything, you don't have a battery or even a driveshaft and your engine is blown up!" Amos appeared just inside Mattie's driver side window and he spoke. "Wanna be next, boy?" Frank froze, unable to move, mouth wide open, eyes as big as silver dollars. Shawn showed himself. "You're a dead man, mister." Frank stiffened even more and trembled. Kim materialized, and when she passed thru the closed window flying directly at Frank, he screamed and ran from the shop, leaving the lights on and the door open. The next morning Frank put Mattie up for sale, he listed her with an agency that advertised in every major newspaper in the state, on the web, and in a handful of magazines. The day those ads started, Frank got a call from a Mr. Joseph McClane in San Antonio.

I turned over in my sleep and my dream continued. I saw myself, at twelve years old, and Paw Paw, as we entered Frank's shop. I saw Mattie way in the back. I was walking toward her, Paw Paw by my side, and I fell in love with Mattie, and she knew it, and she was at peace, she was going home.

I awoke and it was four in the morning, I went directly to the shop. I approached Mattie and Amos appeared to me. "Now you know de whole story, Joey. And it's time to let Mattie take care of you. Trust in Mattie, Joey." He smiled and faded away.

Mattie's door opened and she played a song for me. It was one she had played for me before, a song by the band Deep Purple, 'Highway Star'. "Nobody's gonna take my car, I'm gonna race it to the ground. Nobody's gonna take my car, I'm gonna break the speed of sound..." I sat in her, door open, left foot lingering on the running board, and listened, and when she finished her song I asked, "You going to get me through what I'm going to do today,

Mattie?" She played another song, 'Shut Down', by the Beach Boys. "Tach it up, tach it up, buddy gonna shut you down..."
"Okay," I told her. "We leave at ten o'clock."

I went back to the house, first making sure Dad was asleep, and I packed a suitcase. I took several shirts, jeans, underwear, socks, extra shoes, shaving stuff, toothbrush and paste, whatever I could think of. Looking around for things forgotten, I noticed Dad's picture on my chest of drawers, the one of him in his nice army uniform with all the medals on it. I grabbed it too and stuffed it in with my clothes and things. I had drawn three thousand dollars in twenty dollar bills out of my savings a couple of days before and now I dug it out of my sock drawer where I had hidden it. When I felt like I had thought of everything, I sneaked it all out to Mattie, grabbed a few snacks from the kitchen as I passed thru, and stowed my bag of supplies in her rumble seat area. While in the shop I added a few tools and a couple of extra quarts of oil to my supplies. After I had checked everything on Mattie, fluid levels and tire pressures, I went back to my room and wrote in the journal till I smelled breakfast cooking.

I had considered taking one of Dad's less conspicuous cars instead of Mattie, who was sure to stick out like the proverbial sore thumb, but heeding Amos's advice to let Mattie take care of me, I stuck with the decision to go in her. If I followed my plans carefully enough I would be in Laredo before I was missed here, and I would have Anita with me and we would be across the Mexican border before anyone could figure out what we were up to. I was ready.

I could tell over breakfast that Dad was picking up on my solemn quietness and he tried to pry my thoughts from me. He asked if I had heard from Anita and I lied and said I had not. His look told me he was trying to read me. But I knew there was no way he could. He had trained me too well about body language and poker face and verbal responses in tricky situations. Something deep down inside of me hated to deceive him but my love and need for Anita overrode everything else.

It was Sunday and he mentioned church and I told him I didn't want to go for fear of running into the Cantu family and he accepted that but said he thought he'd go anyway. That was good, he'd be away when I needed to leave and I'd be half way there when he returned home. He asked me what I planned to do today and I told him Mattie had developed a new rattle and I was going to work on that and I'd probably need to test drive her a few times to figure it out. I thought that story might buy me another hour of undetected travel time. He asked if I needed help and I said I'd let him know if I did. I ached to reach out to him, hug him, call him Paw Paw again, be his little boy again, but time had separated me from that stage of life forever.

An hour later Dad was ready to leave for church. I was in the shop and he stopped and talked to me. "Joey, keep your spirits up, son. She'll call soon and y'all can talk and figure things out. At the very worst, she'll be eighteen in another year and free to make her own decisions. I know you're hurting, son, I wish I could help." He patted me on the back and I grabbed him and hugged him, tight, for too long, fighting back tears, choking on words that would not come out. And I thought, if that didn't give me away, nothing would. He left for church.

There were so many things I wanted to tell him, but I couldn't. I loved and admired that man, I wanted to be just like him. I knew what all he'd done for me in my life and it broke my heart to go behind his back this way. I was about to cause him a lot of worry and pain, but maybe, just maybe when Anita and I got married and hid out somewhere for a couple of weeks, her parents would accept that they couldn't stop us, maybe they'd be ready to accept us as married and we could come home and start our life together, build our little house. I hoped for that.

Mattie felt good on the road, she ran straight and strong, no shakes or misses, but that is what I would expect from her. Maybe I was just being paranoid, looking for some trouble to pop up, surely I couldn't expect what I was doing and was about to do to just go smoothly without any problems at all.

I decided to travel Interstate 35, it went all the way from San Antonio to Laredo, it actually went all the way from Canada to Mexico. I would have preferred back roads but they all ran more east and west than north and south so it made more sense to just get on the highway and make good time. I was about a third of the way to Laredo when I spotted the first cop, a deputy sheriff coming from a merging road near a small town named Pearsall. The sight of his car startled me and I jumped in my seat. He pulled in behind me and I knew he must have noticed Mattie. I watched suspiciously but kept my speed constant and he slowly dropped farther back into the light traffic, an occasional car or ranch truck passing him or merging from the little intersecting ranch roads and thankfully putting themselves in between us. A few miles farther he turned off and I didn't see him anymore. I breathed a sigh of relief.

After Pearsall, the drive turned long and boring, one hundred miles, more or less, of nothing but Mesquite brush and flat land, ugly in comparison to my beautiful hill country, and a scattered handful of towns smaller than Las Casas, barely requiring drivers to slow down while going thru. Two more deputies appeared and disappeared without incident, one officer giving me the thumbs up sign in response to Mattie and I waved a return greeting. A few miles out of Laredo I encountered a border patrol check station. They normally only stopped traffic going north, away from Mexico, but this time they were stopping cars going both ways and I surmised they were looking for someone in particular. The thought concerned me. As I rolled to a stop by the waiting officer, I opened my window and turned down the volume on my radio.

He was Hispanic, young, maybe still in his early twenties, strong build, looked impressive in his starched uniform. He peered into my eyes and I wondered if he had been trained to read people like I had. Of course he had, he was a cop, of sorts. His eyes moved around the inside of my car as if searching for some kind of contraband and I took that as a good sign, he was not looking for me. He spoke without accent or cordialness.

"American citizen?"

"Yes, sir."

"Destination?"

"Laredo, sir."

"Crossing into Mexico?"

"No, sir." I lied, being careful to keep my voice tone the same.

"Purpose of visit?"

"To visit friends, sir." Another lie.

"I need to see some form of identification, sir."

I offered my driver's license out the window to him, he didn't take it, just glanced at it and at my face, moved back a step and waved me on without another word.

A mile down the road I let out a long sigh. Ten minutes later I entered Laredo and I was immediately lost. Laredo was huge and sprawling, like San Antonio, and predominately Mexican, also like San Antonio but more so. Mattie was down to a quarter tank of gas so I pulled into a gas station/convenience store to fuel up and ask for directions. The clerk didn't speak English and my broken and very limited Spanish wasn't getting the job done either so I bought a city map from him, paid for it and the gas and drove Mattie over to the side of the concrete parking lot to study the map and find my way to 1021 Nueces Street.

Laredo was laid out in a confusing manner as if no planning had ever been done, even in its early days, as if houses and buildings had been built first and then streets were placed in some random, serpentine fashion to accommodate them. Maybe meandering animal trails had been paved, I mused. So it took a while to find Anita's grandmother's house and when I did I was early, by more than half an hour. I cruised by it, thought about sounding my horn to let her know I'd found her but decided against it, too early, had to stay on plan. I sat in a vacant lot two blocks away, pushed buttons on Mattie's radio too rapidly to give any of the stations a chance to entertain me, and became very conscious of my heartbeat as I watched the time. I studied the city map I'd bought at the gas station and plotted our route to the border crossing. At one twenty five, five minutes early, but she would have expected that from me, I cruised back by 1021 Nueces Street and this time I did honk. The porch light was on and had not been on before, that was her signal to me that she was ready. I made a U-turn in the next intersection and went back, this time I stopped by the curb in front of the house.

As Mattie rolled to a stop, Anita burst through the screen door. She wore jeans, tennis shoes, and a red tee shirt but carried nothing as she ran down the cracked and broken concrete sidewalk toward us. Mattie's door popped open for her and she jumped inside. We hugged and kissed. The screen door flew open again and the grandmother appeared, sixty feet or so away, holding the screen door with one hand, she screamed something at Anita in Spanish and shook her fist at us.

"Adios Abuela, I'm going to get married!" Anita yelled and waved, laughing defiance at the old woman. Anita scooted close to me and Mattie accelerated hard, burning rubber for half a block. I knew it was stupid to call attention to ourselves, but we had pulled this off, so far, and I felt like celebrating, like rubbing John's face in it, sure that he would soon hear the details of our escape, burning rubber and all.

Mattie turned on her radio and played a song for us, an old song, as usual. I'd heard it before I thought, but didn't know what year it was from or who sang it. "Goin' to the chapel and we're goin' to get married. Goin' to the chapel and we're goin' to get married. Goin' to the chapel of love. Spring is here and the sky is blue, birds all sing as if they knew, today's the day we'll say I do and we'll never be lonely anymore. Because we're goin' to the chapel and we're goin' to get married, goin' to the chapel and we're goin' to get married. Gee I really love you and we're goin' to get married, goin' to the chapel of love. Birds will sing, the sun will shine, I'll be his and he'll be mine, we'll love until the end of time, and we'll never be lonely anymore. Because we're..." We listened quietly while the song played, stunned by the timing of it.

I silently remembered when I had heard it before, when Anita and I sat in Mattie and kissed for the first time that day at my thirteenth birthday party, that day I so awkwardly asked her to be my girlfriend. Mattie played it with no radio back then and Anita didn't hear it that time, this time she did.

Anita snuggled up to me and said, "Mattie knows."

Laredo is right on the border with Mexico and ten minutes later Anita and I were crossing the bridge over the Rio Grande River and into Nuevo Laredo, they couldn't stop us now.

This was as far as our plan went, in any detail anyway. Unsure of how to get married in Mexico, we drove around till we found a church, it was a Catholic church of course, a tidy looking, native rock, one story building with a square bell tower and a faded red tile roof, and it looked to be hundreds of years old. We parked Mattie in a small gravel parking lot and entered the building thru the front door. We were in the main assembly room and it was dark, the few dim lights left shadows throughout the room except in the front corners and we felt our way down the aisle. As we approached the altar in the front of the room, front inside but rear outside like all churches, a priest appeared. He stood up, having been seated on the front pew perfectly still and we hadn't seen him there so he startled us. A small man with a kind, clean shaven face, he was maybe sixty years old but moved like a much older man. He looked at Anita and then at me, and at her again, and spoke to her in Spanish, introducing himself as Padre Jose.

Though I had lived my life in a TexMex environment and had taken a couple of Spanish courses, I was still unable to converse well with the Mexicans in their language. They spoke in words from different dialects, used strange clichés and talked too fast. But I was able to at least follow the gist of this conversation as Anita explained to him that we were looking for someone to marry us. He was certain she was pregnant and tried to offer alternative ways to deal with such a situation. The three of us sat on the ancient looking dark wooden pew and Anita explained that she was not pregnant, that we had been in love for four years, worked hard to finish school early so we could start our lives together, but then were separated by her father. He asked our ages. Anita shot me a worried glance and I nodded for her to answer truthfully.

She responded that she had just turned seventeen and I would do so in a few days. His reaction worried me, he wrinkled his brow in a scornful expression and slowly shook his head. "Aw, ninos, muy joven." He replied. (Aw, babies, very young.)

I took that as rejection and stood up. "Come on, 'nita. We'll find another place, someone who'll do it, maybe a judge or somebody."

"No. Sit, please. Let's talk some more." The padre countered. He knew we were determined and must have thought a church wedding would be more proper than one performed by a judge. A few more minutes of conversation gave him more of our situation and he eventually agreed to perform the ceremony. Padre Joe took our driver's licenses and transferred our information to a marriage certificate, signed it and handed it to me. "Do you have a ring for your bride?"

I hadn't thought of that. "Uh, um, no, I don't."

"Yes, we do." Anita cheerfully countered. She pulled the gold chain necklace out of her blouse and removed the gold band I had given her for her birthday three years earlier.

We stood near an altar, in front of Padre Jose, us dressed in jeans, tee shirts and tennis shoes, Anita's hair in a ponytail, me needing a shave, non-English speaking nun as a witness, and said traditional "I do's." I slipped the ring on her finger and we kissed to seal the union. I looked into Anita's eyes and apologized. "I'm sorry, baby. You deserved a nice wedding with friends and family and a big reception to celebrate. I'm sorry we had to do it like this."

I saw no sorrow or regret in her eyes, not even a tear, only happiness, that beautiful smile, those dancing eyes, little girl dimples. She gently bumped her forehead to mine. "I'm going to spend my life with you, Joey. I am now Mrs. Joseph McClane. I'm happy. I am as happy as I could possibly ever be."

Out of the corner of my eye I saw the Padre smile and nod in response to Anita's words.

My mind drifted back to that day, that thirteenth birthday, when I watched that skinny, yet to fully bloom, little girl playing football, rough, with the boys, while the other girls cheered from the sideline, probably making fun of her to each other for her tom-boyishness. And then later her handing me the model car and telling me she bought it with her own money and wrapped it herself, and later still, us kissing inside Mattie in the shop. And from that moment on, I loved her. And now she was my wife, my child bride. I imagined her in a white wedding gown, low cut front, flowing train, veil with her pretty face behind, make up and jewelry, as it should have been, with her mother sitting in the front pew crying tears of joy, her dad proudly walking her down the aisle. But she settled for this, this Mexico elopement, as if the other didn't matter, that which all girls dream of. And now, instead of the wedding announcement, there would be mug shots and a story of an underage runaway couple. I kissed her again and when I tried to pull back she wanted more, pulling me tight against her, prolonging the kiss. This was love, true love.

From the church we took the marriage certificate to a government office where records were kept, and paid the filing fee of five dollars and got the official stamp placed on our marriage license. We were finished with what turned out to be the easy part.

"Now what?" I asked. I pointed Mattie toward the border and Mr. and Mrs. Joseph McClane headed back for Laredo, Texas, USA. Just over the border my cell phone rang, it was Dad.

"Hi, Dad."

"Where are you, Joey?" He sounded worried.

"In Mexico, Dad." It was a lie but just barely, by only feet or yards, not miles, not yet. "Anita and I are married."

"Oh, Joey." A sigh. "I was afraid of that. Her father called here, says you kidnapped her and he has the police looking for you. He's furious."

"Yeah, I figured. He should have done it our way, Dad. He should have known he couldn't split us up. Dad, I'm sorry, sorry that I had to deceive you too. I really am. I love you, Dad, I'd never hurt you, not intentionally."

"Yes, I know, son. Where are you, exactly? Are you still in Laredo? You need to get out of there as quick as you can, and don't come back up I-35. Listen son, I'll come get you if you want me to, meet you somewhere... Please son, let me help."

He knew where we were, more or less, he was too smart to not know. "We're going to hide out for a couple of weeks, Dad. Then we'll come home, right after my birthday, I'll be seventeen, no longer a juvenile, legally. The marriage will be consummated and there'll be nothing they can do about it."

I heard him sigh again. "I can't talk you into coming back home today, can I? I'll help you deal with John Cantu." He waited only briefly for the answer that didn't come. "Okay, be careful, son. I'm so worried about you. Don't lose contact with me, okay?"

"Promise me you won't help them find us?"

"I won't, son, I won't help them. But I'm so worried about you kids, Joey. Please drive carefully. Don't do anything dangerous."

Neither of us spoke right away, we didn't want to say goodbye. He broke the silence. "Joey, your friend Sam, from NASA called, just to check on you. Maybe you could stay there, at his place, if you can get there before they find you. You want his number?"

I did want his number, I liked the idea even though Houston was three hundred miles away, highway 59 went straight there and it was certainly not where they would be looking for us. I called Sam and told him what was going on and asked if we could stay with him for a couple of days. He agreed without hesitation.

We studied the map and found our way to Hwy 59, it wasn't hard, it branched right off of I-35 on the north end of town. Just as we veered onto the entrance ramp I heard a siren behind me, not close but coming up fast. A glance in the mirror confirmed my fears, a Laredo city cop had spotted us. I knew Mattie would be obvious to them. I floored the gas and quickly began to outdistance the police car but another came from a side street, closer to us than the first cop and he gave chase also. As he slowed to cross the curb and the grassy median to get onto the highway, I took the next exit off the big road and turned onto a country lane. We were at least a mile down the road and going well over a hundred thirty miles an hour when I saw the two cop cars turn onto it behind us and I took a quick left as soon as possible then another left, crossed under 59 and over into the countryside, zig zagged through the narrow roads and tried to keep going in the same general direction that 59 went.

Ten minutes later, sure that we had given the cops the slip, we got back onto 59 and tried to blend in with the light traffic there. Laredo was several miles behind us now and I was sure the city cops would not pursue much beyond the city limits. But there were county cops and state cops to worry about and they were all connected through their radios. The farther we got from Laredo, the lighter the traffic got.

We were back in the flat, brushy, desolate countryside of south Texas, just like what I'd gone thru getting to Laredo from the other direction. The next town was Freer and it was sixty miles from Laredo on a good straight road which offered very few side roads for escape or alternate routes. I decided to push Mattie and make some time while we were in an area that offered almost no other traffic to contend with, so we cruised at an easy clip of ninety five to a hundred miles an hour. We passed through a long heavily wooded area and into a clearing and a sheriff car with two officers in it shot out from a ranch entrance, siren blaring and red and blue lights flashing. I knew I could outrun them and I hit the gas and Mattie responded, but then I saw the helicopter to our left. I didn't expect this kind of attention. What did John tell them? As we passed a small side road I saw another sheriff car coming from somewhere down it, still about a half a mile away.

Knowing it was hopeless, way out in the middle of nowhere, surrounded by cops, even from the air, I let off the gas and slowed down. Anita and I looked at each other and she pleaded, "Joey, don't let them separate us again, please."

The police cars were close behind us now and our speed was down to about fifty. Watching in the mirror, I noticed the cars back off a little and though I didn't brake I continued to decelerate. The helicopter closed in to our side and dropped down to almost ground level and slowed to keep pace with us. Downdraft generated by the rotors caused considerable turbulence and it was a fight to keep Mattie straight on the road. Looking over I saw a uniformed passenger in the chopper eyeing me through binoculars and talking into a head set. Suddenly the flying police veered up and away and headed for who knows where in the distance and the two police cars turned down a small farm road and sped away in the same direction, lights still flashing. It didn't make any sense to me.

Looking into the mirror I saw Amos and he threw his big head back and his goatee encircled mouth open and laughed out loud, gold tooth sparkling. Wondering but really knowing, I looked to Anita to see if she heard the laugh like I did, of course she didn't.

"What's going on, Joey? Why did they stop?" Anita's frightened voice begged for an explanation but I could not give her one. I suggested that maybe they were going to set up a road block ahead somewhere. But why would they? They had us trapped. We were even stopping for them.

Amos appeared again and spoke. "Look at Mattie, Joey." I looked out over the hood, Mattie was black, shiny black with chrome gleaming. And I understood. That chopper cop must have not only seen a black coupe but also a black driver, one who probably flashed a big gold toothed smile at him. Amos' words came back to me, "Trust in Mattie, Joey."

Anita scooted close to me and rested her pretty head on my shoulder. "What just happened, Joey?" She wiped tears from her eyes with her fingertips and looked around behind us for the cops, then laid her head back against me. "Why did they quit? They had us."

"I don't know, 'nita." I lied. "Maybe Mattie had something to do with it."

"Mattie?"

"It's best you don't know, for now anyway."

Freer was the town we were entering, a little community of ranchers, smaller than Las Casas and nowhere near any other town in this flat, arid, desolate looking part of the state. We passed thru it cautiously and I noticed a cop in the distance, speeding away from town down a small road that cut across and led, eventually, back to I-35, looking for us, no doubt. Maybe they were thinking we were trying to get back to I-35, to San Antonio. Sure that a town this size would have only one cop, and we'd already seen him, we stopped long enough to go thru the Dairy Queen drive thru and order food to go. We gassed up at the town's only gas station, a convenience store, used their rest rooms and got back on the road.

In another thirty minutes or so we would cross I-37, a major route from Corpus Christi to San Antonio. They would almost certainly be waiting for us there. Anita studied the map and when we were within a few miles of the intersection we took an alternate route, circling around major roads and getting back to 59 a few miles past the crossing. Towns began to get larger and closer together with more traffic. I knew if they found us again they would know for sure that Houston and not San Antonio or Las Casas was our destination.

Victoria was the next city of any size and as we neared it we left the highway in favor of smaller roads. With Anita reading the map and navigating, we zig- zagged around the town and found our way back to 59 several miles on the Houston side, and there we picked up more cops. And they came after us with a vengeance. This time I put my trust in Mattie, as I had been advised, and felt confident we would get away again. But Anita, unaware of what I knew, was not so sure. I returned her worried look with a smile. "Don't worry, baby. They're no match for us."

Her voice trembled with fear. "There's a lot of 'em this time, Joey."

And there were, I counted seven police cars at a glance, just on one side of the road. They were everywhere, still coming from other roads, descending on us, all kinds of cops, even a game warden in a pickup truck. You'd think I'd murdered someone, one of their mothers maybe, the way they swarmed us. Damned adrenalin freaks, I thought. They weren't ready for us when we came up on them and we sped right past them and I floored Mattie and left them behind. I quit the highway and began making frequent turns even doubling back a couple of times and moving farther away from the highway and soon I saw no more cop cars.

We were trying to figure out just where we were and how to get back to at least the right direction of travel and a helicopter showed up, directly over us. Now that I could neither outrun nor hide from.

We passed through a nice long stretch of road where the trees formed a canopy over us and provided at least a visual barrier from the chopper, it almost had a safe feeling to it and I relaxed a little. Less than a mile after coming out of the canopy, several cop cars lined our side of the road, five of them, lights flashing, and the chopper buzzed us. Mattie slowed to about forty and cruised right by the cops, who scowled at us as we passed but did not pursue. The chopper pivoted and flew in the direction from which we had just come and the cops all turned around and sped off too.

"Joey?"

"Don't even ask, 'nita. You wouldn't believe it anyway."

She opened her mouth to speak, hesitated, nodded her head, breathed in and out heavily. "It's the car, it's Mattie, isn't it? She's doing something."

I didn't answer.

"Are you going to tell me what she's doing, Joey?"

"No, I can't explain it right now, listen, Mattie's taking care of us, that's all you need to know."

What I saw looking out over Mattie's hood was no big surprise this time. She was candy apple red with yellow symmetrical flames, not black with door handles, or yellow with Hell Flames. And a peek in the rear view mirror showed me Shawn's face with a 'you know what' eating grin. We found our way back to 59 and continued our journey to Houston. The closer we got to Houston, the heavier the traffic got. We let the hour pass quietly, traveling at a speed that kept pace with the other cars on the road, and enjoyed the cover they seemed to provide. Anita turned the radio on and Mattie played Anita's favorite classic song for her, "Ooh baby I love your way, every day, got to tell you I love your way, wanna be with you night and day…" Anita smiled at me.

Seeing her smile turned my mood happy, like this was all going to turn out all right. She was slumped down in the seat and had her bare feet pulled up under her and was hugging her knees. She looked at me a little sideways and smiled, little girl dimples, black hair falling around her face, and she said, "We're going to make it, aren't we, Joey?"

We entered the outskirts of Houston and I called Sam again from my cell phone. I had been to his house before but not from this direction and he gave me instructions. We exited the highway and began following Sam's directions through the suburbs. Almost there, we attracted another cop. He burned rubber with one back tire as he began his pursuit of us and came up fast, red and blue lights flashing. I wanted to run, thought about it, but with all the cars on the road it would have been dangerous. Looking out over Mattie's hood, I noticed it was red again, with symmetrical flames. I saw a happy Kim in the mirror, in her maroon racing helmet, looking more like a reflection than a spirit. The officer pulled right up beside us, looked me in the eye while talking on his radio, then he faded back, killing his emergency lights. I knew what he saw and it wasn't me.

A few minutes later we arrived at Sam's house, the time was 7:14 p.m., our escape run had taken nearly six hours and covered more than three hundred miles. Sam was outside waiting for us and he waved us into his garage through the already open overhead door. He walked in and closed the door behind us. Anita let out a long sigh. "I'm hungry." She said.

Now safe inside Sam's home, we began to unwind and relax a little. Andrea, Sam's wife had gone into town to buy some takeout food for us all and Sam was anxious to hear all about our trip. We were all over the news, he told us, we had become known as "The

Runaways" and the entire state of Texas was watching the story which was quickly gaining the attention of surrounding states. We had led the law on a three hundred mile, high speed chase, the news said, and fooled them at every turn, we even outran helicopters.

I promised to tell Sam the whole story but first I needed to call my Dad so he wouldn't worry. Sam advised me to use his phone and not mine, in case they were tracking my calls.

"Hi, Dad, we're at Sam's house now, we're okay."

"Wonderful, son! That's a relief. Joey, how in the world did you do it? Everybody was after you, even from the air.   It's been all over the news. Twice they claimed they had you boxed in, were tightening the perimeter and were close to catching you, and you slipped away. How?"

"Dad, nobody can catch Mattie."

"Oh my goodness, Joey, you nearly gave me a heart attack! How about Mattie, is she okay? Any damage to her?"

"No, she's fine too. Mattie's amazing, Dad, she even surprised me."

"Listen Joey, you stay there for a while, you hear me? John Cantu has the police convinced that you took Anita against her will and that you're some kind of a psycho or something. The news people cornered me in the driveway here so I talked to them, thinking maybe I can help with the truth. But lay low for a while, let things calm down. This has gotten blown all out of proportion and the media is in a feeding frenzy, making it even worse."

Seated on the couch with Anita and holding her hand, I began to relate the experiences of the last few hours to Sam. Just as I was getting started, Andrea returned with Mercedes, their four year old daughter, and supper. I introduced Anita to Andrea and she commented that Anita was every bit as beautiful as I had described her back when I was working at NASA last summer. So now with all of us seated around the living room, enjoying the Chinese takeout food in its cardboard containers on paper plates, I began the story again.

Of course I left out the parts about Mattie doing her Chameleon stunts for the cops, which was tricky because that made some of the story hard to make sense of, but I winged it pretty well. Anita didn't contribute to my story and I could feel her eyes on me the whole time. I guess she was still putting the pieces together herself, but she had to know.

When we were talked out and full, Sam turned on the television and found a news program. It didn't take long for our story to come up and we sat quietly and watched. A news reporter who introduced himself as Wayne Hamilton, gave a summary saying that Joseph McClane and Anita Cantu were the sixteen year old south Texas couple now known as 'The Runaways' who, in a very fast homebuilt hot rod, had captured public attention, while somehow evading and at times just flat outrunning law enforcement officers, even when pursued by helicopter, several times during a three hundred mile, high speed chase and were now suspected to be hiding out somewhere in Houston. Police had told reporters that we'd been clocked at speeds in excess of one hundred forty miles per hour. He went on to say that conflicting stories were being told by the parents of the two teenagers and it was unclear if the girl had been kidnapped or had gone with the boy of her own free will. But police suspected she had willingly gone with him since they now had evidence that the underage couple had crossed the border into Mexico to elope and then returned to the Texas side.

Our photos flashed on the screen, underlined with 1-800 numbers to call and report sightings or information to help locate us. While our pictures were shown side by side, a recorded voice, robotic sounding, of a policeman, I guessed, gave our descriptions which were also printed below the pictures.

"The young man, Joseph Raymond McClane III, is described as Caucasian, sixteen years old, six feet three inches tall, approximately two hundred twenty pounds, stocky build, brown hair and blue eyes, light complexion with no distinguishing marks or tattoos. He is not thought to be armed or dangerous."

"The young lady, Anita Rene Cantu, is seventeen years old, Hispanic, five feet ten inches tall, weighs one hundred twenty five pounds, slim build, black hair, black eyes, dark complexion with no distinguishing marks or tattoos. She is not considered armed or dangerous."

"They are traveling in a customized 1934 Buick Coupe, yellow with flames painted on the front half, and a large number thirteen on each door. The car is reported to be extremely fast and has been clocked at speeds in excess of one hundred forty miles per hour. If you see this vehicle or these people please do not attempt to approach them or to apprehend them yourself, as they are prone to flight. Call the number on the screen and give the location and time you saw them."

Wayne Hamilton was then joined by a lady reporter who introduced herself as Bobbie Riel, and they had a live, on camera, conversation about the story. They seemed convinced we ran away together and there was no kidnapping, the lady even threw a romantic spin on the whole thing, calling me Anita's knight in shining armor and claiming that was the now prevalent public opinion. I suppose Mattie was my white horse. Video footage of Mattie on the run, as taken from one of the helicopters, before she performed one of her magic quick change stunts, was shown, and I must admit she looked absolutely awesome in action. I laughed under my breath and Anita elbowed me and giggled.

"We will now show you footage from exclusive Channel 7 interviews of each of the runaway kids' fathers." Wayne announced. John Cantu came on the screen looking as angry as I've ever seen anybody and began to rant and rave and lie his ass off. He practically yelled as he gave his red faced, hand waving version of how he had tried to discourage his poor little unsuspecting daughter from getting involved with this abusive, parentless, white boy from the wrong side of town. He described me as a worthless high school dropout who would beat the crap out of anybody who crossed me, and who had repeatedly bruised his little girl's arms and neck and self-esteem. He said I was "nothing but a dangerous, uneducated grease monkey" whom he would personally see behind bars before this was all over. John was certain that Joseph McClane had repeatedly raped his daughter and threatened to kill her if she tried to get away from him.

"He just made a complete ass of himself." Anita complained. "I'm sorry, Joey. I didn't think he'd go this far."

"It's okay." I replied. "He's just upset 'cause we won, we beat him and he can't stand it."

Dad's interview was next and after a brief introduction as a petroleum engineer who retired early to raise his orphaned grandson, he gave his version of the story. And Dad did great; he spoke well and kept his composure and looked like the educated man of integrity he was. Dad told the reporter that Joey McClane had finished high school via home schooling at the age of fourteen and two years later had earned a college degree in chemistry at the University of Texas and was now working toward a master's degree. "He's a child genius, and a very well educated one." He claimed. "The University of Texas tested his aptitude at 175, greater than the famed Albert Einstein. He's a happy, smart, mild tempered kid whose only fist fight in his life resulted from the town bully saying something nasty and insulting to Anita, and I was proud of how he handled that incident. At the time her father was too. These kids fell in love when they were thirteen years old and her father has allowed them to date for four years now. He allowed Anita to work toward an early high school graduation, knowing all along what they planned to do, get married. But when the time came, John hid her at her grandmother's home in

Laredo. Anita sneaked out of the house, found a pay phone and called Joey and told him how to find her. Even her grandmother says he drove up and stayed in the car while she ran out and got in and left with him, yelling back to her that she was going to get married."

"Okay, Mr. McClane, what about that car? That extremely fast hot rod, where did Joey get that, did you buy that car for him?"

Dad laughed. "No, Joey built that car himself. Well, I guess I did give it to him, sort of, he was twelve years old and it had once been my grandfather's car. It was damaged and not running when we got it back and Joey fell in love with it and started working on it right away. That is his car, he built it, Mattie, he calls it."

"Mattie? Right? The car's name is Mattie? The car has a name? Okay, so how did he have the ability, at his age, to create such a car?"

"Well, he got that from me. I'm a classic car enthusiast and that's what he grew up with. Plus he's smart, he has that natural mechanical aptitude, he just understands how things work. Did I tell you he held a job at NASA last summer? By invitation, because of his academic achievements, top security clearance and everything. That's how bad of a kid he is. This whole thing needs to be put back into perspective, as far as I'm concerned. What we have here are two kids in love who have simply refused to be separated. That's all there is to it."

"All right, Mr. McClane, your son, or grandson rather, is a sixteen year old college graduate who builds cars that can outrun the cops, and he and his sixteen year old girlfriend have run away together and gotten married in Mexico. Pretty incredible story. He may soon have a criminal record too, sir. The police are not very happy about him outsmarting them half way across the state of Texas. What have you got to say about that?"

"Well actually, Wayne, Anita is seventeen, and Joey will be too, next week. These kids are plenty smart, both of them, and I don't think the police will find them until they are ready to be found. When things calm down they will come home and maybe cooler heads will sort this all out. Nobody's been hurt, there's been no property damage, not even any close calls. And I'm convinced that nobody will ever be able to separate these two kids."

"One more question, Mr. McClane. Do you know where they are?"

Dad flashed a sly smile. "I wouldn't tell you if I did."

The camera zoomed in on only the reporter. "There you have it folks, a modern day 'Bonnie and Clyde' story of two young runaway lovers in a homemade hot rod making monkeys out of the police all the way across south Texas and still on the run. Joey and Anita, The Runaways, from the tiny south Texas town of Las Casas. I just hope no one gets hurt before this is all over. We'll keep you up to date as the story continues to unfold. I'm Wayne Hamilton and this is Fox 7 News."

An advertisement jumped onto the screen, something obnoxious, Sam clicked mute on the remote and the entire room was silent. We were in a trance, at least I was, I couldn't believe what I had just seen. How did things get like this, all blown up into some big news event with cops looking for us and everything? We just wanted to get married.

Sam spoke first. "Well, you sure know how to make a good news story, Joey."

I couldn't answer.

Anita looked at my half eaten meal. "You gonna eat that?"

Andrea laughed. "Somebody's taking things well."

Anita smiled at her and answered, "I got what I wanted." She reached up and rubbed my shoulder affectionately.

"Uh, Sam, I don't know where else to go, for a while at least. You think it's all right if we stay here for a few days? I've got money, we can buy groceries, help with the bills and stuff."

"Don't you kids even think about leaving!" Andrea insisted. "You're welcome as long as you need to stay. Hell, I feel like I've got celebrities in my home. Come on, Anita, I'll show you your room and y'all can unpack. You boys go get their things out of the car."

Anita laughed lightly. "Well, Joey was able to pack some things but all I have with me is what I have on. My grandmother was watching me like a hawk, I couldn't even grab a toothbrush."

"Oh, well then we need to go shopping." Andrea seemed pleased with her idea.

"I'm not sure I should go out in public, Andrea, I just saw my picture on television."

"Yeah, well, we could change your hair, put some sunglasses on you, stuff a pillow under your shirt maybe. I'll take you to the Cuban Market, nobody there would turn you in even if they recognized you, which they won't. You do speak Spanish, right?"

"Como no?" Anita replied, and then rattled off something in Spanish I didn't understand.

That night Anita and I made love in a real bed for the first time, and slept wrapped in each other's arms all night. The next day was Monday and both Sam and Andrea spent the day at their jobs while we slept late, showered together, and then watched our story on TV again. The news was getting quite comical as a sympathizing public had begun calling in fake sightings of us all over Texas, even as far north as Amarillo and one from eastern Louisiana. Over two hundred sightings were reported with only five coming from the Houston area. A representative from the state police made a public statement and he was not happy, claiming we had endangered the lives of police officers and the public and they had a long list of criminal charges against me.

Although it was closer to time for lunch, Anita cooked our breakfast, another first, and then began cleaning the house, not that it needed it but just trying to be helpful and show her gratitude. I spent a couple of hours cleaning Mattie in the garage. Anita provoked a wrestling match with me and we made love on the living room carpet. Anita made a joke about calling in a sighting of us in New York and we laughed about it but didn't make the call for fear of the number being traced or identified.

Sam and Andrea came home from work around six and the girls went shopping while Sam and I baby sat Mercedes and cooked supper; grilled red fish, rice, potatoes and corn on the cob. Later that night, about ten thirty, I think, we watched our story on the news again. The police had now received well over a thousand calls of sightings all the way from California to Florida.

The runaways were safe for now, but I began to worry about what would happen when we did go back home. Would Mattie perform her magic and get us all the way there? And what then? Would John still try to separate us, could he? Would I be arrested? I decided to put it all in the back of my mind and just enjoy our hideaway honeymoon for at least a couple of weeks.

As days clicked by, Anita and I grew restless, neither of us used to being cooped up in the house all the time. Anita offered to keep Mercedes during the day but since Andrea worked at the day care where her daughter attended, she gracefully declined the offer. Dad called every day to see how we were doing. Anita wrote a letter to her mother to ease her worry and Sam mailed it in another envelope to a friend of his in Dallas who took it out of the cover envelope and mailed it for us to Las Casas. John found it and turned it over to the police who then concentrated their search for us around the Dallas area because of the postmark. John was not hard to outsmart and neither were the cops.

Early in our second week at Sam's home, we celebrated my

seventeenth birthday. We got brave and went to a movie with Sam and Andrea. Sam and I went in his car, Anita and Andrea in hers. We went into the theater separately but sat together, after walking down opposite aisles and meeting in the middle of the row of seats. When the show was over, we left the same way. It was good to get out. The next night we went with them to a drive-in restaurant. Anita and I huddled together in the back seat of Andrea's SUV.

Dad called the next day to let me know he had hired an attorney who had in turn contacted the Harris County District Attorney and gotten a list of charges against me. And indeed it was a long list. I was charged with speeding, reckless and dangerous driving, and evading arrest in four different counties, flight in a motor vehicle to avoid arrest in three counties, endangering the lives of police officers and endangering the safety of citizens, and taking a minor across the state line, plus taking a minor across the border of the United States into a foreign country. A total of nineteen criminal charges, about half of them felonies. Oh shit, this was serious, I could go to prison. It worried Anita more than it worried me.

By the third Wednesday of our ordeal, we had been holed up in Sam's home for two and a half weeks and Dad called to say that our attorney had hammered out a deal with the state. Being dropped were the charges of endangering private citizens and flight to avoid arrest. Fines totaled over six thousand dollars for the charges of speeding, reckless driving and endangering the safety of police officers. I was getting six months' probation for taking a minor across the state line and across the Mexico border. In addition to the hefty fines, I was to perform two hundred hours of community service within the next two years, and my license was to be revoked for eighteen months. But I was not going to jail.

I jokingly suggested to Anita that maybe they'd drop all the charges if I'd take her back to her father. She didn't think it was very funny.

"So what does the lawyer say about our marriage, Dad, can John have it annulled or something? We're married now, he's not going to split us up."

"Well, that's a little trickier, son. You have to get married again, on this side of the border this time. John refused to sign the consent form but Anita's mother went to our lawyer's office by herself and signed it. He says that'll work. But she wants you to have a church wedding, she wants it done right and with family and friends present. She's already getting it organized."

"When? When will the wedding be? And does she realize we intend to live together between now and the wedding?"

"Maybe you'd better have Anita and her mother talk about that, son. She can call her now, you don't have to hide any more, nobody's going to come after you. Oh, and Dr. Larson says he'd better get a wedding invitation. Joey, Mr. Carson, the attorney, and I will travel to Houston Friday and we'll all go down to the Harris County DA office there in Houston where you'll give yourself up and be booked and then released on bond and a court hearing will make the agreements official. Don't worry about anything though, it's just all legal formalities. I think you're getting off pretty easy, Joey, this could have been bad."

Mr. Carson called the news media in Houston and leaked the story to them, so Friday morning when Anita and I, Dad and our lawyer arrived at the Harris County Courthouse the reporters and a small crowd of fans of the runaways, maybe forty people, were waiting for us. As we walked up the sidewalk to the courthouse building we were cheered, filmed, photographed, and pelted with rice and flowers. Dad had ridden with Mr. Carson, Anita and I had driven Mattie there. I'd get some last minute advice from the lawyer and we would go inside and start the process. As I stepped through the doorway I looked back at Mattie, she had drawn a crowd too.

The booking process in the district attorney's office didn't take ten minutes and after a short wait, maybe twenty minutes, we were ushered into the courtroom. The judge, a robed, heavy, balding, black man about Dad's age, gazed sternly at Anita and me over his half a glass style spectacles. He handed me the official charges, several pages, long pages, legal size. Looking at the judge, I thought of Amos, even though they looked nothing alike. At least a gold tooth would be nice, I thought. Silly thought. The place was dead quiet and Judge Harrison glared a silent hole through me while I was supposed to be studying the pages he had handed me. It unnerved me and I became fidgety and felt my hands begin to sweat.

After a quick scan of the charges, which were just what I'd been told, my lawyer and I exchanged nods, and I met the judge's glare with as humble of a look as I could manage but I didn't look away from him, I stood up straight and looked him right in the eye, ready to take my medicine. I still had Anita and no price was too great.

When he first spoke he chastised us for what we had done, mostly for the danger in it, and the disregard for our families. And then he wished us a very long and happy marriage. In his sentencing of me, he went strictly by the agreement the DA had made except that he dropped the two crossing the border charges instead of giving me probation for them. He claimed they were not applicable in this case. They were meant for an adult stealing a child, not for young lovers on the run. When he finished the legalities of it all, he leaned forward, covered the microphone with one hand, lowered his voice, and smiled for the first time, a sly smile. "Off the record, young people, my wife and I eloped too, many years ago, but we did it in a much quieter manner than you two did. And one word of advice, kids, that burning passion that made you do what you did, don't ever let that fire go out."

Outside the courthouse again, making our way thru the overfriendly crowd that was still gathered, we received the well wishes of our fans and reluctantly spoke with reporters. They questioned Anita about her future plans and she replied that she planned to keep me well fed, well loved, and help me work on my cars. With the same question directed at me, I said that if my new criminal record didn't get me kicked out of school I would work toward my Master's degree and start a business building custom cars.

Mr. Carson had other things to do while in Houston and went his own way from the courthouse. Dad treated Anita and me and Sam and Andrea and Mercedes to supper; steaks and seafood. Anita happily devoured an embarrassingly large meal. We thanked Sam and Andrea for opening their home to us at such a time and they said when we got settled in our own home they'd come see us. I liked that idea.

The drive home would have been uneventful if Dad hadn't succumbed to Mattie's hunger for speed, and he got a speeding ticket forty miles or so out of Houston, near the little town of Sealy, ninety two in a sixty.

"You could have done better than that, Mr. McClane." The cop told Dad as he handed him the ticket.

"Excuse me?"

"Ninety two miles per hour, you could have done better."

"Uh, sorry sir, I don't quite follow you."

Straight faced, the cop motioned toward me with his little aluminum clipboard. "Your boy there got a hundred and forty out of this car just the other day." He gave us a little smirk and walked back to his patrol car.

END

We had our church wedding, at our church, our Pastor presiding, and Anita was so beautiful in that white low cut gown, I fell in love with her all over again. A stern faced John walked her down the aisle and handed her over to me. Dr. Larson served as my best man and Anita's younger sister was her bride's maid. Later, at the reception, beer in hand, looking around more than at me (body language, avoiding eye contact), Mexican band playing in the background (diversion), he confessed he knew we were right for each other, just too young, voiced a weak apology for letting things get so bitter, and pledged his help and support. He was trying to save his own marriage, I surmised. Two news crews came to the wedding, just showed up, but we made them stay outside, to do a follow up story on "The Runaways", a happy ending kind of thing. I noticed John tried hard to avoid the camera, walked way around it looking the other way.

We followed up the wedding with a two week honeymoon fishing and scuba diving in Cancun, Mexico, Dad's treat, where I drove a rented car every day in defiance to my suspended Texas driver's license. By the time we returned home, my first annual inheritance check was waiting, one hundred thousand dollars, a one and five zeros, beautiful, I kissed it.

Unlicensed and unable to drive on the street, I converted Mattie back to a full blown dragster and she was back to doing what she did best. Determined to make her as fast as possible I replaced her 1966 Buick nailhead engine with a modified 1987 Buick

V-6 dual turbo charged engine, replaced her five speed manual transmission with a racing version of a power glide automatic, and found ways to lighten her body weight. The cops couldn't stop me from driving her down the track and I drove her to low eight second times and many trophies.

Very soon after I started racing her, before I really had her at her best, we were running down the track at the San Antonio Drag Raceway and things in my peripheral vision were a blur but I could tell I had a comfortable lead on my opponent and I shifted gears and watched the time board as I passed by it as I always did even though I knew my time wouldn't flash on that sign until I was well beyond it. I could look around at it after I did the turn around and was on my way back to the pits. And I did. 8.982 seconds, 147.66 mph! I finally broke into the eights! I was ecstatic, I had worked so hard for this!

Then it hit me, I had this feeling like I had been here before, déjà vu. My mind went back to the deep daydream of this very moment that Mattie had pulled me into that day when Dad had just bought her from Frank and I was steering her onto the trailer, and every detail was correct, even to a thousandth of a second.

I looked in the mirror, I looked like I was twelve years old, I did a double take, I looked in the mirror again, I needed a shave. Yes, I had been here before, at the very beginning. And this is where Mattie was taking me the entire time. She showed me today, five years ago at our first meeting, in perfect detail, then she brought me here, as if she had planned everything. Could Mattie have had that much control over my life for the past five years? I was so shaken by this realization that I pulled over and parked before getting back to the pit area, and I sat there, staring into space, hands gripping the steering wheel, thinking but not thinking, frozen, trying to come to grips, Mattie rumbling out a fast idle.

Five years flashed before my eyes in random disorder; Anita and Mattie that first day, she was in awe of Mattie and was car savvy and Mattie approved of Anita, she played that 'Chapel of

Love' song, she wanted us together. My studies picked up real momentum at that point and I was propelled thru high school and college at an unbelievable pace and nothing was difficult for me. Anita and I quickly became very physical, especially when we were inside Mattie and our relationship took on a very mature nature for our ages. The history I was shown that all led up to Mattie choosing me... Frank saw it, what was it he said? "I was watching the boy in it and it's already taking over..." The race I just won, the time, the speed, all of it predicted five years in advance. And Amos advising me to let Mattie take care of me, she knew what was going to happen and how to handle it. Yes, Mattie had planned everything, she was in control. Now I knew, what would I do about it?

Her radio turned on and played for me that same song she played for me that first day without a radio; acoustic guitar, drums, violin, beautiful young lady's voice, "Tonight you're mine completely, you give your love so sweetly, tonight the light of love is in your eyes, but will you love me tomorrow? Is this a lasting treasure or just a moment's pleasure? Can I believe the magic of your sigh, will you still love me tomorrow? Tonight with words unspoken, you tell me I'm the only one. But will my heart be broken, when the night meets the morning sun? I'd like to know that your love, is a love I can be sure of. So tell me now and I won't ask again, will you still love me tomorrow? Will you still love me tomorrow?" I let the song play out and watched Mattie's radio turn itself off and her dash lights flicker.

Was I being asked to make a decision? I thought so, and it was an easy one, I couldn't imagine life any better than this even if I was not in control.

"Yes, Mattie, tomorrow and always."

I shifted into gear, headed for the pits.

Anita and I lived with my Dad for a few months, while we had our little house built on the back of his property. We slept together in my room, in my bed, Sparky trying his best to sleep between us under the covers.

Mattie took me back in dreams to fill in the gaps left when she hurried her story through Roy and Kim's times. Dreams came at a slower pace now though, and less frequent, but they came. One night Mattie showed me myself in a dream, I looked about sixty something years old, some gray hair, crow's feet at the corners of my eyes, I looked a lot like Dad, and I was a passenger in Mattie. Driving her was a tall, stocky boy in his mid-teens, and he looked just like me at that age, and he looked like he had fallen deeply in love with Mattie. He gazed at me with watery eyes and said, "Paw Paw, I can't believe Mattie is mine now, I don't know how to thank you. I'll never let her sit outside or get dirty, and there're so many things I want to do with her." I wondered when the dreams would begin for him, perhaps they already had. When I knew for certain, I would give him the journal.

Dad and Anita got to read in the journal, the behind the scenes tricks of Mattie during her run from Laredo to Houston, and they seemed a little surprised but not shocked. We kept it all to ourselves, an unspoken vow of silence among outlaws. Mattie's ghosts still appeared, to only me of course, less often and more subtle, their purpose for me completed now. Just quick, quiet visits from old friends. Mattie still played songs for me, at times, her favorite remained the Deep Purple song, "Highway Star", and once in a while she would play Peter Frampton for Anita.

Our cozy little red brick, three bedroom, two bath, house, with a red metal roof at Anita's insistence, was finished several months after our wedding, we settled in, Sparky came too. Unsolicited calls for custom car jobs came in, a result of "The Runaways'" publicity of Mattie's unbelievable run. Dad and Anita helped me as I built a custom '32 Ford two door sedan for a real paying customer. After four months of work I presented it to a very pleased owner and profited a whopping thirty seven dollars but learned some valuable lessons. Despite the poor start, this was to develop into a good business for me, eventually allowing me to build my own shop and hire employees.

Eleven months after the wedding I earned my Master's degree in Chemical Engineering and declined job offers from The Foundation and NASA. But Dr. Larson and I remained good friends. Three years and four months after our wedding, at the age of twenty, Anita and I were blessed with a healthy eight pound baby boy, you guessed it, Joseph Raymond McClane IV, and we called him Little Joe. Dad was Paw Paw again, pushing eighty, but strong and healthy, moving a little slower maybe. One year later, along came a beautiful brown skinned little girl who would steal my heart on a daily basis. We named her Andrea Rene McClane, she had black eyes and black hair and little girl dimples.

I prayed to God to help me to be the kind of daddy he had given me.

www.ingramcontent.com/pod-product-compliance
Lightning Source LLC
Chambersburg PA
CBHW061307190726

48288CB00002B/396